To Pet

Th

James Edward Parsons (B.A. Hons in Media Production/Animation) studied art and design, and then animation and film production. A few years ago he turned to writing screenplays, then short fiction, and finally novels. He was born in Newcastle, moved to Manchester under a decade ago, and is married.

ORBITAL KIN

This book is dedicated to my wife, father, mother and close family and friends. Thank you.

James E. Parsons

ORBITAL KIN

AUSTIN MACAULEY
PUBLISHERS LTD.

A CIP catalogue record for this title is available from the British Library.

ISBN 978 184963 348 2

www.austinmacauley.com

First Published (2013)
Austin Macauley Publishers Ltd.
25 Canada Square
Canary Wharf
London
E14 5LB

Printed and Bound in Great Britain

Chapter 1

'Slow down the car, you insane madman!' Alan yelled with tense panic.

The young women beside him laughed and screamed louder, enjoying the thrill of the reckless, wild driving of the entertaining and very handsome young man at the steering wheel, Steven Lowell.

'Steven, watch it, really. You okay, mate?' Alan asked.

'It's cool, man. Enjoy the thrill ride, buddy,' Steven replied, smiling, but in that moment a feeling froze his own consciousness while he steered the wheel.

He was almost fully paralysed, gripping the wheel tightly, and in the darkness of night, ahead on the road, he caught sight of a shocking image. There was a tall, naked, muscular man with bright red shaded skin all over, looking right at him with black shining eyes like those of some animal. Alan quickly grabbed at the steering wheel, seeing how Steven was immovably frozen.

'What are you doing? Shit, Steven. You okay?' Alan said hysterically.

The girls in the backseats were still screaming, but then became silent before whimpering in sudden fear as the car swerved from one side of the road to the other.

'What? Blackness... Stars... Planets... The stars around planets...' Steven murmured.

'What are you talking about? You awake there?' Alan asked.

The car screeched along, hitting the curb with a loud wail as it continued.

On the road ahead, the red, tall man was gone from view, and there was only the dark of night and the street lights around.

'Hmm? What? Yes, I'm... I'm here,' Steven told him. 'See that?' he asked and he looked ahead, seemingly refocused in himself and took back control of the car again.

'See what? Nothing's out there. Are you alright?' Alan asked.

'Me? Yes... Just lost focus I think. Stop worrying mate, chill out. Time to relax now,' Steven replied in a quieter voice. He realised that Alan did not seem to have seen the vision that had been out there on the road, looking right at him.

'I would if I didn't still have my thesis test equipment in the car's boot, Steven!' Alan reminded him. Then they all saw the bright flashing lights ahead.

'Oh Jesus!' Alan gasped with nervous anxiety.

'No problem. Sit back, enjoy the ride,' Steven said.

The girls just looked at each other in silent shock as they gripped each other, while Steven upped another gear and the car rushed on. He took it quickly around a number of tight turns, down behind the city streets, then around a few darker, narrower tracks toward the open fields and countryside.

'Steven, just pull over or we'll get jailed and banged up if you don't. That's not us!' Alan implored.

'Relax, good buddy, we're okay. You ladies are having fun, right?' Steven asked to the women in the car almost casually.

'Oh yeah! This is just proper wild! It's crazy!' one of them shouted, smiling.

'Not wrong there...' Alan agreed, quieter.

The car still twisted and turned, the police close behind for a couple of miles until they were gone. Driving down a final few narrow lanes, all was quiet.

'There we go. Smooth, safe parking. We're fine, aren't we?' Steven said, slowing down the car, and looking back at the girls who smiled at him with admiration.

'My God, that was just insane! You are mental. a crazy man, but a gorgeous one too,' one of the girls told him, and they laughed and squealed some more. Alan simply shook his head, unimpressed but relieved that the car had stopped and the police seemed to have lost them.

'What now, Tom Cruise? Mission over?' he asked.

'No way, bud. You fine ladies want a few drinks? Music? Something else?' Steven asked the girls.

'You bet we do,' the blonde told him.

'Okay then. Over to our place now,' Steven told them. He winked at Alan then laughed, like some crazed fool – crazed but wholly confident, and missing no opportunity in life for instant, dangerous pleasure at any time.

Reaching the flat where Steven and Alan lived together, Alan let the girls inside, while Steven hid the car around the back in the closed off parking area. Steven then went in and quickly joined Alan and the beautiful young women who were getting strong colourful drink cocktails, turning on the stereo and rolling a joint. They eventually paired off and Steven and Alan slept with a girl each successfully.

The following morning, both young men got dressed and left the flat with the women. They took them into the city, and then Alan and Steven continued along up to their university's laboratory studios by mid-afternoon. It was cold and frosty when Alan and Steven drove along into the university campus. They got out and walked along by the university buildings to their department.

'Look around. Aren't there a few police around over there? Strange, isn't it?' Alan said.

'A pain, more like. Never mind. Let's just get to our rooms,' Steven told him.

'Very bloody worrying. Pray they don't see us,' Alan replied as they walked in.

They reached their laboratory department rooms and walked in fast, closing the doors behind them.

'You should keep a low cover, calm down more. You know they have hang ups about your father and you these days, let's be honest. They'll try to get anything on him and you if you let them,' Alan told Steven.

'Right, okay... Shit, I'm my own person, Alan. I'm just angry sometimes, and go a little wild. You know me. You love it, buddy,' Steven said.

'Right, yes. Whatever you say,' Alan replied.

They were met there by the other close members of their Master's degree course experiment team – Joanna, Pete and Pascal.

'Hey, you two awake yet? Had enough headache pills and hair of the dog?' Joanna asked with expected sarcasm.

'Hmm? Don't be jealous, Jo. Yeah, not that we need to do much here. It'll sort itself, right?' Steven said, smiling widely. In some ways, he spoke in a way that they just did not understand. Alan believed that it all came directly from his father.

'Don't be an arse, Steven,' Alan suggested as he unpacked documents, his laptop and files by the others at the tables.

'You think you'll easily pass this Master's degree man. So relaxed all the time still?' Pascal asked Steven.

'You worry too much. I know what to do, what needs doing, how and when. Got to play the game here. It's not just the degree – it's the contacts outside and a lot more. You know that by now, mate,' Steven replied.

'Yeah, man, but look – we do worry about your passing even so, you know?' Pascal told him.

'I know, man. Thank you all, you're so considerate to me. Just got to remember to actually enjoy life while it's there,' he said.

'You're not in your sixties, mate. You could slow down a little, just until we're done here' Alan said.

'Hey, every day might be our last. I'm not trying to ever be a pessimistic guy, so I grab life by the big old balls and run with it. I have fun and so does everyone around. You know that to be a fact Alan, don't deny it,' Steven said. 'So, what's up? Where are we up to here?'

'Didn't think you'd remember,' Joanna said, coming to meet him at the desk.

'We're just about done, aren't we? We've collected the list of measures and figures we needed, but we're now shaping the final evaluations together while Alan does the last tests with Pascal now. Remember that?' she asked.

'Of course. Only testing you, babe,' he replied, smiling and receiving her expected vicious stare in return.

Their university degrees in Advanced Physics, Biochemistry and Structural Cell Biology were coming to an end in a couple of weeks. Alan, Steven, Joanna, Pascal and Pete were all desperately still working long hard hours to complete their joint project and individual work thesis papers and dissertations on time. While they worked away, so hard and focused, Steven seemed to just coast along through, always being seen in the popular nightclubs, and known to the vast majority of university students and lecturers for his wild, debauched, rock and roll party antics, and this just shocked and amazed the others. Not that they never went for a few drinks or clubbed like most students, but now, at the end of their hugely important Master's degrees, Steven had seemingly acted like this for close to five years, always the admired, infamous, reckless, party legend. He could drink almost anything at any time of day and all night long, and could be found in most, if not all, of the notorious city clubs, bars and pubs, with the most beautiful women – often a couple at once – and knew students of all kinds; filmmakers, musicians, artists and also a good number of well-known and nationally respected professional scientists, somehow. They had a good idea how.

Steven was unbelievable – almost inhuman, with so much energy, almost dangerous but loyal, mostly entertaining and fascinating. He must have slept with almost half of the university's female population and, if rumours were accurate, even a few men, and he had been involved with the local police in connection with many chaotic and legendary house parties. His winning charm always seemed, somehow, to help him escape successfully to party another day, another night.

'I can't believe that you still haven't calmed down just a little before the end of our education here. It does make the rest of us nervous, you know. You just could have some understanding, a little bit of respect for us. It would help us work better,' Alan told Steven as they sat together.

'Why should I? This is me. You all know me. I manage. I get the grades I need, the marks we need. I just have different ways. You wouldn't have got laid half as much if it wasn't for me. True, right?' Steven said.

'Just... Just focus, please. I want you to pass at the end here. We can't put in all this effort and lose our Master's now,' Alan said.

'And I will. We will. We can't let our parents down, right?' Steven suggested.

'No. How much do you really care about this, Steven?' Alan asked, pointing to the laboratory around them.

'What – science? Totally, absolutely. You know it's relevant, important to our survival, hope, destiny – everything. You know my opinion, mate. We'll work together. It's the plan. We agreed. I guarantee that, still,' Steven replied with a visible, serious certainty across his face.

'Yes, so you have said before,' Alan replied.

'So, we have drinks at Bar Midian tonight. Maybe hit Herbert's Bar and the others?' Steven said. He was unstoppable.

In the grammar school with very highly respected grades in the community, the young girls sat at their desks, quietly sketching, after their teacher had given them their subjects to draw. The teacher walked around the room, seeing what the girls were coming up with by themselves. Some drawings were really simple, and others much more detailed. She came back around the top and stood along by little Lucy. She was then very intrigued by the image she saw.

'Lucy, dear. Can I ask – you drew this yourself, did you?' the teacher asked.

'Yes, Mrs. Cooper. All my own,' Lucy told her tentatively.

'You are sure of that?' Mrs. Cooper asked.

'Yes, Mrs. Cooper. Just me,' Lucy told her.

'Okay that's... Just fine. Lovely, Lucy. Can I borrow it a moment?' Mrs. Cooper asked and took it from her then.

She walked back along down to another girl, Beth, and held the two drawings side by side. Both featured a longboat, both had a town in the background and birds in the sky. Not strange, as the girls knew what the story that Mrs. Cooper had read to them had included. But both drawings looked exactly the same, line for line, executed and composed precisely the same as each other, everything, every line in exactly the same position. Mrs. Cooper was silently shocked and unnerved.

'Beth, can you explain this?' she asked the girl.

'Sorry, Mrs. Cooper?' Beth said, confused.

'Never mind. Very good Beth.'

Mrs. Cooper walked back to little Lucy.

'Lovely drawing, Lucy. You okay there?' she said.

'Yes, Mrs. Cooper. Thank you, Mrs. Cooper,' Lucy replied.

'Right, alright. That's... Good Lucy. Very good,' Mrs. Cooper told her, and she looked at the little girl with confused fascination.

In the lounge of the large family house, as afternoon sunlight shone through the blinds, Steven's father Gordon sat with his youngest child Lucy as they ate a pack of chocolates between them, and he asked some questions.

'So, dear, has school been good?' he asked.

'It's okay. I like it. We were drawing and learning songs,' she told him as she looked through a comic book he had bought her.

'Oh, that's really great. What were you drawing, then?'

'Different things. Sometimes I was drawing animals, or space and then Steven and things,' she said coyly.

'Oh, right. Okay. Seen Steven lately, have you?' he asked.

'Not really, no. I haven't Daddy. But I know what he has been doing,' she said.

'You do? Good girl. Was it fun to watch?' he asked.

'He was driving really fast,' she said, looking mischievous.

'Oh, but he was alright, was he?' Gordon asked.

'Yes, but Daddy, he saw the red man. He did,' she told him and jumped up, excited.

'He did? Alright. That's really good, Lucy. Thank you. Well done indeed, darling. But it's a secret, okay?'

'Yes, it's a secret,' she replied, nodding.

'Very good, dear. Well done. I'm very proud of you, my angel,' he told her and hugged her lovingly.

At the doorway to the room, his ex-wife and Lucy's mother, Beatrice, leaned in to see them.

'Still here? Can I talk to you, Gordon?' she said calmly.

He looked up at her. 'Yes, I suppose. Wait here, Lucy. Finish the chocolate if you like. Good girl,' he said and stood, joining Beatrice. They walked through into the kitchen together.

'Right, look, don't think she loves you as much as you want her to, okay?' Beatrice said quickly.

'Oh, hang on. Calm down Beatrice. Jealous, are we?' he responded.

'Oh, don't bother with such a pathetic response, okay? She is not a project for you in any way.'

'What is it with you? She's my daughter, and I'm spending some time with her. End of story. Tragically paranoid, aren't you?' he stated.

'You can let a work project fall to pieces and others pick it up afterwards, but not her. She is a precious little girl – my girl,' Beatrice warned him.

'I agree with you. She is so precious indeed. My girl too. Always will be,' he said and walked away, then turned back.

'I'll see her again as usual. Calm down.'

'I know you have plans still, old ideas,' she said.

'Do you? Poor Beatrice. Get out more, get laid,' he told her and winked. He walked down the hall, entered, kissed Lucy goodbye and went on his way in his expensive car.

He took troubled thoughts with him as he drove. He no longer loved Beatrice, but he knew then that she most definitely was right about him. She always had been.

In his car, Steven drove along with Alan through town in the mid-afternoon, but Alan thought that he seemed sombre and unusually quiet.

'You alright now, Steven?' he asked.

'Me? Hell yeah. Why you asking, sweet thing?' Steven said.

'Right. Back last night. When you were driving all crazy, scaring the girls, you kind of blacked out or acted weird. You were talking about space, the stars and stuff like that. Got some things on your mind?' Alan asked.

'We all have concerns, mate. No, I'm just great, you know me. Don't know about all that last night, though. Just being freaky, scaring you and the girls a bit, you know?' Steven told him with a leisurely smile.

'It was so damn dangerous, though. You really shouldn't do that all the time. All this mad shit in the clubs, at the pubs, around. You don't have to,' Alan said.

'Hey, I know that. It's not for anyone but me anyway, alright?' Steven retorted. 'Well we're safe, and fine, thanks to you, I suppose. You want some Mexican food for lunch now?'

'Can do, I suppose. Good idea,' Alan replied quietly, and looked out of the car window at the town around them.

As like most nights, right then, Steven was out in some popular bars and clubs around town. He was meeting many others he knew from university, college and just from all over. So many people knew him, in the bars, the pubs, the clubs and he knew them. He was famous and infamous equally. He hugged, kissed, and laughed with many of them, buying drinks and accepting them. Some were always waiting to see what his crazy act would be that night, or his classic joke. It was never desperate attention seeking, but he always ended up with some unpredictable tale for others to recount. When he moved from bar to bar with a core group of friends, he was angrier than usual. He tried to keep it below the surface, hold it back, but so much wanted to get out, be released. He downed another shot, then a pint, then a shot.

He was so pissed at his father. Not that he expected money from him freely, or really wanted it or his unquestioned respect, all the time. He did want attention and understanding, which was sometimes rare and had to be requested. They all knew just how busy Gordon was. Steven, his brother Nathan, and little sister Lucy all knew. They knew that, but it was something in the way his father responded to him, which was different to Nathan and Lucy. His mother Beatrice was the same with Lucy, and both parents were very protective and strange around his sister. He understood that Lucy was their only girl, and still so young in her first year at secondary school.

Something was being held back from him. Did they not trust him? he wondered, not for the first time. Why not? Just why the hell not, ever?

But the real pain, the bigger issue, was that Gordon had snubbed his opinion a couple of times and it was just continuing. Gordon had shown him plans for some confusing, outlandish, and more radical research experiments with patients. Steven could not believe the kind of thing Gordon was discussing. It had really given him a different view of his father, whom he had usually admired like most other people did. He could not easily believe that it was really what Gordon would decide to do for success, but then had he done similar things before with his research production company? Steven had been wondering. It had made him wonder and question all of the years of the success of Gordon's science research and pharmaceutical exploration. Gordon was so fucking stubborn, he thought. Steven needed to know the truth, and he wanted honesty from his father. If this was Gordon, a man who forgot morals and human ethics in science and experimentation, then perhaps he was not the father he wanted. But he just was not sure of any of these feelings, and it filled his mind painfully.

'Alright then, I've a damn good idea right now,' he said to his friends around in the crowded bar.

'This is it?' one asked.

'Too right, it certainly is,' Steven replied.

There was some thought in his mind, some conflicting crowding of emotions and other forces. He kicked open the fire exit by the wall in the corner and began to pull out tables from the bar onto the road outside.

'What the hell, Steven?' one friend said in amazed shock.

'Follow my lead here, will you?' Steven asked.

They proceeded to drag out three large tables onto the road. Steven then returned to the bar and collected drinks, chairs, wine bottles and more girls, who then went out and sat on top of the arranged tables in the road while he sat in a chair and poured out wine for them, all of them laughing hysterically and loudly. In seconds, cars approached and piled up, their confused drivers angry and not slightly amused. Seconds later, police came along to the surreal, decadent scene. They arrived and showed bemused faces, totally lost for words. Was it a joke? Some stunt for television?

'Okay all of you, stop this please. Cars need to pass. Let's get this all moved, okay?' the lead police officer told them.

The girls were drunkenly dancing on the table tops, swinging the bottles around, and Steven was pretending to play a piano in his lap.

'Yes, what the fuck is this?' Steven joined in. 'Appalling behaviour. Youth of today! Can't believe my eyes. Why, decent, civil folk would never actually ever have the balls, the fucking imagination and chutzpah to do such a thing!' he cried out dramatically.

'Who the hell are you? Right come on...' the next officer said, stepping forward. But right at that instant, he seemed to lose his thoughts.

'Yes, what's the trouble, Dibble?' Steven asked with a wry smile.

Many of the drivers from their cars had stepped out, meeting Steven, the girls and his friends.

'You're fucking mad, lad. What is all this about?' one man asked with a blood red face.

'I'll fucking move them, damn bloody students,' another then said.

They quickly walked right up to Steven at the tables. Like the police officers, in the next few seconds they too became speechless. They all still looked at Steven and stared at the scene on the road, but remained silent.

'Hello? What's stopping you all?' he asked apprehensively.

All of them then gradually moved back, returned to their vehicles and drove away. It was a highly bizarre reaction, but one he had encountered a handful of times now. But it was surely still a mystery. What just happened? he thought. He was pushing it and testing the limit of this strange occurrence, one of many. He looked around and saw the girls on the tables, the chairs and drinks from inside the bar. The bar staff, who he did thankfully know well, stood nearby, watching.

'Can we get all of this stuff back inside please?' one of them asked.

Steven nodded but then walked off by himself, thinking and wondering.

In the highly expensive, private surgery room of the doctor, Gordon sat relaxed but listening well enough to the advice and questions asked.

'You do get the suggested regular exercise, don't you Gordon?' Dr. Pearce asked him

'You know I do. I told you so before. I enjoy it – the gym or running in the park with friends,' Gordon replied.

'Right, you did say. I remember that. But you take time out from work and thinking about work, don't you?' the doctor asked.

'I would say so, yes, when time allows it,' Gordon responded.

'You know that the mind needs to switch off. Take breaks away from pressure at times. I understand that this could be difficult with the pressure and heavy workload from your company and the business projects you oversee,' Dr. Pearce said.

'I have to control so much at work, you know,' Gordon told him.

'I know, and I am very impressed, certainly. But you know the importance of what I am saying?'

'Yes, of course I do. There are so many projects, though, and people counting on my decisions. Right now I have just come to see a much desired personal project regain the attention and interest that it deserved long ago,' Gordon told him.

'Well, that's very good. Please though, Gordon, take good care of yourself. It will be worth it,' the doctor explained.

'I very much agree with you, I definitely do,' Gordon said with a sly smile.

Dr. Pearce looked down through his records on his laptop, over many older files and reports covering the health and wellbeing of Gordon for at least a decade and then before with previous doctors. He looked again at documents which he could not forget when he had to meet Gordon. Although Gordon was a very successful businessman in the world of science research and medicine production testing, he had a medical history which held some grey areas. There were years not covered from when Gordon had lived in America nearly two decades earlier, before he had returned with his wife, and they had soon gained another girl along with their two older boys. There had been a number of periods over the last few years with Gordon where his own mental stability had been questionable. A nervous breakdown and slight depression, all before he refocused and his company found the enviable, enormous success it was now internationally known for. Dr. Pearce was not totally sure that Gordon had completely recovered from those unstable mental difficulties, and from recent events and meetings, he believed that there could be serious danger for Gordon very soon. While he might have spoken out and warned him much more seriously, the money Gordon paid him ultimately bought his silent agreement and neutrality. Gordon and Pearce shook hands and then he watched Gordon leave, smiling and as positive as ever.

Chapter 2

Gordon entered the house, exhausted but thinking, as focused and constant as ever.

'Beatrice, I'm in. You there?' he called out.

His ex-wife, Steven's mother, came into the hall to meet him.

'Hello, Gordon. Have you spoken to Steven recently?' she asked, with accusing agitation.

'Not for a couple of days. Why?' he said.

'Really? A couple of days? Because we're both his parents here. You and me have brought up our children to be honest, strong, morally good people, okay?' she told him.

'Yes, I agree with you. Christ, what's with you? You okay?' he said.

'Me? Look, I spoke to Steven. You have to think about what he thinks of you. How much do you tell him? When? He's getting older now Gordon, he's going to finish university finally. He's a grown man now. But how much are you telling him?' she asked.

'He knows, what he needs to know, for now. Why? What's he said to you?' he asked.

'It's nothing he's said, specifically, Gordon. It's… it's just we have to...' She cut off her speech.

'No. No, it will be time soon enough, honestly. I promise. Didn't I promise so long ago? Just leave it with me. I care for my dear son, alright? Along with paying for everything here,' he told her, waving around at the house, the furniture.

'You're not a great man these days, Gordon. And you know I left my own career for three children. I raised them, and you were just acting like an arrogant fool. Some great scientist. So great, what great mistakes,' she said. She had begun crying a little, he noticed.

'Oh God, come on now, Bea. I understand. You know me. You know I understand. Don't you trust me still?' he said to her in a sweet, manipulative tone, his arm now on her shoulder.

'I... I do, but tell him, Gordon. Tell him about America, about when he was small, and when the other two were born,' she begged.

He hugged her gently with close affection. They did row often and they had separated some years ago, but they did still try to support each other and raise their children together.

'He will know, he will,' he told her reassuringly.

Alone in his office in the city, Gordon sat at his computer looking through emails, messages from various clients, partners and associates, business requests, notes on meetings coming up soon, and changes to current project time structures. Then an unexpected email came up. It came from someone else, a person who he initially struggled to think of. Then it came to him, the name, with the face. A very old professional friend from years earlier, from a time before his children had been born. Before he had come back to live in England and before his own business existed.

Against his first instincts, he opened up the email. It began in a friendly manner, recapping on time passed between them over the years, asking about Gordon and his wife and work. Further down, though, it then changed. 1982 was mentioned, a significant year for both of them. Some very secretive scientific projects were written off, things he had not personally spoken about or even thought about seriously for such a long time. He had been a much different person back then, a younger, more naive eager scientist then.

The email continued, reminding him of old chances he had taken, a specific project so ambitious and dangerous with absolutely unforgettable consequences. It was not good, not at all easy to confront any of it so suddenly. Gordon finished reading, and then suddenly deleted the email. He turned away from the computer monitor then, with a serious look over his face. He moved over, reached down and opened the lower side desk drawer. He took out a large bottle of whiskey, unscrewed it, and necked it for a long moment. He gasped, shook his head at the strength of the drink in his mouth, then instantly threw the bottle hard on the edge of the desk, held the broken cracked neck of it and threw that over against the wall, smashing it into pieces loudly.

Whiskey and blood mixed on the top of his desk, and his right hand stung as he looked at it. As it began to shake, he looked at the cuts there. The open wounds glowed, pulsed, absorbing the blood and whiskey in the moment, like he knew it would.

The family home had been small and bleak. Never too much money to spare, Alan's parents' wages only just barely managed to cover the bills and rent every month. While Alan grew up with continuous warm encouragement and guidance, both parents providing positive words with schoolwork and his interests, giving him reliable advice and knowledge of the world, their values, beliefs and opinions, he struggled to connect with many others but ultimately rarely needed to do so. He had his fascination with everything science related; animals, biology, chemistry, the planet, the human form and nature. His father had told him about his own interests in sea life and scientific research through the late sixties and seventies. Lack of funding had stopped his father from pursuing a definite career in science, but he very much urged Alan to try his hardest to gain such a path if his own grades and studies would allow, with more readily available funding and grants out there now.

Alan soon enough got his own tropical fish, and various insects. These silent creatures were as strange and unique as him; they were there to hear his thoughts and problems when no others would. They watched him learn more, and to examine more as he grew.

He then also soon learned more about the planet, agriculture, weather and chemistry from his grandfather who he only saw once or twice a year. He was a dear, loving man before he then died of a viral sickness in some way less than three years ago. Before he reached university, Alan had built up a compulsive, non-stop addictive need to learn, to research, test and debate theories continually, and was ongoing and extremely impressive to his lecturers and teachers around him.

After losing a number of girlfriends who found his continued unending reading, researching and fascinations ultimately intolerable and bizarre, Alan resigned himself to only being with his close few loyal and understanding or at least tolerating friends, and his pet fish and old wrinkled lizard, Eddie, in the flat he shared with Steven. Once at university, Alan did finally meet a few women who actually also saw the fascination and extreme social importance in his scientific interests which finally boosted his confidence and hope in a believable long-term romantic relationship again after too long.

'Alan, I've always been just so amazed at how you just seem to soak it all in and remember so much about the plant structures, human biology, growth and all the things on the course so quickly.

It's just so impressive,' Lucy told him with honest admiration as they sat together in the university's Union bar.

'Oh, well, thanks, Lucy. Well I don't know why, I just have to know these things. I love it all and personally find it just such important stuff to know, and if I get to work with this kind of information soon, that'd be great. It's always been really fascinating. I've not much social life because of it I suppose, but I accept that. It seems just important that I learn it when so much can be done, using science techniques and research to help so many people. I mean, I get drunk, and socialise sometimes. I do. You know, I see people... but I... I have to learn this stuff and get a good career now,' he explained almost apologetically.

'Oh, no, I agree, I do. I understand. No, it's great that you are so passionate and dedicated. I should spend more time around you, it might rub off on me. The dedication, I mean. Look, I have to go meet some friends. See you tomorrow, maybe, then. Take care, bye,' she told him.

'Yeah, see you too. Great to see you. Bye,' Alan said and sighed quietly to himself as he watched her leave.

He watched her walk away and felt bad about his lack of cool, his pathetic way with women. She was such a beautiful and lovely intelligent girl, similar enough to him, he thought. She seemed to understand complex academic work and actually enjoy it, and she appreciated his science Master's degree, but still he was a silent nervous wreck, finding it difficult to relax and just talk easily in conversation. He could not help but look at her cleavage and her legs before him as she spoke to him, and then lose his words quickly when his turn came around. His work was a reliable companion, he remembered. Science was always there for him, always fascinating, engaging, unendingly amazing. It always lifted him up, and took him away from the depressing facts of life around him. A good textbook, some '70s rock albums and occasional porn and weed was there in between the science.

Along with a usually sex-free personal life, Alan found his scientific study and fascination had been heightened by a small number of very significant personal experiences – which he very rarely told anyone about, actually, other than Steven, but even he only ever had heard small pieces of truth when both were extremely recklessly stoned or drunk at weekends. Looking over a pile of academic textbooks after waking from a short nap, Alan refocused his gaze over them, observing diagrams and notes with great detail.

A memory came to him then from around ten years earlier, with his grandfather out near Devon, in the southwest countryside of England. Time spent in the beautiful countryside, the epic blue skies and vast green fields around, and the farms and hills near his grandfather's own fields. A year of good beginnings soon found problems – slow growth after stilted weather, bad germination and crops which found difficulty in maturing well. As ever, Alan listened well to his grandfather, the news and troubles. His grandfather was in no way nearly a scientific man, only knowing the processes and procedures and techniques of his farming business in well-learned ways from his own father before. Alan liked to hear about it all, a real example of processes he was reading about, knowing plant life, various patterns in growing techniques, weather conditions in farming production quality, and expected obstacles and outcomes involved, but here he saw it all first-hand.

He occasionally viewed the machines and areas around the farmland and crop fields, with his grandfather explaining the past work there. This one occasion was when he had solved the problem. He had helped the farm to survive another year when the future seriously looked in question. The solution came to him; the right farming, growing techniques, levels of water, soil regulation and fertilisers came to mind as he spent time there. It was a way to try things he had only read about and he offered his help to his grateful though surprised grandfather, who soon was forever grateful. A few weeks later he got a call thanking him so much. He knew why, but he felt uncomfortable about the praise. Two more unexpected occasions similarly boosted him on, and with little financial support but continued outstanding grades, Alan reached a well-respected university. Somehow though, with thoughts of his influential father, Steven also joined Alan right there, and they found their bachelor pad to live in through their university years.

The music pumped and throbbed through everyone with loud repetitive beats. Steven was with two girls and a male friend, Nicko. They danced on, moving to the beats and the time changes, like all others, sweating but euphoric. He was lost in it, happy while in there, and away from the work of daytime life. The music and the drink and even some drugs took his troubled thoughts from him. He danced on. In the darkness, while neon lights flashed on and off in all directions, he suddenly caught sight of a strange person. A figure tall and of the kind he had seen only a handful of times. The man, it was of that gender, had burnt red skin, with almost hypnotic shining black eyes.

'Oh hell, what the fuck?' he muttered. He didn't need this, he thought. These people, or whatever they were, returning, following him, watching him.

He moved away through the club, trying to seem relaxed and casual still. He sipped at his bottle of drink again, smiling at others. He chanced a look behind and it was still there. No one else seemed to see it at all in any way, which scared him even more. Then there was another one, appearing behind the first. Both moved through the dancing clubbers in his direction slowly. Two now. Two red skinned naked people, their black eyes unflinching.

'Get away, please' he said quietly under the booming of the music.

He moved faster then, past many more people, out to the main cloakroom and toilet area. He leaned against a wall, and sighed to himself.

'Alright there, mate?' one guy asked, leaning in to look at him.

'Me? Yeah, man. Chilling but fine. All good,' Steven told him.

'Okay then, mate. Nice one,' the man replied and walked off.

Steven looked around, then decided to get some air, and walked back out onto the main street.

'What do they want? I'm mad aren't I? Mad or possessed,' he said to himself in the street under his breath.

'They show you...' the voice from inside his mind then told him.

He looked around, surprised and nervous.

'Show me?' he asked.

'They need help... Our fathers...' it told him.

'What? I don't get it' he said.

No answer came, no more reply. He walked along the street and texted his friends in the club. They came out and met him in another club in a short while, but for that night he did not see any more of the red people and he was grateful.

In a quiet weekend between next stage preparations of the projects at their university, Alan took the opportunity to return to the north of England, going home to Sheffield for a family visit. The journey took a few hours on the coach, and grim heavy clouds welcomed him back to the cold parts of his childhood. He took the bus alone, down through grey narrow roads and streets where his early year memories remained for him. The family home was there waiting – quiet, comforting, in its expected humble and ramshackle way. His father Tim and mother Valerie greeted him fondly at the front door to their home. They asked about his studies, his flat, Steven and even the weather down south. They settled in the house exchanging news and recent events. To be back home, Alan felt comforted but equally sad. There was also an uneasy feeling of it not really being time to be back there, as if he had not come back with the most impressive news of amazing careers and Nobel prizes.

This was where he came from, though. His place of origin, his upbringing, a place of beginnings. He did though, see his parents still there, struggling with difficult job situations, and managing to live to a decent level, with worsening health issues, with the crime and the unemployment rising around them depressingly. Alan felt like he was abandoning it all every time he went back to university, ignoring reality and his own family problems for romantic urges to be a highly respected scientist. His mother just told him to forget about it when he tried to admit his feelings, and that he was making them so proud with his studies anyway.

When he did return like this, usually every month or less, he could often see the town with different eyes. He began to see the town from a more objective view; the businesses, passing of history, the contrast of classes, the fracturing of the community, the youth tribes and fear in the eyes of older folk, but also the fields behind, the allotments there still. They were tended in good condition somehow, despite all modern distractions of today. He appreciated this in a new strange way, he found. He took the time on the Sunday morning to walk along down to the small patch of allotment he had personally claimed there many months before starting university. His parents did not know of it, and he had kept it very discreet for professional reasons. At the place he had taken up, he had divided up the soil area and had set up a small number of tests involving a few plants, wheat and vegetables. As he was away, he had arranged an agreement with Bob Glendis, a regular around the allotment; a kindly man near the place with his patch. Bob and Alan regularly spoke over the phone every couple of weeks, with Alan guiding him with the growing procedures and testing he had planned. Bob felt very helpful and keen to be involved in what seemed very important academic research.

Once there, Alan had observed how things had changed. He compared his earlier notes and very quickly saw some surprising and interesting changes. The plants had begun to bloom but the leaves were fascinatingly unique with irregular markings, unlike how they would be. He took small samples very carefully in a box from inside the shoulder bag he had brought with him. He was pleased and felt that his home town held now a positive, hopeful and useful connection to his bold, new, different, academic life elsewhere in the country. Science was connecting both places for him, back and forth.

In the mid-afternoon one day, Alan passed time with his mother and while she baked some kind of cake and scones, he talked to her. She then made a tea for herself and coffee for Alan as he continued with casual questions.

'Oh, mum, is this the one that I put together?' he asked.

'Yes. Still drinking it and you know, I really did feel the difference to my back and hands. It's unbelievable,' she told him.

'That's great. I'm really pleased. Just a couple of things I combined, sometimes thought to potentially work well together for remedies,' he told her.

'They definitely are. You're so smart, my love,' she replied.

This was another immensely pleasing and positive personal success. It probably did confirm a few small theories he had with certain biological and chemical mixes from several plant compounds he had experimented with on a quiet, personal level.

Chapter 3

The following week, one very long afternoon stretched on in the laboratory at the university. Steven lounged around, his attention gone from work, eyes looking around aimlessly for anything to amuse him. He grabbed a nearby magazine and idly flipped through the pages with frustrated boredom. The doors opened, and Alan stepped in with extra equipment and files carefully piled up in his arms.

'Hello, genius, rock star, lover man,' Alan stated with a tired smile.

'Oh, hey. Everything in order?' Steven asked casually, not entirely interested.

He dropped his load down onto the lab tables. Then he looked across at Steven who lay stretched over the long, old, tattered sofa chair at the back of the room.

'What are you doing there?' Alan asked, having foolishly hoped that Steven might have continued to do something useful while he was away elsewhere.

'Well, look... I'm just thinking about... things,' Steven told him, looking at the various pages of the science magazine.

'Look, hey, what do you think it takes to be involved with this? Look...' Steven began suddenly then, catching up with some interesting thoughts, finally continued. 'Limb transplants, cutting edge medicine, climate change... Flying to Saturn, black holes, Mars, living on other planets... What do you think?'

'We can't do everything, and we can't be involved with every simple notion that comes into our heads – not every single thing. We have to focus on the things that we are doing, things we can make real immediate impact upon, Steven. The things we are studying here,' Alan said.

'Oh, yeah, right. Living on Saturn or Mars, or reaching other galaxies, quantum mechanics all that...' Steven said, kind of dreaming.

'It is very interesting, yes, but you know me – things have to be looked at in terms of priorities. Those things are extremely fascinating, but we are studying other things here. We therefore will soon have a more immediate impact on these areas rather than black holes, climate change or travelling to distant reaches of space,' Alan told him 'How necessary is all of that? You know, what will help us first? You on a siesta right now?'

'No, no. Just couldn't bear to work without you. Give me a few seconds here. You're back, so let's go, right?' Steven said.

Alan nodded with unimpressed, silent agreement.

In a city building in Bristol, five floors high, a handful of scientific research developers and business people talked together in a very important conference around a long wide table.

'Hello, welcome, my friends. We are due to come to a definite decision about this new venture we are looking at with great seriousness this morning, right here, finally. What do we think, then?' one man at the head of the table said to all before him.

'Well, the man is certainly very interesting. He puts up a good proposal for sure,' one said.

'This Gordon and his company I feel are maybe not the right thing at this time,' another argued.

'No, look. He is a strange kind of bloke, that's true, maybe too mouthy and forward, but he knows his stuff here. He seems to really know how to communicate and bargain with many others, and he knows his stuff too in scientific terms,' one said in defence.

'Where was he from? His background – do we know exactly?' another asked.

'Yes, well, only so much. His company is extremely successful, continuing to make big progress internationally. He comes from up north, around Sheffield,' one said.

'Yes, but him – what about him?' the other woman enquired.

'He... he is actually a bit mysterious when we look into it. There are a few things unclear or missing, but it is his company which impresses us in a great way, really. Some personal contradictions, but let's go on his actual work and what he is achieving. We probably can't afford to let him go from us,' the other warned.

'What are the contradictions?' one asked.

'This Gordon – he could be from outside of this country. We think that is a possibility, with also some unresolved political history to his work past,' the other told them.

'But he sounded so English,' the first said.

'Right, yes. Look, we certainly are not going to make any racist small-minded comments; we embrace all ethnicities, all cultures. He could have been born here but worked overseas. Or that might not be it either. Doesn't really matter. It could also be that he is just from up north, born here, eventually set up his company and here we are. The rest we know,' the other argued.

'Very strange,' she remarked.

'Exactly,' he told her definitively. 'But even so, thinking of his work we know about, what say we?'

The faces around the long table nodded eventually in unison.

'Yes, we'll join with him,' the other grand man near the front end agreed.

'Yes, we all agree now,' another said.

'Alright. Yes, that's it then,' said a woman to their left.

They all agreed that this curious but impressive businessman of the science industry was who they should now join with for the future of their highly secretive and financially bold plans ahead.

While Steven and Alan and their group studied hard at one end of the campus, across the other side some highly serious financial meetings were being played out. Between dozens of enormously stressed hardworking teachers, academics and students, the heads of departments and leaders of faculties at the university were organised deep in the closed up meeting rooms for a late announced but highly important meeting with influential outside beneficiaries and supporters to the university courses.

'Thank you very much for coming here today so soon. Apologies about the quite short notice, but that was due to our timing. I think you understand,' announced the university governess, a smart and steely eyed lady at the centre of a wide table which they all then sat around. She seemed very certain of her words and wise with her age. 'We will, I am sure, now come to some satisfactory agreements concerning the things which have been mailed out and discussed over the last two weeks,' she explained.

'Do we have to do this now?' one outspoken woman suddenly asked.

'Angela, please. Gentlemen, ladies, please do not interpret this in the wrong way, Angela is only worried over the timetables, schedules and wage issues of the last few months. Only a small few have felt nervous but have sat in discussions that explained our reasoning with these meetings. Angela, you did hear our thoughts, didn't you?' she said.

'Of course, but...' Angela said.

'I hear you, Angela, you know that. You agreed with me yesterday, didn't you? You also have a lecture very shortly, don't you?' the governess reminded her.

'Yes, fine. Good day everyone. Hope you all get what you need,' Angela said dramatically and then stormed out of the room with aggression.

'And so, to this arrangement which has been suggested. Would you like to now elaborate in final terms the detail of it all, please?' the governess said.

'Yes, gladly we will. Well, as you expect from what we spoke of over the phone and in emails, this is simply a supportive offer of stability for at least two years in the amount which we spoke of to you,' the lead man said.

'Right, okay. That is right, but only so much was understood from those messages. Yes, we did agree so far and things do seem very plausible. That did sound to us certainly very interesting. We are most definitely grateful for your consideration in this deal right now over other choices possible. I must now though, speak of some issues, firstly, which I think need to be discussed, really,' the governess began. 'You see, I think you of course understand how a university like ours usually survives, or at least expects to usually get by financially every year. The current problems, the strained relations to government and the education board checks on many levels. We have to be most careful, indeed, when it seems that we connect to specific outside organisations, companies or institutions for periods of extended time and the exact circumstances then involved,' she told them.

'Yes, we do certainly see what you are concerned about, and very rightly. We understand this. This was expected, but you all need not panic at all, we can assure you. We lay this out for you in complimentary terms. It goes more near advertising, praise and support for both us and yourselves in business terms and your own fine higher education establishment here. Here is the final briefed whole document, which you may now view for clearer decision of your own,' the second businessman explained as he took out the document from a briefcase and placed it over the wide table.

'Oh, right then. Very good, yes. Yes,' the governess agreed as she took from them the files presented.

The Deputy University Area Head looked up at the three men and one lady then with apprehension.

'This deal, the connection of yourselves, is also between Solar Invert Industries and the ones we already met with headed by Gordon. That company is still certain in its claims from earlier isn't it?' she asked.

'Yes, Madam. The company, Gordon too, they mean to follow up certainly exactly as stated, as your departments will produce the number and range of science based research cited within the larger profile. That is still the clear basis here,' the man told her.

'Okay, then, only checking. You expected that, I am sure. This is all very stuffy, right? Overall, we are very much interested with this move,' she replied.

'Oh, Janet, really,' the governess said quietly in disapproval as she quickly skimmed along the documents before her.

'Yes... Besides, Gordon's own son is working with us here, a postgraduate project. A good thing, very fine brave work they are doing it seems. Steven, he is a great young man to his successful father for certain,' the governess commented, smiling with exaggeration for the businessmen and lady ahead.

'So then, governess, should we leave the two of you here with more time for you to finish studying the papers?' the front businessman asked.

The governess stood then, looking satisfied with reading not even half of the documents in her hands.

'Oh, no, this I think... This is fine. Our decision is a certain yes to your generous offer. We thank you very much for the opportunity,' she told them.

'Well, governess, we thank your good selves. Okay then. If that really is your choice, please then sign these final papers... Here,' he told her taking out the other documents.

The governess did as she was asked, while Janet beside her looked on with some slight visible discomfort at her agreement. They all shook hands, joked a little and then the group of business representatives left the meeting room finally.

One morning, as Steven made breakfast in the kitchen of the flat, Alan walked in from the corridor.

'Oh, morning. Sleep alright?' he asked.

'What? I suppose I did. Coffee? Toast?' Steven said.

'Good, yeah, nice one. I began to pack a few things last night. Still going over to see your dad's business offices today, aren't we?' Alan asked.

Steven turned to see him better but then looked away, stirred the coffees and put the bread in the toaster.

'No, Alan, it... We won't be going now,' Steven told him while looking at messages on his phone.

'Really? Why not?' Alan asked.

'Oh, just problems. My father, the business. It's just really busy, no real time for us at the minute it seems. He wasn't feeling so good too,' Steven told him.

'Again? Is he really bad or something?' Alan enquired with concern.

'Look... No, it's just... I think that he doesn't have time to take us around the place again at the moment. You know how busy it can get there,' Steven explained.

'Right, yes, I know. But Gordon, is he resting then?' Alan asked.

'Maybe. Something like that. I'll probably go across in a couple of days. So just us back to our own grand epic work at university,' Steven reminded him

'Okay then. You okay though?' Alan asked, in a friendly way.

'Me? God yes. Let's get dressed and do what we do best. Come on, have this breakfast, drink up and shower, you smelly bastard,' Steven told him with a joking manner and a nudge in the ribs as the morning light shone on their closed window curtains.

After a short train journey, Steven arrived in Cheltenham and then travelled by bus to the town centre and toward the building which he was to meet for a very significant arranged appointment. He had a meeting to keep up, arranged days before. This was one of many interviews he had lined up for promotion of their University academic project and work ahead, which was looking for much funding and financial support. He reached the pub and, after looking around, saw the man he was to meet with.

'Hello. I'm Steven. We spoke on the phone. Derek isn't it?' he said.

'Yes, yes. Hello. Drink?' Derek offered.

'Alright, thanks. Carlsberg,' Steven told him.

Sitting with drinks by the front window in a couple of minutes, they soon began the professional interview together.

'So, now we're here together. Let's begin. Tell me about what it is exactly that you and your group are working on together?' Derek said.

'Okay then. Well, I did tell you just a very small part on the phone and email. Be excited, be interested now, I tell you. This most certainly is a hugely new bold direction which we are headed in. No heads stuck in textbooks, or nervous stuttering, wimpy half-baked ideas crap. We have very specific hard results which define our direction and defined, certain targets. We will save thousands of lives, improve living for so many, do things which others have given up on long ago,' Steven declared, with no lack of assertion. He was a dramatic, captivating and extremely confident character whenever the opportunity was there such as this.

'You certainly don't lack strong ideas and self-assurance, that's obvious. So when you mentioned saving thousands, how? The cell experimentation, medical tests in chemical alterations you stated?' Derek said

'That is simply only the very beginning for us, believe me. Be sure of that. We'll be on the news in less than four months, on the television, Internet news, everywhere. No limits. These medicines first, then very soon after branching further out, other problems confronted using these findings straight after. Only our own thoughts will be our limitations. All other science groups are simply too scared or too lazy compared to us,' Steven declared boldly.

'You know, you of course still just are a very small handful of university postgraduates tinkering away right now – no offence. No doubt you have very clear plans it seems, though. You could, though, be careful not to be too ambitious to begin with. You also should think of gaining guidance in your careful new direction with these results you now have,' Derek told him.

'No, see, that's what I mean. That kills off all great endeavours immediately, for certain. No offence. Forget that. I am a confident, young guy. I talk, I meet, I make deals with the new, radical science findings we hold. I get it done for the others. I'm contagious, don't you think?' Steven said, smiling cheekily.

'Okay, I really can see that much. Right then – the project itself. The figures and results you provided me with – explain them to me in some more detail, please, could you?' Derek asked.

'I could. I probably should. You can imagine how it will be. I tell no lie here, I'm not wasting my time or your own. This, our work is unique, sensational stuff. Do not miss the chance to be one of the very first to be connected and support us, to be known as one of those who 'discovered' us early on,' Steven explained temptingly.

He had won this meeting, he knew. It was in the eyes of Derek, his interest his desire to accept and take the chance right then. It ended well enough for Steven.

Alan came into the flat after shopping locally on his way back. He put the food away in the kitchen, then went to relax in the lounge. He put his feet up and looked around the room. Over on the coffee table, he saw some new books among other things. He leaned in, picked through them; some DVDs, books, comics of various kinds. Steven then walked into the room, smiling at him.

'Oh, good evening, bud. You got some bread and things, right?' he asked.

'Yes, got your text. There are some curious new books and things here, yours?' Alan asked.

'Oh those. Yes, just wanted to read some different, fun stuff. It's great, interesting stuff, you know,' Steven said.

'Well, yes could be. I've seen a couple of these writers and directors around. You don't always go for this type of thing though, do you much?' he said.

'Right, okay, I know. I can explore stuff though, can't I?' Steven asked.

'Oh yeah. But really, so much science fiction. I mean, you and I like to watch a good movie sometimes but some of it just...' Alan began.

'Look don't worry about it. Just some escapist entertainment. Want to watch this one now?' Steven asked, picking out one of the DVDs.

'Well, right, okay. Fine. Looks good,' Alan responded.

They sat down. Steven fetched a couple of beers and started the movie.

As the group of Steven, Alan, Joanna, Pete and Pascal began with their interesting bold Master's final degree project after only a couple of weeks, unexpected things came to happen. Their tutors, professors, and lecturers at the university were continually helpful and hopeful of their young scientists, and soon they expressed it. As they worked, one of their lecturers, Philip Keys, paid them a visit.

'Good afternoon, Alan. May I talk quietly with you, please?' he said

'Oh, Philip, hello. Yes. Of course. What is it?' Alan asked as they began to then walk around and out of the room to another smaller quiet area.

'Alan, you know I am still very impressed by what you and your team are doing, and have been doing for three years here now. More recently, things have been much more fascinating and I am honestly very proud so far, I have to tell you,' Philip said.

'Well, thanks very much. That really means a lot to me, and to us. We do try to find new things, want to look for things that really, honestly, would be helpful to the world around us,' Alan told him.

'Right, yes, and that is what we definitely have encouraged, you know this. Alan, I am pleased to now tell you, in a discreet way you understand, there has been a good amount of serious interest industry-wise,' Philip explained.

'Oh, really? Like from who exactly, can I ask?' Alan said.

'Now, don't get all giddy. You do need to continue with the whole entire project with the same highly dedicated professional focus planned,' Philip said. 'I have been contacted by four significant companies so far, and only because I spoke with some industry friends about the planned work and the early results you provided in the initial proposition tests,' Philip told him.

'Okay, that's great to hear. But you can't tell me who right now?' Alan asked.

'No, not just yet,' Philip said.

'So will that change anything for us now?' Alan asked.

'No, and I will not tell you the names of the companies right now. You all must simply continue on, please. It all looks to me very promising, and is very exciting to myself and many others right now. Let this simply drive you on even more, and more confidently. Let it be a strong indicator that you are on very significant paths scientifically with your outlook, skills and individual and joint ways of working,' Philip said.

'Okay, great. But it's good then, isn't it?' Alan asked.

'Yes. Okay, Alan, now just listen. I will be around for advice, you know this. And look, I see how Steven is with his flamboyant, eccentric, hyping up of things. Be careful. Alan, is he... is Steven okay right now?'

'Steven? Yes, he's fine. He's doing a lot of communication and networking for us. But he's still very involved in the test too,' Alan told him. 'Why, what's up?'

'Yes, there are big companies, and big investors very interested in you, but do not feel the pressure. If any contact should come, remember – this is, firstly, only your Master's degree work. A project, just an extended project for information. Get your qualification, then see what comes to you all later,' Philip said with serious caution.

'Right, okay then. Thanks Philip, very much. I do really appreciate your advice, and always have done. We appreciate it, the team. I will remember it, I honestly will,' Alan told him.

It was good news, definitely, but it also gave him a strange heavy degree of new thought about their work going on now. It was only his higher education, his qualifications firstly, and scientific exploration. No immediate need to join corporations, to make deals and earn vast millions without thought of the serious, ethical implications involved. Alright, he certainly knew that in the modern world, scientific research and new breakthroughs could create huge sums of money, blur people's individual concepts of right or wrong morally, make them forget the needs of society, humankind, the original basis of their projects and could also sway the focus of personal ethics. When science could potentially create much money, then many jobs, and deals internationally, sometimes the original ethics of the work so easily are forgotten. That would not be him, he thought. He was his work.

To get to the university laboratories on time, Steven had to really try hard to get rid of the large group of affectionate, flirtatious young women around him in the car park.

'Look, I'll be in the Union after. I'll see you ladies there in a while. I do have to do some boring but very necessary scientific experimentation now. Get the drinks in for me, ladies,' he told them.

As he turned from them, he caught sight of a strange couple of men at the other end of the car park looking his way. Could they be lecturers at all? He believed that he had never seen these men around the university campus at all. Maybe they were some people connected to university funding? Perhaps, but probably not, he realised. He saw then that they did watch him too, then quickly looked away and in seconds moved off over through the far doors, gone somewhere from his view. The sighting made Steven actually feel uncomfortable. Police he could deal with, and cars chasing him, coppers accusing him, but strange unknown men just simply watching him from afar? Something not good was taking place, he thought to himself.

A morning spent watching the mind-numbing low brow talk shows on television ended when Steven looked across out of the front window of the flat. Some attractive young women passed, and a flabby grey-haired man, and then he noticed the post lady approaching. He hoped she might be bringing that new, highly rated RPG game he had ordered online. She walked along and then another man came up toward her. They stopped, and he spoke to her as she looked through her post collection in the bag strapped to her shoulder. What was that guy asking her? Steven thought. Maybe she had the guy's weird fetish magazine in her bag, he thought, and he was just too keen to get his hands on it. That bloke was not a local though, he thought, watching him then. The post lady was nodding as he spoke to her, but she seemed to then disagree. Then, no, she looked thoughtful. She looked over at the flat's front door and was telling the man something else. The man seemed to be agreeing, seemed pleased and asked a couple more questions. She said something else, then they both smiled at each other and she continued on her way. The mysterious man then took a glance at the front of the flat, the window, then walked off away quickly. It disturbed Steven a little. Who the hell was that man, he wanted to know. He waited a second, then stood and walked to the window and carefully watched the man walking off down the street. He had simply no sure idea of who the man was, but he was probably some kind of trouble.

Chapter 4

Within the tall, deep and impressive company building in the city, the scientific medical production research company that Gordon owned continued as efficiently it always did. Managers, executive supervisors, and deputy control staff all continued their individual special tasks, but this particular day would offer uneasy difficulty as a small number of the more executive head department supervisors tried to go through regular communication and deal meeting negotiations.

'Hey Rodney, is Gordon in the building yet today?' Scott asked.

'Actually, no, I don't believe so. Can't say I've seen him around. You know how he can be, though,' Rodney replied.

'Right, I know. Suppose so. Okay,' Scott said.

The two men attempted to continue phone calls and emails to other research departments. A woman entered the room abruptly, looking worried before them.

'Where is Gordon?' she asked them.

'He's not in yet,' Rodney said to her.

'Oh, shit. Fuck, we need to find him right now,' she said.

'Why? What's the matter?' Scott asked her, not catching her.

'The Ronson and Figgis deal... There's a real problem now. They are saying a load of bad shit about Gordon. They're so paranoid and being just manipulative. Crazy talk really but that could really cause a lot of real problems for us,' she told them.

'What kind of problems, exactly?' Scott asked.

'I shouldn't say, he needs to talk to them really soon. The whole deal could go sour and nasty and could even stir up a load more problems up ahead for us very easily,' she warned.

'You think so? What do they know?' Scott asked.

'Enough, I guess from what it sounds like. I don't know... It's just... Gordon is missing so much right now. He's so... elusive,' she said, then quickly turned to leave the room, distracted by some other serious thought in mind.

'Tell him to find me if he comes in soon, will you?' she told them as she walked off then.

'Yes, hopefully we'll see him soon,' Scott replied.

'She's right about Gordon,' Scott said to Rodney quietly.

'You can't say anything like that. What? You think there is some weird stuff going on with him?' Rodney said.

'Could be. Might be the usual clichés; mistress, gay boyfriend, other business deals... I don't know, he's... You know, you've seen him. Big, really successful guys like him... So much pressure and work is like an addiction to them,' Scott said thoughtfully.

'But he's not your regular mega-ego rich bloke though, is he?' Rodney said.

'Exactly, yeah but it's all about the thrills. New kicks, new highs, dangers, excitement all gets bigger, grander, better than before...'

'So you think he's doing dangerous things?' Rodney asked.

'I think he could be. He might not think it is dangerous, but he could be in danger somehow,' Scott said.

'Bet it's a bloody great, exciting, wild kind of danger though'

'Hell yes,' Scott said.

They both seemed to have a look of admiration over their faces at the thought.

Between one and two that afternoon, Gordon had still not made it into the company building. Scott walked along to the main office area that Gordon used when there. He knew the door code, having observed Gordon discreetly previously, and this was to be the first time he dared enter alone. It was a long wide room, and around it were placed a number of very visibly exotic and obviously quite expensive ornaments. Some modern art prints – Warhol, Bacon, Lichtenstein, Pollock – hung over the walls around him. A framed photo of Galileo and another, bizarrely of Lenin, right next to another of his family. Gordon, his wife, Steven and the other two children. This was the room of a very powerful, successful but often mysterious and strange man, he thought as he looked around. He stepped across to one side, noticing the computer monitors, and a stack of files and books on the desk beside them. Then he felt inside himself suddenly, some tickly, strange niggling feeling nagging him. He turned and reached down.

He opened the lower drawers of the long desk and looked down. Inside would sit known guilty secrets, embarrassing obsessions of a respected, wealthy northern science research businessman; the fragile workings of his brave, bold psyche. Some vodka, Prozac, a literary novel, some executive toys. In the other, some magazines of various intellectual level interest. But much closer inspection revealed them to be science periodicals, journals specifically about space travel and exploration, the galaxies around us and the known planets outside of earth. Strange, he thought. Not very shocking or valuable as bribery material. Well, many of the greatest men were often just simply great nerds; sad, boring souls with barely any juicy secrets, ultimately. It seems his boss was just one of those same pathetic nerds. He looked around a little more, though now deflated and feeling frustrated, then walked back out of the room again.

It was quite a discreet bar out on the higher streets of the city centre where Steven sat with a double malt whiskey and Coke, his personal thoughts brewing slowly. He clicked his fingers on the glass while he waited for nearly fifteen minutes by himself, which was never enjoyable after more than ten minutes, usually. After that, his father showed up, all wise smiles and swagger.

'There you are, son. How are things now, then?' Gordon asked him, sitting by him.

'Where are you? Every damn day, where are you?' Steven suddenly said with aggression.

'I work, Steven, very hard. You know this. I gave you the life you know. I help people live better, you know that well enough,' Gordon told him.

'No, not when no one knows where the hell you are. No staff, no one at your company, not me. You show up, you vanish later. I need... It is better if you show up, you know,' Steven told him annoyed.

'It is very good you feel that way. Just what I need from you,' Gordon replied, smiling.

'No, I need reliability from you. You want a son to follow you, a good scientist in the family after you, in your amazing footsteps? So, let that happen then, will you?' Steven said.

'You... You are doing well enough. I know. I watch your moves. I like it,' Gordon said.

'What? Where have you been? I don't feel very fucking included right now. Tell me,' Steven said.

'Trust me. Respect me and my experience, my son,' Gordon told him with a quiet seriousness. 'Now, let's order some lunch shall we? A fine steak and a strong drink?'

Late in the afternoon, Alan took a couple of important project documents along to the lower laboratory offices to hand in. He walked down corridors alone, turned a couple times, continued. All was quiet as usual. The strange, deathly, hospital like quiet had grown on him in the time there and would hopefully be his continued familiar environment of work in future. Turning another corner, then, he almost walked right into a mysterious tall man.

'Oh hell... Sorry, I'm very sorry,' he said feeling almost embarrassed.

The man, in his expensive fine dark suit looked back with quiet interest at him.

'This is the place of the bio-channel observance testing department, yes?' he asked Alan.

'Yes, absolutely it is. I work there myself. Well, I study there. Can I help you at all?' Alan offered.

'Your name?' the man asked him.

'I'm Alan. You?' Alan said.

'And the others on your course? Other young men like you?' the man asked.

'Yes, why do you ask exactly?' Alan said.

'Thank you, Alan. Have a good day. Good luck at work,' the man told him and then he walked off with quiet focused confidence, disappearing around the top corridor. Alan observed him leave and was then very confused and just a little apprehensive about this strange person.

The house looked too good, as it always did, thanks to well-paid cleaners and staff. A gargantuan mortgage, with far too many rooms vacant, but there for guests who occasionally stayed over when the grand dinner parties took place. Steven walked in, sighing with reluctance. He preferred really not to visit too often these days if he could, but he knew where the money for it all came from, and how he should regard it personally. His father Gordon was, he knew, an immensely hardworking, dedicated businessman in the world of scientific research and funding.

In some ways, the house uncomfortably made Steven consider his far future, and how it could possibly mirror his father's life. Not just the impressive grand house and expensive cars around them, but how much he might even repeat Gordon's successes. Would it be from his own hard work and dedication or the unavoidable offers of help and guidance from him. This would surely be good but most likely not really impress his father, he believed. There was never any sure way of knowing what ultimately impressed Gordon, Steven believed, especially from his own actions. So he simply enjoyed himself, and everyone knew about it, about his wild actions. Gordon knew, but rarely expressed any opinion, except with more money and offers of powerful significance in the business world.

Science was in his family. Gordon had made very expected developments through the '80s and '90s, establishing the family wealth, business, reputation and comfort with his focused work in the scientific fields. The wild attention-seeking events of every other day in the life of Steven could be interpreted as frustration, but Gordon remembered his own youthful actions being not too far from what he saw Steven doing. A wild, talented son from an experienced, calmed, talented father.

Entering the vast open hallway then into the first study, Steven met with Gordon, who was with a pair of business friends, talking with whiskeys in hand.

'Good morning, my wild child offspring,' Gordon said, seeing him enter.

'Morning gentlemen, and father. Calculating infinity and more beyond?' Steven replied.

'Well, business never stops,' Gordon told him.

'Yes, business, not science these days is it?' Steven said.

'Science, like most everything else is business. You know this,' Gordon told him.

'I know your opinion, that's certain,' Steven said.

'You know how lucky you are too, don't you?' Gordon asked.

'Okay, funny that. Can I help with anything here?'

'You tell me, son,' Gordon said. It seemed that possibly Steven had entered at the wrong time, and had walked in when Gordon did not wish him to be there. That was such a regular occurrence anyway. So what? Steven thought. These moments gave him great pleasure.

'Show not tell, right? That's us,' Steven answered.

'Certainly. University's almost over, isn't it? Almost five long years hiding from the world of real work. Making me proud, are you?' Gordon asked.

'Does that matter?' Steven said.

'Oh, don't start that. I hope you come out well. Car running well now, is it?' Gordon asked changing subject.

'Yes, just about. Runs very well. I get around' Steve said.

'Good. Okay, Steven, this is Lucas and Davies. You've met them before, right?'

Steven took a glance casually their way, smiling a novelty sarcastic smile.

'I believe so. Some party, a few months back now, wasn't it?' Steven said

'Sounds about right, yes. A new venture we're talking over. Interesting thoughts and possibilities. Investors offering toward tests concerning some unseen medication procedures, new direction in immune system control theory... Of sorts,' Gordon told him. dramatically. 'Your kind of thing. Is it worth giving your exclusive attention? We are discussing this with strong opportunity ahead of us.'

'Long term jobs, results, exclusive rights, safe production with good ethical practices?' Steven asked.

'Perhaps just.... Perhaps,' Gordon told him resentfully.

'I'll go my own way. Come this autumn, my own plans will support me very well. You know this. Sorry guys,' Steven told them.

'Oh, that's fine, your choice of course. Always will be,' Gordon said.

Steven picked up the large bottle of highly expensive malt whiskey and sloppily necked a few strong mouthfuls. He then began walking out of the room, only stopping to turn and give them all a defiant look before leaving. He drove away from the luxurious residence at great erratic speed in his car, pissed off and distracted with insecure thoughts more than ever.

Since his early teens, Steven had felt the manipulative influence of Gordon and had observed the work his father had done with hesitant curiosity and interest. Gordon, when asked, would tell him about great men such as Einstein, Galileo, Newton and Machiavelli, and he himself was involved in scientific exploration and testing, always of some radical nature outside of the strong business company which allowed it. Some fathers simply paid the bills without grand ambition, worked nine to five, just happy to have enough and know they and their family were alright. Gordon knew of the world, knew of how scientific discoveries helped the world, cured diseases, explored space, broke boundaries and saved societies through technology. His family looked after, he then continually sought to progress scientific discovery in health, disease, evolution and progression. What Steven had seen over the last few years as he grew up, his thoughts maturing, was a father who in one way was influential in science and in another, influential with money and business deals. The two sides of Gordon confused Steven and continued to disturb him.

Being his son, Steven did feel the not unnoticeable pressure of Gordon's success. Should he personally feel the need to continue easily into a waiting career in scientific business ventures alongside his father? It might not be worth ignoring or avoiding, Steven often thought. But he was his own person, with his own beliefs, opinions, desires and ambitions – wasn't he? He often wondered just how many of his own opinions were truly his own and which had been gradually shaped and bred into him from Gordon through his teenage years and earlier. He would find himself, and Gordon would see that.

Steven had a younger sister, Lucy, and a brother, older by two years, Nathan. Either of them could be another success in scientific work, though this was probably unlikely. He knew Lucy was only in secondary school, even though she was special in her way. Nathan too, had seemed to have missed his first chance; he was now unemployed after art college, spending his time writing and painting. If it was going to be anyone, Gordon most definitely had his sights firmly set on Steven.

While Gordon was obviously extremely influential and respected in most scientific areas, he also had influence and interest in the work Steven was doing at the university, even if he rarely showed it clearly. This had been welcomed and watched with caution equally when finally noticed. Of course he valued the input and views of his father who had worked with science of many kinds for over twenty five years, but there were always things to be wary of with Gordon. He had offered his views, guidance, opinions, support and opportunities a number of times, and Steven had taken six months at one of Gordon's business headquarters. Steven had learned much of great value toward his Biochemical Business degree, but did try to be aware to keep his distance between himself and his father, even while working in the family business for that short but interesting time.

Steven wanted his own identity and his own achievement, and he could almost sense his father coming too close, almost stealing his original thoughts, making too many decisions and choosing too many paths for him. As his science Master's degree had continued, Steven and Gordon came to spend less time together as their opinions separated, polarised it seemed. Gordon had told him a number of times how he almost envied the academic, unseen freedoms of university work; the open experimentation and opportunity available. He explained how when money and business come into play, much less exciting chances were allowed, contrary to belief. Gordon himself had many personal complex theories and ideas, and occasionally aired concepts that seemed bizarre and too radical or just simply entertaining sound bites spoken to shock or fascinate. Those ideas stayed dormant, untested, forgotten now that he put all of his time into working for multinational, financially backed research and production companies, producing a series of successful medicines and legal drug remedies, mostly. Steven often could see the occasional sadness there, collected deep in his father's tired eyes.

In significant contrast, Alan went through his late teens and early twenties in much more difficult, uncomfortable circumstances. Though not extremely dire, things were certainly working class and depressingly bad for his family financially and socially, much less privileged and with many more problems. Alan almost liked and embraced the near poverty at times, his parents showing him that great character can be born from difficult challenges in life and hardship to overcome as they found ways to get through and appreciate what they did have. He then worked extremely hard, studied constantly, valuing the opportunity to be on his university course having come from such a bleak, poor background economically. It paid off by the end of college and his degree, granting him access to a Master's degree, alongside his close friend Steven. While economically they had been opposites always, they shared interests in simple things like '70s rock music, video games and fine women.

Together, Alan and Steven hoped to make new progress in their own unique scientific research and experiments as a strong, bold team. The wild, opinionated stance of Steven along with the deep theoretical focus and discipline of Alan worked so surprisingly well for them at college and then university; praise and respect coming their way often enough as teachers and lecturers noticed how different and interesting their ideas often were.

Throughout college and university, Alan was surprised and often wondered if Steven would one day jump right into a position with Gordon at the family business, which seemed too tempting to ignore. There was a fascination from both Steven and Alan about the pharmaceutical and medical research company Gordon headed. It had the business tag and it produced new drugs and medical technology, but there were always other things going on they had seen. Steven knew of these more mysterious projects.

'You're making mistakes, Steven,' Alan eventually commented.

'I'll get through. Look, this is still only university, mate. There's more to come. The real science, the big thrills are waiting. Just waiting, passing the time, going through the rituals of education,' Steven said.

'Going through the rituals? I'm not. I'm using the opportunity to prove myself, to test theories early, show what I am capable of now,' Alan told him.

Did he need to feel jealous of Steven? Was that the truth? he wondered. He was depending so much on Steven, their final year projects needing the efforts of both of them and the others to come out successfully. Every day it was worrying Alan, Steven's distant, nonplussed attitude to everything about their Master's degree work and the importance of it. He often felt like a nurse, being there for his crazed, wild friend. He honestly admired and respected Steven, but there were just more and more strange times when Steven was too careless, risking himself. It had to change, Alan thought. For his sanity, if no other reason. Was Steven getting ready to join his father much sooner than after university ended for them?

If that was to be, Alan would be going alone, different new projects, alone or with others. Would that happen? he thought. There was no way that he wanted it to be like that but it seemed to be coming anyway.

'I'm sorry, mate. We will move on together. You and I. Both of us,' he told Alan.

'Three weeks left now,' Alan told him.

'Three short weeks... Then the world should watch out, right?' Steven said, as confident and relaxed as he always could be.

Alan was nervous but hopeful as well somehow. His erratic, wild friend would take them somewhere and find unexpected but definitely eventful and interesting opportunities ahead for them. He would still have to really watch that the specific ethics and the science involved would be respectable, but Alan knew he and Steven worked extremely well as a team – maybe too well.

Chapter 5

The three weeks passed, with tension but hope. They graduated. Parties happened, stupendous amounts of drinking, drug taking, clubbing, sex and eventually job interviews and meetings with various project organisers. Alan, Steven, Joanna, Pete and Pascal were out, highly qualified in complex and respectable academic scientific practice. No more education, time for real practical work in among the real world and the highly professional science industries around the country and elsewhere. They could challenge the establishment, begin really important socially and scientifically relevant projects, and feel their own efforts being seen and considered.

In a matter of weeks, Steven, Alan, Pete, Pascal and Joanna formed a legitimate, real independent research test team – business accounts, company logo, the works – and set out working in loose connection with other local universities and bursaries for funding and support. They discussed their initial few major proposed projects and, in the main, Steven and Alan directed and controlled it together. Their post Master's, professional outside project looked into further studies and experimentation on immune system boundaries and cell division limitations, with other chemical additional exposure. They engaged in tests on blood, skin tissue, samples from hospitals and local morgues. Their new highly ranked Master's degrees gained them frequent continued interest and funding quickly, without them really having to do much of their own work contacting companies and others. They were impressed and so were their families proud. They were beginning to make their mark, the world of scientific research and testing noticing these new brave and bold young people entering the scientific community at large.

As they conducted interviews and pitched themselves, their theories and proposed projects and ideas, known major scientific companies, businessmen and woman of influence took notice and considered how to work with them. Gordon watched and heard of the choices and statements of Steven and Alan over the beginning time. He was proud as he saw Steven becoming a responsible man, entering into professional business dealings in the science world. He watched Steven and saw the still strong potential, even if Steven was reluctant to join with the family company. It was to their advantage, however, that Steven decided to work within the project team as they moved ahead professionally together.

The early weeks became unexpectedly tense, with an uneasy seriousness weighing over the young group of scientists.

'We just can't tell them anything at all,' Alan told them.

'We're not, are we?' Steven said.

'It might sound like that. This is the beginning, our first impressions,' Alan said.

'And it's a good one. The best!' Steven excitedly cheered.

'I'm not sure,' Alan sighed.

'He might be right, in a way, Steven,' Pascal interjected.

'Oh, you think so, do you?' Steven said not keen on his opinion.

'Just calm down, boys. We're doing well. We are. Let's look over our options again, okay?' Joanna said to them all.

'Do we need to? We can't just fall back and get scared like soft, little kids – forget that!' Steven said with obvious anger and resentment .

'You have to stop acting like that,' Joanna told him.

Steven quickly looked back at her, then he threw out his right hand and knocked some lab equipment to the floor, smashing some of it easily to pieces.

'Oh, great,' Alan said, watching it shatter.

Steven walked right out of the laboratory rooms, not stopping.

'He's just a crazy man,' Pascal said aloud, shaking his head.

'Some of the best scientists in history were... eccentric too,' Alan offered.

'Eccentric, but not psychotic,' Joanna added.

Alan knew they all wished that he would stop making excuses for Steven. He did too.

As a new, young group of postgraduate scientists, they continued on. Interviews came and they began to see what they could do together; how they should work better together in the real world as professionals in order to make their mark. Individually, they each specialised in specific areas of science and research, and this they had to try to use to their advantage. There were certainly many great problems and issues which they could look into helping and investigating through experimentation; issues which they greatly cared about, including illnesses – diseases such as cancer of various kinds, motor neurone disease, neurological problems and more – following on from a number of areas which Steven and Joanna had focused on with their final degree test projects.

Even as reckless and wild as Steven could get, he did produce half a dozen truly fascinating and challenging examples and results to give them much to show around to others and use to progress their work. While all four of them had produced exceptionally high theories and results continually, Alan and Steven together clearly stood out to them as the two who produced the most interesting and useful results.

Steven had worked through a final project which studied and examined differences in the modern human immune system in Western living, and diseases and viruses which broke through it and why. He was looking at radical views for understanding, beating and controlling illnesses which weakened us continually through our lives. Besides normal expected medicines and drugs which usually only went so far to help, he was trying to take the illnesses and immune system attack down to the basics and study it minutely. Alan, meanwhile had a final degree thesis which focused upon unusual rarely studied areas of medicine, chemical and biological combined and systematic healing experiments. These two very separate areas of investigation were decided to be where the whole group would and should forge ahead and seek out financial funding.

As they expected, Steven took the lead. He used the tactics and talk he had observed from his father for years. He began to find the group certain interest and negotiate financial meetings and gain interviews and formal meals to discuss the work itself being proposed. In the matter of only a few weeks, they rented a small office area on the edge of the city, converted it into laboratory rooms and set out beginning tests toward briefs which Steven and Alan agreed, with the head managers of two chosen national medical research science companies, along with help from the university which they had all graduated from.

'The budgets are working well, aren't they? I can almost barely believe how fast this is all happening,' Pascal said as the four of them moved equipment one afternoon through the laboratory rooms.

'Oh, hell yeah, of course. No problems. We're on a roll now, guys,' Steven told them with assurance.

'We need to keep a close watch on it, even so. Can't just get carried away. This is all for the long term haul. We don't want to buy way too much equipment and then find it all grinds to a halt before it has really begun,' Alan said.

'It won't happen. Have no fear,' Steven said.

'You're right, Alan. He's right,' Joanna said, looking at the others.

'Trust me, trust us. We're going to make headlines, win prizes, no doubt of it,' Steven told them, not for the first time. They all looked at Steven, grateful but with silent, nervous scepticism. They were truly all close friends in the group, or close enough, but they each held their own individual private views on how Steven wanted to work with them.

The familiar cramped, small flat that Alan and Steven shared remained so while they began working as professional, legitimate scientists. They had their unusual 'odd couple' style of chore sharing between them, but often Alan ended up getting the worst end of things, involving cleaning grime and filth away. He did not really mind, as he relied on Steven ultimately for advice on how best to lure women and show them an outstanding time. Because of this, they knew each other so well, and were so close, like real blood brothers from one family.

On waking one morning, Steven entered the lounge room, half waking up, to see Alan watching the morning early news with close concentration.

'Morning there, mate. Look at this, it's just real bizarre...' Alan told him, not taking his eyes from the television screen.

'Oh, right, what is it?' Steven asked and sat down beside him on the worn down sofa.

'... This unexpected sickness is to be studied and monitored very closely. It is hoped that there are no more expected cases to be found like it in the near area. It seems a one off occurrence so far. The doctors suggest not to be panicked right now. Police...'

Steven heard the television news reporter say it live before them.

'So, what was that then? What is it?' he asked looking at Alan.

'They had a guy – he was ill – but it was apparently a very unusual and bizarre sickness or symptom. He seemed to almost die and then came back, but some senses were heightened, and others almost totally gone. He is now almost totally blind. How just really weird is that?' Alan told him. He was clearly stunned and fascinated himself at the report.

'People get sick in all kinds of ways. It... happens,' Steven replied in a strange casual almost uninterested manner.

'That doesn't happen. It's really fucking strange, Steven. Come on, we could look into that. It's worth checking,' Alan suggested.

'No. That's police work anyway. Forensics, like on television, really. I mean... Look, we can't try to begin solving everything. There is not enough time, not for our humble little team, at least not at present. What's on the other news channels?' Steven asked.

Alan gave him a look but changed the channel anyway. Would he be able to cope with having to ignore many serious bad situations and sicknesses to only deal with a select few in his work ahead? he thought. What kind of frustrating torment would that be to live with? Could he deal with Steven being so emotionless in work, so detached and objective, and only thinking of needed results and procedures? They had to be professional.

After the unexpected wild scenes across the town streets, the second ill person with similar symptoms was caught soon enough, taken with great secure speed to be studied by highly qualified doctors and a few government representatives. This was a curious, strange beginning illness which had possessed the person, a woman, possibly in her mid- to late forties. She had calmed down, though was in a heavy daze, and was dosed up with strong sedatives to a secure degree. Two doctors took the expected samples and tests of blood, eyesight, urine, heart rate, skin and saliva, and then moved on fascinated and puzzled. There was something else about her and the first one like her; they could not help but continue to investigate her strange ways, afraid, quietly and simply confused. What had caused this average woman to suddenly become wildly rabid, increase in strength, running demented and chasing others, then just as suddenly, become speechless, confused and motionless.

'She is just so strange. Weird. Her blood, the temperature... Then what is that with her skin?' one doctor noted.

'I know. It's... It's so perplexing really. Very, very bizarre. No clear answers I can find immediately. What sickness is this?' the other said.

'Could it be from overseas – some new virus or disease that has been dormant for decades, or longer?' the first suggested.

'Maybe. Possibly. We'll check who she is, her medical stats, and if she's been overseas recently, as usual,' he said.

'And she seems similar to that bloke, really.'

'But he was not contagious, was he?'

'Well, no, not so far, that we are aware of, at least.'

'We can't have her here, can we? What do we do now?'

'Hospital, I should think.'

'But we could do more, given time. We could find out what's wrong with her ourselves.'

'What can we do? We just don't have more sophisticated equipment here, now. Only the usual. We could call some friends. If you think she could be such a find for us?'

'She could be a very significant thing right now. Very interesting, very valuable, I'd say,' the other doctor said. They looked at her and then at each other without saying any more. One of them then reached for his cell phone from his jacket pocket to phone a useful friend who could be very certainly interested with their situation, he believed.

Chapter 6

While Gordon had to spend so much of his working days in redundant meetings, on the computer and in webcam discussions, he still had kept many areas of other scientific research and study open to explore occasionally. As time and years had passed in his life, with a very small handful of close associates, he did organise investigating a couple of more provocative, dangerous theories which most were not willing to listen to, and which would openly pose immediate threat to his established life. But he pursued the most careful ways of looking for the right help and support available to him. These were concepts and theories that, when discussed openly in the science industry, were repeatedly frowned upon, and labelled morally and ethically as extremely questionable. Gordon though, in some ways, did think that there were some bold figures in times past who had gone beyond the majority outrage for the greater ultimate benefits that others could not dare comprehend in the present through lack of courageous daring. There was always distrust for the real bold, brave thinkers and always would be, he believed. It was expected, and he was to expect it himself as part of his work, as just a hurdle to climb.

He had reached a time when he believed he could finally make some very significant experiments and progress with his secret personal theories at very long last. It was to be highly secretive, but it was to happen now he knew. It all could wait no longer. The time was right now, he thought.

Over the previous decade, he had gained the trust and confidence of a number of influential and interested men and women who worked in similar areas of science research on such large international scales as himself, with medicine, technological breakthroughs, and other fields of study. He had begun the task of organising times, names and places. If the slightest things went wrong, he knew someone might inform authorities, police and others ending everything. His life, his work officially would end for sure. He knew doctors, investors, biologists, physicists and more who were now finally willing to offer some level of help to him. He had tempted them with offers of great discoveries, small favours, joint acclaim, reward and now it was time. It was all coming together after over a decade of silent waiting.

The lunch was a satisfying break, and now coffee was needed. Alan and Steven walked back up to the laboratory entrance.

'Were the doors left open?' Steven asked.

'I... Well, no, they were closed. Weren't they?' Alan replied.

They shrugged and walked with slight confused ambivalence. Things looked alright and untouched on first glances. They walked around, set up the computer programmes once more and boiled the kettle for strong coffee.

'You working now, then?' Alan asked, slyly teasing Steven.

'Yes, damn it. Don't you start, slave driver. I've got my thinking head on. Joanna coming back too?' Steven said.

'Think so. Maybe later on, though,' Alan told him.

He sat down at the computer, and opened files to then check through a list of results then complied theories. They were still at a stage of preparation, and many elements going forward were uncertain still. Alan looked at the figures presented on screen. He knew that to move on in good time, they had to find something. They were stuck around a particular area. While they had begun to build a pleasing pattern of connection with new found medical compound synthesis, more needed to come to them, and fast. They could, he knew, just simply face a few months more of trial and error as usual. He had to just relax into the slow pace of testing again after their initial unexpected burst of testing success. He saw a sudden arrangement then, before his eyes. What was it? The figures were looking relevant, and he was seeing some new connection, a link between numbers and estimates so far unseen.

'Hey, Steven, get here. Look at this now,' he shouted loudly across the room.

He began scrolling down the pages on the screen and scribbling rough notes in a small pad at the right side of the desk.

'What? The coffee's here,' Steven announced, bringing it over as he came.

'I can't believe this. It's here. This looks very good to me. Check it out. It's all we need. The path ahead is much clearer now. Right, here, I see it,' Alan told him with renewed enthusiasm.

'What's that then?' Steven asked still not entirely captivated.

'The next step, more steps ahead. I see a lot of it all here. Look at it, see?' Alan said pointing to the computer screen then.

'You do? You do. Great. Good. That must be a great moment of personal epiphany. Well done. Fancy a good beer now to celebrate?' Steven said.

'No, let's just get this nailed down clearly. Can't lose it. Focus, before I lose the train of thought here, and the path ahead' Alan said with great seriousness.

'Alright. Here's your coffee, champ,' Steven said and smiled, patting Alan on the back.

A long lunch break enjoyed, followed by a couple of international top quality chilled beers, Gordon and his close, small management team quietly talked between each other in a relaxed way about plans for the company, international market expectations and even family problems. As the four colleagues around him laughed and joked, finishing their drinks before heading back to the company building, Gordon felt a tight strain in him. A heavy pull in his chest, pulling down. His eyesight blurred a little, but he still listened to his friend Gareth talking. He coughed and leaned to one side. A sharp pain distracted him then.

Gordon stood, knowing he should leave them then.

'What's up Gordon? One of them asked.

'I'm... I am fine. I... will meet you... out at the cars in a few minutes,' he told them.

'Okay then,' his colleague replied.

They watched him walk out to the car park, each with their own opinion of their boss to themselves. They spoke quietly to one another.

'You know how Gordon acts about his family? Strange, right?' one said.

'Big, rich manager types like him rarely talk about their family truthfully, and then when they do, it's their jokes and nothing else,' the other said.

'He's very, very tetchy if you ask anything, I found,' the first said.

'Well, it's because he's divorced. Didn't go too well, I think. Tries to see his family, and his children when she lets him,' the other replied.

'She a real bitch?'

'Well don't know really... It seems it's very complicated for him. Just one little girl. His other two are grown up, I think.'

'I think I hear she's got some disorder – maybe disabled or something. Don't say anything right though, yeah?' he said.

'Oh, right, no problem. Of course not,' the other replied.

In a lively local city pub, Steven sat alone with his third pint of lager, taking time away from the research project; the pressure and nagging he felt from the group was stressing him too much. He looked around at the early evening people around him, drinking also, enjoying time out and relaxed conversations, and escaping work and their own individual pressures in life. There was a long, flat screen, plasma television up on the wall to his right side and right, then news of the startling street attackers came on; some people around began noticing it, and they then began offering their own mumbled opinions. Steven heard them, their fear and disgust, ill-informed anger and hatred, misunderstanding the real causes. They would surely be much more grateful, Steven thought, when they knew completely. Yes – these events had been obviously tragic but for the greater good in moving ahead for society. That was his opinion, what he had been thinking so far.

'Dirty street scum, those ones. No need for that behaviour at all. Diseased and drugged up,' one man spat out, looking up at the news report.

'Should jail them, beat sense into them. Lock them up. Take their drugs away, sort them out properly. That's those video games and crazy music doing that, makes them mad in the head, ultraviolent,' another lady said in agreement.

Steven turned to view the opinionated soapbox regulars, there near him with their narrow views and stereotyping thoughts.

'There's often three sides to every story, you know,' he said calmly and quietly.

'Oh, sorry lad, who are you? Prime Minister or something?' the older man said.

'It is obviously very sad what's happened, but they might not be doing the worst thing here. Could be some good outcome,' Steven suggested.

'Really? Are you mental, son? Did you see the victims, or hear the reports properly that's coming in? Listen to it all. Bloody bruised, beaten so badly. Disgusting. Pray it don't happen to you,' the older man spat back at him.

'Right. I suppose I don't. Of course, so true,' Steven replied quietly.

A young bar girl walked near him then, collecting the pint glasses around and leaned close by.

'I'd leave it now, honey. Forget them. I see your point, I think,' she told him discreetly and then winked.

'Okay then. Thanks. Lovely eyes, by the way,' he told her.

'Oh, not too bad yourself, either,' she responded and winked as she then walked away. He finished his last pint, then also walked away from the jaded, simple soapbox drinkers all around him.

In a locked cubicle in the men's toilet of the expensive popular lunch bar, Gordon propped himself up against the side wall, waiting to throw up. He waited a long painful moment, but after a few minutes, nothing came out. He was dizzy, nauseous, and pissed off. He understood the signs, he knew his body, his own secret, personal ticks. Was he just too stressed? He reached into his jacket pocket. No, he knew his own history, the events. From a small box there, he quickly took out a handful of pills, then from another pocket found some different yellow ones, and necked both small handfuls rapidly then washed them down with a drink of tap water at the sinks. He stepped out, lurched up to the sinks and looked at his shaking face, pale but knowing. His own eyesight was hurting him, focusing was a difficult chore, considerably. Trying to look hard at himself, the image he found was unexpected.

He saw before him some surreal, distorted variation of himself, an alternative, a wish fulfilment dream self. The skin was some kind of luminous sinew, a vile shape, almost sweating but not actually. His eyes seemed to just about fluctuate in shade and colour. How could that be, he wondered? No, he hated this. Always had, he remembered. He could control it, with his special pills. As long as he had those sweet, special pills.

Around five minutes later, he came to meet the others out in the car park by their cars.

'Everything okay, Gordon?' the woman in the red coat asked him.

'Yes, totally fine, thanks. Let's go earn our wage, then, you clever hardworking bastards,' he yelled with a broad smile and arms wide. He winked to them all before then getting into his own car. He drove off as his sense of reality returned to him, with the unnatural occurrence over.

There could always be things he could not predict, Gordon thought. With science, with life. But there were things he knew which were so unique and special to him. Time had let him secretly think many things about these rare but powerful strange changes in his body, his perception. He had many theories, and a few which became extremely obsessive over the years. As close as family, as far as darkest space. It pleased him now, as he reached his late fifties, finally.

So they were out. It had been miscalculated just enough for it to become dangerous and, in a big way, uncontrollable. He did not know when or if it would happen, but now it had, it could be controlled he believed. If not, then at least covered up or excused away in the industry. There were messed up people out on the streets, failed ruined experiments. They just could not work but someone had to, at some point soon. There were only so many paths left for him, and the ultimate most obvious one was lined up right ahead, like he knew it would be eventually.

No real doctor seemed able to do any damned thing to help, to get this fucking strange unknown disease out of him. That had been his initial want years earlier. Right now though, it had inspired him so much, and had revealed many things he believed. It was his problem in many ways, he knew. Many years had been passed as he learned more, tried more, believed more significance came from the strange pains, visions, feelings.

It did seem to him now that the first two had escaped in such wild, violent ways. His colleagues had given him wise advice. But why would he have listened to them? They were not like him – they envied him; his position, lifestyle, wealth and achievements and could honestly not really understand his work that they had been helping him with, in more ways than they knew. Now, he would begin the process he had held back against his better intuition. There had been an even more secretive idea, phone calls made, connections with old friends in Britain, America and other countries overseas. It was to be a much more difficult and extremely more ambitious plan which would, he knew, certainly now endanger his entire company. But it was his company which now allowed him take this most personal huge risk. Now he would begin the process; now he would return to outer space.

As the day drew on, with serious mapping of figures and testing progressing, Alan and Joanna watched carefully together on opposite sides of the laboratory.

'Watching still, yeah?' Alan asked across the room.

'Eye on the levels, going steady still,' she replied.

Then Steven burst in, a big proud smile on his face.

'Hello, darlings, give me a round of applause then,' he said.

'Quiet. We're timing things out carefully still,' Alan told him.

'Three more interviews, feedback from two more investors and meetings for the next week. Alan, still following the new direction? Those great figures with the new compound tests?' he asked.

'Well, yes, it seems just the right way. Perfect timing. Just perfect. Fate, even,' Alan said and surprisingly laughed out loud.

'Exactly right. Good, great. I'll just look at the notes we've got this week,' Steven told them as he moved around the room between desks and tables.

'Fine, just be quiet then,' Joanna replied as she and Alan both watched their work, not even glancing at Steven for a second.

Chapter 7

While darkness fell near nine o'clock, Steven walked along the estate, past industrial buildings he knew well. It was quite an unusual area. Some vacant factories, others that all produced their individual mysterious products just as his father's laboratories did their special work inside. He approached finally, not really in the mood, but he had answered the call from his father and agreed this time. All around was silent, and only sparse, distant streetlights marked out the surroundings for him. He walked close up to the opening of the fence around the laboratories and caught some faint sound behind somewhere close to him.

He turned, a little nervous, then. It was increasingly difficult to make out almost anything with the thick dark of night cloaking the area. But there was some sound, some footsteps, even. Then a brief flick of light, small somewhere. It shone on something maybe ten feet away from him. Then, again, he was sure he heard some footsteps. He turned and walked on faster, entering the gates around the building.

Two police detectives walked in toward him, as quietly as they could. He knew. Steven turned back again and looked into the dark behind him.

Their minds changed. The detectives saw Steven, and he saw them. They stopped still, confused expressions over their faces. Both then moaned and gasped suddenly, freezing motionless and uncomfortably, but then turned around. They slowly walked away together, away from the laboratories and from Steven. Steven watched them go. He seemed in a daze as he stood there. A voice in his mind spoke lightly to him, or simply spoke from somewhere.

'Going, gone. Going, policemen, away.'

Steven blinked his eyes, shrugged and shook his head, focusing his eyes and then walked on again toward the front doors of the building and pressed the buzzer. The door opened after a brief moment and he entered.

Much later in the evening, Steven watched Alan while they sat watching a comedy DVD in the flat together with a few lagers.

'This is classic, this guy, unbelievable. Hilarious stuff,' Alan told him, laughing and pointing at the actor on the television screen before them.

'Right. I know, he's a total... He's a real madman,' Steven replied in a more sombre tone.

'You alright? I love this film – it's bloody funny, isn't it?' Alan said.

'Oh yeah. No, it's hilarious mate, I know. I'm good. Really good,' Steven told him.

He finished his fourth can of lager and looked out of the window, out up at the deep dark night sky above. The distant stars waited for him, for them, the planets out there too; all kinds of hope and secrets, always ready and waiting.

Too early in the morning, there was a hard knock on the front door to the flat. Steven stumbled out of bed, dressing gown pulled on haphazardly, yawning as he walked to the door.

'Hang on there, calm down,' he mumbled.

He opened the door and saw his mother looking at him.

'Steven, have you seen your bloody father?' she said.

'What? I know – he's an arse, isn't he?' he told her.

'Steven, language! No, really. Have you spoken to him in the last couple of days at all?' She continued.

'Come in, mum, please,' he told her.

They walked into the main room together quietly, Steven rubbing his tired eyes and waking still, slowly.

'Yes, I think I met him Monday. Can't you contact him?' he asked.

'Doesn't seem like it. There are some very serious issues right now, he and I have to discuss,' she told him.

'Oh, what do you mean? Can I know?' he asked.

'You know how he has been before. I have to look after your sister and your brother is out. Look, I know you and he have spoken about some things – he mentioned it in his way that he does,' she explained.

'What do you mean? Mum, come on. What things? Is he alright?' Steven asked 'Look, I know things won't be the same with you and him again, but he still needs you, as a friend – you know him. No one else knows him like you, even if...' he said.

'He's a grown man, a foolish man. Your father... He's alright. You know him, Steven, these days – you know him better. Be there for him, will you?' she said.

'Yes, you know I will. I think he's an arse, but I can still learn a lot from that crazy scientist businessman,' he replied.

'Don't be a foolish man like him, Steven. He might be too far gone, but you can hold back,' she said.

He could see that she seemed extremely worried and serious in her words. He was shocked in a way, and surprised. He knew how strong she could be. She was a very tough, independent, modern woman, but human still. While his father had been the incredible business prodigy of science, she had supported the children, raised them, and had given them ideals, views and ethics. She made sure they survived the divorce.

'Be there for him,' she repeated.

'Okay. I will, he knows I will,' he said quietly, guiltily.

'Yes, he does. Even so, be there,' she said again.

She kissed him and left the flat, leaving him to think of his successful father and his own future. Then he thought of his mother and how she really felt toward Gordon after all these years.

As Gordon looked over emails and messages, reports and more at his desk, his intercom buzzed.

'Gordon you have Mr. Reznor and Mr. Claypool to see you here. Shall I let them in?' his secretary asked.

'Right, yes, right, let them in and no others while they are here, alright? At all, you understand? No one at all comes in,' he told her.

'Yes, of course Gordon,' she replied.

He stood and looked nervous then, even frightened in some sense.

'Come in,' he said as he opened the doors, greeting the two men.

They entered and smiled back silently as the doors closed behind them.

'Please sit, both of you. Drink? Whiskey? Vodka? Wine? Coffee?' Gordon asked quickly.

'No, thank you, Gordon. Relax, please. You know us well enough, really,' Mr. Reznor told him.

'Yes, I suppose I do. We do. Just... Finding it a bit... There's lots to think about, you know?' Gordon said.

'Yes, that's right but you will know what to do when it is the right time. We want to just check things now,' Mr Claypool told him.

'Which things exactly, then?' Gordon asked 'Because there are a lot of things that are not really ready around here just yet. But I really do mean what I told you, you know that. My son, and... and my daughter. I just have to change some things...'

'Okay, slow down, Gordon. Calm down. You seem to know how your son – Steven? – will step into his part of things. Now then, little Lucy – you need to be so sure of what we discussed. Do you think you are now?' Mr. Reznor asked him.

'I think so, yes. I think I would say so. Absolutely so,' Gordon replied.

'Really? We'll let you make the final decision there. But time is running short. Like we asked, Gordon. Other news now, Gordon, includes the very promising places we have spoken about. Remember the places?' Mr. Claypool asked.

'Oh, absolutely. I am very interested in those places, you know for certain that I am,' he told them.

'Of course you are. You should be, you know that,' Mr Reznor said.

'Yes, I am. It will be beautiful,' Gordon added.

'Thank you for the special work you have put in with us. We understand the time taken, the pressures, and the wait that has been involved,' Mr Claypool told him.

'But it helped, didn't it?' Gordon asked anxiously.

'Yes, Gordon, you know it did. You will be rewarded, deservedly so,' Mr. Reznor told him.

'Just do these last things. Make these decisions, Gordon. One week. Much has been done. Incredible things, just a few more things left now. Make us very proud, Gordon,' Mr Claypool urged.

'I will. You will see that, really you will,' Gordon said.

'Yes, you do that. Have to, don't you?' Mr Reznor said, almost smiling but not quite.

'Goodbye then, Gordon, we'll be in touch, like we do. Take good care now,' Mr Claypool told him.

'Yes, alright then, gentlemen. Thanks very much now. See you soon, goodbye now,' Gordon responded as he led them out of the door.

Door closed, then locked, Gordon fell back against the wall behind him, a distraught face. He sighed and returned to his desk slowly. He opened a lower drawer on the left of his desk with a key from his pocket. From inside, he took out a piece of paper, scruffy, slightly marked and tattered. It was a child's drawing in crayons and pencils, fairly simple images. It depicted very basically the sky, black space above, twinkling stars and some planets above in the blackness of space. A simple picture, it had a phenomenally powerful effect upon Gordon. He held it and almost broke down, some tears forming, welling around his eyes as he looked closely at it. He placed the picture back inside the desk drawer and then took out a single sharp gleaming razor blade, holding it between fingertips. He brought it close to his opposite wrist for a brief moment, looking at it silently, calmly. He then returned it to the desk drawer, breathed a deep breath, and returned to his desk's computer screen. He pressed his intercom.

'Sally, get me a good cappuccino please,' he ordered.

Chapter 8

Steven was enjoying leading the team officially now in the real world of science experimentation, but found his skills to continue in entertaining and convincing the financial backers, governing boards and academics. He was best in really taking people along – bringing the complex, academic scientific phrasing and terminology down to layman's terms, mainly putting things across in the most tempting, dramatic ways, gripping them with the best offers and projects they had heard in a long time. A salesman of science, future potential, a PR man of medical and scientific hope to all. He loved the attention, the suspense and negotiating, and it fuelled him, encouraged him in his escapades professionally and at night on the town.

On a Wednesday night, he met his father Gordon for an expensive, exotic meal at an exclusive city restaurant. He drank the wine and enjoyed the fine courses.

'Everything going well for you and your new team now, with your original brave projects?' Gordon finally asked him before the second bottle of fine wine arrived.

'Things are very good, thanks, father. And your own work? Any... interesting events to speak of at all?' Steven asked.

Both seemed guarded and careful with their words.

'There may always be things for you to know. You know that. You are interested now?' Gordon asked with a sly smile.

Steven took a swift drink of expensive wine, then replied.

'You will always be a strange old cunning shit, really. I am sure I will know all of it in time,' he said.

'You have a certain question? Something to know right now?' Gordon asked him.

'No... Yes. God no. Not at all, actually,' Steven growled at him, frustrated.

Gordon laughed out loud easily, then leaned in closer, speaking in quieter tones.

'You want to know more about something you've seen recently? Some curious thing, a thing connected to your hardworking father?' Gordon asked.

Steven was quiet, silently looking around them, and hesitant.

'My work is well, Steven. We are proceeding with many things that have been waiting such a long time, piece by piece, bit by bit. A dream in many pieces coming together. We don't hold back. Some don't take the chances, making us wait. We don't hold back, and neither do you,' Gordon told Steven firmly.

'Don't think you know all of me, my own mind, my own thoughts. Look, just... Be careful. If it is anything like I think, watch how far you go. You'll get sued to hell and back or worse, and I won't save you,' Steven warned.

'No, I know many men of power and influence. I get chances, but with you... If you take the chance, Steven...' Gordon offered. It was possibly the kind of exclusive offer set only for his most talented son to take. Steven could view it like that.

'I am taking chances, Dad. My chances. My own and I'll damn well not do things as...' Steven said but did not finish his speech, to avoid offence.

'Things as...?' Gordon prompted.

'Things too dangerous, goddamn twisted,' Steven told him. He finished and stood. He necked the bottle of wine, took another forkful of steak, and then left the restaurant in haste.

Over the next few days, Alan and the others observed Steven join them in work in a surprisingly quiet and focused manner, quite out of character. They wondered if he was alright in himself. As they worked as a team, each studying rates and changes in equipment, Alan spoke to Steven discreetly.

'Hey Steven, we're working well here. Really appreciate your input, mate. Thanks for getting us so far. But apart from all this, how are you doing?' he asked.

'Me? Grand, my fine buddy. Actually I'm just very concerned with our tests here. Got to be sooner or later, right? We need to get some impressive results,' Steven replied.

'I know, you're right. But you, how are you? You're a bit... not yourself,' Alan quietly observed.

'Is that a crime? Look, I did get a Master's degree, like all of us. I do work every so often, in a scientific way,' Steven told him, his temper rising slightly.

Joanna and Pascal looked over at him then, hearing him and seeing his strange behaviour suddenly.

'It's okay Steven. It's good you're into the boring serious side of this all as well,' Joanna said, smiling encouragingly. They all then continued with the careful monitoring of levels on screens again.

On a bright morning, Gordon looked out of his office window across the city horizon. There were so many office buildings around, where people were working so hard, long hours and pushing themselves. He liked drive in a person, ambition and hunger for more. He had it, and he needed it. It had taken him so far from his troubles, away from the dangers of his past. There was a knock on his office door and he welcomed the people inside. Two of his closest management team personnel stepped in to meet him, Charlie Vale and Annette Shepperton.

'Come in, you two. Take a seat, please, relax,' he told them.

'So, everything going well down there today?' he enquired.

'Good enough so far, I'd say,' Charlie responded.

'We'll get more out of them by this afternoon. Slow start, but it'll pick up,' Annette said.

'Right, good. Look Charlie, Annette. You're coping very well with the projects off loaded onto you both in the last few weeks. Well done. Very well done, okay? Sorry about that, but I did like the results,' Gordon told them.

'You're very welcome. Glad we were given the opportunity. Don't want you kicking the bucket just yet, you know? Kind of used to you around here,' Charlie said.

'No, thanks again, Gordon. We always want to help ease your work load. It's about us, the team, really. After you owning the business, we're here to take it on with you,' Annette added smiling eagerly.

'I know, and I'm glad you both think like that. You know I've sometimes spoken about the future here, some possible plans, changes we could envisage eventually,' Gordon told them, settling back in his large, leather backed armchair.

'Right, okay. Is something big on your mind at the minute, Gordon?' Charlie asked.

'Could be. You know how we have a number of successful, reliable international deals going, good communications overseas waiting on us. It's going so well these days,' Gordon explained.

'It's taken some good effort and some time. You've done so much here for nearly a decade. So amazing, the results we've achieved, I think,' Annette commented.

'Absolutely, good, I know. Very pleasing results. I'm proud of myself, proud of all of you, the team and the many below down in the lower floors doing the tests, packaging and preparing. I'm proud of you two very much. So, I like to think you will do much more,' he told them.

'Like what, then?' Charlie dared to ask.

'You know, I might just leave in future – not for good, but on longer breaks, maybe work elsewhere, bigger projects which could be developed and while I am gone there, the two of you could do so much here for me,' he told them.

'When are you thinking this might happen, Gordon?' Annette asked 'Not that we want you to go soon but...'

'No, it's okay. Like I say, just possibly in future, ahead. I might go far off and I'd need reliable help here. But by then, well, there could also be my oldest son Steven with us working here. Just possibly. His degree is of a high standard in chemical strategies, but he could step in with his skills here. He knows that,' Gordon explained.

'Right, that could be very good,' Annette said.

'Yes, he's a nice young man, from meeting him, I remember. Okay sounds... good,' Charlie said.

'Not right now, okay, but... sometime ahead. Just maybe sometimes,' Gordon stressed then.

'Okay then, we look forward to this grand plan,' Annette said.

'We'll just put up with you until then,' Charlie joked.

'Yes, you will just have to do that,' Gordon replied with a wry smile and leaned back.

On an evening, returning from the laboratories, Alan and Steven sat around in the flat with a couple of cold, cheap beers and simply relaxed after a very long day of testing. Alan needed to talk to Steven about something that had been on his mind, just a vague issue, but it would not leave his thoughts easily.

'I've seen more strange things in the news. You know, like that thing a few days back – the bloke, sick then blind, but changed in other ways, remember?' Alan said.

'Oh, right, okay,' Steven replied, not entirely listening closely.

'Yeah, someone else now. Another one – similar but different. Unexpected. They are being more concerned now. It's a serious strange occurrence,' he told Steven.

'And it happened where, exactly?' Steven asked.

'Down around Bristol, then closer to London,' Alan said.

Steven was quiet then, looking around.

'Alan, are you happy with our new science work in the real world?' he asked.

'Me? Yes I am, certainly. Why'd you ask?' Alan said.

'But if we did get some opportunity to do something else, similar but... different maybe, more sort of special so soon, would you want to?' Steven asked.

'Steven, we're doing our work. It's ours, just ours, exclusively. Ours alone – we own it, no one else but us. At least right now,' Alan told him. He was very proud of that personally.

'You know, many big, wild, mad, science fiction things might happen sometime, even in this cold, grey pessimistic country,' Steven suggested.

'What, you want to build robots, fly in space, and fight aliens like in your favourite movies now?' Alan asked with mock cynicism.

'Hell yeah. No, really. Hey, there have been rumours around like that,' Steven said, apparently serious about something he had said.

'What? Robots and aliens?' Alan asked confused.

'Us, the British going into space, moving out, taking bigger steps...' Steven told him.

'Well, yes but just really speculative, vague, hopeful rumours. Just university and academic speculation, theories and suggestions. It fills the magazine pages. Nothing more I think. I'd be interested but I don't believe any of that is going to be here, so soon just yet. We might possibly prevent serious diseases, but no space suits and moon pubs for us any time soon,' Alan argued.

'Can't you take me seriously sometimes?' Steven asked.

'What? Of course man. You know I do,' Alan retorted.

'Well, show it and listen to me, will you?' Steven said.

'I do but what you're talking about... I just can't see it happening really soon. I'd find it amazing you know that,' he said.

'Right. Yes, you would. Okay,' Steven answered and he stood, beginning to walk around the room slowly and then walked out to the kitchen.

They seemed to realise that between them they both had a serious divided opinion in some areas of scientific speculation. It worried Alan, but Steven was not so bothered just then, not with what he was considering.

Chapter 9

While Steven travelled between libraries and laboratories with a few strong drinks at random bars, Gordon called him on his mobile phone. Parking the car in by their laboratory car park, he answered the call.

'Finally. How are things, my lad?' Gordon asked.

'Yes, good enough. I'm busy at the minute. What's up?' Steven asked him irritably.

'Want to see something topical and interesting?' Gordon offered.

'Really? I doubt it?' Steven responded.

'Oh, ye of little faith. Come by my office building, level 0.2, as soon as you can,' Gordon suggested. There were troubling ideas tormenting the mind of Steven now that Gordon was being much more open.

Less than half an hour later, Steven entered the large, impressive, secured research and production business building where Gordon worked most of the time when in town. Steven was escorted down a lengthy, bright corridor by a very beautiful, young lady in a white coat, who was friendly, though professionally distant.

'Your father seems in good spirits today. Much work going on, it seems,' she told him as she led him on.

'He likes to think so, that's for sure. I myself have started my own new scientific research production group recently. We'll be huge. All very progressive, challenging, contemporary research, you see,' he told her proudly.

'Oh really? That's interesting. Like father, like son, then?' she suggested.

'Hey... Well... Maybe, yes,' he admitted uncomfortably in agreement as they finally reached the room.

She led him to his father, who waited down the quiet hall in a wide, expansive room. One of the several highly equipped rooms, used for testing, research experiments and more. Gordon sat down at the far right side with two others. He stood when he saw Steven enter.

'Okay, there you are. Come, see what we're working with today,' Gordon said to him.

Steven walked over cautiously. He did not ever want to seem simply in obvious admiration of his father's work, without questioning the moral and social ethics of it, even if it really was fascinating to him.

'This is Alec, our coordinator and Donald, our administrative regulator in this department,' Gordon explained. 'We have been examining some very interesting findings to have come to us today. I thought you might just be interested, really. You won't see this very often. This is an example of actual, real, radical testing in progress.'

'Really? Well, that depends. Go ahead and impress me,' Steven offered.

'Now, please, you know how I personally like to look further, and think further than some every once in a while...' Gordon said.

'Yes, right. So?' Steven said.

'So, keep an open mind, won't you?' Gordon told him.

'I do, you know I certainly do, father,' Steven replied.

'Alright, then. Please come over here, follow me,' Gordon said, leading him off to another side of the long room.

He moved out around the desk, then led Steven along past a couple of the wide covered cubicles, toward the end row.

'You know you can come here for advice and my opinion any time, don't you?' Gordon reminded him. There was a detectable sense of sincerity, but Steven simply found that he had to keep a distance from this place, at least so far in his life, in order to shape his own scientific opinions.

'I know that. What do we have, then?' Steven said, wanting to get through with the event quickly.

Gordon nodded then took the door handle to the end cubicle room and swiftly opened it up. He stepped inside the smaller room and turned around to face Steven. The room was filled with many more professional and severe gadgets, apparatus, and tools of the trade, some looking like hospital devices possibly alongside the monitor screens and computers along the right side of the wall.

'Come inside. I want you to see things that I have had in mind for a very long time,' Gordon offered with a proud tone.

Inside, Gordon stood alongside a long stretcher bed table. On it, lay a person – probably a man judging by the outline – moving and shifting slightly, but tied down with restraints and held fixed in position to the bed.

'What the hell is this?' Steven asked suddenly shocked at what he saw. He had not expected this kind of thing right then. It was a joke, that had to be what it really was, he thought. His father was playing a really wild trick right here.

'This is good news,' Gordon told him smiling back.

'I... I really thought this had ended long ago,' Steven said.

'Steven, come here – look at the readings we have collected,' Gordon offered.

At first, Steven could not move, and did not want to accept what he saw. He only looked back at the man he knew as father. Gordon pointed down over at the table with several small monitors and screens bleeping and flashing intermittently.

'What exactly?' Steven then finally asked moving a gradual step closer, hesitantly.

'Very good findings. This man here, Steven, is extremely sick, very ill indeed. Early form of nervous neurological diseases, now though, with our help... He is a much, much healthier man. So much healthier now. Healed,' Gordon said, looking at the man who slept.

'Why? What have you done, if I will not be appalled, at all?' Steven asked.

'These are new techniques, my techniques. Thinking in a different direction, not of budgets, not of branding or sales,' Gordon explained.

'So, what was wrong with this one?' Steven asked.

'Originally, not so much. A couple of days ago, near influenza, fever, along with the diseases progressing that I mentioned... He has conquered them almost totally. Still here, unlike others. You saw the others?' Gordon asked with playful mystery, but Steven understood.

'In the news?' he asked. 'That was very serious, Dad. The guy, blind but different, his senses changed and then two more...?' Steven said.

'Correct. What do you think? With this example I've secured meetings with a couple of people with very significant influence who can help take it much further. It is a direction I have only occasionally prepared and made notes on in the past, eager to pursue but never having the time or knowing exactly how until recently. I will hopefully impress others who have usually been so negative, so resistant when I have barely even begun to suggest similar projects,' Gordon explained honestly.

'I have seen the previous... tests. This is... it's interesting, definitely I agree. But I do have my own work now, my direction ahead, you understand?' Steven told him.

'And your work – it will be so successful, will it?' Gordon asked. How could a father be so mocking, so critical? Steven thought.

'In time' Steven said. 'So, this isn't the first. Why like this, why?' he asked.

'Sometimes you do what it takes, my son. Whatever leads your curiosity despite the naysayers and uneducated fears of others,' Gordon told him. 'Do you want to help us?'

Steven walked around the operating bed, looking at the man lying there. A victim, a patient, apparently helped and cured from serious illness in some new secret ways. He was aware of the pressure of competing big businesses, as Gordon worked with many such ones regularly. Could his father actually be more successful than those with millions of pounds poured into experimentation?

'What? How do you mean?' he asked.

'We've more to do now here. Not done yet,' Gordon told him. He turned open a long flat bag, revealing a collection of elaborate sinister knives, and apparatus, ready to use. Steven observed the man on the operating bed – half awake, bruised, strapped down. It was most certainly ethically wrong, and horrendously so – wasn't it? It could be worse though, he considered. The man was better, wasn't he?

He saw what his own father would do, had done, for science, for a better society in general. An extremely hard working, disciplined man his father was. But what was the good if nothing was questioned while pushing so many boundaries continually? Was that him also? he wondered.

'Steven?' Gordon said, bringing him back to the situation before them. He then held out a shining, razor fine knife toward him. Would Steven join in, take the next step with them, whatever it takes? Whatever...

'Not today' Steven told him. He walked away from the horrific, disturbing scene.

'Steven...' Gordon said walking a couple of steps after him then stopping by the doorway.

'Don't worry, father. You've been successful,' Steven said, not looking back but leaving him to continue the experiments without him.

The night was dark and deeply comforting, Alan sleeping well after long hours in the lab. The crash and clattering erupted unexpectedly around from somewhere close, shocking him into sitting up immediately in bed.

'What the...?' he said aloud, looking in the darkness of the room.

Then more noise continued, unfocused muffled smashing and banging around. He stood a little nervous, then eventually decided to investigate, picking up a heavy Bunsen burner. He quietly stepped along and into the lounge room. The sight inside was completely unexpected and saddening to him.

He saw Steven there, bloodied hands as he held a chair leg. Around him were their tables, lamps and glasses all smashed, lying in dozens of pieces over the carpet.

'Steven? Hey mate, how are you?' he asked in a kind, quiet voice as he moved closer.

Steven stood upright, coughed.

'Holy shit, not very civilised of me,' Steven commented, looking around.

'Want to talk?' Alan asked.

Steven shook his head slowly. He sighed.

'I'll... get new stuff. Better stuff. So last season,' Steven said joking.

'Okay, fine by me. I'll put the kettle on, yeah?' Alan offered.

The very pleasing progress which was being made in the laboratory rooms was now being stifled for Alan, his focus lost generally. In a greasy spoon diner in the city around lunch hour, Joanna sat with Alan, ordering desert. She was good company and always had a joke to tell, offered affection to all her friends and Alan needed it right then.

'So, you're going to see that comedy tomorrow night still?' she asked.

'I suppose so. You're going this time?' He asked.

'I might, if I can. Steven?' she asked.

'Oh, probably. Got to relax sometime, haven't we?' he said and looked around uncomfortably as he stirred his coffee.

'Definitely. We're doing important research but we need down time like anyone else, we're only human,' she agreed. 'Alan, you ever get crazy ideas in your mind?'

'What kind of ideas?' he asked.

'Things like... Well, we're scientists now officially but... Well science fiction things. Mad implausible stuff. Got to have an open mind, right?' she said.

'Question everything, right. I... I do agree with that,' he told her.

'You feeling okay today?' she eventually asked him.

'Oh yeah. Not too bad. I think I'm getting too focused, need to step back a bit,' he told her.

'We do. Can't go solid all the time. Got to have fun. I need to see some guys, and you need to see some foxy girls, right?' she said.

They both smiled at each other and looked around them momentarily.

'I mean, isn't it amazing just how far things are advancing but just in some countries; Internet, genome, stem cell, mobile phones, nano-technology... So many things. What would you do if you could?' she asked.

'Me? Well... Too many things to begin with. Cures of diseases, maybe more global balance with medicines, drugs, and technology to help disabled people,' he told her.

'What about space? Other planets?' she asked.

'What do you mean? Why say that?' he wanted to know.

'Oh, I was reading a couple of articles in *Science Advance* magazine. A few scholars, academics discussing more unheard of theories about other life forms, possibly living on other planets if we needed to, with fossil fuels running low on Earth. Imagine it, though,' she said.

'It's too far. I mean, interesting of course but... we haven't sorted things out down here yet. Maybe we have to do that first,' he suggested.

'But what if we find answers out there? All kinds of answers?' she argued.

'You think? Are they saying we are thinking of doing things in this country?' he asked.

'Didn't get that specific and confirm anything. Interesting stuff, though. Yeah, we have a lot to do first, I suppose. Here's the tiramisu,' she told him, seeing the waitress arrive with their orders.

Chapter 10

In a block of business offices at the bottom end of the city, people worked for wages, busily focused on computer screens, sending emails, negotiating and taking notes. In among a series of cubicles, one woman coughs suddenly, sniffs alone. She thinks it must be her hay fever at first – yes, that must be it. She tries to continue with her work but the irritation simply is too much, the coughing a distraction. She falls down forward onto the walkway beside her desk. No one sees at first, then a short balding man turns to find her.

'Oh, Helen, are you alright?' he asks and walked around to help her up.

'I... Yes, just... headache I think,' she tells him. 'Just go... freshen up I think...'

She walks along down to the ladies toilets. Inside, she is alone in the quiet space, seeing her pale, exhausted face in the mirrors along the wall.

'Too... soon. Too soon...' she says quietly to herself. She looks down at her hands and sees shockingly strange blisters have formed. She takes out her phone and made a call.

'Hello, is Doctor Marks there, please? Well, Doctor Lowell, Gordon Lowell?' she asks anxiously 'Yes, please...'

She waits, then after a long, nervous moment he speaks.

'Hello, Helen? It's Gordon here. How are you?' he asks.

'The... effects... It's happening but not right... It's gone... not good... I'm at work now. Feeling... coughing, my skin...' she says, confusing him as she tries to explain her fear of her illness.

'Please calm down, Helen. Everything is going to be okay, really. We'll send someone out to get you. Take the day off, go home, rest well. We'll have a good look at you. I'll be around with help. Nothing to get too concerned over. See you soon,' he tells her.

But there is, and she is extremely worried. She looks at her deforming hands, her skin sagging, reshaping on her bones. Her cough is painful, but she feels a kind of change inside.

In a smaller part of town, down among quiet, poorer streets at an old, council house, Mr. Derek Larson was in the front room, smiling to himself. He had been very sick in recent times, frail in ways and sad because of it. Many doctors he had seen, a few different types of legal, prescribed pills and medicines he had tried with no real satisfactory results, after many months. This time it had been different, that was for sure, he thought. With the help of Doctor Gordon Lowell and the other scientists of a largely unknown project research group, he had regained his independent freedom and better overall health. He had agreed to the tests, the experimental methods and drugs, injections and had been made known of possible unusual side effects and dangers which most likely would not show, but had to be discussed anyway.

He smiled as he looked down at his bizarre new skin, his potentially reptilian texture and changed fingernails. This was some novel mutation, inside and out. He breathed differently and felt he saw in a new, perhaps even better way. His strength seemed much increased, he was more confident and even wildly alive like he had not been in years. He felt the need to leave, to be outside, to show himself to the world at large, to celebrate, escape and be alive in his new changing body. He opened his front door and, looking at the setting sky overhead, he then ran out like some freed beast, loose and wild.

Days later, in the city of London, Gordon and two others met with another group of respected science research investors and government representatives. This was a quiet, low key arranged meeting, to discuss issues which rarely were seriously considered but always were at the back of official files and minds. It seemed they might now hold some present potential interest finally, thanks to Gordon.

'Good afternoon, ladies and gentlemen. We are here to discuss again the steps we have taken so far. This project has still remained entirely known only to the people in this room. We know that many just did not ever want to trust in these ideas or have faith in them, which is their loss entirely. We all know how important our project could be. So, Gordon, how has everything been moving along?' the man at the front of the long glass table asked.

Gordon looked at them all, then stood, smiling wide.

'I have certainly very good, interesting news. The patients have been responding how we have been hoping they would. The changes are very successful, and the cells, genes, DNA, are all connecting extremely well. We can be very excited in our steps. Big things will be happening in a short while,' he announced proudly.

A man to his left spoke.

'But Gordon, what... What about the calls you had – Helen and the other one?' the man said meekly.

Gordon glanced down with powerful disgust.

'We have been taking the patients along through the steps. You see, as these are all extremely unique new procedures they have been just a little nervous, naturally. But what we have seen suggests very great progression. We can be very hopeful in implementing the discussed following steps,' he told them.

'Okay, from the documents here and photos presented, we can clearly see impressive change. Well done Gordon and Charles and all of us. We've not been expecting to go anywhere near these forgotten ideas for a long time, but now it seems we can,' a tall man opposite in an emerald green tie and tight green suit replied.

'We need to be careful, is what I am suggesting. You all know the absolute secrecy of this right now,' the man on Gordon's right declared.

'Oh, don't worry, not long now. And I may have more trusted help to advance it along, also, very soon,' Gordon told him.

'Oh, really? Be sure it is from a very safe trustworthy source. Glad you're so relaxed,' the man told him.

'Simply confident and professional, my friend. So, can I ask in other matters then, about the eventual final resolution of our proposed project? These patients, doing well, should eventually meet the level that was talked about in order to consider the other plans. What about that?' he asked the man and two women opposite.

They looked back with blank, expressionless reactions. One of the women then spoke.

'You trust us and our connections overseas and around Europe still. Yes, we have spoken and contacted a number of associates. The subject has been discussed with careful, increased seriousness over the last couple of weeks now. We do, we can now say, have satisfied interest from some who can most definitely open certain avenues for us, if we impress them enough from here on,' she told Gordon and the others.

'Well, that really is very pleasing news. Thank you very much. There is no doubt in my mind that we will not fail to show them things to blow their minds about the future for us all,' Gordon exclaimed with deep satisfaction.

The following day early after ten in the morning, a disgruntled and agitated man entered the tall business complex offices of Gordon's company and demanded to speak to him immediately.

'Sir, could you take a seat? He will be available in a short time, thank you,' the attractive young female receptionist told him calmly.

'A seat? I must see him right now and he'll want to see me. I really must speak with him this minute, you hear?' he told her with intense conviction.

She was slightly intimidated but knew her job.

'Sir, really, if you simply sit down he will meet you soon enough – in a few minutes, that's all, really,' she explained.

He looked at her carefully, then simply stormed down to the doors at her right.

'No, Sir, hey, you can't just... Sir, come back!' she said, but he ignored her pleading and walked through.

He entered the office ahead and found Gordon with a client.

'Okay, Mr. Ashley, we'll speak again on Friday, if that's alright,' Gordon told the client and then noticed the intruder. 'Hello there, Frank' he said as he began to show the client, who was shocked at the disturbance, to the door.

With the client gone, Gordon closed the door, leaving only the two of them inside, alone.

'Gordon, the woman has bloody changed. She's so fucking sick – you did this. You did it and it has gone so damn wrong. We said not like this!' the man shouted.

'Hey, Frank, sit down. Whiskey?' Gordon offered.

'What? Shit, no. She is different too soon, too dangerously. I agreed to this with you, with our specific understanding and agreement – you know that,' Frank told him.

'You agreed for a nice fucking sum of my money, Frank, you know that. Remember? Calm down. This is the beginning, that's all. We protected ourselves. No trace of bad practice. She agreed too, the signatures, the agreements. She signed up willingly; they all do. Trust me in this,' Gordon told him.

'How... How can I? It scares me, Gordon. I didn't know, didn't expect it like this. I mean... for her to...' Frank said, trying to explain his fear.

'We're dealing in big games now. Brave games, We'll be brave. But they're games with rules. We'll respect these rules, even if most people are unaware of the games happening. Trust me. She's okay though, isn't she? Alive, breathing, moving?' Gordon said.

'Oh, yes. Alive, but like I told you, changed. Her skin, her behaviour, it's fascinating but... strange Gordon, so strange,' Frank said. 'Well, look, I don't want to fucking lose my damn job, Gordon. You have your empire, you're safe. Any seriously bad shit here, she's yours. And who knows what she'll do or who she'll go to if she falls to pieces or something,' Frank suggested.

'Can't. She can't and won't. You won't either,' Gordon told him. This was no advice but a serious order. He lifted a glass of whiskey up and suddenly threw it violently hard towards the wall on his right. It smashed loudly into many pieces, glass scattering around them while Gordon continued to stare at Frank.

Chapter 11

Alan approached Steven, one afternoon, while he monitored some tests with chemicals in their group laboratory.

'There's a report in the paper here. It sounds similar to that other thing... that sick person. People reported some sick person again, seen having some attack or even attacking someone else. Doctors say it was a medication mistake of some kind but some speculate other possibilities. They're in hospital now. Press say it's not contagious, but could be connected but the doctors don't say much. Curious report,' Alan told him.

'Yes, very. Doctors probably gave some miscalculated dosage or wrong pills. Glad I'm not old yet. This test is steady. You going to help us here, Alan?' Steven said.

'Right, just found that interesting, wanted to tell you.'

'I find you not working hard, right now, kind of difficult,' Steven replied.

'Alright, easy party animal,' Alan said, joining him at the tables with the equipment.

Many, soon enough, had caught sight of Mr. Derek Larson – only briefly, but that was certainly enough time to shock and horrify them. He roamed along through the back of the town fields, the narrow areas, past drug addicts on the streets, gang members, and teenagers drunkenly kissing; all seeing him, all stunned and confused. They looked on, seeing the sight of his unnatural skin, his green glowing eyes, the wild leaping through tall grass, chattering and roaring. He fled off alone, excited and most definitely dangerous.

In quiet, academic rooms, a group of very intelligent, scientific researchers sat together in heated discussion. They themselves were educated, and most worked in areas concerning astrophysics, space exploration and bioengineering.

'Gentlemen, we have to make some choices about recent communications. Certain suggestions have been looked into now. We need to decide upon how we react to the offers we have gained. Are we prepared?' one man, Blake, asked as he stood looking through a folder containing various documents.

'The main offer – the deal of Europe and support of extended American individual monies – is shaky, and possibly not guaranteed, Blake,' one man said.

'No, it allows it, it seems. Real space travel from right here, finally. For us and major breakthroughs at the same time. It's meant to be. Only with this kind of individual backing and the knowledge of these people who know all the right contacts,' Blake told him.

'Blake, this could fall flat in our faces. Millions, more gone, if it doesn't work out.'

'Have some balls, will you? Besides, two years of preparation has helped secure this already for us. The location across the lower south is ready; we just need to agree on what the greater plan is and dates and times. And it is this biological, preparation project. Revolutionary, necessary and looks very impressive, believe me,' Blake answered.

'This Gordon guy up north – he's a bit up himself, isn't he?' the other asked.

'You know of his business skills. Very experienced man, always has had many ideas ready and an open mind. And what's that to do with anything? He gets things happening. Bold, brave scientist, really. Got balls,' Blake answered. 'Well, if everyone here agrees?'

'He works with a large team, including several doctors and biologists. We're convinced by now, right?' another said.

'Certainly. So, in a month now, while he and the others do their part, we arrange the first actual British space mission from the United Kingdom itself,' Blake told them.

They all looked at each other. Positive and proud faces, confident and ambitious people who were willing to do anything it would take to make the country proud.

A short number of days later, the next radical, painful, secret progress began.

'It's happening?' A voice asked.

'It's happening now, that's right,' Gordon replied.

A series of short rapid phone calls and a car drove out from the lower car park of a building. A brief time after that, it arrived at a house near Sunderland in the north of the country. The front door was answered quickly. Moments later, the woman was escorted into the car, which left immediately. At that same time but further over in the northwest, another car arrived and took a man from his home. They took him and the woman separately further down the country. Less than four hours later, the two people were escorted deep into a mysterious building of some kind of research or another – it was not clear from any sign or logo on the outside of the building – and down into specially equipped observation rooms, individually, finally, secured and held in position.

These people had already shown bizarre physical changes of various kinds, biologically – genetic modification – and now these altered bodies were to be tested in ways which may have seemed sadistic, unnecessary or senseless, but were actually vital. These were tests to find how well these individuals would survive in their state, not just where they were, and where they lived, but in space and further.

Taken into individual test chambers, the two patients barely knew what to expect, but were almost grateful for a variety of strong drugs to sedate and prepare them. Various observing scientists watched, counted down and began the significant starting of the new testing processes. Among the small group stood Gordon, pleased and fascinated.

'Here they are, brave soldiers, keen helpers. This should be absolutely fascinating,' he told the others as they began preparing them together, initiating the beginning.

'This is going to last for a good few hours, Sir,' one of the scientists turned and told him. 'That will be okay for them?'

'Oh, yes, don't worry. We'll stop if they look like it might seriously threaten their lives. If we have to. Go ahead now,' Gordon said. 'I'll observe the beginning now, but then I have other things I need to do.'

Locked in, strapped tight in place behind the thick glass walls of the chambers, the woman twitched at the start, being injected and prepared continuously five times. He coughed to himself and turned away, taking out his cell phone to make a call as he walked off down the corridor alone.

A month of serious hard work on their very first professional scientific research project had passed, and the group of young promising scientists were coming to the end of their first initial study experiment. With Alan finishing it, they came to find unique distinctions between medical healing processes and modern known drug substances and healing through potential synthesis, combining elements of plant biology and human tissue and cells. Alan and Steven took the final evidence to highly respected government science boards of certification after consulting their academic lecturer friends from their university.

'This is certainly... different, we can tell you that. You have been only doing this for a month?' the government scientific official questioned them.

'Yes, but not just that, not really. We finished our Master's degree projects in the summer, and these results have come from extended theories now fully tested at first stage. So, almost two years, in reality or more, with our team of four, so far. But please admit, these are truly, honestly very promising results, my friends,' Steven told them, using his great friendly charm which was like that of a highly successful salesman.

Alan felt so uncomfortable, out of place and awkward. They were going to reject them, he could feel it coming he thought.

'You certainly have admirable spirit, Steven,' one of the officials commented.

'We must be confident and we work our arses off, only bringing the freshest, most valuable findings to you now. Do you agree?' Steven told them.

They looked at each other, then down at the evidence on the desks, presented over the laptops and overhead projection.

'We are then pleased to agree Steven, Alan, and accept your most interesting current test result findings. There is evidently much useful hard work here that we can look into further investigating,' the first official told them with a friendly smile.

'Thank you very much; it means so much to us. Thank you,' Steven told them.

'Yes, it really honestly does mean so much. We accept,' Alan agreed.

'Absolutely, outstanding. This is the right thing for you. We guarantee it,' Steven added.

Alan, Steven and the team all headed for the town that night, in celebration of finding a pleasing business partnership to allow them further funding and research testing. Joanna and Pascal with them, they drank in a number of busy and loud bars and clubs around the main town streets. They laughed and danced around like crazed, overexcited fools, drunk on the good news and excessive amounts of vodka, gin, cocktails and shots and endless pints of lager. Steven entertained like he always did; starting drinking games, singing, karaoke, joking and chatting with strangers. He introduced them as an incredible, super scientist team, destined to create all kinds of magnificent mind-blowing medicines, technology and breakthroughs, and he convinced most people. He did it so effortlessly, that was his thing. It almost embarrassed Joanna and Pascal, but they knew to accept and ignore it if they were out with him; it was just his way, and they did not mind much on such a special occasion.

With new funding taking the projects further, they then extended their research team with a couple more scientists fresh from other universities nearby. After this, Steven began to soon be missing from their laboratories more and more. He had seemed to be growing into his persona, becoming more of what he seemed to think he was expected to be. He was, they knew, doing more work in attaining attention for their work, getting them noticed and respected in the science world. They continued on, Alan mostly leading their efforts in the tests and project steps now. He himself did wonder where his loud, close friend was disappearing to so often, as Steven was remaining fairly mysterious about his actions.

For Steven, he found that he could not help but be drawn to know more about what exactly his brilliant, scientist, business, philanthropist father was achieving from the things he had been shown days before. He was of course very concerned for his father, but he knew these ideas had been around for a long time. He knew Gordon had thought very carefully about the practicalities involved and, in all honesty, Steven was probably envious and intrigued to begin with. He followed information and messages left for Gordon and the basic things he had been told so far. Gordon was seemingly pleased – it appeared that Steven finally was taking the kind of hoped for interest a son should have in the successful family business. Steven knew that he had different views to his father; they did not see everything in modern science in the same way which was to be expected, as they came from separate generations, decades apart. Gordon had, though, taught Steven many things as he had grown up – lessons in science, judgement, analysing tests and experiments. Steven had grown and chosen his own personal scientific heroes and inspirational breakthroughs to inspire his own work. He wondered what had made his father become involved in science, to be the super successful scientific businessman he now was, as Gordon had never fully revealed his own youthful years and education completely. And then he wondered if he would really be just as good, or if he should be even better, or nothing at all.

They met together, finally, at Gordon's home during the week, the two of them leaving their individual, secretive meetings and private agendas. Steven entered the house and found Gordon drinking a gin and malt whiskey in the back room, watching cricket on the wall-wide plasma screen.

'Afternoon, my busy father,' he said in greeting.

'Well, hello son, the scientist,' Gordon replied, not taking his sight off the television screen, but moved to the table by his side and easily poured out another drink for Steven.

'Thanks. You've been travelling. I've missed you once or twice this week,' Steven told him.

'Wanted to meet me? Sorry, yes. Meetings away from home. Business is good again,' Gordon said.

'Same here, actually. All fine, honest hard work,' Steven said.

'Glad to hear it, Steven. I'm very proud of you right now,' Gordon told him.

'Only now? Are you? Proud of yourself too, I hope?' This was met with silence from Gordon. He suddenly laughed a little, then sighed, looking at Steven finally.

'You'll only get so far, the way you are now. You're picking it up slowly, just in time. Believe me. Everything you know – your easy living, the clothes, your car, education – thank me and the risks I've taken. Not all the time, not every day but once in a while. Big risks, they paid off. And if you understand me, join me,' Gordon explained and offered.

'Damn it father!' Steven exclaimed.

'So, what was your work, right now?' Gordon asked as if he had possibly forgotten.

'Well, with the team it is biochemical, genetic immunity stimulation research. It is successful so far. I've been able to get us secure funding and stable interest and support now this last week,' Steven told him.

'All original, is it?' Gordon enquired. Silence. 'Well?' he asked.

Silence still from Steven who only looked at him. Truth was in the room, a truth hidden for a long while. Both men knew they needed each other for the work they had, to be the successful men they were now.

'Thank me later. Or... do me a favour, if you feel you should,' Gordon suggested.

'So... what have you been doing?' Steven asked very quickly.

'Glad you asked,' Gordon said, smiling ruefully. 'I've arranged very impressive plans. My helpful volunteers... They will be going so much further, so much further very soon.'

'What does that mean?' Steven asked.

'Would you like to know?' Gordon offered.

'Yes. You want to tell me?' Steven replied slowly.

'Then join me. Tomorrow come with me to see the progress, alright?' Gordon said.

Steven looked around. He felt trapped, frustrated and anxious. He had never allowed himself to be so close to his father for a very long time. He wondered what his mother would think of it.

'Thank you,' Steven told him in a sad, humble voice and drank the strong, fine drink Gordon had offered.

The laboratory became a tense place in a very short time. All eyes were on Alan while Steven was just barely there every few days.

'Alan, can I ask you – where the hell is Steven? Is he even really involved with us anymore?' Joanna asked while they proceeded with testing.

'Yes of course, he... He's getting us attention, recognition, support. You know he got us meetings, keeping us in money for equipment, talking to the right people. It has been working, you can't deny that,' Alan told her.

'No, no, that's true. He's just not around too much. We're just wondering, that's all,' she replied. 'But really – all this time? Alan, are you sure?' she asked.

He looked down at the readings coming through on the monitor screens. He worked on, not knowing how to give her the answers she was looking for. He was worried about the direction of the projects privately, and if he could keep them on course while Steven was so absent. His thoughts too often drifted toward other ideas; his own thoughts of more vague biological plant and chemical compound research.

At that moment, Steven suddenly walked into the laboratory, arms wide open, a huge wide grin and bright shining eyes.

'Well, good afternoon my hard working sci-fi folk. Hope all is well in the lab. We are on track. Keep it going strong, as ever. Many interested newspapers, journals and more want to talk and discuss our work immediately. Believe me,' he dramatically exclaimed aloud, walking around between the tables at which they sat.

'Hey, Steven, what you been up to all this time? Don't like the real work anymore? we could do with your input here, you know,' Pascal told him.

'Sorry, did you not have your ears open right then? Okay, chill. I'm with you guys. Someone has to keep us alive in the media, keep us connected. You do understand that, right?' Steven said.

'Okay, let's ease up on him now. He's doing his bit, in his own way. We couldn't do any of that as well as he does, right?' Alan said defending Steven, as he walked over toward him then. He leaned close toward him.

'Steven, let's talk, yeah?' Alan said carefully looking at him.

They walked through to the almost claustrophobic rest room to speak frankly.

'Want to tell me anything?' Alan asked.

'Like what? What do you want to know?' Steven said.

'What do you think? Listen, don't bullshit me. It's me – we're close enough, aren't we? Look we need you quite a lot here, you know that. We know and I know that you are doing some very useful things for us – that's the truth. Just, can you be more open with us, please?' Alan asked.

'Right, yes. That it? Whatever, fine. We're all working hard together, you're right. I understand that,' Steven told him.

In some sense, Alan knew that he just did not fully believe his answer. He actually expected that; he did know how Steven acted. It saddened him, but he felt that really all he could do right then was to observe the actions of Steven and be ready for what might happen.

Chapter 12

Within the corridors of the city police station, many officers walked through beside each other, all kinds of minor local crimes and troubles on their minds to be dealt with. Danger and trouble was often, in actual fact, usually very exaggerated by the local media, and the police both constantly helped and blocked their work as much as they deemed necessary. The smallest possible scandals were soon taken and stirred up to outrageous always dramatic levels whatever the incident. Some investigations were simply baffling and slippery for ongoing weeks, months, or much longer. Other cases were regularly left, and then only ever occasionally reopened. Most cases, even for the police were, with their best efforts, still too confusing, and those with too many complications were then forgotten. There was always a suitable excuse to end it. But sometimes there were officers, Detective Inspectors who held onto these puzzling cases, just too personally fascinated, or curious.

Here in this city, there was at least one veteran police inspector who now had given time to something which he often remembered, a suspicious man who troubled him still. There were lingering rumours which would not leave a man who they all knew. They knew Gordon, the very wealthy respected and highly successful local businessman. A bold gentleman of impressive talents, originally a scientist of some sort, who continued financial endeavours and grand deals internationally, with his now large business research and production company. But history had given him some suspicious tales and connections, many of which could, in ways, make him seem a man of some strange crimes potentially on huge financial international levels if he were ever one hundred percent proved to be guilty of any of the number of incidents.

Some of the officers knew what Gordon was doing – there were regular articles in the local and national news broadsheets, sometimes telling of his expensive deals, millions risked on new projects, and special experiments his company was taking part in. The inspector Heinlein and a couple of his professional friends every few months would quietly discuss their known theories concerning Gordon, the perfect local business icon, an example of rags to riches success. They knew Gordon had apparently spent many years earlier in America until less than twenty years ago, when he had returned home and then built up the stunning scientific research and production medicine company which he now controlled and owned personally.

There had been at least four times over the last decade or less when Gordon had been almost in some way linked to some serious accusations. What had got him off had always been sheer luck, and very good lawyers at the last minute. Always someone, something, came up to release him, protect and save his perfect reputation. But they remembered, the police – it was their job. Some of them at least remembered. Here again with the end of a recent case involving international smuggling allegations, possession of illegal chemical compounds, and possible bribery, Gordon had come into the story. It had been possibly going on for five or six years if Heinlein remembered right, since he last almost pinned Gordon down, last almost took that big gamble to claim justice. With any major wealthy business people, things always had to be checked, researched, backed up extremely carefully each time. This time, might be the time.

Earlier on in the day around noon, Inspector Heinlein received a call from a friend which brought some fresh interest suddenly in the dealings of Gordon. Finishing early at the police station with ease, Heinlein then drove off along to a small pub down the side of the city. Walking in, he soon met up with two friends who also worked in the police force in other departments. There was Jack Troworth and John Seagrave.

'Come to know more, Gerry? Good choice. Sit down,' Jack said with a warm smile on show.

They sat at a table and began to chat casually, discussing their lives, families, and crimes on their minds.

'Crime still crime, right?' Jack said.

'Doesn't change, like the local MPs we have to wait on. You two busy then, that it? Got some very interesting news for me finally, remember?' Heinlein – Gerry – asked.

Jack nodded back with a mischievous grin, taking a sip of his pint of ale.

'There does seem to be something happening we think, Gerry,' John said.

'We are going to be very careful, aren't we?' Heinlein reminded them with serious caution.

'Right, of course. Goes without saying, that does. But, you have to know though,' John said.

'Okay, thanks. So... go on,' Gerry said, prompting him.

'We have been informed of a few charges at a bank he has accounts with, and they could be suspicious. Some purchases that do not make sense, conflicting origins. That, and even better – deliveries to his buildings. A number of very unusual deliveries,' Jack added.

'That is not enough. Right, so, if that is what it seems it could be, we then get warrants, set up our inspections and begin. Anything else at all?' Gerry asked sipping his lager.

'Yes, yes. Hey we wouldn't just waste all of our time here. Not at all. Look there seems to be connections between the two, and this makes it now even more of a thing to definitely be involved with,' John said.

'What connections? It has to be really solid, John, really sure. A real thing before any move on him at all. You remember the past? It was almost the biggest disaster, right? We can't have that at all now,' Gerry told him.

'Okay, calm down, my friend. Yes, we wouldn't be here talking like this otherwise. Your good friend Michael on security, him and his pals, they have given us these tasty morsels,' Jack said.

'And he has seen these curious things now personally, has he?' Gerry asked.

'He certainly has, he says. This could be it. Finally take this conman business creep to pieces, to justice,' John told him.

'He's not just a conman, I've said... We'll need to be so careful. So what next?' Gerry asked.

'Michael is going to keep us updated, and you can call him if you want to. He's expecting you. That okay to begin, then?' John said.

'Okay, good. Fine enough. Thank you, guys,' Gerry replied, a smile steadily spreading over his face.

Soon enough Heinlein did call the security man, Michael. They met for drinks the next day, arranging what could be done in monitoring Gordon, locating scandal, crimes that must be there, waiting to be found, and to take him away from his grand position finally. The following night, Michael drove to his security shift at the company laboratories building where he worked, which was owned by Gordon. His security firm sent him to many different places every few weeks, and so he would not lose his own job, he believed. He knew the corridors, exits, entrances, locks, alarms all around well enough after three weeks back there. He had been a couple of times before and seemed still the same mostly. He could check the deliveries again, get into the rooms he needed to, check calls with the secretary Amy who he had slept with twice so far. She was often open enough with gossip he seemed to find. She could exaggerate, the tall tales, but he would know the difference, he could tell by now.

He did the shift, doing his usual routine, his hours alone, casually reading the sports section in his newspaper, then checking with the other security guards across the building as usual. He checked for what he might have missed in the last forty-eight hours since his last shift.

'So, Amy dear, looking so gorgeous once again. Always such a beauty. Any strange activity around? Strange phone calls? Bizarre packages, or people today at all?' he asked, touching her curling smooth long silky brown hair, and looking into her deep blue eyes.

'Oh, wouldn't you love to know, darling Michael?' she replied. 'Certainly there have been deliveries, some strange, some boring, so far,' she told him.

'I am not so sure a simple security guy should be aware of these little things' she said.

'Security. Your security, the building's security, Amy. I have to know to keep us all safe here, don't I?' he said. 'So these packages from where, when, what size, shape?'

'Some from Bristol, Tyneside, and London. Some always come from there at the minute. Then Germany, even France now, though,' she said.

'Oh really? Fascinating. So they looked strange and unusual, did they?' he asked, more serious now.

'I would not say that, well, maybe I suppose. Just equipment, parts, lab stuff. The usual. Different suppliers now, I think. Some chemicals too, though. Signed about six times for all those,' she explained.

'Where were the chemicals from?' he asked.

'They were Germany and France,' she said.

'Okay, right. Anything else? Calls?'

'Yes. Still interested?' she said, teasing him.

'You know I am. Definitely,' he said.

'I am free tomorrow. You?' she said.

'What? Oh hell. Yes, maybe. Yes, the evening if you like. But the calls...?' he asked.

'Well there was...' She looked around, seeing no one else around, and looked back a few pages in her organiser and on the computer screen beside her.

'Mr. Shallton, of EndStart company. Mr. Arndale of Genseever company, Ms. Locktern of BridgeSource company, checking the meeting here Thursday. So?'

'Right. Good, good. Thanks very much Amy, my dear,' he told her, and then held her hands, touching her hair again.

'Tomorrow?' she said.

'Oh, well, we'll see. Call then, okay?' he replied and walked off, giving her a wink as he left.

Nothing more unusual came during the shift for him. Simply one more boring predictable night, like all the others it seemed, securing the mysterious building of this mysterious rich man's work. He did enter a few rooms, searching discreetly. Eventually he found codes, numbers, and messages which seemed relevant for Gerry Heinlein, he guessed. The following day, Michael spoke to Gerry Heinlein on the phone.

'Okay, look. Here's some news for you – the boss has received packages from Germany and France. New suppliers, and some of it could be a bit dodgy. Some equipment, and chemical deliveries too. I'll send the specific detail over to you now if you want, all the stuff I've got here,' Michael told him.

'Yes, I would certainly appreciate that very much, Michael, very much so. You will be rewarded, of course,' Gerry Heinlein said.

'I know I certainly will, Mr. Policeman, Sir. It's people like myself, you lot always depend on in the end, isn't it? Funny right? Our great proud, honest police force,' Michael said with casual sarcasm.

'We all play a part in upholding the laws and justice of the land,' Gerry said.

'Right you are. I'll be expecting my reward, Gerry,' Michael answered then ended the call.

The longer he worked there, the more he did think about the questions, the strange deliveries, the work going on deep inside the special scientific laboratories in the building he helped to guard. He knew that he himself did not really know too much of modern scientific breakthroughs at all. Security work could be anywhere you were told to go at any given time. He knew football, dirty jokes, old movies, good women. He just happened to be there then, but he could have been anywhere. He was though, happily making much welcomed extra bonus wages from Gerry Heinlein easily, which was great news. The thing was, now along with the unexpected money, he also had some unexpected questions. Did he need to think about any of it? Know about any of it? He was quite cynical of these big rich businessmen types like Gordon. All their unending money, lifestyle, confidence, arrogance... How did they get it all? Why them and not ever people like him? he thought.

The arrangement was difficult, Heinlein was well aware. How could he be simply throwing money away to this manipulative young security guy, buying lies and yarns so useless. He was obsessed, he knew. He just could not let it go, after a number of years. If there were any serious crimes involving Gordon and his businesses, he should find it sooner or later – that had always been the thought which kept him going. Gordon should pay for it all. He should lose it all, Heinlein thought. For justice. He checked the product names, details, addresses, and delivery posting he had received from Michael. Eventually, finally, no success came. No satisfying truths there. Just legal, regular equipment, it appeared in the end. There was something there to be found, he thought. It was there, deeper, waiting still. Just hidden still, covered up. Protected, protecting Gordon like always.

Low key traditional Asian music played in the background somewhere while Alan and Jane sat together in a reliable recommended restaurant, enjoying a course of fine Indian food.

'You know, I usually keep putting off opportunities of romance – not that I exactly get loads of offers, of course. This is very much a lovely time,' Alan told her, obviously still quite nervous.

'Well, I really do enjoy your company, okay? You're such a sweet real bloke. So genuine and honest, I really need that, Alan,' she told him.

'That's me, just a simple honest geek. An almost professional geek full time now, give it a couple of months,' he joked.

'Hey, I'm there too, count me in Geeksville. Two of us, together with the project going well,' Jane said.

'Yes, but you seem to maintain being a more regular non-nerd young woman much better,' he told her.

'Everyone is different. So you and Steven have been living together through university all the time?' she enquired.

'Yes, around four years now. It works most of the time. We'll both get our own places in the next couple of years or much sooner, after our Master's degrees are finished,' he said.

'Same here. The girls I'm living with are great friends mostly, but I might even move in with a guy eventually. I'd like to feel like a proper woman, in a grown up relationship maybe,' she said. 'I do all my sports and things, I know. The gym. My father puts so much pressure on me. But it's my own life in the end,' she told him.

'Absolutely. That's what you want? I wouldn't expect that. Well, look, I mean... No, well not like you shouldn't be married or even...' He tried but tripped over his words as he flustered.

'Don't worry, I know what you mean. People get older, move on, grow up after uni. I'm no little girl anymore. I'd like a man with me more of the time,' she explained.

'Oh, okay then. That's great. Right,' he said, but looked around uncomfortably. 'I really like this curry. It's pretty hot but it's very tasty as well, isn't it?'

'Very tasty, Alan,' Jane replied with a romantic smile.

They held hands across the table. Alan even managed to pour the wine very carefully. He was finally with a woman who accepted how he was – his life, work, and all of his ways. He realised that he was very happy with Jane. There was an easy connection between them, he felt, warm and loving both ways.

Another week passed, and dozens more interviews with journalists and reporters for papers, radio stations, web interviews, journals concerning business ventures were proposed, secured and completed. Things were as busy as ever for Gordon, as he liked then to be. These interviews were useful, necessary even, and he knew also greatly enjoyable to him. The attention, adoration, respect always there for him now. A good positive sign. It had taken years for it to be like this. In every interview he still almost revealed real truths, shocking well-hidden deep personal secrets, like some confessional time. Guilt, shame, pressure all in him; an endless tension which held him how he was. That was fine enough for him. It had made him what he was now.

The projects and work which took place within the walls of the building, were often quite secretive and highly valuable exclusive work. He had got into the habit long ago, of putting out false elaborate information about what was happening in the laboratories at any particular time. He was not the only one he knew to do this, but he did it very well. He probably put way too much effort into it than most, but he knew he also had a difficult personal history to protect, and more; which validated and justified it all to him. He was almost certain that no one who entered the building or left it, had a truly real grasp of the truth of the work inside, and the past inside him, unless he wanted them to – and he definitely did not.

The trouble was, he himself was beginning to forget what his real truths were now. Steven knew that was what he relied on. His loyal if sometimes difficult elder son Steven was there with him, almost all of the way now. Whether he wanted to step up, and join in properly with Gordon. He was certainly welcome, Gordon thought. He believed that Steven deserved it after how he had helped Gordon so far in a number of ways, sometimes aware and other times just there simply obeying his father. Steven had become a wild, dangerous, rebel offspring youth at times. Gordon had done his part in making him like this, while some of it was just hormones and lifestyle choices, but it all suited the uses of Gordon. For Steven though, often it did threaten his education, and strained his sanity and his identity but he continued after enduring a number of police cautions, fights, arguments with friends and threats all still hitting him hard and regularly. All for Gordon it seemed, ultimately.

Business was well, profits high, international deals forthcoming still. Gordon could rest pleased but other things now sought his personal attention. In holding things together, in such ongoing successful ways, he had to meet with a group of associates who knew some very deeply personal facts about him. They had all worked well together for over a decade, each trusting the other, seeing potential in their research, the talent in the work of Gordon that he had then set up and created so boldly almost alone with mostly only their money and contacts.

Things were changing; the world of medicine, pharmaceutical productions, research experimentations, costs, materials, international markets, deals and distribution. Some were considering looking elsewhere, and this would not help Gordon at all. He met and confronted the questions, the propositions put forward.

In a serious business meeting between himself and a handful of close long-term industry associates, they discussed the issues which were troublesome then.

'You need to give us more now. It is how things will move on. This is all too vague,' one man sitting at the middle of the large round black table announced with the other three around him all facing Gordon.

'We've helped you for years, Gordon. Kept you in the country, built your business for you, you know that,' another suggested.

'I am always so very grateful, but this is all very delicate. We agreed on the time. Steven, my son, is not ready just yet. His project has not been finally agreed with the university board,' Gordon explained

'Oh, that's the small detail, just the covering, Gordon,' they told him. 'We can't guarantee that we'll forever be able to keep the authorities away, understand?' the first man argued.

'Right. I'll make arrangements. Count on me. The board will listen, this week,' Gordon told them.

'And Gordon, what's more pressing are the actual tests you told us would be happening, producing what we asked for. We got you the right equipment, which meant pulling some questionable strings, remember?' the first man said.

'I know that. They are just about to begin. Really. Just checking the security, that is all – the safety,' he told them.

'That is covered though, isn't it, now?' the man in brown jacket to the far right asked.

'Yes. By tomorrow, yes. No problem now then,' Gordon agreed, but to himself felt extremely uncomfortable.

He believed he had convinced them. He needed to know that he had convinced himself, but other things troubled him too much to think clearly right then as he left to return to the ones who listened to his orders.

There was an increasing frustration in Steven, his life he felt being pulled and pushed against his will far too much. He had Gordon pressuring him with family and unsettling business offers, then there was Alan and the group wanting too much from him, not understanding what he was doing for them and their work. Still, his brother Nathan and little sister Lucy, were in his thoughts. It was a long day, he thought. They all were now. As evening came, he sloped through the town centre toward the multiplex cinema. There were the usual rubbish big budget movies showing, he saw. He could walk along to the art-house cinema four streets down for a more stimulating challenging film, but there was a movie here he needed to see, he was almost sure of it.

He did not pay too much attention as he stepped to the counter and asked for the ticket. He paid and walked along in. He sat in the darkness for a few moments, the trailers flashing by and then the movie began. He almost forgot which one he had picked but watched anyway. It was a kind of mystery tale. Some confused characters, some technology, paranoid discussions. Then space travel; spaceships cruising the galaxy, an alien race, misunderstandings, a power struggle. It impressed Steven, fairly good special effects employed, but screenplay predictable, stereotypical and lazy but he watched still. Some part of him really enjoyed seeing it. Some part of his mind spoke to him.

'All the space... Stars in space...'

He heard it in his own mind. Not his own thoughts at all, he was sure. It was not unusual, but strange and depressing in a way.

'Stars in space... Up in space...' he heard.

When the movie ended, the voice in his mind ended too. He left the cinema relieved.

Chapter 13

On a cold wet Tuesday afternoon, Gordon sat in his lounge with his daughter, little Lucy. She was staying over for a couple of nights as she did every fortnight. Gordon would often take her shopping, get her ice-cream, see animals at the city farm. Every two weeks, Lucy helped Gordon with some special tests and she always gave him fascinating results, always inspiring him further in his private most secret work.

'Alright Lucy, choose the game today,' he told her.

'Name game,' she replied breezily.

'Okay, good one, Lucy,' he said. He took a moment, a deep breath, and then began the experiment.

'Okay then Lucy – the name is... Philip Richmond. So what do you think?' he said and waited, watching her closely with his writing notepads at his side on the table.

Lucy looked around, seeming to wait for inspiration.

'He works in... a place... called... Legion Security?' she told him eventually.

'Where? Do you know where yet?' he asked.

'Maybe close to... Middles...borough, Daddy?' she told him.

He walked over by another long table beside the front window. There were a couple of small notebooks there which he picked up. One had a special lock which he opened up. He thumbed through quickly, finding the right pages. He looked up, then smiled.

'Very good. That's correct Lucy. Here is the next – Oscar Billminson?' he said.

Lucy looked away thoughtfully, down at the floor, then giggled a little to herself.

'He does... He works for... Um... Research insurance?' she said, sounding unsure.

'Yes, he does. But where does he work?' Gordon asked.

'Is it... Southampton?' she said.

'Close, very close. Try again, dear,' he told her.

'Maybe... Poole?' she added.

'That's right. Well done, darling,' he said and hugged her fondly, then looked at his precious girl. She then suddenly wobbled slightly to one side.

'Oh hey, Lucy darling, hold on' Gordon said and he quickly rushed over to her catching her as she began to fall to the floor. He took her gently and sat her carefully up in the chair near her. He knelt down by her, watching her closely then.

'Lucy dear? Can you hear me? Lucy?' he said.

'I... am okay. I'm okay, Daddy. Just... tires me out,' she said slowly and looked up gradually at him.

'Oh, I know, dear. Relax now. I really thank you for helping me so much. We'll get you another horse soon, right?' he told her. 'Listen, princess, I do still need to have some blood and the usual, you understand?' he said.

She nodded silently and then smiled at him. She seemed to still have the special skills that only she had. His special little girl. His gift from years ago, he thought as he looked at her. She sat and picked at the bowl of sweets on the table by her. While she perked up again, Gordon reached off into a drawer and brought out a bag, which opened out to reveal a number of medical instruments. They were startlingly sharp, clean crafted pieces of metal made to cut deep precise incisions. Little Lucy sat sucking on her favourite sweets quietly as Gordon took some samples of blood from her left arm, then swabbed saliva from her and even took a few strands of her pretty long blonde hair.

'You okay there, my little darling?' he asked as he finished up.

'Yes Daddy. I see people, you know...' she told him casually.

'Yes, you really do. Wonderful. You will help them, you are my helpful girl,' he said, patting her head with affection. He packed away the blood and other samples, then returned to her. He took her hand, and led her out for a lunch at her favourite pizza restaurant in town.

As Gordon drove the car back into his front drive, he saw Steven waiting by the front doors. They went inside together.

'Any troubles, son?' Gordon asked as they walked down the hall together.

'Oh, my problems, always my crazy problems, right Dad? You'd know,' Steven began.

They walked together into the lounge.

'So what's up? Where've you been just now?' Steven asked as they settled into some chairs.

'I've taken your sister Lucy back to your mother's house,' Gordon explained.

'Oh right. She stayed over?' Steven asked.

'Yes, it was this week. I took her to Alfonso Pizzeria. Her favourite around here. It's really great quality, you'll have to go with us some time,' Gordon told him.

'Yes, I know. I hope she enjoyed her stay this time,' Steven said.

'She did – she does. How are you really, Steven?' Gordon began 'Your university work's going okay right now, is it?'

Steven grabbed him by the shirt collar, and pushed him violently fast up against the side wall. Gordon quickly got his own grip on Steven.

'Hey, steady on, son,' he told Steven.

They held tight to each other. Steven let go and quickly managed to throw a fist, hitting Gordon in the stomach. Gordon lurched, but instantly grabbed Steven at the neck. He looked him the eyes.

'You can't do any harm to Lucy,' Steven told him with fresh seriousness.

'I never will. That... that is the solemn truth, my son,' Gordon replied.

He let go of Steven, who then turned, kicking a chair over and stormed across toward the wide windows. He looked out silently then looked back over at Gordon finally.

'Don't worry Steven. Concentrate on your good work at the university. Such superb work that I do honesty admire so much. Stay focused, son,' Gordon told him.

'Ha, oh, I wish I could. It is my work, at least,' Steven replied. 'My decent, honest work. You've lost your way, do you know that now? It's only me who has the balls to tell you though, of course.'

Gordon watched him, nodded and sat down in his high back grand chair.

'So, what is troubling you?' Gordon then asked.

'Oh, look, I'm just getting caught up with the bloody police too often, really. They're on m case with just no damn thing better to do at all. Sad losers, really. Can't get enough of me, that's it. Some local coppers keep meeting me now, asking around for me,' Steven told him, almost bragging.

'Well, you haven't done any really seriously bad things though, have you, really?' Gordon asked, with much closer fatherly concern.

'I wouldn't say so. Just average things, just some fun. Hey, look, I'm just any regular young bloke having a good time. I like women, booze, wild times. I don't start fights, sell hard drugs, steal or crap like that. Just...' He stopped, looking caught out.

'Just what, Steven?' Gordon asked.

'I'm... fine. You'd back me up though, right? With your influence, right?' Steven said, and Gordon nodded eventually.

'That is right indeed. I would. Correct. Let's have a drink,' Gordon suggested and moved over toward the drinks cabinet, Steven looking embarrassed and grateful.

Rain spat down over the window before Gordon as he sat thoughtfully alone with a double espresso before him.

'Bad weather, isn't it?' a voice said near to him.

'Could be worse, I think' Gordon replied, only looking into his dark black coffee.

'Could be much better in Washington, U, S of A, right?'

It was a medium built man beside him then, looking out at the heavy rain on the other side of the windows of the coffee shop.

'I wouldn't know. Too busy here, actually. Much too busy. Much too successful,' Gordon said, with an audible waver in his tone of voice.

'Really? Of course,' the man agreed as he quietly sat beside Gordon.

'See these crazy sick people in the news? Some disease, very strange?' he said.

'I see them,' Gordon replied quietly.

'Find them interesting? How they came about?' the man asked then turned to look right at him. 'You haven't changed Gordon. Not enough.'

'I agree with you there. I really do,' Gordon said.

He finished his coffee and then quickly left the man, a man who he had known for a long time.

They drove along with Mary in the back of the van. She was tied tight and secure.

'This is not right. She's so ill, she should go to a hospital now,' one of the two men in the car said to the one driving.

'You agreed to do this now. We know Gordon, he'll pay up, really well. He will. So much cash, my friend,' the other said.

'Fine then, bloody fine. Your idea. I need the cash, is all,' the other responded.

They drove on through daytime traffic, streets of urban people, with everyday concerns of health, money, relationships, and safety. This new disease was driven on through between them, all unaware for now. The pair in their car stopped at road lights, waited anxious and nervous.

'God damn lights, change you bloody things, hell,' the driver said.

'Alright, easy... Wait here... There,' the other said. The lights turned and they drove on finally.

As they moved along another car roamed out a few yards behind and tailed them straight casually for the next three roads. They then picked up speed where the road opened up out, and so did the other car.

'Hey, look in the mirror there,' the passenger said.

'What? Shit, who the hell is that?' the driver said.

'No real idea. Not police but... I mean, maybe or well...' the passenger said.

'You do think they're following us?' the driver asked.

'Don't know, but just move, man. Speed off or lose them somehow,' the other said .

The driver then changed gears, pushing up rapidly on the roads ahead. The other still followed it seemed, even soon gaining smoothly and keeping right on them casually.

'Shit man, they want us. They're fast as hell, stuck on us good,' the passenger told him. 'Go faster, somewhere, just lose the fuckers!'

'Right, look, I'm trying, okay?' the driver replied.

The car moved on faster, the other so close behind, locked on straight and hard. They turned on two roads in quick succession, even jumped a road light. All other cars gone, open road had them, desperation weighing down heavy on them. In the back of the van then, Mary made sudden moans, noises frightening to them.

'Oh, what's up with her now?' the passenger asked.

'She's diseased, man, like toxic ill, all mutating probably,' the driver said.

'Oh God, oh Allah,' the other responded.

'She won't stop man, it's freaking me. Gordon will have to pay so much for this,' the driver told the other man.

'Shut her up. Will she just be quiet?' the other asked.

The other car forged on with a sudden hard burst of speed again.

'Right, blitz left now.'

'Back around, the right, okay? Nail it, just go man,' the other said almost hysterically.

The other car came only yards behind then, the engine so loud, as they moved around, chaotically turned and then suddenly swerved, hitting a streetlight or something. They drove on, seeming surprisingly free from the pursuing car finally. A gun fired out, and a bullet flew out somewhere behind. They drove off away, somehow escaping on the roads, back on track once more.

In the calm family home, Steven's mother, Beatrice, was in the kitchen tidying things when the doorbell rang at the front. A few seconds passed until she reached it.

'Oh, Gordon, why are you here now?' she said, seeing her former husband standing before her.

'I was nearby and wanted to visit my children. Are they in now?' he enquired.

'Yes, your daughter is in the living room. Go on through,' she said with forced welcome.

They walked in finding Lucy watching the television – some teen drama programme. She saw her father and quickly got up to hug him affectionately.

'Hello Daddy. Why are you here?' she asked.

'Oh, I need to check on my princess, don't I?' he said. 'Had lunch yet?'

'No, not yet,' she told him.

He soon enough took her out down to the city centre, along to a modern cafe, where they ordered Panini's and drinks.

'School is okay now, is it? No boy troubles right now?' Gordon asked her.

'Oh no, Daddy, just my friends Simon and Mark. Don't be disgusting. They're just my friends, Dad. Anyway, I mostly only see Michelle and Jennifer when I do see anyone,' she told him.

'Oh right, that's okay then. Hey, I might be travelling soon. Maybe overseas – America, or Europe again. A special little girl I know might be able to come along with me,' he suggested.

'Me, Daddy? We can go travelling?' she said.

'My company is making some contacts in other places, and I need to visit new people in different countries. I could be gone a while, really. You could visit, at least. See what Mum says, I suppose,' he told her.

'Really Dad?' she said, amazed and excited.

'Definitely, darling. Of course, honey. We'll see what can be arranged, okay?' he said.

'Daddy, have you seen Steven much?' she then asked.

'Sometimes I do, yes. He is very busy too at his university. All that very clever important work he has got to do,' he told her.

'I miss him, Daddy. He's not around much, not now. Like you,' she said.

'Well, that's no good. I'll see him, have a word. Tell him his special sister wants to see him. He has to think of you, he really does,' he told her.

This made her smile and she hugged her father again fondly.

He leaned in closely, looking much more serious.

'Lucy, have you had the fire dreams again, darling?' he asked her.

'Daddy you... you didn't want me to talk about them,' she said.

'I know, but really, Lucy, tell me now. It's okay – have they come back to you?' he said in a such a caring manner.

She looked away quickly, sobbing a little.

'Hey darling, what's up?' he asked and put an arm around her.

'No Daddy, it's Nathan...' she began.

'What? What's Nathan up to?' he asked.

'He said I should be quiet about seeing things, even to you,' she told him.

'Well, Nathan is wrong, I'll tell him about it. You must talk to me about things, I'm your father,' he said.

'I know that Dad,' she said.

'Is he still watching? Does he still ask you about it when you see things?' he asked.

'Yes, Daddy. Nathan is my brother, though,' she said.

'Yes, but he still must know what he should not do. I should see him soon then. I've been forgetting about him I think,' Gordon said.

'And Mum,' Lucy told him.

'Oh, your mother? I suppose so,' he said.

Gordon sighed to himself.

'Good, fine, yes. Okay, Lucy, let's walk back to the car now,' he told her and they left the café, his arm around his precious sweet little girl.

Chapter 14

In the flat, Alan sat reading textbooks with some classic progressive rock sounds on behind him when Steven came in suddenly.

'Oh, hello there. You alright in here?' he asked Steven.

'What? Hmm, yeah fine. Just getting a bite to eat. Got to go see my shit father. Arsehole,' Steven told him.

'Steady. He's not that bad, really. He's alright, isn't he?' Alan said.

'Sometimes yes, other times no,' Steven said.

'I get you,' Alan replied, watching Steven disappear into the kitchen, and reappear with a quickly slapped up ham sandwich.

'See you later for drinks and Xbox battle boogie showdown, right?' Steven said, before leaving with a loud door slam behind him.

The car ride was easy to navigate, but difficult emotionally as ever it was. The night sky had darkened in by the time he pulled in near the street where Gordon lived. Interestingly, at the other side police were coming out right from beside the house, and into their own parked cars, where they drove away. After knocking at the front door, only a couple of seconds, Gordon greeted Steven quickly.

'Were the police just here right now?' Steven asked immediately.

'Come on in,' Gordon said, opening the door to him.

Strong expensive whiskey was poured into two glasses, one each, and they moved into the lounge room together.

'So tell me why they were here then?' Steven asked again.

'Calm down. They were just making some local enquiries, really,' Gordon explained.

'Oh really? They haven't found your secret monster hidden in the basement, Dr. Frankenstein?' Steven said.

'No, not yet. These ones are no CSI big wigs. My secret is safe,' Gordon said.

'Funny. Okay but really tell me what they wanted?' Steven said.

'Nothing to worry about,' Gordon said.

'There is plenty for me to worry about. I think we all know that. When they come here, to your house, to see you. That will worry me,' Steven said.

'You don't worry. You watch and learn. Admire. Relax. A little danger is what?' Gordon said, waiting for the reply.

Steven looked back, and drank his strong whiskey in one.

'A little danger is... expected, a bit more is a good sign,' Steven told him. It was obviously a kind of mantra which he had been taught from his father in the past.

'That's the answer. Checkmate, son of mine,' Gordon said with a fond smile.

'I just... You're a father too, remember. It's not just me and Nathan looking after Lucy okay?' Steven told him.

'That's right. I know.'

'Yes, you do, don't you?' Steven said. 'So, have the police been before?'

'Surprisingly not. Shame, right?' Gordon remarked.

'Oh, absolutely. That's right, father,' Steven said.

'So what about you and the boys in blue?' Gordon asked.

'Let's see... Last time they got close was probably after a party a few days back... Some kinky game, someone got scared, someone with no sense of humour...' Steven explained.

'Excellent, good effort. But clean get away, then?' Gordon asked.

'Of course. All cleaned up, no final evidence at all.'

'That's my boy,' Gordon said.

'Look, I'm going to go now, but just think about your family more, will you?' Steven asked.

'I could say the same thing. Don't forget my offers, okay?' Gordon reminded him.

'How could I ever?' Steven replied. He gradually moved to the door and walked out. With the sharp smell of good whiskey on his breath, he drove away speedily back through the city roads to the flat and Alan who waited there for him.

The lower secret locked rooms where Gordon walked were a place of great guilty thoughts, and nervous potential dangerous events in wait. This was no regular working laboratory, but perhaps it really was the environment where Gordon and his own work did belong all the time, all along. The truest, most valuable projects, even outside of the known work which had earned him thousands and even millions. He walked inside, quietly greeted once more by the two trusted close partners who sat observing the people then bound down on tables who they, in some sense, viewed as their new patients. Gordon walked around the room, viewed the running steady monitor screens, incoming results, and the expressions of the patients who slept, casually sedated.

'Going well, is it? Going good now?' Gordon asked the first partner quietly.

'Yes, interesting. Slow, but very interesting so far,' he replied.

'Okay, okay,' Gordon said pleased then moved along over near the other man, who stood by the second strapped down person, watching and reading on a number of small devices connected up to the person.

'And here? What so far?' Gordon asked with optimism.

'Yes, steady careful results coming through. You seem to have a good theory set up here I'd say, Gordon,' the man told him.

'Thank you. Means a lot, really. Continue on then, please. Be bold and brave. No limits here,' he told the man.

Gordon looked at the patient lying there helpless, eyes shut and relaxed so far.

'Don't give me those eyes, will you? You asked for it. That's right. You know I should do this. I have to, you said so yourself. Just... relax,' he told the captive man lying before him.

Gordon looked back to his close partner friend, a Joseph Hillwell, and whispered carefully.

'My daughter was returned safely again today, wasn't she?' he asked.

'Oh yes, of course, no problem at all. No worries there at all. We would not let anything happen to her,' the man replied sincerely.

'Right, thank you. Okay then. I'll return later tomorrow, but message me if you have to, you know. If anything different comes up problematic at all,' he told the man.

'You're the boss here,' Joseph replied, smiling back at him.

Gordon walked away back out, away from his captive special patients, with personal fraught concern for his so precious young special little daughter Lucy.

Only now that parts of his plan were actually moving along as intended, he was feeling the added pressure on top of his duties controlling and managing his business company. He walked along, thinking deeply to himself. Gordon spent time observing the two hidden special patients at the Midlands laboratories, vastly intrigued and fascinated at the sight they were seeing there. Suddenly his phone vibrated in his pocket, and so he answered.

'Hello, Frank? Alright?' he asked.

'We need Helen back. Locals have been gossiping, speaking to police. They've seen she's gone... Journalists are sniffing around, Gordon. It's no good at all,' Frank warned.

'No, no way. Not yet. She's so impressive so far. We need her here, now for a while longer, we really do,' Gordon told him as he looked back through the long glass window at Helen being monitored still.

'Gordon, please. Come on. Your business, your company, all under threat – she has to return now,' Frank advised him.

'Oh, come on, a couple more days?'

'We really shouldn't do that, Gordon, it's too much. There's no time,' Frank answered.

'Okay then. Leave it with me,' Gordon said.

'No Gordon, wait...' Frank began, but Gordon had already turned his phone off. He was walking back through to the laboratory chamber to look at Helen and her most unique biology.

Chapter 15

The garden was such a huge overgrown wild looking place, but it was extravagant for Lucy to play in when she was not at school. This was the best time for her and Beatrice, who would watch her beautiful little sweet girl, who gave her such simple joy, like nothing else in life. She had left Gordon, but she kept Lucy to herself. She took care of her precious, lovely little princess, and here in the garden the secrets were on show, only deep behind the tall trees and thick bushes; and this is where they remained. It was here that Beatrice encouraged little Lucy to blossom with all of her unique talents she had found over time. Although they had three treasured children, Lucy was the one they watched and waited for now. Gordon knew something from when Lucy came to the world, he had real feeling of some strong importance that little Lucy would provide at some point. There definitely was something supernatural about Lucy, but it was still only just gradually beginning to emerge occasionally. This special potential in Lucy was most likely what split Gordon and Beatrice apart. Gordon seemed to view Lucy as perhaps the most exciting future project he could have connected to his own work, and as such, it ruined his relationship with her. Beatrice though, loved her Lucy so endlessly and took so much inspiration from her in many ways.

As they watched Lucy grow up to her current eight years of age, Gordon, Beatrice, all of them had at some point seen some strange unexplainable things around perfect little Lucy. Gordon knew and thought many things about this. Steven denied anything he had seen, only visiting every month or so. It only made him drink and do drugs more frequently. Nathan, as an artist, spent much time in some way being inspired by the apparitions or visions around his little sister. He was not sure what the real cause was. He had spoken to Beatrice about it, and spoken to his father, and the answers never explained any of it clearly, and never satisfied him or Steven. His little sister provided his stories, and artwork of many surreal kinds. Perhaps the artwork could eventually reveal more truthful answers, he often hoped.

Again Nathan sat with a sketchpad, paints and pencils, waiting and watching his sister. She was happy as she skipped, danced and played around, thinking of fairies, sprites and magical worlds. The happier she was, the more likely it often was that visions came, he knew. They never though she was any kind of mentally challenged child, disturbed or ill in the head, with problems psychological or any disability such as Autism or Asperger's. She could be whimsical and unfocused, but then she was only small still. Angelic and inspirational to watch always.

They came suddenly as she danced around the colours and shapes came up, emanating up in magnificent clarity. These stunning figures moved out around airily, joining Lucy in her dancing around. She moved like they were familiar friends – perhaps they were to her. But it never left the garden. Outside the garden things were tragic and flawed, but never inside with Lucy.

There were dark skies and heavy rain hitting down on the windows to the university laboratories while the group worked through together. By this point, they all had specific duties over several test procedures, documentations and preparations. Things were set out, conducted and worked through steadily and in a very focused manner. Alan, though, was apprehensive about something around them. As the project was more certain with stronger funding and financial backing eventually, due to the work of Steven and his persuasive meetings, they officially employed two more members to the team – Philip Burns, and Jane Hurley – as they often had to follow tests through on a twenty four hour watch, they later found.

'Steven, there is different equipment around the lab today. I don't know where some of it came from – new pieces, devices,' Alan said.

'Oh, well. Must have been the technicians and others. Finally doing something good and useful instead of pretending to have other better things going on, and being jaded and wishing they could start over,' Steven replied smiling.

'Well okay. It's just strange,' Alan said.

He accepted the response and saw that he could simply be just tired now. He had pushed himself perhaps too much once the project had begun, just to want to be sure it started right. He had to let up on himself, he realised. He had to listen to Steven more when it came to living and working, just to some extent.

Down the lower northern town, along toward Helen's home, a police car roamed and finally parked up. A moment passed and then two officers stepped out and walked up to her front door. They knocked and waited. A brief moment passed, and neighbours looking from twitching window curtains across the street. The door opened then.

Helen appeared to the police officers, looking calm and friendly. At the end of the road Gordon watched from his car, and satisfied, finally drove away.

They were already gaining much increasing interest locally, but much more rapidly, Steven found he was needed for many more interviews and meetings, more even than he had knowingly arranged personally.

'Yes Mr. Broodstock, if you really want to have a drink and discuss our project you are very welcome. Yes... Monday? Yes, at say, eleven. Thank you, goodbye,' Steven said over his cell phone.

He approached Alan over by the data boards and computer tables.

'There we have it – yet another interested party. This is just astounding, almost unmanageable, unbelievable. So many people have read about us or seen the website. They're gagging to know more. We'll be set for a long time. Very big opportunities ahead, Alan,' he informed him with huge enthusiasm.

'It's fantastic, I agree. You're the one, big mouth salesman scientist hotshot man. We owe you, I believe,' Alan told him joking, but honestly grateful.

'No, not like that. I'm with you guys. Us versus the world, that's it,' Steven said. He looked down at the work on screen and beside Alan then.

'Hey, Alan, what is this stuff you're viewing here?' he asked.

Alan suddenly seemed to panic, his cheeks turned red slightly, and flustered at the question.

'Oh God, no Steven, it's only... This is just some smaller personal stuff, notes, theories. Just taking a break. I should get back to the real thing. Like you do,' Alan said.

'What kind of stuff is it, though?' Steven said, still interested.

'It's just some loose ideas left over from university, really. No specific thing. Just some thoughts in other areas, you know – the weird biology stuff I found interesting some times. Crap like that,' Alan said, sounding casual.

'Oh, right. Well, let's just work now then, right?' Steven suggested.

Alan nodded in agreement as they both then quickly turned to the main project work once again.

'First of many things. You should think about changes,' Steven suggested.

'I do. I think about how to change mistakes around us, mistakes inside of us,' Alan agreed.

'I want to make an offer with you. We could continue. Like before, both our ideas,' he said. He seemed keen to see Alan react positively.

'Steven, we've been worried about you,' Alan told him frankly in a low voice.

'Don't worry. You worry way too much. That's why I've come so far, Alan. I just go with my intuition. You know that,' he said. He was frustrated.

'We're different, Steven. Probably why we separated with our work,' Alan told him.

'Aren't you listening to me? The offer I have? Join me at the front of real, genuine progress, my father will always let us in there, with them,' he said. As he spoke Alan noticed him limping on one side, his left leg slightly rigid. He also seemed to have a bizarre twitch or tic, only noticeable over his face every so often.

'Are you okay, Steven?' he asked with honest concern.

'Okay? I'm... fine. I'm really good. Really damn good, okay? Yes, I am okay.' He stopped and they stood looking at each other for a brief uncomfortable moment.

He quickly walked down the drive to where his car was parked and got inside. He did not look back at Alan again before he drove away. Alan watched him go and thought to himself that something was going to change very soon. Steven was changing, himself and things they knew well. Alan knew that Steven always had the opportunity to step into his father's company, where he would have guaranteed wealth, success and respect.

Alan had difficult sleep that night and was haunted and troubled for hours until finally the sunlight greeted his weary eyes. Somehow he left the house as normal, knowing that work demanded him, and some hope continued to draw him as ever it did. Upon arrival at the laboratories, he was met by Jane and Pascal waiting for him.

'Alan, they've been,' Pascal said with an instant seriousness. Jane approached him.

'Jo's been taken in. They suspect us of doing some kind of serious subversive dangerous work here. Really radical stuff. I don't know why,' she said, holding his hand.

'Who? Who has been here?' he asked. He thought they meant the police, but could not be so sure.

'Them, the ones who work with the government. If we're not doing the right type of scientific research in their view, we're closed down, locked up even, maybe. We could be seen as criminals,' Pascal told him with a certain pessimism.

'But we're not that kind of science. There's no danger for us or from us. Where's Jo then?' he enquired.

'They won't say. They just took her. They'll be back, to speak to you, and to look around,' Pascal said.

'What do you really know about this?' Alan asked. He just did not care about being subtle anymore.

'Why should I know any more than you? You just can't trust me at all,' Pascal said. He was not shocked, just nodding.

'I just thought you might know something else. Something more. You seem to know many people all over, let's be honest,' Alan told him.

'"Honest"? Late for that isn't it Alan?' He said and walked away then. Jane then came up to him.

'What now?' She asked.

'Who knows? We don't need to feel guilty of anything. Our work will only help mankind in a careful way. No danger. We're not guilty,' he said.

'Alan, that might not matter at all. I've heard some rumours...' she began, hesitating.

'What rumours exactly?' he asked. She looked to check that Pascal was far over at his corner of the lab before continuing.

'Alan, things are changing. We might have to adapt to different ways soon,' she said.

'Why? What do you mean by that?' he asked. At the same time, a loud bizarre commotion erupted outside the building, like machines demolishing the walls. They all looked at each other and then quickly walked to the doors. Alan opened them and looked outside with nervous caution. The sight astonished and shocked at the same time. Jane gasped next to him.

'Close the doors,' Pascal said quickly. Alan sensed the strong fear in him then. He was also afraid though there was a different strange tone to his voice.

'It's more of them. The attackers, the sick ones. A group... Look at them...' Alan said stunned by the sight outside of the lab windows. He was fascinated by the scene out there, its grotesque random chaos. There were four of them. What they were doing was surreal and quite disturbing. They attacked a group of businessmen and women on the street with what seemed their bloodied fists, and anything they had found to inflict damage, which included shoes, knives, and wooden posts. The others simply waved their arms and scratched out violently. They all seemed drugged, sleepwalking or in a trance as they fought, while the businessmen and women screamed and defended themselves.

They could see that they were a new breed of attackers, shockingly violent and yet with dead vacant eyes on their faces as they ran at them.

'Close the door, Alan!' Pascal told him again, louder and impatiently.

'Do you wonder why they're doing it, Pascal?' Alan asked him.

'That's for someone else to think about, not us. But the police will sort it,' he replied and closed the door for him.

'It still could be contagious, those people out there,' Alan said.

'Not necessarily. They'll figure it out, because they have too, and they've the money to do so. It's down to the police and doctors. Cancers within, disease and tumours. Trying to keep one step ahead of nature. Nature is a tricky bitch,' Pascal said.

He took out his cell phone and dialled the police's number. They showed up in a couple of minutes, as the crazed fighting outside began to fragment – some business men fighting bravely, the women managing to run away mostly, besides a couple of horrific casualties beaten and bruised. Alan, Jane and Pascal stood safely within the laboratory watching by the window side, eventually deciding to return to their work.

'What have you heard about the space flights, Jane?' Pascal asked her minutes later, as if nothing had been happening.

Alan could barely believe that Pascal or any of the others were seriously interested in the new sudden hints of news from around various reports and journals, some businessmen and science research individuals commenting on some kinds of space mission from right there in the United Kingdom. It would be really great, a proud thing even, but he did not believe the country had the money, the equipment or international support for it to actually happen in reality. Just hyped up news reports was the truth, he thought.

'The space project? Quite a lot actually. Good and bad news. There is an amazing possibility that we could actually go with them soon,' she announced.

'Really? You mean as we are scientists?' Pascal asked, suddenly seeming quite happier and interested. His mood swings though were grating on Alan's sanity more and more.

'No, we can't,' Alan said breaking in, and they both looked at Alan.

'Really? Why not exactly?' Pascal asked immediately.

'It's us. Not enough money, or influence. Same as ever,' Alan told him, fairly sure of his opinion, even if he did not want it to be true that he did believe it so.

'No, Alan, that doesn't matter. It's just time. It depends on the jobs we have, our research, how we pitch it to them, our skills and the opportunities. And if you see that old friend of yours anytime...' Jane said. Alan took an uncomfortable deep breath and looked at her.

'Who?' Alan asked.

'You know. You worked with him. He's in a science research company too, isn't he?' she asked. He almost felt sick inside.

'No, Jane. No chance. No need to... Just... I can't see it happening. Let's just keep focused on real life anyway. Look...' he said, trying to keep both of them calm. Pascal though did not help.

'But Alan, what is real right now? What should we be doing as research? Space travel is real, is necessary. Our perfection as a race, our future. This planet is turning to shit. It's falling apart because of fossil fuel dependency, industrial living, toxic waste, chemical waste, globalisation... The human race has to move, look elsewhere. It's happening, and we could be right at the start of it all. Priorities, Alan. Imagine it all,' he said confidently.

'Don't you start, okay? We've got work here. Important, relevant work still. Things to do still. If you think otherwise, or want to ruin it all...' Alan replied but quickly lost his focus, his thoughts mixed and distracted.

'You're doing fine by yourself, big man,' Pascal replied. Alan stepped closer to him then, their faces only inches apart.

'They're coming back for you after Joanna,' he told Alan.

'They can do that if they want to,' Alan said.

Pascal looked at him, then at Jane, and then he backed off towards the doorway.

'Fine by me. I was only wasting my time here with all this. You'd better say goodbye to him, Jane. It's nearly over,' he said, and then opened the door and left them. Alan was glad he was gone, but he was suddenly curious as to what that meant. He would need replacing on the team, or they would have to take on his work along with their own, he realised.

Alan could not be sure that their work could continue without one or two of them. But then they were being taken apart and investigated then. Changes were happening.

'Alan, I'm just a bit scared now. What do we do?' Jane asked quietly.

'We're not doing anything wrong. Don't worry,' Alan answered, but doubted that he had convinced her then.

'Not unless they decide we are. The rules are changing, and the laws concerning experiments, ethics, government funding. They're changing to suit corporations and money men. We're fucked now. Plead guilty, we'll have to,' she said sombrely.

'What? No. We're not guilty of anything. We're no criminals. Is this what we get for working so damn hard to help our country and others? Isaac Newton, Einstein – were they criminals?' He asked.

'It's relative to the times around us. You know that. This government choking our scientific freedom to explore and test for the better. They'll be back here very soon now,' she told him.

'We stand and defend our work,' Alan replied.

'Really?'

'What? You want to run?' he asked. The idea was just insane. A scientist running from the police like some serial killer or drug dealing thug. They were highly educated, civilised people who were contributing hugely to a better world, he thought.

'I don't want to be put away. Can we defend ourselves? The work? I've heard some of what they were saying earlier – they are talking about things differently. They view it all in a different way. Our work might actually be deemed criminal,' she told Alan.

'Why? We work with chemical mixes, microscopic structures, time, elements... No animals, people or drugs are involved... Well not really anyway,' he replied.

'I don't know their reasoning, or why laws are changing. Maybe it is because of what could potentially come from our work...' Jane guessed.

'We could appeal to their needs,' he suggested. 'The government always really bends to science if we can offer something to help medicine, or something like that.'

'What? How? I don't see it happening soon enough,' she said.

'The attackers. We work on them for the government. Just for a short time, long enough,' he said. He did not like the idea even as he spoke it to her.

'Alan, I just want to leave it. Leave this. For a while,' she told me.

'Let's leave this building then,' he replied.

They walked out along town quietly, discussing their options and thoughts.

'This just might be a good time to put the project on hold. Just for a while. Take a break. A sort of holiday' Jane suggested, smiling at Alan as they walked along through the city. 'You're so stressed out all the time. It'd be good for you. For us both,' she said.

'Okay. Really? I don't know. We were doing something. To stop now... Maybe just in a while longer, just wait some more...' he began.

'Always a while longer,' she said.

'Yeah, I know but really, I was beginning to observe something, some difference I'm sure, the structures, the reactions...' he explained.

'You always do. Let's take a break, Alan. It'd be wise right now. Pick it up in a while, a few months or more. Come back fresh. Besides, it's just any science is dangerous right now. We don't have to forget it all – just take a break. I like our life together,' she told him. He remembered those words for a long time.

They stopped down by the canal side bridge and went to a quiet familiar cheap restaurant for lunch. It was the last romantic meal they would share before their lives were changed in so many ways. The meal was good and allowed them to decide upon their path to take. They chose to return to the labs. Alan had somehow convinced Jane, and he was so pleased. After a short while thought, the men did come back in the afternoon and Jane and Alan went off without resistance.

They were individually interrogated but stuck to the answers that they had decided to tell them earlier. They asked them about the research project in great detail, the objectives, the potential risks, costs, and results so far. They already knew all of this, Alan was quite sure, but they wanted to hear it from them. They let them go that night. It was unexpected but they were relieved indeed. Alan met up with Jane and they cautiously returned to his flat.

They were nervously quite as they entered the flat. Paranoia filled their minds, unease and mild fear. Then Jane spoke.

'So we're taking a break then?' she asked.

'I... suppose we are,' he replied, looking at her briefly.

'They didn't ask you to be a part of anything else? Anything related to the attackers?' she asked.

'What makes you think that? No, and well, I didn't offer. Just glad we're free and together,' he said. He put his arm around her and hugged her warmly then.

'We're free, yes,' she agreed.

They slept deeply together that night, relieved and secure finally. In the light of the following bright cold morning, Alan awoke alone.

Within seconds Alan became scared, worried and got up to look for Jane. He stood and looked around the bedroom, then called out her name. With no immediate reply, he walked out toward the main room and kitchen. 'Jane?'

He went and looked around but could not find her. That was how it remained. She was gone. Her clothes that she was in were gone, others still there but that did not give him hope. Her phone was gone, so he called it and waited. No answer came. He spent over an hour calling up her family and friends. Her sister did not like him and so was just as guarded and cold as usual. A close friend of Jane's did speak in a cautious manner eventually.

'So have you heard from her?' he asked again.

'She's a free woman Alan. Let her be,' she told him.

'Look, I'm just bloody worried, Megan. So she's okay? Has she told you anything? About me and her?' he asked, desperate for information.

'Enough, all that she wants to. Just don't worry, but think about other things,' she said.

'We were taken in by the government squad yesterday. I'm just worried that she is okay,' he told her. 'They have her again.'

'Is this bullshit?' she asked.

'No, absolute truth I swear,' he said.

'Call me back in half an hour,' she told him.

Before then he decided to call John, to see how he was after being grilled under pressure alone the day before. Like Jane, he received no reply from his mobile. Calling his landline gave no answer either. Alan went on the move. He left his flat and drove off. If he was simply being paranoid well, he would bear the embarrassment, but if not he needed to find his friends and Jane as soon as he could before some serious injustice happened to them.

Alan was nearly ninety percent certain that he knew where John lived, so he drove to the area and pulled up at the street that seemed familiar. He had been there may be only three times in a year, so his mind was very vague. He stood in the street, but struggled to recall the actual house he was at, and then tentatively stepped up a few doors. His time was short and he had to simply take a chance. He hesitated and then walked up to number sixteen.

Was it the right house? He would find out. He pressed the buzzer and stepped back. The quiet moment was ominous. He looked through the frosted glass panel window of the door for anyone coming.

'John? Are you in? It's Alan,' he said. 'Can we talk?'

He was feeling embarrassed and stupid. He was concerned that someone might be watching, following or observing him. The whole government thing was unravelling his mind.

'John, please come to the door. Answer your phone. Anything,' Alan said with depleting confidence that anyone was coming. He was feeling desperately alone in the situation. Not long ago, he was part of a strong team dedicated to discovering breakthroughs in specific areas of disease and virus growth. They were now tempted, bought, sold, blackmailed, threatened into inaction. Were they simply that weak? he wondered. Was he just meant to accept the end so soon, so suddenly?

He used to think that a good scientist did not accept the problems of the world around but strives to find solutions. Where were his solutions to all this he wondered?

He drove to a local petrol station to fill up the car. Doing so, he walked into the kiosk and the young man on the counter was focused with eyes down on his newspaper.

'Excuse me there,' Alan said in a friendly tone.

'Hey, have you seen it? Lucky geezers or what?' the young man said to him.

'Sorry?' Alan said.

'The astronauts. Well, they're not all proper trained like that. They're sending up another mixed bunch of them,' he told him.

'Really?' Alan answered. His interest was barely there until he glanced at the photo spread in the newspaper before him on the counter. He took it from the young man and looked closer at it.

'Hey, are you going to buy that?' the young man asked.

'What? Fine,' Alan said, handing him a five pound note. The thing that took his full immediate attention right then was who he saw in the photograph.

She was going up there. Jane was going to space but had not told him. Perhaps he should have expected that but it still felt shocking. Men lost their women sometimes, people moved apart, but to space? He knew she would go. She must have been planning it for a long while without telling him a thing. Did that mean that she just did not care about them, their relationship?

It was scientific research to her; this was her exploration and discovery. Small tests and routines in the bland, quiet laboratories were never enough for her. He knew that.

Alan did not think that she was as selfish as that. A part of him wondered if she had been influenced by someone else. It had been a recent urge of hers, or so it had seemed, but it had been for most of rest of the population of the country as well so it was not entirely strange.

What Alan began to soon wonder was could he actually follow her if she went into space? He really did not know an answer to that then. He was just about sure that he did love her and that he might just do anything at all to stay with her. But then how selfish of him would that be?

Alan had the rest of mankind to consider, the rest of the nation to think of first before his own actions and love life. They would be travelling to some space station and conducting new, extremely essential experiments he knew. Was his simple lustful desire more crucial than their successful space knowledge, information and progression? More important than curing serious mental and physical diseases and ailments if their own research soon enough had the breakthrough that could be very near them in their work?

His mind ached with the serious personal and ethical dilemmas which he saw that he had little time to resolve, but which had to be confronted. The newspaper held the details of where and when of the next shuttle launch to the space stations. His mind began to clear. He forgot the science project briefly, and focused on the news of the brave space mission project being arranged. He only wanted to save Jane.

They could shut the project down if they wished, they really could. Something inside reminded him, maybe some distant memory from his father. He remembered that sometimes people with real love, love found between two people, was more precious than any rare new found mineral, any new technological breakthrough. It was a memory, not personal knowledge, but it always had been in the back of his mind. Jane was his real love, he did believe that.

Chapter 16

At the far end of the long beautiful garden behind the grand detached house, Steven could see his brother Nathan and little sister Lucy there as he entered to meet them. Nathan saw him and walked up to meet him as he came in.

'Here's my wild Casanova scientist brother for some reason unknown, yet, on a break from his many slutty lusting groups of young women everywhere,' Nathan remarked.

'And hello to you too, my good brother. Everything okay with you?' Steven asked, ignoring the tired jibes.

'So you're actually bothered now, are you?' Nathan asked.

'Oh, you know I am, always. Stop it with all that, will you?' Steven said. 'How's Lucy anyway?'

'The question should be "how's mother?" really,' Nathan told him.

'Well, so how is mother?' Steven asked.

'She's so bloody weird really. I mean really now, Steven,' Nathan said more serious finally.

'But Lucy is okay, right?' Steven asked.

'She's as interesting as ever. She's doing alright in her way. I watch her, you know I do,' Nathan said.

'I know. Thanks Nathan. It will change,' Steven said.

'So you keep saying… You always keep saying that,' Nathan told him.

'But you believe me, right?' Steven asked.

After only at first staring back at him, eventually Nathan did nod in agreement.

'What about Dad now?' he asked.

'Well, good enough, I suppose. Still very difficult, but you know our father,' Steven said, sighing as he and Nathan then walked back up the garden toward Lucy who played alone at the bottom of the garden, lost in make believe daydream tales. She saw Steven coming, and quickly ran up to meet him with affection.

'Hey, little pixie, you playing out here today? I've missed you,' Steven told her.

She smiled back as she hugged him.

'I've missed my bigger brother too. You shouldn't go away. Don't go away all the time,' she said loudly, looking cross but then smiling again soon enough.

'Oh, I am so sorry, Lucy. You're right, little sis. I have to do my important university work though. You know that. My special science projects, like Dad does, remember?' he said to her.

'Hey, Steven – don't, yeah?' Nathan said. 'Right. Okay then, shall we get ice cream now?' Steven asked Lucy, who beamed back up at him.

They all entered the large home of their mother Beatrice, taking Lucy into the kitchen. In there, they looked around in the tall many-sectioned deep freezer for a flavour or two that pleased their little sister.

'This is just a special treat now okay Lucy, just because Steven is here, right?' Nathan told her.

'I know. Special Steven visit ice cream' she replied.

They found some rocky road and orange sauce, which put a huge grin over her face. As she dug deep in enthusiastically, Steven and Nathan sat back talking.

'Didn't want to see Mum just yet then, did you?' Nathan asked.

'She doesn't need to see me. She only needs to see Lucy, and you mostly still,' Steven replied.

'It won't keep like this, this easy you know?' Nathan began. 'Dad won't let it; he won't let you know it.'

'We'll see, we will. Things are looking very good for me. My research team is getting some great interest, great results at the university now. Stunning results, even,' Steven told him.

'Great. I'm happy for you, I am. My own life is still down the pan. No damn prospects, wasting away, but an honest artist still, that counts over it all,' Nathan said with no total conviction.

'Oh, hang in there. You will get picked up, you're bloody talented. Get something going with those friends – the graffiti guy, the poster bloke or the comedian girl. Some new project, maybe,' Steven suggested.

'I might sometime, don't know. Right now though... you know how it has to be. Just here mostly. Have to be, right?' Nathan said.

'Look, don't blame me now. We know how things are. You and Lucy, you know her best. Just relax, I need this, how this is,' Steven told him.

'But does she? Does she really?' Nathan asked.

They looked at little Lucy who played with some spoons on the kitchen table, after enjoying her ice cream.

'She's still... How is she?' Steven said.

'Yes, Steven. Very much still like how she is. No different. She can't get hurt. She won't, will she?' Nathan said very quietly.

'Oh God no, Nathan. Stop it. Right, look okay that's fine. Very... fine,' Steven told him.

Steven then turned and crouched down near Lucy.

'Hey Lucy, have you seen the red ones recently again?' he asked her. She looked up at him, then away.

'Not really, I suppose. I have just been myself, haven't I Nathan?' she said and looked at her other brother.

'Yes, you've been just you, that's okay. I'm happy with that, no problem,' Nathan told her.

'Mum and Dad will get back together soon? For holidays?' she asked them.

Steven and Nathan both looked at each other and then back at her.

'Yes, our holiday. That's it. Sometime soon,' Steven said.

'Oh, Steven, really,' Nathan said, not keen with his statement.

'Look, I'll talk to Mum. I will, really. She knows what we think about things,' Steven said to Nathan.

'You know her answer. Same as ever,' Nathan told him quickly.

'No, it'll change. Really, finally. Not long to go. Not all about Dad for long,' Steven said.

'Right. I hope so, Steven. Hope you show me,' Nathan said.

'I really will. Our holiday time soon. Really,' Steven said in a defiantly determined manner, and he then winked at Lucy who looked up with admiration.

Every day for Gordon was another day with endless paranoia, concern and dread now. For a highly wealthy, successful man, he certainly behaved to himself like some homeless lost soul – the desperation, confusion, fear, and regrets. He hid it so well still. And as Steven grew up, he even began to shift the attention of curious local authorities to Steven and away from himself. They could be watching – always could be, and should be probably, he would like to think. Gordon had made such a miraculously lucky escape all those years ago; he knew that for sure. He was lucky and had certainly continued to be, his business ventures and so were his family. It was luck with dangers that only he and Beatrice knew clearly. He had regret in spades, so much, but it was ultimately outweighed by stronger dreams and desires. Three loved children now of his own, how proud he was. Steven and Nathan now grown young men with their own dreams and beliefs. Then there was his little angel, sweet little Lucy.

It was becoming much harder for Gordon to spend time with Lucy now. Partly because of the control that Beatrice had, from their agreement over the children, but also of his own choice. Lucy was very delicate and special. So different from Steven and Nathan, in way that mattered so much to Gordon continually. He believed she should be with her mother, at least while she was still so young and innocent in the world. While Gordon had bonded more easily with Steven and to some extent Nathan, he knew how important it was to keep such close watch over his precious daughter at all costs.

One evening in the house, Gordon sat before the television, some old western movie playing on screen. Strong potent masculine men, quick to draw, shoot down the bad men, and save the women and the people around them. He liked those movies, but they could be stupid sometimes, he thought. He sipped on a cold vodka and lime drink and spoke to some friend on his phone as he watched the familiar old movie.

'Yes, things are good enough. Yes, at the university, the other a stubborn arty dream child of some unfashionable kind. Lucy? Yes, she's lovely. Angelic to me. Yes, her mother has her mostly, still... I know I should, damn woman...' Gordon told his friend over his cell phone, the drink inflaming his usual latent angers.

He seemed to begin to look uncomfortable sitting there, refilling his vodka drink soon enough, to keep his mood going strong.

'She is still fascinating?' the voice asked him.

'Very much so. Yes. Maybe more so now. Always fascinating, the things she mentions, the things around her,' Gordon replied thoughtfully.

'You are still thinking the same thoughts then, old friend?' the voice asked him.

'I might be, yes. Just good, uncompromised scientific research for the best, boldest results to change it all,' Gordon said with lilting drama to his words.

'It could be so much more dangerous, Gordon. This is your family,' the voice told him.

'My pride and joy. That's right, isn't it? It should be...' Gordon replied.

He reached across the desk at his side. There were a group of framed family photos from birthday occasions, and family holidays as the children had grown up. He picked up a framed photograph of Lucy with her mother, looked at it quietly and carefully. He then quickly stood and left the room.

There were certain cars always around when Gordon was holding numerous business meetings in the city. He knew they still found him, monitored him after years passing by – they must be so frustrated, so bored with him surely he often thought. In a way he almost did not mind them following him, his actions and movements around, waiting for him, for mistakes and clues. They would have no luck so easily. They wanted to find the Gordon of twenty years ago, the man who had made a huge mistake but escaped. They were watching a different man now, a wiser man. He was so much better than that. He was grateful for Steven, who made things much easier finally in the last couple of years. It had been such a long time of waiting, but now things were moving along.

'I think I've seen the undercovers around us again, Gordon,' one assistant manager of his company commented to him discreetly.

'Don't worry, we have no need to panic, they're most likely the press, journalists or the opposition right? Our success is desired by so many others. It is just inevitable that we will be watched, viewed often enough,' Gordon told his employee.

'Doesn't this get to you after so long? Like private invasion?' the man asked.

'With any level of good success known publically, in business of all kinds; others want to know your secret, or even then your weakness. Even if there really is none other than sheer, actual, very good hard work, really. It is even like a kind of compliment, if an irritating one. Let us continue on now,' Gordon told him as they walked along through the main corridors of the company building.

The initial tests were beginning well enough, Gordon believed. His mind was now focused on these immensely secret works which had been in the planning for months, probably years now. Defiantly years he knew. These were possibly the most delicate, dangerous but undeniably significant and important research tests he had ever worked on in his life. He tried hard to only focus upon this while he knew there was another serious danger still close and perpetually there.

There were once again police officers and detective inspectors, so close now. It had come around once more, after another long quite period. So many things seemed suspicious apparently to them. But he knew how desperate and paranoid some police could be, hoping for the case to give them the promotion, the award or recognition needed. He had set up Steven well enough as the main distraction, too well really. He could see that Steven was in danger of seriously harming his own career soon, but it just seemed the right trick to disguise the project among other things.

These were names which Lucy had provided, names of specific police officers, constables, inspectors who were starting to find links in new ways that threatened Gordon and the work in a seriously big way. He had thought about his options, and considered a few specific interesting possibilities. While down in the lower hidden laboratories, he greeted the two patients who had offered themselves to be part of his brave bold secret work. He knew them each well enough beforehand, had checked their details, statistics well enough. They had told him that they certainly did trust his vision. So that had opened up the paths of opportunity, finally. The secret project was bigger than the laboratories, it was many elements of his own life which all needed to be balanced and finely monitored for it all to come together well. But there were negative elements which needed to be stopped. There were ways, he thought. New thrilling ways there for him now.

As night had come, Gordon alone took the two patients along out back into his van with blacked out windows. They were sedated and calm for the drive, as he took them out along the motorway in the right direction. He felt very uncomfortable taking them like this – it was not really kidnapping, he told himself. They did put themselves in his care, that was the truth. They wanted to be useful to him, to be part of what really could be so historically significant, and this was now just part of their use to him. Yes, that was very true, Gordon thought as he drove.

He took them out along to a safe place, sat them there, and took off their ropes on their ankles and wrists. He prayed no one would come to find them, and it was a secluded area, he was absolutely sure of this. He turned the car around and drove along the motorway back home. He drove faster than normal, probably too fast. Could he remember where the speed cameras were on that stretch of motorway? He did not give a short sweet fuck. He had to get home as soon as was possible, do the checks, and the security procedures. He drove straight across the pathway and down into the drive. He ran out, up and into the house quickly. He stopped, looked around thinking, and then ran up the stairs fast. He stopped at the third door and knocked.

'Hello?'

'It's me, Gordon,' he said.

A plump woman opened the door to him.

'Hello, Sir. Everything is fine. Lucy is reading her new book now,' the maid told him casually as she let him inside.

'Right, right. Okay, well you go finish up downstairs, then you can go. See you tomorrow now okay?' he told her.

'Oh, okay then, Sir. Are you sure?' she asked.

'Yes, yes. Don't waste any time. Please, have an early night. You deserve it, really,' he told her. 'I'll finish reading with Lucy myself now.'

'Okay then, Sir,' she replied as she made her way out and waved goodnight to Lucy. Gordon sighed and walked over to her.

'Been a very long night, my dear. But a good one,' he told her and put his arm around her.

Gordon waited, locked the door and sat down close by Lucy.

'Good evening my darling. How are you tonight?' he asked.

'I like my new book, Dad. It's good, a princess, but she fights dragons with two brothers and they travel over mountains for days. Then elves and beasts come more and more and battles...' she began to tell him excitedly.

'Oh really? That sounds really exciting. Darling, I have a thing happening now, I told you yesterday, remember?' he said.

'Your patients, Daddy?' she asked.

'Yes, that's right. They're in place right now,' he told her.

'For the police people right?' she asked him.

'Yes darling, that's it. You ready to do it now?' he asked in a quiet tone.

'I think I can, Daddy,' she replied.

'Okay, if you're very sure, please start now, Lucy,' he said.

She dipped her head, sat still and began her task while her father watched.

Chapter 17

With the small collection of newly volunteered patients in the quiet laboratory rooms, there would be so much to observe. That was what Gordon hoped. All kinds of new beautiful results could be found hopefully, now that time had passed. It was almost like being some kind of real regular doctor, with the examining, the quiet questioning, and waiting. But these were new careful moments, possibly extremely significant times. These were very lucky individuals right here, and they should know that. Just possibly, but they knew the chances – or almost.

'They look peaceful still,' Joseph in the laboratory told Gordon.

'Yes, you're right. That will change. Don't be alarmed, be extremely excited when it comes,' Gordon said positively.

He moved around the room. Over a long flat table top, he had laid out a selection of specially prepared chemicals and compounds. Some waited in syringes, others in various forms of capsules. These had taken such private and close dedicated work for long months, so many months and attention from Gordon. He was already proud of these highly secret artefacts before him, even before things here began to take off in any impressive manner.

Leaving the main laboratory rooms later in the night, Gordon walked down the corridors and spoke on a cell phone.

'Is she with you?' he asked.

'You know she is. How is Steven now?' Beatrice said over the phone to him.

'I suspect he is well. He follows my footsteps still. Like he should,' Gordon told her.

'Now Lucy is better, yes? She is returning to school work again?'

'Yes, she will. Not that you distract her in any way, as ever.'

'Nathan is home though, isn't he?' Gordon said.

'My Nathan is home, at my home. My Lucy is there, where she likes to be. Where she belongs, safe as she is. Aren't you losing precious time away from being the mad scientist genius?' Beatrice said.

'Goodbye now. Steven will be around soon,' he told her then ended the call with anger. Only Beatrice could really drive him into a real rage, and he knew she would be smiling to herself then.

'Gordon what do you think about these people who have been caught attacking others out on the streets? They're saying they're sick people, like it's a virus, neurological mental sickness going around?'

'You know, we often don't appreciate how fascinating life can be, even the worse situations – illnesses, tragedies, bad events, diseases,' Gordon told him.

'Yes, some said these people are unstable, not themselves deranged in the head. Could it be some contagious thing, or are they really just violent sickos?' the man asked.

'Yes, I've heard that. It could be some special disease, virus or something similar but unlikely I think. They could be full of surprises though.'

'But they're hugely dangerous – not gang people, not psycho people, it seems. But they were hunting people, beating them, but randomly, in really unexpected ways.'

'It is interesting, I agree. Many good things are sometimes found in extremely bad circumstances, you know. This is a fact of living,' Gordon said.

'Don't you feel sorry for the people who've been hurt so far?' the man asked.

'Of course I do. There is, though, a very interesting view of these reports is all I am suggesting, you see. The police and doctors should be finding the useful information to explain it all, I hope,' Gordon told him.

The team of scientists drove along, back to the labs at the university campus after lunch at a local cheap pizza restaurant. The roads were busy as the mid-afternoon return to work spread back out. They watched cars move along, some in a hurry, some driving more casually. Many cars were on the road there around them, all kinds of people inside – hard to guess from the outside the characters within.

'Are we being followed?' Joanna asked.

'What? By a car?' Pascal said.

'Yes, behind us, up the road there to the left,' she said.

'No, come off it. Bullshit. So paranoid. Really?'

'I think so. Don't you think?'

'It's Steven's vast legion of adoring women folk. The last one wants her virginity back. Or an STD test,' Pascal commented.

'Oh, hilarious stuff. Congratulations. So fucking funny you are. No really. Round of applause. But anyway – don't be so paranoid. What car?' Steven said.

'Really Steven are you slipping up with the local police more than usual now?' Alan said.

'Good God no, will you all just relax now, yeah? Bloody hell. We're really just very loner geek academics, okay? Drive,' Steven said.

'Yes, that's about right, I'm sure,' she said.

Alan tried to casually take a couple of glances to the road up behind them. There were a few stylish cars there, he could not really make out one particular suspicious one alone though he thought.

Many drinks and good private thoughts shared like they only dared between each other alone again. Alan still threw up painfully into the kitchen sink, as he had done dozens of times before.

'Oh, easy now, brother. You'll get through, just one too many shots again this time. Not your style really, is it?' Steven told him standing there, concerned but slightly amused.

'I... I appreciate it. You... you know that?' Alan managed to say.

'Right, oh for sure, mate,' Steven replied.

'No... The things about family, your family, I'm sorry...' Alan told him.

'That's just fine mate, really I don't mind. Forget it really,' Steven said.

'No, your problems with it... Your dad is such a... fool, good brother, and sweet little Lucy...' Alan muttered between retching in a stop-start manner, into the sink still, lurching gasps

'Right. Fine, forget it. Glad I see you and your good family,' Steven told him.

'No, mine is shit too. Very... very shit... sometimes... good actors. Good...' Alan stammered.

'Well I know acting too, my fucking dad and his ways,' Steven responded.

'You see Lucy? But your mum is weird about things right?' Alan uttered.

'True bud, very... true. Yes, I do my bit, I certainly do,' Steven told him and thought about it himself then when Alan seemed to have finished being sick finally.

Gordon leaned in close, fascinated and with detached study. He watched the eyes before him, so human, weak, and regular. Any eyes could see things of life around them, the greed, hate, confusion, fear. Human conditions all. These simple eyes had not seen what Gordon had, and the person here could not imagine his sightings in his own life, his valuable personal secret memories which he held to so precious. He moved his hands over the eyes, watching carefully.

'You see me? Just me now? See anything else? Tell me if you do. Go right ahead. I understand. I wait,' he said.

The testing continued on. Some words came forth, some utterances not completely coherent but holding worth, he believed.

'Show me what I need, please. Reveal what is hidden. You could be anything. You could live a beautiful dream. This world is corrupted, the west, the east, but you are the ones. Like me. New dreams, secret dreams opened up, revealed, given hope, different chances,' he sighed, looking at them with wonder and hope.

'We're not going to harm them really, are we? I know they have agreed to help us, they agreed to this but...' one assistant said to Gordon.

'No, they'll be fine. No harm, no guilt. They'll thanks us very soon, for this opportunity here,' Gordon told him.

He stepped outside of the room. He took out his phone pad and scrolled out photos, pictures of his family – Nathan, Steven, and then Lucy. He suddenly made a quick gasp, stifled it, and sighed to himself again as he looked at his sweet little special daughter.

As Steven and Alan walked back up to the flat together, Alan looked around behind them, down the street. There was some audible sounds, people somewhere close talking, an argument, someone joking maybe. Other sounds also rang out faintly though very close. Some unnerving strange sound caught his attention. It could be the long hours at the lab, distorting his perception, the stress of Steven and pressure to find the results they all wanted.

'It's loud out tonight, right?' Alan said to Steven as they walked up the steps to the door.

'Could be I suppose. Let's get inside,' Steven replied, not quite aware of the sound which confused his friend.

They hung up jackets, put down folders, bags and sat slumped down on their old beaten sofa together, both tired.

'Oh my God, I'm so worn out,' Steven said.

'Really? Good, good to know,' Alan told him.

'What's that mean?' Steven asked.

'Oh come on, Steven.'

'What? I've got some shit stressing me with my family,' he explained.

'Really? Never usually gets to you easily,' Alan remarked.

'Well, it does but I hide it, remember? But if I'm honest, and I will be with you, I'm going mad dealing with my bloody father and them right now. Only ever me doing anything,' Steven told him.

'What's he up to now?' Alan asked listening well.

'It's not just him. Him and mum, they just don't let up on each other. My poor Lucy. I'm so worried for her mate,' Steven told him.

'Does she seem okay?'

'Yes, she is I think. I mean, she's mostly oblivious to any fighting, arguments around her. She always keeps me happy. So sweet, an adorable little princess.'

'At least your family has a pulse – mine just drift along. Happy but emotionless shadows of themselves. No spontaneous emotions. I'm here for you mate, really,' Alan said.

'Yes, I know. I'll try to keep my head on our project, just real professional and focused now,' Steven replied.

'I do understand. This is your family mate. It's your parents who have made the mistakes. You, Nathan and little Lucy just dealing with it all. You and Nathan are watching Lucy still, right?' Alan asked with an timid curiosity. 'Your dad... he is just a strange old soul. Fascinating, absolutely so, but... you know. Let's kick back now, okay?'

Steven sighed and stretched out, yawning.

'God, yes. Beer up, get the console multiplayer on my friend,' Steven told him with a fresh smile.

'But look, did you see anything weird outside before, when we came in?' Alan then asked him.

'Like what exactly?' Steven asked with a curious look.

'Well... Oh, forget it. Nothing. We're just too tired that's all. Beers now, right?' Alan said, as he stood to enter the kitchen for a night of much drinking and bonding as they did well.

The house was deathly quiet while Gordon sat looking at Lucy as she sipped her slushy drink, sitting restlessly flicking through a comic book next to her on the rug near the lounge windows.

'Lucy, I need you to think of your brother Steven. He is at university now. He's been in trouble again. Very mean men at the police station, the one in the city we drove along by, they want to tell Steven and punish him. They can't do that. I'm his father and they are confused you see. You understand, Lucy?' he told her.

She nodded slowly then looked up at him thoughtfully.

'Yes Daddy, I think I do,' she said.

'Okay now, carefully think of the police officers there, in the police station now. If they are thinking about Steven, any of them, discussing him now. They must not. They must forget about him. Have you got that, Lucy?' he asked.

She nodded again and closed her eyes. She sat still, her breathing calmed then and quiet. Gordon watched with great interest, waiting to see what she did next. It was always such a very fascinating time when he asked her to do these special tricks which she was so good at to help him occasionally. It had worked well in the past, and she was such a clever, good girl, he remembered. He waited, so anxious. Eventually after a long moment, Lucy opened her eyes and looked up at him again.

'They were thinking of Steven, Daddy. Wanted to find him, talk to him. Not now, not any more now. No way. Not today,' she told him with a smile, pleased with herself. She then yawned and did look quite tired.

'Wonderful, Lucy. Thank you my little lady. We have to look after our Steven, don't we? He can be silly, getting into trouble sometimes. He'll be grateful. You just sit and play there. I'm just going to get a coffee dear,' he told her and walked off to the kitchen. He depended on her so much, more and more day by day but would not accept just how much to himself, not totally.

It felt good to get away right then, Gordon thought, as he stood alone at the long side tables, mixing up compounds in preparation for the coming patient tests soon. Everything had to be so exact, extremely carefully measured out to the last drop, the final millimetre, the perfect volume. It was his own levels of special chemical combination, his own theory of potential outcome. He was lost then in his private thoughts, his mind drifting, calm but optimistic on the task he was preparing before him.

A strange noise around him somewhere then.

A voice somewhere, perhaps in the room.

That can't be right, he thought. No way.

Then again – some small whimper, utterance or whispered words from somewhere close to him.

Behind him? He stopped his task then to cautiously look around. The room was empty of anyone else there, just himself still. He waited a moment, then eventually returned to the work. He was very proud of this special formulated mixture compound he thought to himself again. It really could be a revolutionary thing, finally, after such a long wait for so many years. Not the perfect way, but a way at least, he thought. Possibly the only ever way. So he took it.

His thought taking him so emotionally, he then saw that he had spilled some of the precious special mixture, only the tiniest amount, but every drop was to be accounted for. He had touched it, rubbed it in between his fingertips. He walked over by the laboratory room sinks, washed his hands with a dreamy observation as he did so, then returned to the work once more.

The voice then came back nearby him, close enough. Was it the same voice from earlier? He was not sure at all. This was a familiar voice, female words coming to him.

'Daddy, stop working too hard,' he heard.

'Lucy? Here?' he said confused, and looking around him.

'Daddy wants to go away,' she said.

'No, I just... I...' he began.

'It is okay, Daddy. They know now,' the voice told him.

'What? Who knows what now?' he asked.

He did not turn or look around now. Only listened. In the mirror on the wall, he saw the image behind down to his left. He shook his head, moaned quietly, then laughed nervously. He stepped away. He looked behind then, and saw no person there. He sucked in the air, and looked over at the equipment on the tables. He could rely on the equipment if not his troubled tired mind, he thought.

Chapter 18

The city hospital was as crowded and depressing as usual on a Friday evening when they brought in Derek in a shocking, bruised state. He was aware of himself, his name and identity, but he was fairly dazed, and disturbingly there was a lot of blood over his trouser legs, shirtfront and sleeves. He did not seem hurt personally, but when doctors checked him over gradually, they came to find the most bizarre marks and forms over his arms, skin, and neck. Almost like scales near his neck, loose but defined marks, and his breathing and blood very strangely unusual and different.

The doctors began to discuss the findings, and just then the initial doctor returned with another. As he walked out toward the car at the entrance, two men in suits met him that instant.

'Mr. Larson is being taken care of now. He is stable enough. Do not ask, thank you. Please take this envelope and look inside by yourself. Good evening doctor,' the first man told him and promptly left again with other as they closed the car door on Derek and took him away along the motorway. The doctor watched, confused and speechless.

In his private office, the doctor took the opportunity to take a private look inside the envelope given him – inside, he found a cheque for a surprisingly substantial amount of money, thousands, written to him. He then had to personally seriously think about his own deep ethics and morals and how they stood that very night.

Down south, along from Dorset and before deepest Cornwall, many trucks and large long vehicles were speedily transporting vast unknown cargo toward a private location. Agreements had been made, only between a very small private and select handful of powerful people, nationally and internationally. Even so, it had begun this process of huge secretive scientific operation almost instantly and unknown to the population of the country at large.

Over the following days, in absolutely tight high security, the cargo of the many huge trucks and lorries, taken to their southern hidden locations, was arranged between forests, parks lands, and close private land. No one at all was given any real information, or were even largely aware of the goings on in any clear way. Soon after, at the right time, the people who had arranged the delivery of the unknown massive equipment and secret giant cargo then contacted others – one of which was Gordon. A larger, ever more ambitious event was being prepared, and he was a key figure within the secretive highly powerful group of people making deals concerning the most expensive height of modern scientific technology.

Alan came into Bristol and the flow of the traffic over the roads changed, still packed tightly but opening out more. He took deep breaths and calmly navigated his way along with good progress. There were large lengthy crowds lining the side streets and sides of the roads from the town, the closer in he got. People were celebrating the space travel, enraptured, curious and proud in equal measure. It was like the sight of some religious cult pilgrimage or festival happening. The roads and signs led him out along the outer side of the city to vast open field areas.

There it stood. Beyond the crowds and the tallest city buildings, behind it all and now towering in grandeur was the shuttle. Unbelievable. After the long unknown private incubation, this very secret yet now proud patriotic symbol stood towering over the problems and despair of the people of Britain.

Alan could only drive the car near the ends of the fields and so reluctantly had to then continue on foot. He got out and ran along, well aware of the precious minutes drifting away. People moved around all over the fields up ahead in their many bulging crowds, security maintaining a level of peace and controlled anticipation.

He pushed through between them, with no time for good manners and beyond them all he could see the shuttle which stood magnificently tall, waiting for that grand time. News reporters flocked around maddeningly, ignorantly scrambling between each other and the many scientists and officials at the closed off launch site area. So many reporters, blocking his path through. Alan reached a group of official security men near the main launch area boundary lines. Around there, there were then at least a dozen or so large white tents, mobile rooms and the official large stage for announcements, the kind used for Reading or Glastonbury music festivals. He came along near the white tents quickly and looked around.

'Excuse me, how can I get to talk to one of the astronauts, Jane?' he asked a suited man taking with the security at the entrance to the first tent by the enormous stage. He looked blankly back at him.

'Sorry, who would you be exactly?' the man then asked him.

'I am Alan Blake. I work with her in a science research project just outside Sheffield,' he explained. They looked back, then gave each other a look.

'So, do you have any passes?' the suited man asked him.

'What?' Alan said, dumbfounded.

'This is an extremely high security area. Can't let any nutjob stroll in and mess things up, obviously,' he stated.

'Well of course you can't but... Here, take a look at these I.D. cards,' Alan told him and showed them two of his lab security cards. They murmured between each other. The suited man then spoke.

'Let me just get a check on one of those,' he told Alan. He stepped away, talking quietly into his radio. Alan looked around beyond them, tense and desperate to get past them.

'Can you just let me pass through? That's me, that's my identity. My face there, I'm a postgraduate PHD qualified scientist. There isn't time and I really need to see her,' he urged then.

'I am very sorry, my friends, but I've been told that I still cannot let you pass. Go and watch like everyone else from down the front there,' the blond guard explained.

'What? Come on, that can't be right! Who wouldn't let me in? I'm a work colleague!' Alan told them.

'I'm sorry. Look, we're very busy today,' the suited man told him.

'So am I. Do you see the freaks on the streets? The ones running loose? Random bloody violence? Is Mr Steven Lowell in there?' Alan said.

'Sorry Sir?' the suited man said.

'Mr Chirico, did you speak to him? I know him. Known him for a decade, and spoke to him only minutes ago. He works with me. Is he there?' Alan asked. He really did not want to speak about him, but he had a disturbing feeling that he could be right there, in deep with the whole launch right then.

He was willing to find another way through if he absolutely had to right then, but he waited for the reaction of these simple and aggressive muscle men before him. They looked at each other once again, then at him.

'So do I pass through yet?' Alan asked.

The blond radioed through again. He listened, nodded then looked at Alan. He listened some more and Alan wanted to grab the damn radio receiver from him and talk to whoever it was himself.

'Yes. You can go through, Mr. Blake. Phil here will escort you. You'd better be quick though,' he told Alan, who would be as long as it would take to get to Jane.

'Thank you very much,' Alan replied and then followed Phil, the pumped up security guy, through down the corridors at the side of the stage between the many tents and mobiles. They twisted and turned in direction as they passed more guards, security and press reporters, and other men and women connected to the launch. He did not urgently wish to meet Steven, whatever he had to offer then, he was simply hoping to save Jane.

As Alan followed Phil, he quickly looked around.

'Hey Phil, any chance I can see Miss Hurley first? There's not long before the launch,' he asked.

'I'll take you to Mr. Lowell, and if he wants you to see her, you will,' Phil answered in a flat tone of voice. He was so obviously enjoying doing his job and restricting people like him, taking out his own personal resentments.

They passed many doors, a mobile canteen, some smaller rooms and piles of obscure equipments of all shapes and sizes. Alan began to think of any quick possible plan he could put together to get to her from there as Phil was only taking him to Steven. He checked that Phil was looking ahead and took his chance, and immediately made off and ran away down a narrow corridor to his left.

There were fortunately some signs mounted along the walls of the corridors which directed Alan where he needed to go. One of the signs thankfully led him down a short passage and into a room marked 'Astronaut Preparation Rooms'. He entered with quiet caution and two men stood in the recognisable space suit outfits.

'Who are you?' one of them asked seeing him enter.

'Hello. I'm Jane Hurley's boyfriend and her co-worker in her chemical fusion progress immune project. Is she around somewhere?' Alan said.

'Oh right. Alan, she spoke about you. She was getting ready in the next room through there. We're going out in a few minutes. Aren't you watching it?' he asked.

'Well, I'm here now,' he said then walked over and through the doors which he had pointed toward.

The doors opened up to him, Alan stepped in through and his heart sank immediately. The room was empty of people but the doors opposite were open. He could see through across a short corridor to the launch area. Walking across to it were some of the astronauts, and Jane was among them then. And so shockingly, so was Steven. Alan ran out through the room, passed the doors and was quickly blocked by more tall, imposing security men.

'Guys, let me go across to Miss Hurley, please, I'm her research partner and her... her fiancée!' he shouted out in desperation to them.

'Really? I don't think so, mate. No one passes this, not now. Too late,' the closest tall guard told him. The other two astronauts were escorted past him, as Alan stood there, watched closely by the four security men.

'Look, it's absolutely damn well vital I speak to her! Honestly, I really have to right now, please!' he protested. They looked down on him, down at him with a lack of care, of reasoning and were probably amused.

'Sorry. Enjoy the launch, Sir. I advise you enter the crowd out front to have a decent view of it,' the guard told him flatly.

Alan could see the group of astronauts walking along a ramp up to the loading entrance to the shuttle behind the guards a few feet away from him. The group looked down at the swelling gleeful frenzied crowds around on the fields and roads below. They waved down smiling. They next moved around up there a little, posing for photographs briefly, and then... and then Alan saw Jane.

She was there amongst the group, suited up, prepared for brave space travel, exploring our dark galaxies above them. She smiled and had a look of confident hope over her young, beautiful and focused face. She caught sight of him then it seemed, a brief couple of seconds. He thought she did anyway. It seemed like it, and he truly hoped so. With hundreds or thousands in the crowds his hopes were high, but he was nearly positive she looked back at him. A look of uncomfortable optimism. His expression changed ever so slightly in that brief moment as they were all then ushered along toward the shuttle entrance.

They moved around some more, all of the group looking down at the crowds of supporters, proud and curious masses of citizens before going into the giant tin can to seek a different life away from the exhausted earth. They moved around, and behind Jane he saw him again for the final time. Steven looked out at the crowds, standing tall and triumphant. A man sure in his achievements, respect and power. Right then Alan had an even stronger desire suddenly to get up there and stop the launch himself, somehow. Could he do that? What would he be prepared to risk, he asked himself?

His daydream of anarchy was futile as he saw them suddenly crowd into the shuttle to a thunderous applause from all around the area. The countdown began and as panic and anger buzzed through him, Alan could only stand numb and watch all of the life that he cherished leave, the love he had, go from his planet that he clung to for increasingly confused reasons. The shuttle ignited, amazingly thrust up from the base, into the sky and away. The crowds cheered, enthralled, and Alan turned away alone.

PART TWO

Chapter 19

The space stations contained more than anyone on earth could have imagined or known about to begin with. There was an advanced form of social rules, experimental civilised life social structure, respect, relaxation and observation of space and planets all around them.

All the scientists onboard were given individual roles and long term duties while they would be there on the space station. They were all to be working at the station for at least three months, potentially around two years depending on the success of the project ahead of them. They were there to explore many aspects of existing out in space, away from earth life. In a unique step, they had a number of small retrieval pods and robots which they were to send out to the nearest planets to collect samples, which they would then study and examine over the course of their time.

When Jane reached her specific station, it was over twenty four hours later. Time could not have passed faster. In her life for years, since a child – a tomboyish young girl, intelligent and always curious – she had been fascinated by the mysterious expanse above and beyond earth known as 'space' and the other planets quietly floating in the never-ending blackness. She was gone.

No more traffic jams, no more bad weather, gossip, hay fever, pollution. All of the mundane, predictable, soul-crushing annoyances of earth life were behind her finally. She and all of other very privileged astronauts, guests, and a number of wealthy elite could now start fresh in a new perfectly designed and highly controlled artificial environment. The half dozen secret space stations had been quietly in production for over a decade, with a large number of people already out there building, constructing and preparing it all unknown to the public back on earth. Many of earth's respected architects, scientists, physicists and psychologists all offered time and opinions until finally people could go out and inhabit the stations. The time for the number of launches to the space stations over just two months was perhaps very carefully or prophetically orchestrated. There was a larger grand plan which it all was a part of, but which not would learn of until much later.

There was more than the general public on earth would get to know for years happening. So many more people were actually up in the space stations and so much more reason for them to be there than on earth. In the weeks after the final shuttle launch which Jane was on, the state of the United Kingdom and Europe changed in spectacularly horrific ways. The illness that had caused the sick people who had attacked and murdered many across the country, rose up again this time with much more contagious power and horror. England was finally quarantined in days by the rest of Europe and the west. Any kind of regular daily life for anyone ceased to exist. The atmosphere was like that of the old wars, except that this new enemy could creep up and enter you, in your veins, chemically or in other biological ways. You then were the enemy of others, and on it went.

In the first few days after the launch, Alan simply tried to rearrange his scientific project. In one way, it kept his mind away from becoming so negatively depressed over Jane and thoughts of self-blame, anger, but also he thought of other possible uses of the results which the project had only recently begun to reveal. His outlook was much wider open to more chance possibilities now that she was gone. He felt that there was less to be so concerned over, and just simply tried out any theory at any time from then on. He could lose nothing much more valuable than Jane, who was gone already.

The work was simply passing the time in a creative and constructive way to cope with the emotional loss. Or so he told himself to remain casual about things. He had been too hung up on things until then. Nothing should seize his full attention completely from then on. Not much could, if he was honest with himself. He was jaded and cynical as he noted the dangerous events across the country and violent attacks continuing amid space travel celebrations.

As he remained casual about new research and experimenting alone from then on, the government science watchdogs kept away. He was now merely viewed as a non-threatening single scientist with no real new dangerous breakthroughs to stop presently. It was all just a highly educated hobby from then on for him. He had reverted to working with school labs and local chemical authority boards for money to pay the rent and bills. Until the news reports changed.

Never one to immediately believe everything he read or saw on the mainstream news media television or tabloid newspapers, initially without thinking of the other sides to a story or report, he took it cynically when arguments of the mental virus causing the creation of the increasing attackers sprang up again. Leaving his flat revealed the unbelievable truth, and he could not avoid observing a significant challenge that he just had to understand better.

The new citizens of the space stations were shown to their apartments right away after a tour of the place they would now call home away from earth. They were all there to conduct research, observe and be observed, study and be studied. There were many extremely important new experimental means of social structure and lifestyle as well as space exploration as the stations orbited the surrounding known planets and known further galaxies. There would be many new things to do, ways to live and explore life that had only possibly been on hold until mankind had moved out far enough, and taken such bold courageous chances.

At this early stage, life on the space stations was still very much an experimental cautious level and all citizens had their special specific roles to play. This was consciously known before they all had journeyed out there, and most were calmly happy with the jobs and taken given and dictated to them. Jane had her set of official routine jobs concerning monitoring exercises, psychological tests on others and social progressions among the carefully optimised and defined atmospheres within the space station environment. As weeks and months passed she became comfortably acquainted with many of the other scientists and astronauts around her.

The atmosphere was relaxed though continuously professional. Between work and relaxation Jane did inevitably come to meet Steven a number of brief but ominous times. It seemed that on board these acutely new democratic peaceful socially and scientifically progressive floating galactic islands, Steven had lowered himself to the regular level of most other people. She had seen him doing manual labour on some construction sites, and then also driving through area zones like a humble taxi driver to others. She believed that Alan might be pleasantly surprised to witness his old friend so human and selfless up there.

The space stations were another environment copied like similar successful cities from earth such as Madrid, London, Washington, Berlin and Tokyo, but they were in such a strange new location which offered new opportunities for all. Jane began to view life on the station as wholly exciting and fresh, unlike any other time in her life. She felt so special and lucky to be up there. Blessed, even. Alan was forever in her mind, but she did see new ways for herself to exist, think, behave and live. She was still herself, but this was not earth, and so she could perhaps rise beyond what had been keeping her back before. A new start, a different way.

So much had been left behind, some of it for the best, some of it missed by some. Jane happily said goodbye to celebrity pop culture and the advertising everywhere, and had never much liked cats or dogs so their absence was fine too.

The space station that Jane lived on was sectioned into five large areas of small communities with between twenty and thirty people in each. She was in area three, street two. She was housed in a reasonably finished and likeable apartment bunker with five others, men and women. These were all scientists such as herself, and they were all posted on to a project of work which monitored outer station atmosphere effects and communications with the other stations with some monitoring of health of all on board their station. It was constant work though they took shifts and were all still simply in awe of the views from outside – earth and other well-known planets such as Mars and Jupiter parading nearby, yet so far still from themselves even then but closer than ever before.

The new environment and projects brought Jane a renewed sense of pride and satisfaction into her life. She was proud of her work with Alan before on earth, but on the space station the work was obviously successful and ground-breaking to begin with, important and many other people around were just as happy and proud of the historic events which they were personally involved in then.

Everyone felt part of one large pioneering new age scientific enterprise. They knew then that people back on earth were watching and waiting for any and all news and reports that they sent back and it pushed them on every day. Although this made Jane happy, she did regularly think of Alan back down on her home planet. She did not completely rule out returning to earth in the near future, though she did not know when that chance might actual happen. So far, she had signed up for at least two years. Depending upon the safety and success of the space stations project she and the others could potentially remain – if they wished – for maybe half a decade or longer as there were certainly great complex plans to build upon the initial half dozen stations very soon.

'It's like a new life, like being reborn really, isn't it?' said Donald Vernon. He shared the same small living area with Jane and the others, and was also physicist and bioresearch professor.

'It is if you want it to be, I suppose. It's definitely a fantastic experiment,' Jane replied.

'You think it'll show us all how to live perfectly?' he asked.

'What? Eradicating all disease and negative elements of living as a society? In perfect harmony like one big love in?' said Jules Pearson from behind, with sharp playful sarcasm.

'Not exactly, but it's the idea, isn't it?' Donald replied. 'With that fucking mad plague thing spreading down on earth, the violent attacks all over wiping out dozens and dozens more daily, we'll have to develop the cure up here real soon,' he suggested.

'From up here?' Jane asked, surprised.

'Yeah, one of the things that's happening here, right?' Donald said.

'You sure about that? I think we're looking more at the space and planets near us here, not back at earth,' Jules said.

'Why from here?' Jane asked. This was fresh news to her and seemed strange to work on cures for that so far away in space.

'Well, we're going to be looking into keeping these space stations absolutely germ free, disease free, safe and peaceful for all, all the time. We'll be sending our findings back down. Some of the scientists here are looking into eradicating the new bio-plague thing. We've the template for a perfect way of living here very soon,' he told them.

'Big responsibility, isn't it?' Jane said thoughtfully.

The weeks and months that passed were certainly enjoyable and stimulating, possibly more so than with her previous team of scientists led by Alan. Jane now was working alongside many of the most respected and talented British scientists of modern times on the station. She felt more pressure and responsibility resting on her than ever before and it in turn made her feel very significant and important and a part of the whole team made up of physicists, biologists, astrophysicists and chemical research scientists plus many more specialist men and women all collected there.

They worked steadily for many months over several areas as they studied and monitored the social health both physically and psychologically, and the increasing potential to adapt to the environments of planets near the station in time.

As they worked they also simply lived, calmer yet in many ways much more satisfied by the detachment from knowing the goings on back on earth as closely as they used to. As a worker on the space station, Jane was happily engaged with work constantly, and proud of the advances they were making with each day as a member of the new population which orbited away from mankind's original home planet. Even so, beneath the contentment, she could not ignore the stirring mixed anxious feelings which she did eventually begin to dwell upon privately, alone, mostly at night in bed. Her love for Alan stung her painfully, but she tried to focus on socialising with her new colleagues and neighbours in her area of the space station. They were all very interesting, charming and friendly people mostly, and conversations were good, the talk positive and pleasant. But her love was left behind.

The forms of entertainment and relaxation allowed to them on the station were as ground-breaking and new as the research equipment which they used daily. There were the usual ultra-realistic mega graphic interactive 3-D connected and fully sensitive videogames, some chipped and linked to nerves and senses with small pads and clips to the skin and fingers. All of these games and the devices which could be used for daily exercise and motor reflex stimulation as well as the research work machinery and were equipment over all the station were powered by breakthrough reuse of liquids, oxygen, gases, chemicals, light and waste. No fossil fuels were being used long term and essentially the population lived by the use of their living and lifestyles.

After days of serious study and observation on the changes to citizens of the station and environmental interior atmospheres, Jane was found regularly in the company of Jules and Donald as they played out elaborate fantasy games or fast paced mind stimulating games on the console equipment in their shared living quarters.

'Your scores are getting better Jules – it's about time,' Jane told him, joking as they played the games.

'Helps when I've got good competition like yourself here,' he answered.

'It's funny – I didn't really relax like this back home. I was spending so much time on the projects that I was involved in. We were so sure that we would get the breakthrough that we needed and deserved eventually. Sooner or later. I mean, we needed to find some changes, even small changes, proof, but there wasn't enough time or we couldn't see it... Then the inspectors came along...' she told them, thoughtfully thinking back.

'It's not just you. You'll find that a large percentage of the scientists here on the station were all desperately striving away on many different types of experiments hoping to make their own breakthroughs, cure diseases, find new and better advancements for mankind,' Donald told her.

'So, what were you involved with before you came up here?' Jane asked, curious.

'My work with a group of others at Bristol University laboratories included the researching of animal behaviour and diseases, and human emotional response to and from technology in everyday life. Of course it was relevant completely until I left but well... things change, don't they? The greater good, right?' he said. She sensed a level of uncomfortable regret in his voice. 'I will, though, return to it all when I go back down and this is over for us,' he continued.

As she spoke with her new close colleagues and neighbours, she began to feel that it was not just her who had left a life which she greatly valued. She saw that there were others who also felt unfairly pushed away from important work, threatened and scared away from doing what they knew was meaningful research.

'Jules, have you got unfinished work back home?' she then asked.

'What kind of scientist would I be if I didn't have?' he said, smiling back. 'Yes, there were things I was working closely for a while, I worked with a number of well-known respected writers, thinkers, and others. It was a type of bioengineering that we explored over the last couple of years. It kind of fell apart after the large company who is co-founding this endeavour became a huge success in the field. This just flawed the rest of us. I'm not too jealous – they have hired me as a bioengineer observer and assistant along with research duties here for any discoveries that might come up,' he explained. 'Your own work, Jane? Was it anything different to ours?' Donald enquired.

'Others might not think so – perhaps it wasn't. I don't know. I know what you mean about the company and bio-healing organic progression technology breakthroughs, and it did come close to some of my team's work in some ways. We looked at other things also though-health, stamina, aging, body structure, DNA… perhaps it was simply meant to happen like this when it did. It seems so. This whole project right here in space – this is our evolution, our turning point finally isn't it? It's so marvellous,' she told them.

They gave each other somewhat unconvincing looks and moved apart uneasily to their individual quarters then. Days were different on the space stations, not just simply the change of day to night, sunrise to sunset. They had these changes, artificial of course, but they knew this; they knew the false reality mimicking the old way of life. Could they all really adapt permanently? And was it going to be really worth it?

All groups and committees aboard the stations experienced this feeling, although it was barely acknowledged at all. Counselling was offered in some situations but most thought of themselves as unshakeable, highly intelligent strong willed men and women who could not let simple personal nerves distract from unique work happening then. In one of the lead groups of supervising guardian squads made up of the much respected and more politically and financially connected figures, was Steven.

Chapter 20

Work shifts were irregular, often one area of the station working while another rested, and vice versa across the station. Alternated work patterns, though eventually some did notice unusual organisation. Somehow, after a few weeks, the shifts were of a strange order, cut up, rearranging, not making obvious sense to them but they continued, the work being their main concern.

After a shift one afternoon, Jane walked along to meet Deborah in the next separate blocked zone area of streets.

'Deborah, how are you?' she asked, seeing her walking along near the perception view report booths.

'Oh, hey Jane. I'm good but well, tired. Still very fascinating all this, isn't it? Still amazing every day when I wake. Same for you?' she asked.

'Well yes. Certainly,' Jane replied.

'And the men, not too bad. One guy – mmm, he's a sweet talking smooth one,' Deborah told her, winking.

'Glad you found a good one. Deborah, can I ask, have you been put to work on some really unusual shifts, different jobs, tasks, and recording times?' Jane asked.

'Yes, we have, but it was expectedly mostly. It's down to the different kinds of work anyway, right? It has to be like this, I'm almost sure. A little irritating but the way it is. You getting along alright then?' Deborah asked.

'Yes, no real problems yet,' Jane replied. She looked off, feeling lost and sad.

Jane observed the happening of the shifts between station groups across the station area zones as the weeks passed with dedicated interest and worry. Yes some groups were working on observing the growth of food, plants, and basic chemical changes which she understood, but for all of the groups work like this, in such illogical, complex fashion was continually troubling to her. She did almost want to laugh at her continued paranoid thoughts. Things were operating much differently to back on Earth, she knew that. This was one giant living experiment, a trial in a strange place far from regular life. To survive successfully, they obviously had to exist in more irregular patterns of being for however long it would take to find what they needed.

People across the separate station areas were all definitely enjoying their very complex, focused scientific endeavours there, most just simply going along with it for the experience and fame of being in space – such a once in a life time opportunity to tell the family about and be known for ultimately. Whether the experiments were finally a success or not almost did not matter to some of them there. For Jane, being there might just be a tragic mistake, she began to think to herself eventually.

Connecting the dozen separate station areas were a highly dedicated small selection of people who communicated information, messages, changes, regulated smooth transition of workflow and experimentation across the space station. There was Brian Lessing, the manager of projects daily, Suzanne Worthing, the –sub-deputy manager, Andrew Planter, the executive processor of communications, and then Steven, overall networking consultant of science experimentation synchronisation. Between them, the whole entire project moved along according to the initial early plans laid out on Earth months earlier.

Steven may not have had the official position of manager over the entire project with the others, but he did have huge personal influence and effect over decisions, and they all were aware of this though he had, it seemed, slipped back in his prominent involvement after a couple of weeks up in space. Most of the many dozens of scientists up there had seen him introduced at the beginning, heard of him having played some reasonably significant role in making the mission possible, but soon forgot his prominence as he drifted back, with less regular interaction with them as time went on.

The changes and times of work across the station Steven was very aware of personally, he made sure of that. While he seemed to have disappeared to most people, he was, in reality, very much focused on the shifts of work, the schedules, the changes of personnel to duties, experiments and testing routines across the entire space station. Once he knew the flow and position and pattern of daily routines, he then considered how his private plans were to then be begun without unnecessary disruption and smoothly worked in without immediate detection. It was all the perfect place and perfect setting for such trials of radical experimentation so close to the many mysterious grand planets around.

Early meetings had taken place where they officially met each other, discussed the prepared grand space project and their official individual roles, how they would work together and how they were to manage and oversee the entire population onboard and make the time a fantastic legendary scientific accomplishment in human history like none other.

'Alright, good day, everyone. I am Brian. I'll be officially leading us with Suzanne, as you know, but together are the whole management team. We are no better than any of you, we all have respectable education in our relevant chosen fields of science, but we were simply democratically elected and we will do our best to do our best in managing this unique British space mission and exploration. This is an exceptionally unique and brave adventure we're on now. The others depend on us in many ways, but then we also depend upon them. I hope that all of us in this large conference room area, can work extremely well together as one big team to get the best results and return safely to Earth on time successfully.'

'We will individually oversee the operations of one area each, and then cross-communicate results and observations back. We will synchronise and supervise the whole work together in the ways we already excel in personally. Everyone confident now with it as it has begun?' Suzanne asked the enormous crowd of scientists gathered in the conference room.

'Absolutely. With the training we received and between us it is going to be highly enlightening, without meaning to sound too much of a New Age hippy type,' Andrew agreed.

'Yes, I am happy with our roles and the beginning of this huge, fine project together.'

'You, Brian, are pleased to work alongside with us, in balance, all of us cooperating as the project moves along?' Steven asked then.

'I certainly am, Steven. I can be humble enough to know your opinions when problems may arise. We do understand that you yourself had a very important amount of significant influence with the very recent beginnings and early organisation of the project, with the launch and wider financial and industry backing. We are impressed by that, thankful, but it is very much back to full-time challenging dedicated scientific research and testing here right now,' Brian told him.

'Right, absolutely, Brian. That's absolutely true. Well, let us begin this space odyssey, shall we all?' Steven suggested and walked out of the meeting room, smiling as he left them.

'He's a strange one, but a very entertaining young man, that's for sure,' Suzanne commented.

'He is, but also unexpectedly talented with it. He seems to be able to charm people, get media attention, and give good speeches but also produces fascinating new results in his work too,' Brian said.

'Yes, his own father too is a well-known very respected man who works in areas of international scientific research and production,' Andrew added cynically.

'Alright, Andrew. We're here as a professional team, and many people are hoping we do very well. The population of the United Kingdom, Europe, and well, the whole world below, are listening and watching our success now. Let's amaze those back home with our highly professional, successful team results,' Brian said, and the three of them walked out together to the separate areas of the station.

Steven walked the corridors alone, between station zone areas. He was not completely pleased to be forced into the team among Brian and Suzanne, but it gave him a very powerful position on the station which he absolutely needed for what he had in mind. His thoughts were on things only he knew – his future plans alone. He had his own private reasons for being there, and no matter how interesting the station project findings and tests became, he had his own experiments to begin and watch closely. His father was in his thoughts against his will continually. Gordon had inspired him, but now things had changed so much, all this fantastic space travel had barely been envisioned months before.

For days, Steven had been trying to understand what exactly Gordon had in mind for when this was happening. Gordon was safe now, and no police or government would catch him in space. But now that they were all there on the space station, was it right? Steven wondered to himself. What Gordon had been involved in was a disturbing thing that Steven had witnessed and so wished he had not ever known anything about. It had made sense disappointingly, to him, but it also showed him something about what could be possible. When he considered space and the other mysterious planets around, with what was already known of science, many more possibilities revealed themselves if he decided not to consider some of the dangers to individuals.

He walked then into the secret allocated area, entering his private number codes and opening the locks in a manner only he knew how. No others knew this area to be in use at all, as a small number of rooms and passages on board the space station were still free and so far not assigned any immediate use. Inside waited the dozens of patients, confident in his continuing secret tests. He reassured them, supplied food and water, and reasonable living facilities and quarters to them in wait of his proceeding plans.

No other on the space station could know anything of these people, these troubled, confused, physically mutated patients just yet; before things were ready by the standards of Steven. He had paid off so many, made promises and countless bribes so far. He was now sickening himself, the things he was thinking and considering doing with the many scientist around him over the station. He knew them now, had spent much time with a number of them, at meal times, helping out with jobs and duties around areas. He was a fun and friendly person, and always would be, but to remain successful in original ground-breaking scientific work he had to detach himself and his emotions and just do what was considered necessary – didn't he? Was this how Gordon had been too, he thought? Years of difficult decisions between personal emotions and professional choices?

As the space station project continued on, Steven then started to visit the five other areas of the station. Andrew managed the food and crops and chemical testing areas, Suzanne managed the social and personal health and endurance area, Brian the medical observations as well as overall station management, while Steven personally only managed research records, data and theory compiling areas, which was fine with him. He knew that he needed more time to be with his patients secretly, and it seemed to work easily.

Between the long, focused work shifts and sporadic down time, Steven got to know Andrew, Suzanne and Brian more closely, they came to discuss individual histories, theories and opinions of science. Steven did not want to simply use and manipulate these very intelligent decent people – scientists like himself, with mostly much more experience. Could he trick them convincingly with elaborate, well timed, clever plans in preparing his own operations ahead? he wondered. They did not know from the beginning of the trip, and they had no idea at all of the hidden patients, or his plans yet, but it was only passing of time before he could be caught out, just one slip up...

What would be done to him? he thought. He would be made an example, shown and punished in legendary ways, humiliated, deported back to earth, jail and life inside waiting for him, his built up scientific career lost forever from him, he expected.

These six separate research areas of the space station could all individually provide him with exactly what was needed to finally perfect the design of the patients, who had only so far morphed into highly dangerous, bloodthirsty and still unpredictable specimens on the streets of Britain down below. This could be avoided with careful planned study, a collection of chemical compounds needed and brief tests, he knew it could. Gordon had suggested with great statements that it really could, and should happen. It just needed some special time and attention. And now, here on the space station, no laws prevented that any longer.

The work in the station areas was beginning very confidently – each had around ten scientists working and monitoring tests, and swapping roles every other day so that most people got to experience the various areas of work and stay fresh and interested. As Steven monitored and recorded the overall incoming results coming through, at the start he had time to look around, study the station layout, and make personal secret notes to himself concerning the areas, corridors, escape routes, passages. He soon visited Andrew working firstly, among the food and crops area zone.

'Hello Andrew, everything working out well here?' he asked as he entered the large open artificial field and test crop area, where scientists toiled and planted together.

'Oh, hello Steven. It's going well, yes thanks. Everyone has their role, their duties clearly provided, they all know how we're working, so it seems to be beginning very positively so far. You must be waiting for the first real batches of data and results to reach you I expect, right?' he asked.

'Well yes, there are things I am busy with though, but just thought I'd take a quick look at it all beginning for myself,' he replied.

They walked along around the top of the field, watching the scientists all around them.

'They seem very passionate about it. This is a lot of physical labour that people like us would not normally do, but I suppose we all know what has to be done, and how extremely useful this work will be to us soon enough. Everyone seems focused, working as one almost already,' Steven said.

'Yes, I hope so. That's what we need. If we all understand each other, better results must arise from that shortly,' Andrew told him.

Steven was impressed by the unity and the calm but focused dedication, and almost felt strongly jealous of it before him then. There were chemicals used in the food crop growing process which Steven saw could possibly be of great use to him. He walked on, with plans shaping in his mind.

After another fifteen minutes, he then reached the next area zone. Walking along these next two zones where places of more philosophical testing groups relaxed, chatting, discussing life, others took part in mental tests of many complex kinds. They observed how they all viewed living, being now with wide open deep space surrounding them in place of fields of green grass or huge grey buildings of comforting regularity. Their homes, friends, wives, husbands, and children were all many, many miles away through space. The human race continued on like it always did – the wars, peace, technological breakthroughs, famines, capitalism, pop culture – with them so far away from it, so disconnected, out of the picture, unaware of events and no longer able to interact like before in any way.

Steven looked around for a brief moment and then eventually noticed Suzanne in her own work area zone. To Steven she seemed a very certainly self-assured, confident, capable, opinionated, disciplined, feisty and strong woman, equal of any men she worked with at any time. She was admittedly attractive, with her long blonde hair curling over her shoulder and green shining eyes. But he was much more fascinated with the very unique and strange methods in this zone area. The complex mind tests were also being stimulated with small doses of specially created highly concentrated chemical drug stimulant enhancers and boosted vitamin and mineral supplements. This he could use, most certainly, he believed. No, of course many wild grand thoughts came to mind when looking at how things were happening here but he would need to be extremely cautious he realised. This was potentially the most detailed, delicate testing area, with individual minds and thoughts pushed to controlled levels, pressure and investigation of the human psyche strained. Controlling the area, Suzanne watched over it all, balancing levels on monitors, and keeping the testing in check.

'Suzanne, good day,' he said. 'You think we'll find much from these kind of tests? Not to be negative, you see?'

She looked him up and down, obviously very clearly interpreting his words and actions. Very observant and careful a woman, with no chance of simply coasting through on her flawless beauty.

'The things happening in these two areas may appear just a bit unusual, but sometimes the best science is, don't you think?' she asked.

'You know, I really do agree with you on that point. How long have you been doing this kind of work?' he asked her. He could enjoy spending time with her, her challenging, fascinating personality and opinions. He sensed they quite possibly shared some similar beliefs and attitudes, even though he knew his own plans, and could see what she did and what drove her in life. He found that a rare thing, especially from a beautiful woman like her.

'I've been doing this actual strand of work and technique over three years now. I changed direction over time. I was simply a tutor before, kind of waiting with my impressive qualifications for inspiration or the right path,' she told him, revealing personal detail unexpected until then.

'Oh, we all need to be honestly inspired and when we are, we have to go for it, can't ignore or be scared of inspiration and great ideas, they'll just disappear too soon,' Steven told her.

'Good observation – very thoughtful, and very true actually,' she agreed surprised at their connection then. 'Very deep view.'

'Every now and then, I suppose,' he said.

'Weren't you actually really quite involved with this finally coming together in some way then?' she then asked him.

'Possibly. Some people think so, and I did do quite a few things which allowed the parts to come together, meetings, chats with special people – that's my thing sometimes. I did contact a few big names, maybe got them thinking it was time. But we're all here now, and we can definitely make use of this amazing opportunity. Do you mind if I come around again soon? We're neighbours aren't we?' he suggested.

'You are right, I think. Yes, come by. You'll have to anyway, with the result collections, data checking and monitoring work,' she said.

'Okay, see you very soon then,' he told her and marched off with a playful smile to himself.

Suzanne was puzzled by him. He was definitely strange, a little handsome, yes she admitted to herself, and arrogant definitely, but there was some hidden side appearing which fascinated her now. Perhaps she could get to know that side better – she actually did want to, she realised, just a little more, just enough, she thought as she watched him leave then.

Eventually Steven arrived down at the medical and diagnosing area. In this area, any and all strange unknown or unexpected symptoms, illnesses or pains of any kinds would be investigated, examined, recorded and treated with Brian at the helm. It was his area, and while it was not perhaps the most obvious important and significant on first viewing, it could later reveal things which may tell them much they needed to know. Brian as well, needed more time, as he was, by and large, in charge of the whole entire space station project with just the four others. He was a much praised scientist on Earth, many years with acclaim, awards, respect and admiration for his efforts and work over two decades. Some urged him not to leave, to remain on Earth, saying he was too valuable to lose. He personally, after much difficult deliberation and contemplation decided that he had to go – he needed to meet this grand colossal challenge, lead the project and it most probably needed him, he believed.

He, like many others on the station, had a family back on Earth – a wife of ten years, and three children. They waited now for their father and husband to come back, successful and safe from harm. They gave him strength, hope, and courage now out in the fantastic black loneliness of space. Steven caught Brian dealing with a collection of test tubes and apparatus at some tables.

'Hello Brian, you're starting to find things already are you?' he asked, stepping closer.

'Just preparing everything for when things come my way. Actually, I'm spending most of my time right now just coordinating all zone areas, schedules, and communications between us all. I may need more help here in future – let's hope not really, but if so maybe you'd like to step up?' Brian suggested.

'Me? I'm not sure I know too much about illnesses, diseases, and all that side of things,' Steven told him.

'Didn't you do some project looking at our immune system breakdown, alternative biological remedies, cell strength, gene altering tissues, that sort of thing?' Brian asked. He seemed to actually know a fair amount about him, Steven thought.

'Well, some of that, in a way, yes. My project team – we were sort of still finding our direction. We had only just started our first real big project after getting our Master's degrees. Guns for hire, fresh out, you know?' Steven explained.

'Oh, okay then. But still, if you have an interest and the time, you'll be welcome to help out soon. So, you getting used to all this yet?'

'Out here? Space, it's amazing isn't it? Like a dream, like I'm daydreaming every day now. Astounding really,' Steven told him.

'I know, exactly. Better than any dream, though. So you're okay in your area are you?' Brian asked.

'Yes, yes, just getting into routine, I suppose' Steven said.

'Well, enjoy it, I know I am,' Brian told him with a friendly smile.

This man too, he is a most intelligent man, a leader, strong and experienced. He is no fool, wise observant and able to judge me, Steven thought looking back at Brian. So many cautious steps on my path toward the great goal of our age. Others will be offended, confused, shocked and will disagree, but I know I have to move on soon whatever reactions come to me, he thought.

Chapter 21

Over the next two weeks, Steven quietly watched the activities of all the zone areas of the space station. He made notes, contemplated his actions and devised his grand scheme needed to take things in his direction, to get control, to make the whole station his entire experiment, his way.

As he did this, he looked to Gordon for guidance. He did no longer pretend that he could do without it, finally acknowledging his father for the fascinating, powerful scientist he had been. Within the hidden rooms Steven listened carefully.

'There are a number of ways I could take control – perhaps I just don't need to do as much as I could...' he said aloud.

'No, NO! Take them, take everything. Understand? It is your chance. Only chance. This time here is special. And extremely rare opportunity that must not be missed in any way, you hear me?' Gordon told him strictly.

Steven looked away, feeling small and uncomfortable.

'Father, you did what you could, back home... You did your best, what you'd been waiting to do, trying to do so long,' Steven said.

'Now you. My good son,' Gordon replied. It was an unusual comment of affection given.

'I'm not going to waste this time here, really. I won't at all,' Steven told him.

'That's right, son,' Gordon answered.

Steven could no longer look right at his father like he used to, mocking him, and staring right back. Now there was just too much different. Gordon looked so ill, sick and thin, a contorted mask of disease, ageing, older and withered unlike ever before. It seemed like death held Gordon up, life having left him at some point.

Life was beginning to feel like some kind of historical flashback, Jane thought. She was spending the first month she learned in the food and crop zones area of the station. They were to grow food like anyone would back on Earth to begin with, the subtlety and gradually expose it to a variety of elements from space and planets outside of the station, observing changes over time. It was humble calm kind of work, at least to begin with, really quite simple yet sweat breaking and honest work with science sown in at the end stages. She felt she could have done this back home, in another life-could have been self-sufficient, living from the land, possibly working on a farm, peacefully, simplistically, respecting nature. Did she not respect the natural ways of Earth in her own scientific views? she came to gradually consider. It was a big, difficult question to answer immediately, she found. She hoped that she did, even understanding the issues of globalisation, capitalism, third world starvation, and the hypocrisy. She hoped that she knew how these issues could be balanced and understood between nature and scientific advances back home. The station could help, she thought.

Suzanne was in charge of these zone areas, a woman Jane admired now greatly. She had only twice spoken to her personally, one to one; very briefly, but that was enough to see an obvious admirable character. Jane might have possibly got the impression that Suzanne was extremely focused on her work, but more than that was evident. There could almost be a negative kind of hierarchy here, even among such intelligent, liberal people, Jane realised. They were all definitely extremely intelligent, mature and level headed adults, but these kind of people could often be insular, detached, work and goal focused to extreme lengths, even if not consciously, she thought. She knew, as she was guilty of these traits herself from time to time.

Between shifts and taking walks around, Steven came along by the time source duty room and met Brian inside.

'Hi there. How goes it now?' Brian asked.

'Good enough I'd say. You?' Steven replied.

'Yes. Good. Hey Steven, look – I need to be honest, I think, okay? Let's sit down,' Brian offered.

'Alright,' Steven said.

They moved down to a table over to the left and sat looking at each other.

'I respect that you have done really a lot, taken some very large risks since your father's help and involvement,' Brian began.

'Right look, I have done a great deal just by myself you should know. There's been a huge lot of shit against me, and yes my father does have a very respected company, but I did take my own path all the way here,' Steven explained.

'If you say so,' Brian replied.

'I do. He would not have got involved in this anyway – too much happening for him down there.'

'You think? He didn't say more? Right. Maybe not now. He certainly was in the past,' Brian told him.

'Meaning just what?'

'You know just how amazing it is that this space station has been created, so soon and so secretly.'

'We all have been wondering that for weeks, but don't seem to care so much as we're here anyway now,' Steven said.

'You should. Your father really did.'

'Why then? Tell me what you're hinting at, will you?' Steven said, losing patience.

'You know him, right? Well, his company, then the OtomoVision company, also OxfordKensi company, PalmQuantum Tech... He did so much, so did each of them, in making this station a reality now,' Brian explained.

'Say what you want, just... Whatever. I've got things to do now. My things,' Steven quickly responded and stood. He then walked away, vexed and in a state of confused anger.

After a while, Jane did strangely wonder just how safe they all were up there on the space station. She remembered the horrific bizarre attacks on the streets of Britain before they had all left – the danger, and the random and mysterious unexplainable attacks from sick people with no immediate reason or excuse. What if that disease or illness could have made it up onto and into the space station in some way at all? she thought. Was she being simply too paranoid? Was her mind idle and just running away with her? There had been no explanation before they left, and most newspapers and experts simply more interested in the space mission itself to give much more attention to the attacks after a while. It disturbed her, and made her incredibly uneasy to think about it. They were civilised people on the station, but people nonetheless. There was no kind of protection like down on earth – no hospitals, no police. They had medical facilities of course, and some doctors, but could they really cope if something like that should somehow break out? They all simply expected each other to be healthy, behave, look after themselves, to be peaceful and calm during their time in space. Would they all remain that way? she wondered.

No previous space exploration had turned nasty as far as her memory told her, no specific shocking events ever, she thought. Her mind must just be wandering wildly, escaping her rationality, without the earthly diet of digital multi-channel short attention, hyped up drama and advertising bombardment which slowed our own personal thoughts. Things would be fine, she decided. A pleasant, one of a kind, special lucky experience. Then she would return home, and talk things through with Alan, sweet Alan. They could get closer, think about a future together, and she could just maybe even apologise.

During a lunch break, Jane spent time with others from the crop growing zone, discussing their thoughts about the project as a whole, and possibly futures from the results they would find.

'This is just a crazy privilege, you know?' one man – Jack – told her and the others.

'Don't get too distracted, okay?' a red haired lady – Karla – suggested, winking at him.

'We'll take the results back home, and who knows? Do you think we'll cure something like major cancers or ageing in a matter of weeks or months after returning?' Jane asked.

'Could actually take years really when we get back,' Jack said pessimistically.

'Oh come on, no. Surely we'll work with the many other scientists left down there, and we'll discover something really useful in no time,' Karla said.

'Then there's the attackers,' Jane added.

Karla and Jack just looked at her, not responding immediately.

'What do you two think is happening with them back on Earth now?' she asked.

'I just am damn glad I'm not there right now,' Jack told them.

It really seemed that others were simply trying to forget about what was happing down there, blocking out the terrible events on Earth, and not wanting to confront the disturbing truths at all.

The night was a rough uncomfortable time of sleep for Steven, but it held the most unbelievable dream. Steven paced around, looking in all directions as he stepped out. It was so unbelievable. He walked the surface of Mars easily, with no space suit, no breathing apparatus at all. No pain or danger came to him. He was the alien there, exploring unlike any human ever had before. The land was certainly a rich red hue, the sky over him smoky in greyness cloaking the space station far above him.

He saw something, a figure some distance up ahead. That was just impossible, he thought. No one else was ready, or capable of being there then. Bu then neither was he, and yet there he stood. He was the one, the only man who could walk so easily on this mysterious wide uncluttered planet surface. No other could take that from him. But he watched, and saw the dark shape grow in size. It seemed like the dark silhouette of a man, an unknown man, walking toward him, then running, fast.

'Hey! Hey, wait!' Steven called out, or at least he thought the words left his mouth but he was not entirely sure of it.

Making sure exactly that his time was right Steven, one late evening, stealthily crept down into the first zone of food and crop areas. He had to choose a good enough part, somewhere prominent. He knelt down by a patch of sown soil in a divider, and took out a very small vial of liquid from a pocket. He poured it over the crop area and watched it sink deep in easily. He then though he heard some sound, someone approaching maybe, from nearby then. He turned quickly, panicked and anxious. No one near he saw, but he stood and ran along up the dark corridor even so.

He knew food would be picked and used in a matter of days, and each scientist had their own patch assigned to them. He had a clear idea of who would take in the mystery chemical sown into the soil there. He would be waiting, watching for results.

The next day, he spent time moving around in zone area three, chatting to a few scientists casually, and seeing their interesting work progress. Here though, he began to sow seeds of doubt and confusion, mistrust and paranoia. By simply moving a small number of personal belongings and shifting the position of furniture he watched the double takes, unsure glances and comments arrive a short while later.

'Hey Jerry, where's my torch now?' one man asked.

'Huh? I don't know. On the desk next to the doors,' his friend suggested.

'No, it's not there. You got it?' Jerry asked.

'What? No, I haven't used it. Don't blame me okay?'

This was the first of many similar arguments provoked by the subtle actions of Steven. He then returned to the hidden chambers carefully with his news. He moved along between the rows of small bunks, quarters of the mutating patients of his.

'How are you all now? Feeling better?' he enquired with mock concern. 'I bring interesting news now.'

'Sick – sick and trapped. Let us go out, walk around, please,' asked an agitated desperate looking man in front of him.

'I am sorry, my friend, still too soon just yet. Patience please. Just a short while longer to go. But listen, they are weakening now, I am getting ready for us to go out and begin what is more important.'

'So you say,' the man replied, not convinced easily.

'We'll probably rot in here, will we?' another asked Steven, but there was a severe look of vicious malice in her eyes. All of them in fact could be said to look extremely ready to take out their tense built up cabin fever.

'That's not my intention at all. Just rest, and enjoy the trip. The view around,' Steven suggested, and pointed toward the tiny row of extra strengthened windows, revealing the dark depth of deep space outside the space station.

'We're not animals. We're not going anywhere. But neither are you, not out there,' one of them nearest Steven told him threateningly.

'You're very wrong there, pal. We'll be venturing out – that's the point of the station – new ways, new exploration, new experimentation. If Earth is ruined for good soon enough, we will move out, and this one could be the place,' he told them.

'What? Mars? Live on Mars? Us?' the man asked.

Steven simply looked out of the small windows thoughtfully to himself.

That was what Gordon had told him, anyway. That was what mattered more than most other thoughts. He knew of many things that could possibly happen up there. He had not planned some of it, he said. Not alone, with a few others back and forth over a few years. Some had abandoned the group, too fearful and scared of ruining their reputations, losing their careers, never allowing the most radical – some said dangerous – ideas to come into being. Those ideas were there, Gordon said, waiting for someone. His own time passing, ageing and growing older, his children were the first choice, Steven the perfect gifted son, eventually.

His ageing and fragile father. Was there even ever so much difference between Gordon and the couple of dozen study patients Steven had trapped away in the murky chambers? he wondered. They too were mostly very intelligent, wealthy people, offering themselves for greater scientific advancement. Gordon, like them, was ill in a most terrible way, possibly incurable, but then Steven could not stop hoping. He both pitied and envied them equally, but he knew his own personal responsibilities, and they all, Gordon especially, counted on him so desperately.

Hours passed and Steven began the next step of the secret procedures carefully alone. He waited, watching the rooms located between all zone areas. There among them sat the regulatory maintenance controls desks for the entire space station. Continually monitored by two alternating people, Steven approached one of them who sat quietly watching pressure levels, fuel meters, oxygen, water and all balances onboard for their continued health and safety.

'Hello, how are things? My word, there's so much to keep on top of here, isn't there?' he stated.

'Hello. Definitely. You're Steven aren't you?' Melissa asked.

'Yes, that's me. Is it any fun?' he said.

'Has to be done, but it is good to do, very interesting. A big responsibility. You are quite very much involved with the station aren't you? I remember seeing you at the beginning,' she told him.

Steven sat down beside her then, and leaned across the table beside them.

'That's true in a way, along with of course Brian and the others. Yes, just ask if you need any advice at all. Was it the shortest straw you picked? Being here?' he asked her.

'Oh no, we're just taking turns. I'll be in a zone area in a couple of days. That'll be more interesting,' she told him.

Steven looked at all of the many boards, switches, valves and buttons across the wall and control panels over the table.

'So it's separated between the zone areas – all safety, power, fuel, air con, everything – is that right?' he asked.

'Yes, look – all divided here... On screen you bring them up, select, highlight, set times, changes, checking them against each other and so on. It's mostly like that, but so much of it kind of is tedious, but essential stuff. You've got better things to do, right?' she asked.

'I could have but then maybe not... It's a little lonely where I work too, honestly. Not much to look at,' he explained.

They looked at each other, and smiled at each other slowly as he stepped closer toward her.

'That's a shame. Come for a chat anytime if you want to. I need some company myself here. I'd like that very much,' she told him.

He moved around then, standing and pacing a couple of feet from her.

'Well, thank you. You are certainly one of the most welcoming, warm people I've met up here. Good to know someone like that,' he told her. 'We obviously didn't leave all of the most beautiful women back down on Earth, thank God,' he said.

She blushed instantly then, and giggled a little.

'I'll definitely be back, then,' he told her and then walked away, smiling fondly as he went. It was like a separate, disconnected moment, an instant of lone intimate warm meeting, and honest emotion between them. He felt a unique connection there, not simply sexual chemistry but an honest affection to her, and from her. He had to keep that far from him, he thought. No simple emotion could ruin his work so easily now.

Chapter 22

Nights passed with too much tension, Steven trapped in with Gordon like had not been the case for years. He felt his father's accusing eyes, pained breathing, and taunting legacy in scientific business empires bearing down on him constantly. He paced around, planning, thinking, and trying to keep focus.

'Don't waste your time,' Gordon whispered near him in the dimly lit quarters.

'Don't criticise me now, damn it. I'm not, I have to wait, can't rush it, just can't,' Steven responded.

'I did not rush through my years,' Gordon told him.

'Well, this is me, my time. You know that,' Steven answered aggressively.

He suddenly left the rooms, rushing down the area corridors. He stopped along by some tables, then kicked them, cursing the space station, himself, everything. He continued, breaking the tables' legs, kicking at them repeatedly, splintering the tops while swearing loudly alone in the wide corridor. He walked away exhausted, maddeningly frustrated.

As he walked on in blind anger, Steven came to find Melissa by the control observation rooms again.

'Oh hey, you alright? You seem unhappy,' she said to him as he approached with his tired, dour face.

'Well, could be better,' he said.

'Missing things back home? People? Friends? It's really hard, I know,' she said, and put a hand on his arm with affection.

'Good to have some caring people like you around here,' he told her.

'Oh well, I'm glad you're here, I really am,' she explained.

'You're still working hard here?' he asked.

'I am, yes. But I could do with a distraction I think,' she told him.

The room was a closed off very quiet area. No one else had much need to drop by unexpected and Steven knew that. He also could see how anxious and keen she was for him. She had wild, seductive young eyes, just like his. She kneeled down, unzipped him and began to put a much bigger smile over his face. As he enjoyed her actions, he casually reached over the controls area, and quickly looked through the various area zones condition levels. He quickly and discreetly made some slight changes and then returned his attention to her pleasurable efforts below. He had missed women like this for the last few months, and he was glad to know there certainly were some very stunning ones like her on the station. She finished and stood, then kissed him and stroked his shoulders, smiling at him.

'Want to hang around longer? I'll make some coffee,' she suggested.

'That was really great – you're great – but I must go. I will be back soon though. No way I can't be,' he told her and left her waiting for more.

While setting up his cunning secretive plans, eventually Steven came to learn of the couple of off station exploration rocket shuttles. People were actually going to launch out from the space station in them, hopefully landing on the relatively close surface of Mars. Once there, there were a number of options which were being discussed. He returned to the hidden chamber rooms, needing to know the opinion of Gordon.

'This is... excellent, like... I hoped for. But... it should go much further, once... there,' he told Steven.

'How much further? On Mars? Exploring landscape, geography?'

'Even further,' Gordon told him.

'Really, can we?'

'Already have...' Gordon said cryptically.

Steven looked around, then back at Gordon. How much truth could there be in those words? he thought. Always Gordon was cryptic, surprising, confusing.

'Just what do you mean?' Steven asked.

Gordon looked back, his sagging pale skin, and rotting flesh beginning to smell sour now. He said nothing more after that.

Another crew of scientists sat in the canteen area of their designated work zone on the space station, taking in a hearty breakfast meal before beginning a long shift. Various scientists walked through the zones, passing equipment or messages often but generally the atmosphere was relaxed yet positive as work progressed.

'You know I really don't want to say it, but I do think that I'm getting some regular strong headaches. I'm feeling a bit down increasingly now too,' one guy said.

'Just the adjustment thing. We're all here for each other remember. Just talk about things, we'll all listen, we're all in this big thing together,' another told the first man.

'I know, I know. But it's just physical I think. Just bad sleep too. I'll get through it I'm sure,' he said.

'I feel kind of well, anxious or nervous still,' the other said.

'You do? Just knock one out. Or then some say Jill is a real friendly entertaining lady, even Mark Anderson, if that's your way too,' the man suggested.

'What? Oh right. Leave it. No I mean, I get some weird urge to go further, soon, much sooner,' he said.

'Well, we're all eager to progress here.'

'No I mean, I know what you mean, I feel like that as well. We need to get moving here. Really need to move along. The whole project, we need to be at Mars now. That's it really, we're all thinking about it, aren't we?'

'You're very right, I think.'

'Is he? It's going to take great care and preparation before we eventually do it the way we have in mind.'

'Whatever, don't you want to be there? On another planet?'

'Yes, you know... I do really, I do.'

'We should talk to the project managers about it.'

'Should we? Do we have to?'

'It just might not happen soon enough if we don't.'

'But look, can all of us go there, around the same time?'

'It's two by two, like the ark, isn't it?'

'Right. Whatever you say.'

'We'll talk to them. Didn't Steven just go by here a couple of minutes ago?'

'Yes, I spoke to him a little.'

'Well, we could catch him, see him about it. He's very approachable, a more friendly one than the others,' one said.

'Yes, he does seem like he should have more responsibility doesn't he?'

One long peaceful month passed, everyone working well, in a place artificially home. Then Brian, with agreement of Andrew and

Suzanne announced that they were defiantly then ready to make the long awaited test journeys to Mars. Everything would need to be checked, planned well to the last degree, and monitored exactly. Over the next few days people were selected for various roles involved and everyone else waited highly excited to witness the event soon enough. Brian and Andrew chose Mark Bratley, a physics researcher, and Natalie Brookman to be the ones to travel to Mars first. It was only two people to a rocket pod, there would be two separate trips to start with. Steven made sure to see how they worked, their controls, the potential. Andrew showed him, talking him through the mechanics of the space pods with a small group of others. Later, Steven caught Mark Bratley alone at work.

'Congratulations Mark,' he said to him.

'Thank you very much, Steven. Sorry you are not going yourself just yet. I'm sure you're too busy here, right?'

'Yes, that's about right. Too much to keep track of around here, but I hope it goes really well. It will, I know it. Look, look out for anything... different,' Steven told him.

'Won't it all be kind of different really?' Mark said.

'Yes, but I mean... Something might not seem right, if you get me. But it's another planet any way. See you around anyway,' he said, leaving.

'Okay, thanks,' Mark said, seeming grateful but confused.

There were deep secret hidden quarters far inside the space station – within there Steven, unknown to others, spent regular time, planned, and organised so much. His mind though had enormous levels of guilt, pressure, confusion and paranoia heaped upon it, and he could barely understand his own true beliefs and opinions after so long. Perhaps even his perception of reality upon the space station could not be so easily trusted right then. Or would that just simply be an easy escape from his fear?

Gordon appeared to him then, still seeming proud and smug.

'You are so very busy, my son,' he commented. He stood facing Steven in shady, darkened room, half cloaked in shadow. There was a kind of frailness, something in the face of Gordon which seemed to have changed in a disturbing way. All of the meetings, travelling, stress of business wearing on him so heavy finally showing worse than ever.

'Now we set it up, no more laws which hold us back, laws that simply suffocate human progress because of insecure fear, am I right?' Steven said.

'You are right indeed.'

'I'm taking your plans now father, as you wished.'

'You want to do so?' Gordon asked.

'As you wished, father,' Steven said humbly.

'What do we have then?' Gordon asked.

Steven walked along to his personal desks, with laptops and monitor screens. He opened up files and scrolled down them.

'We have the initial main chosen large group of scientists for the space station-biologists, physicists, chemical engineers, analysts and more totalling sixty two. Then a number of administrators, doctors, a couple of sociologists and anthropologists and others, observing and documenting our time here. Then lastly, my own secret number of helpful patients which you know about very well,' Steven told him.

'You will do what is needed, yes?' Gordon asked him.

'I have to, right? Have to proceed with this grand venture in our progression,' Steven answered.

'Our adaptation, exploration. Forget what you've heard before. It is worth it, totally worth... everything,' Gordon told him.

'Yes. Looking tired, father,' Steven observed.

'I've... a good right. And that's reason again for your... special work, with your talent now,' he told Steven.

'Right, yes my father,' Steven agreed.

He continued to look through many documents on his computer monitor screens with stronger focus, knowing he would not stop now. He was going forward on a steady path – no others could derail him from the purpose, he believed, not out there in the darkness of space.

Chapter 23

Days began to pass pleasantly enough as the areas of the station and their small separate groups of scientists worked on research and observation with calm and dedicated interest.

Jane had begun to spend some time with a couple of women there – Stacy and Deborah – and they sat around in the evenings as much as they could decide when that was, and talked about their personal interests, hobbies, lives, men and science.

'So Jane, what do you think of the guys up here? Any who've grabbed your attention yet?' Stacy asked her.

'Men? Well, I was really kind of with someone you see... it might be... We were very close. Almost... I don't know,' Jane said in a way embarrassed or unsure.

'Well hey, look we're a very long way from home right now. I might find some gorgeous guy or guys here. Got to get what a girl needs sometimes,' Deborah told them with a sly grin.

'Okay, you're right,' Stacy agreed.

'Do you think we'll be living a lot differently here soon?' Jane asked.

'What do you mean?'

'Some say that's a part of being here – not just observing space, gathering samples, but living very differently, social testing,' Jane told her.

'What, like some commune, some new age things? Hippies or communist style weirdness?' Stacy asked with a disgusted look.

'No, not exactly just more... just living but with space around us, affecting us. And the other planets. We're in separated areas on the station, these kind of very small village sort of set ups. It's kind of ready, I think, to happen,' she told them.

'Okay, well I'm just going to do my job, enjoy being here, and go back home as someone who was out in space,' Deborah said.

'So you miss your bloke back home then?' Stacy asked looking at Jane.

'I... Okay, yes I do. Hope he misses me too,' Jane replied.

'He's a nice guy is he? What does he do?' Deborah asked.

'Research scientist as well, mostly in biological experimental studies. We're part of a group, you know – pushing boundaries, like many of us here I suppose,' Jane told them. She thought of Alan then, back on Earth by himself still watching experiments and carefully judging figures and tests without her.

With close timed guidance, Andrew controlled the first launch of rocket pod one the following day. Everyone stopped to watch the momentous task, nervous but mesmerised. Natalie and Mark strapped in, flew out with steady speed and power pushing them on.

The time passed so slowly. To begin with, everyone watched them leave, amazed and hopeful. After the longest time of suspense, they reached Mars. Safely the pod landed down with tentative care. After the initial checks, Natalie and Mark stepped out, with the closed in space masks and protective flight suits on. They communicated back everything that they saw out before them. They were simply amazed and almost speechless but continued to describe the landscape around, and the marvellous mystery of the world known as Mars.

They proceeded to collect many samples in small containers and pocket vials. Mark even stopped and thought about what Steven had told him, his strange words of dramatic caution. No, Mars still seemed isolated, desolate and devoid of life forms so far as they could see. More time passed and Mark and Natalie eventually returned to the space station safe and proud with their samples.

Everyone wanted to ask them what Mars was like, what it had felt like being there, a planet mankind had not been born on, visitors briefly. They were all amazed, talking about the experience for many hours and days. Jane was stunned at just how far from home she was then. It suddenly really frightened her. She was not the only one either, she knew that.

'Who's going next time?' she said when talking with Douglas and Donald, two male scientist friends in her living quarters she had come to know well.

'The next ones to be on Mars are going by related work and qualifications aren't they?' Donald said, looking at Douglas.

'Right, that's it. That sucks too,' Douglas offered.

'Well, we're here seeing it all close as it gets at least,' Jane said positively enough.

In quiet private evening time to herself, Jane opened up her personal laptop and looked through old emails which had accumulated in the last few weeks and months. After a few minutes of becoming homesick, she suddenly found a new email from Alan she had copied only days before leaving earth. It had only previously glitched, and would not open until right now. It was quite long, and seemed to discuss some unusual things as she began reading it.

"Dear, sweet Jane,

Please read this email with serious attention. Take great caution in future. I do not wish to scare or shock you and please do not immediately think I have gone insane in some unexpected way.

You are leaving soon. I have just learned of this. I am not mad at you really, I know how space captivates you so much. Not only you, there will be a good many going with you. But be wary. I wish to tell you of a very serious thing I have found. I now believe I have come across a connection which threatens us extremely seriously. As much as we have trusted Steven, there is trouble from him. Not strictly his own fault, but he is a problem or even a danger.

The people attacking others, the 'attackers', the sick people – I know they are connected to work of Steven's father, Gordon. It looks like police and officials just do not understand, and I myself only have the vaguest understanding but enough to be concerned. I tell you as I have lost Steven. He is missing now, but I suspect where he has gone. Perhaps we should continue our project without him ultimately. What do you think?

Be careful, my Jane. Be so careful of where you go, what you do. Please come back down to earth, to me in time. Please return. I will wait until you do.

Alan."

Alone Jane cried unstoppably in her room. She was confused and sad at her own decisions. She did not absolutely know if she had done the right thing. Life was like that though, she told herself, clearing her eyes and taking a deep breath. Sometimes we have to just take chances, she thought.

Within the hidden locked up chambers, down through the corridor, the trapped attacker patients began to stir, and they moaned. Some feeling tugged within them, as they moved in deep space away from earth, some urge pulled, called with them. One or two of them could see up out of the small round windows, they saw planets beyond out there. There was Mars. They raged as they caught it in their sight. Mars was so hypnotic to them. It called to them, it mocked their human existence. It meant something vastly significant in some unfathomable way to them, that much they could feel, even in the condition they were in. A couple of them began beating themselves violently then up against the walls until they bled, cuts and bruises on their faces and arms. They wanted Mars – they wanted to know it closer, personally, to be there, right then.

The first few weeks of adapting to their professional work on the space station were personally extremely tense and painful for Steven. So much had to be held back and reigned in still, unmentioned, kept so quiet. Gordon was in his thoughts, guilt was on his mind, and deeper, darker possibilities tempted him continually. So close now, to all kinds of opportunities, he thought. His dreams were becoming horrifying, recurring nightmare experiences, he feared. He dreamed, when he let himself finally drift off, of a kind of Mars, in space ahead. Swirling deep colours, hallucinogenic surreal landscapes and concoctions of beings, things, life unknown to mankind, moving, searching for him as he walked the surface naked. He would wake sweating, uttering prayers of mercy, anything to keep the nightmares away. Now a small handful of prescription pills steadied his alarming thoughts and visions, and helped him through the days as the real desired plan ahead began.

With two brave scientists sent out together in the exploration pod mini-shuttle, they eventually reached the surface of Mars. While they were instructed in getting out, observing, testing and collecting samples, another unnoticed figure moved out, away alone on the Mars landscape behind. Though, like most all other near planets Mars seemed uninhabited, bereft of life, species or any sort of signs of alien forms, one person knew it to be only a very impressive trick of human observation. As fast as was possible, Gordon lurched out over the crusted dunes of Mars then stopped. He closed his eyes, breathed slowly. In some amazing way, he sank down through the land, deep down, and was gone below in seconds. In minutes, his sight briefly obstructed, he passed through below, and re-emerged into some never before human viewed or even perceived form of being, in an astonishing secret lower underground environment. It was a kind of village or community – tunnels, but not soil and earth, tunnels of some other cosmic organic substance. Buildings of the kind formed from heat, energy stood strong, physically manifested as structures but opaque and still malleable. He floated over, viewing the sight, humble and curious, feeling so small, inferior and ignorant but eager for more. It was an experience taken early from him decades early in his own life. Now he had returned, he found the real unknown hidden life of Mars once again. He was there to offer himself properly this time, apologetically. He felt himself taken, pulled. Some intermittent sounds flashed by communicating in a kind of cryptic manner.

'My humble apologies to you. I am back, I've returned finally, I of Earth, an offering of humankind. Help me, and I... will help you in... any way I can... undoubtedly,' he said aloud to no visible audience.

His whole body flashed and boiled suddenly, was remade, deconstructed and returned effortlessly in a moment. The feeling was in parts sexual, euphoric, confusing, painful, delightful, and unknown to any man or woman before. With a sudden gasp, and a blink of his shocked ageing old eyes, he stood again out on the wide vast vacant surface of Mars like only minutes before. The two scientists eventually returned to their pod shuttle and were launched back toward the space station.

The morning so far had given Steven yet another uncomfortable headache and dull pain in his troubled mind, after a restless night once more. But this day was due to be a much different one, with a big mission for the station. He pulled himself together and walked on through corridors between the area zones. While there were many specific certain tests and procedures being carried out by the many dozens of people there, he wanted to do his part personally.

He came after a few minutes out at an open communal area, and found Gary Absalom, one of the next to be sent to Mars in the coming days ahead, with a group of others, just talking and discussing the planned trip over to Mars.

'Hello there, Gary, hope you are calm and getting ready in your head, focusing well,' Steven said to him and put out his hand to shake.

Gary smiled, shaking hands and replied.

'Yes, not very long to go now. Keeping focused best I can. It's a great job really, a great opportunity, honestly.'

'Good, so you should think so. I'm very pleased for you. I'll see you before it happens later on then,' Steven told him, smiling back.

He walked away, off down another corridor and looked at his right hand which he could feel stinging strangely somehow. The skin was slightly swollen and at the touch tender and sore and extremely sensitive. It was done, though. Preparation executed well enough, he thought to himself. It should be very interesting to see what comes next.

A meeting was called up between the four lead managers of the space station with unexpected short notice, Steven getting the call from Brian on text alert suddenly while checking area data. He reached the meeting chamber, where he found the others waiting for him.

'Hello everyone. Hope I'm not too late, am I?' he said.

'No, just on time – we're only just beginning. Steven, we want to talk about the journey tests to Mars. As we are planning two in the next three days, then another two in maybe a week after, we so far believe we are ready to go ahead. You are happy with it as planned?' Brian asked.

'Well we all were, weren't we? Why? What has happened?' he asked with concern.

'We need to really look at the possibilities ahead in such great detail before it happens. We have, yes, but we just need real certainty. Really think about what we really could do without being too nervous or afraid now,' Brian said.

'Meaning what really, Brian?' Steven said.

'Well we are thinking, just discussing the bigger idea... the thought of many more of us going to Mars much sooner. Just maybe perhaps we know enough really to make a much bolder move forward now. Maybe it is safe enough is what some of us think,' Brian said. 'So, your thoughts?'

'Well, tough question right now. We need to be careful still, I would say' Steven replied. 'No, look, I mean – well look can I have a say? This is really unexpected. Not totally professional now either is it?'

'We just were discussing it casually and found that we were coming to some new shared opinions together but we are talking with you now also. We do want your opinion too, of course, before making any big changes ahead,' Brian told him.

'Well, no. That might sound strange coming from me. Yes, I am really keen to get there, to know so much more and soon but... safety first. One step at a time. So do you all hate me now?' Steven said.

'God damn it, you bloody coward,' Suzanne suddenly, let out to the quiet shock of the others.

'Hold on, see, I knew it,' he said.

'You hypocrite. Until now you seemed desperate to get there, and now this? No balls, all talk, no guts in reality at all. Should have guessed,' she said, mocking him.

Steven looked at them, shocked.

'What's going on here?' he asked, honestly confused by their gathering and announcement.

'Are you sure of your opinion, really, Steven?' Brian said. 'It's just we could – us, here – go there with just a matter of a few small changes. Maybe we don't even have to tell the others around the station,' Brian announced.

'What? This is crazy, man. It's just wrong. For all the things that we are attempting to do with this space station, all of the immense amount of work all kinds happening, everyone here... No, not yet. Not like that. That's my opinion. Do not do anything like that,' Steven told them.

'Okay then. Alright, fair enough. We respect your decision. As a team, we will then continue on as we previously had planned so far,' Brian replied.

'Right, good. I really did not wish to cause such a... discussion. But thank you then,' Steven said.

He looked at them sitting there all casual, amazed and slowly turned leaving the room alone. He could waste no more time now if this was how the rest of the team were feeling. He had not expected such things, but it was no big deal. They were all still so small in their thoughts even together, he believed as he walked away to sort out his plans ahead.

With a kind of tormented luck, Gordon moved around, waiting for Steven. Mars had taken him, after decades of quiet waiting. A savage intensity, a blind fearful but adoring lack of understanding, fuelled by individual greed. The tragic mistake from decades earlier, hidden possibly by shame and, of course, fear, resulted in this long delayed but eventual devouring of his fragile human body. Was his precious soul gone from him too? Had it been stolen decades before, leaving a thin lie of himself ever since? He was death now, however presented. He was every sin, desire and guilt of the confused human mind, and the result it gained in the deep unrelenting punishment of mysterious space.

It could be a glorious heretical but violent cosmic space death end deserved, and it still held back absolute revelation to Gordon. He was now an emptiness, the final weak phantasmagorical energies left roaming in hope of cursing his naïve son. As he slowly ebbed away, remotely consumed in full by inner Mars energy, his consciousness was given many myriad glimpses of some other existences somewhere, somehow. It was the life of Mars – the societies, the species, history, culture and hidden present population within and around somewhere. He was seeing the thing he had been questioning for many years alone, but even this did not accept him now. It used him, finally, in every way it could. It took him from himself forever.

Chapter 24

At a time when the many busy separate zone areas were now filled with scientists in positive expectant moods as they waited for the first explorers to return from the surface of Mars, Jane had now more ominous and disturbing thoughts filling her own mind. She made her way along toward the specific main management rooms. Jane got there, took a nervous breath, and then knocked at the doors.

'Hello, can I help you?' Suzanne asked when she greeted Jane at the door with a sceptical and irritated face.

'Yes, possibly. Listen can I talk, in private. Is... is Steven here?' Jane said.

'No, he's not right now. Do you want to see him?' Suzanne asked.

'No, I don't. I want to talk to someone else, about all of the really strange things. I think I have come across some serious and important information that your team really should know about,' Jane told her.

'Oh really? What information is that then?' Suzanne said.

'You want to hear? It's all from back on Earth, actually. Out of all of the people who came up here, there is serious danger which we could possibly stop soon enough,' Jane said.

'That could be true in some way now. Jane, isn't it? I doubt though that you can offer much of any relative present importance now that we're up here. We're playing our parts here – that's how it is. We as a management team really are considering all of the specific real dangers on the station now. You may not like that, and I thank you for your thoughts now, but that is it. It is how it is. We have to go on with it. We will all be safe I promise you. I am sorry. Anyway, look – is your station area working well still?' Suzanne asked.

Jane was silently insulted, infuriated and shocked at the response so readily given to her, but did not let it show easily. What an unbelievable bitch, she thought. Arrogant bloody woman. She had been still willing to let Suzanne reveal some latent compassionate side, but it seemed she was just a mean and steely individual simply intent on climbing up the ladders in the workplace.

'Well now, spit it out if it is anything to help at all?' Suzanne then said.

'No... I think now I was wrong, actually. Never mind. I'll be returning to my area work schedule I think. Sorry to have taken you from your work. Goodbye,' Jane replied and then made her way out again, with a fresh view of how she was to continue.

During a long quiet shift in area two, a couple of scientists were very rapidly rushed along to medical rooms, as they exhibited serious and alarming ill symptoms, vomiting, changing of skin colour, eyes dilating and their senses blurring. All others around observed this, shocked, and wondering what the cause could be. They were not back on earth, there were only less than one hundred people on the station, and they had all seemed in very good health before boarding all those weeks previously.

Leaving some debating scientists in the open canteen area, Brian walked in determination onward. He approached the consoles, switchboards and computer monitors, and quickly began flicking across, altering levels and tests inputs. Suzanne then came inside and was confused by his actions which she could see.

'Just what are you actually doing there, Brian?' she said.

'I'm making some necessary changes okay?' he replied.

'Without consulting the whole team at all?' she said .

'We did discuss this. It is the expected bump in proceedings, the early growing pains being ironed out, the fluctuation period before the more delicate testing really begins,' he explained.

'Okay, listen – that's fine. I understand, I really do,' Suzanne responded.

'Look, they are finding some confusing samples, and the data returning with them needs to be very seriously considered before they return back in with us, you know that. The others agreed also, time can't be wasted,' he told her.

She backed away then silently but more sure of the lines of ethics of the space station being drawn up around them. She would most definitely cross the lines with no care of causing any level of anger in others.

While debates passed over what was the more serious troubling concern on the station right then, Brian and the management held another meeting. In only minutes the initial direction of the meeting had lost course, each person adding their own dramatic opinion against the other, some personal point of view or troubling issue, soon talking over each other noisily.

'... There may be not much we are really capable of doing if we admit it...'

'... Gary is not right, he's too laidback in his view, no real appreciation, or serious ambition over others...'

'... We need to separate and monitor all onboard now, we have to be serious...'

Then Suzanne added a point of her own clearly over them.

'There is someone I believe who is actually seriously acting with great suspicion. I'm not just being paranoid – you know the interest in space projects such as these, this size, scale and ambition. Things could be found which many would do almost anything to either get themselves, or ruin completely if they don't. So many would like to know first-hand what we're doing, how we're doing it, what we find and why,' she explained to them.

'What are you saying?' Brian asked, interested.

'There is a person, could be working with others, possibly or not, who makes me highly suspicious of their actions and movements around here. These accidents could very much have been set up, attempts to do real damage or to steal information,' she told them.

'But Suzanne, you know how seriously intense the prelaunch interviews and background checks were, even on us here now. I just don't think there really could be chance of serious conscious threat, someone setting out to do something against us...' Brian was attempting to say.

'There is always chance. Come on, even in science, absolute chance if proven. We don't know every outcome, always – right?' she argued.

'So who then?'

'I... Just for now, I will not say,' she told them.

'Well, that itself sounds just pathetically paranoid and basically useless. Why even warn us like this then?' he said. 'No, remember, we can't just accuse anyone out of the blue. Okay, look don't do anything crazy. If it really is so highly important then find some way to tell us. Please do. So what else?' Brian asked.

Within the securely locked, bolted and shut up hidden chambers, there was little light enough for some to begin to even see hope in their neglected darkness. Though he knew the ones in there, silent, waiting had been mostly wealthy, learned people; Steven had begun to eventually treat them with decreasing respect empathy and lower human regard as they appeared to visibly devolved. He left out bowls of simple processed mushy food, dirty damaged drinking bottles, and kept the heating turned off for most of the time to lower suspicion around them of their existence. He gave almost convincing excuses for all of these terrible conditions, but they knew he viewed them now as less than they had ever been before it all started months before. They were almost all aware they had become in a pathetic sense tragic cast off remains of failed tests, simply ready for more potential hurt if even that would come. They had agreed to it, they knew – it was their own fault in many ways, vanity and greed the cause. More money than sense, some might say.

Some had taken to mostly sleeping constantly, but others now had fevered desperate savage thoughts occupying their ruined and tortured minds. Some could not sleep at all, some thought only of revenge now or some kind of justice for Steven and Gordon, the duo of vile demented scientist oppressors. They stared up out of the very small round windows, seeing glimpses of moons, Mars, and other planets far around them then in the silent dark of space.

'I once could see, but now... but now...'

'I am blind... I could see... but now... I once could...'

They murmured to themselves, among themselves.

'Forgive me, my Lord, my estranged God. Forgive my wicked ways, have mercy on us, please,' another begged.

'No mercy... no mercy for him, for the father, or the son.'

'Or the heathen spirit,' another added with their combined focused maddened anger building finally.

On a quiet evening, in a canteen room alone from others, Steven sat pouring wine, and looking at the cannelloni he had prepared for two on the table before him. Melissa came minutes later, smiling fondly as she saw him welcoming her there. A young and innocent female scientist whom he had noticed soon enough.

'I'm very glad you have come,' Steven told her.

'You're very welcome. I very much like your company, you know that. What's all this here?' she said, sitting down at the table in front of him.

'I put together something different for us to try. Wanted to offer you dinner. Hopefully this could in some way appear to look romantic, do you think?' he asked.

'It is, thank you. Steven, what do you think about what others are talking about – the strange accidents around the space station?' she asked.

'Well, I think people are exaggerating. Some might be bored, in need of something to talk about, some excitement, some thrill. This is good for me, it's different. I am trying to be... a different person, I think. We can always try, can't we?' he said.

'Do you need to be?' she asked him.

'Yes, I think I agree, most likely. I mean, everyone has some faults, the chance to try again, better themselves right? Not that I'm being hard on you or myself, but I have come to the view that things will get better if I try to change, however much it is not my usual self,' he told her.

'So will I not see the you I first met anymore from now on?' she asked.

'No, you have only seen the new version of me. I am ashamed to say I've been quite a lousy womaniser until very recently. Just dozens of lustful, dirty meaningless one night stands over and over until coming up into space here. No real effort put in before, never really thinking about feelings, chances, romances, love... Just sex and thrills. I don't want to be so vacuous and hollow any longer. I don't wish to miss things others have, better things, real things, like you. I like this. I haven't scared you totally, have I?' he said finally.

'No, you actually comfort me here. This is really nice. You're also a very honest, lovely guy,' she told him, touching his hands as she looked into his eyes.

'Right now, I am. You've got me at a better time,' he said. 'We can't be here forever, as good as that might be,' he told her with an obvious sadness suddenly.

'But while we...' she began.

'While we are, we can be anyone, anything. Forget our past, our sins, even our future maybe. Just live in the now,' he said, finishing her words. It was a lie to himself and to her, but they both wanted to hear it then.

'Do you want to tell me anything?' she asked.

'Best you maybe don't know. If you like me now, how I am here, and I certainly like you too,' he told her.

They finished their meal together, watching each other with quiet affection between them. There was undeniably an honest spark of deep passion between them, tragic chemistry. For Steven it was a ruined romance, the first genuine one, and he could not have it for good. So he enjoyed it, and her right then. No better love than out there in space, he thought.

They spent the next twenty four hours together in her bedroom, simply relaxing, talking, making love, and kissing. They slept together and made love over and over. They were honest and understanding with each other. More kisses, sex and romantic eyes between cooking, drinking wine and dancing to slow, beautiful music. He treasured it, the most intimate shared moments with a woman he had experienced for real that he had come to know. He was proud of himself for it, feeling so lucky, worthwhile and warm. Then he said goodbye with heavy pain in his thoughts, left her with a sad mournful kiss and walked back to his doomed plans ahead, alone again as it had to be.

Even while some of the hidden patients prayed and spoke meaningless nonsense, they were still definitely dangerous and they knew it themselves. There were attackers still, very much capable of huge violent force and damage in unpredictable ways at any time. They did still have a good degree of self-control and awareness, but they knew their own inner biology could at any time fluctuate horribly. This might be natural, or provoked by something or someone like Steven. Time would tell, they knew that much. The hidden chambers were soon enough filled with incredibly tense arguments whenever Steven was away from them. The patients, still self-aware and capable of intelligible opinion and decision, argued back and forth with deadly seriousness over their predicament and how things were going to change. They argued just what Steven was planning really, as it seemed too obvious that he was now not entirely sure of the planned surgery and tests on the space station which he had told them would happen.

A form of subtle but highly enraged mutiny was taking place. They also had not seen Gordon for weeks now, and this was a thing which now was extremely confusing them. It had been heard by a couple of them that he had been intending to go out there along with the couple being prepared for Mars sample collecting. Some believed though that they had heard Steven talking to Gordon still, somehow, or at least it seemed that way, but most could no longer fully believe that. Did that make sense at all? they wondered. What did make sense to them? Not much at all now, it seemed. They had been used, tricked, abused, left to die possibly. Anything could happen.

'I think we are a useless experiment. We are a rich man's folly. Something to be hidden, denied. We're a waste now, they're no longer interested,' one told the others.

'What if we are contagious? Deadly to others? Too dangerous to ever go back among other people like before now? Poisonous, like lepers? We'll be killed off quickly when others know about us. For everyone else's safety, but not ours,' another said.

'Just keep calm. Steven is looking into things. It's just going to take time still that's all. Have faith in him,' the other replied.

'But we're sick, we're dripping, poisonous sick now. You are – admit it! We sit here, we're getting worse daily. Falling to pieces now. Tragic examples of wasted mistake. Bleeding, coughing, madness, we're ruined people because of those two who now desert us here,' the first said.

The other two watched him anxiously, weary of his next move. They knew by now that he had a strong, wild temper on him, this other patient who would no longer wait for the cure and remedy from Steven and Gordon.

'I'm not sitting here like a fool much longer. No way. I might have been to come here, but I don't have to stay that way now,' he told the others.

He walked around, eyes looking over their surroundings. He seemed intent on finding something useful, some vessel to abuse, break or attack in his pent up rage. Then he suddenly grabbed a chair near him, overturned it, and began kicking at it, with extreme violence, one foot on the bottom leg. It eventually snapped once, then again, breaking, splintering, and he pulled it apart noisily. It was a stump a couple of feet long, jagged and sharp at one end.

'What are you doing Richard?' the patient nearest asked quietly.

'Me? I'm going to make sure we are helped out, and looked after like we expected to begin with,' he replied, tapping the chair leg in his palm.

'Steven doesn't deserve that,' the man said.

'No? I think Gordon definitely does, and his son, well – like father like son. He probably used him. Both deserve so much now, a high level of bruising,' the man said.

He stepped around the table, looking thoughtful, thinking through his actions, he would carry out with some sadistic vengeance.

'You're not up to this. You have been ill too, you know that. Hurt them, and we'll all be in an even bigger even more desperate mess than we are now. We will,' the other man warned.

'I may be sick, but it needs doing, I swear and none of you seem to have much spine right now,' he said, pointing the chair leg at them.

The two men looked at each other with tense animosity between them. They waited, then eventually quietly nodded, in some silent agreement. Two then suddenly rushed at the one with the chair leg. He tried to strike out at them, shouting and swearing at them. They all fell, coughing and wheezing painfully while punching at each other. They struggled to stand, muscles aching, coughing drops of blood around them each in turn.

'See... see, how... how we are. Richard?' one said while standing up then.

'I... know... you fool, but still...' he answered with anger.

The other pulled the chair leg from him, very easily then. All three of them were obviously exhausted by the struggle, like many decades older than they actually were physically. They were all angry with their dire situation in their own ways, but honestly just wanted to take back what had been taken, what they had agreed to months earlier. For some it might be too late, but some still had in them a burning wild anger, and Steven knew little of it.

For a talented but arrogant wealthy man in his mid-fifties, Richard now felt like a man nearing eighty in his physical body, a few of his senses deteriorating more and more because of these mad bastard scientists businessmen, he thought. Perhaps he did not have the energy to physically threaten Steven or Gordon now, but what of the other ways? he wondered. He was a very intelligent man, who had in lifetime managed his own business of trading and producing electrical appliances in computer industries. There had been times he had been very callous, fast thinking and even nasty to fellow businessmen and women who trusted him. His company had to come first, even while he did feel bad initially years ago. Times changed, people hardened up, had to think quick, take risks. He could see how Gordon and Steven worked, admired some of it he thought, but that was them, and this was a very different situation. He was a commodity to them. It changed everything. He remembered a good few tricks he had used in his own work, and he took time to consider what might work now.

Did he pose a threat in more unrealised ways to them? Did they not even see that he thought? It really could be possibly that he and the others hidden away really were poisonous, contagious disease ridden vermin, just as many thought of the known attackers back down on earth. Steven would not want to be like that would he? Wild, savage, memory and senses disappearing gradually, intelligence and personal character lost to uncertain primeval thing? That was his threat, Richard thought finally. But was it absolutely true? Well, Steven did always seem to keep his distance from all of them when around, never really seen to come too close to any at all, Richard thought. Steven must believe it himself, or at least fear it to be very possible. That was enough, he thought.

Evening arrived on the station as determined by computers and clocks around, all other patients resting quietly mostly, while Richard remained wide awake silently hidden, waiting and listening for the return of Steven. He hid close to his room, calm and thinking of his words, his moves to take when the time came. So much time passed so slowly, minutes filling with wasted paranoid ambition. Where was Steven he wondered? Would he not return this night at all? God damn him, Richard thought. He really thought he had the bastard nailed, that he had been able to predict the movements and comings and goings well enough. Then a sound, a click and opening, and light spread out thinly over the wall to his right in the dark room. The door was opening, someone entering. Steven, it had to be, he knew it.

The person stepped in quietly, moving carefully. Richard moved in close and silent then, the time finally arrived.

'Listen to me,' he said in a low but aggressive whisper.

'Who is it?' the person asked.

'This is Richard, Steven. You know me. You will listen to what I am going to tell you,' he explained.

The door closed behind then, both then in total darkness, unaware of where each other stood precisely.

'I will listen gladly,' Steven replied in a calm manner.

'Yes. We know more than you think. We are not pleased here, not now. We feel forgotten do you realise? Lied to, tricked in many ways. We will not take this easily now – do you understand me?' Richard said.

'I understand. What do you want then?' Steven asked.

'What can you offer now, without more lies?' Richard said.

'I am sorry, but I still offer what I have promised. But to get there you could be more involved I suppose,' Steven told him.

'What do you mean?'

'I am encountering some frustrating difficulties I admit, and so, well, if there are some possibly such as yourself who would be willing to help me simply take what we need when we need it, you will all receive what you desire much quicker,' Steven explained.

'I may agree to that offer. I shall consider it. We will meet tomorrow, and you will know my decision. We may be not in the best of health now, but be warned we are sharp people – we can be a force dangerous still,' Richard told him.

'I hope so. Goodnight. See you tomorrow then,' Steven replied.

They parted in the dark shadows in the doorway area, neither seeing the reactions their words brought to the other.

Richard had made his threat, well enough, he believed. He knew Steven seemed a stubborn self-centred sort, and his decision would be his fate. Was he afraid of Richard now? The thought of becoming of one the wasted, obsolete attackers in only hours from the moment? He should be, Richard thought as he returned to his solitude.

Chapter 25

It had all seemed now to have been so much prolonged exhausting effort, struggling against the approaching numerous wild and unpredictable attackers now sadly with them out there. I should give up, Jane thought. Part of her considered it, throwing the towel in, let things just fall to pieces. Others would have to then try to solve the problem, they should. Why should she do it all alone? she thought. It would be just so easy, satisfying in some helpless, regular way. She sat down alone, thinking of her next move and casually felt around in her jacket pocket. There was something in there which she did not remember collecting. She pulled out then a piece of paper. She unfolded it curiously to find a handwritten letter, addressed to her.

"JANE-

I have been quietly impressed by your strong spirit and determination recently. Alan certainly should be thinking himself a very lucky guy. Yes, I have made mistakes here, I think you know what I mean. You know enough, I think you will survive now.

Honestly,
STEVEN."

It was a shocking find, and pleasing somehow. It disturbed her, but she supposed made her now more confident in some way. She had been right, he knew it. But how much did he know, she wondered? Was it a trick he was playing, jealous and desperate to keep her down she wondered?

She would know very shortly. He would know her response, if he had not also guessed it himself by then.

Steven had seen the journey out to Mars, thought about what that could allow. He urgently needed to talk to Mark, to ask him closely about what he had witnessed, if there had been any strange things, shapes, places, anything. He had to know this, and soon. He knew the pods locations, knew who was going next, and had an idea of what could be gained. He just needed to really know the importance and relevance of Mars, in connection to his father. If it was special for Gordon, it was special for him now. It had to be.

The next pod journey began like the previous one, same build up, same launch. Two more scientists were taken out there, and they too were just as astonished. They stepped out, onto the strange landscape of Mars – something happened, though. There was a problem somehow. The male scientist there, Gary Shields, found his air mask had ripped, and immediately he panicked like crazy. So did the female scientist Jenifer, who tried to see the problem. She radioed back to the space station.

'His mask is broken! It's damaged! Shit, holy shit, help us!' she yelled.

On the surface of Mars, two humans stood running as much as was possible in circles, hysterical fear and dread controlling them, losing their minds or even lives in the next few minutes.

The moment passed. They did not die. Gary, after panicking in a manic fever, eventually found he could somehow breathe as easily as normal, standing there on Mars. Jenifer simply stood in similar shock looking back at him, trying to comprehend the meaning of it.

'Why? How? What has happened?' he asked.

She shook her head, no words that could explain it in any way to him.

Brian, Andrew and others at the space station messaged them.

'What's going on? Jenifer? Gary? Gary?' Brian said in confusion.

'He's alive. Fine, breathing,' Jenifer told them.

'He's fine? Really? Gary, you okay there?' Brian asked.

A short wait but finally the reply came.

'Yes... I... I feel just normal. I feel okay,' he told them all back at the station.

'Okay. Well, look don't take any chances, get back inside the pod right now. Jenifer you get samples, if you want but very quickly. Monitor Gary, then return back to us, okay?' Brian told them.

'Yes, of course,' Jenifer replied, her voice delicate and faltering.

When the pair did return hours later, everyone was silent with awe, amazed to see Gary, all wanting to look at him, talk him, close up, face to face. He was taken to be observed, tested and to rest from the unexpected trauma. Elsewhere, Brian and Andrew sat with Jenifer to discuss the occurrence.

'How do you think it happened?' he asked immediately, understanding that she had been also severely shocked on Mars beside Gary.

'I've no idea. Our suits and masks obviously can't be trusted totally,' she said, guessing.

'Right, okay, that is possibly true,' Brian agreed.

'Possibly? We almost died over there, from some mistake with the production of the suits to blame,' she argued carefully.

'We need to think of Gary,' Andrew reminded them.

'Like he's a useful specimen? It was an accident. He's just... Leave him alone. That's not the point of all this, being here,' Jenifer said, but was unsure of her own words' truth as she said them.

'No, maybe not but then... We should consider all new evidence, new findings in any way, wherever they should arise from, in all honesty,' Andrew told her flatly.

'No, we just... got it wrong. Look, at least Gary is okay now. That's the point,' she said. She felt tears beginning to fall from her eyes, and then stormed out of the room in unrestrained anger.

Another room held Gary, relaxed now, though contemplative in mood. A mixture of drugs eased his anxious fear and confused anger to the events. He still managed to have some simple wonder at what had happened, why and how he had survived on Mars. Was it him, or was it Mars? Was he different or was Mars different to the things they had believed for decades previously about the environment and chemical state of the planet? he wondered dreamily.

Suddenly then, Steven and Suzanne entered the room, with sympathetic smiles as they approached him.

'Hello Gary – you are looking very well, thankfully. How are you feeling?' Suzanne asked.

'I feel confused, embarrassed, but grateful really. I don't know. Damn lucky maybe,' he told them.

'Don't feel physically different?' Steven asked.

'Physically? Well... I do feel better now, I think. Maybe more awake, kind of. Not sure. Better now though, I suppose,' he said.

'You were scared, up there immediately?' Suzanne asked.

'What? Well yes, I thought... I mean, it was scary. Very. Brave enough to be here, in space but not to just freely walk on Mars...' he said.

'But... You perhaps just did that very thing,' Steven noted.

'Yes. Who knows how?' Gary said.

'Okay, well, look – we're going to give you some injections, vitamins, stabilisers, and more... Make sure you metabolism is right, blood sugar you know? But please call for us anytime if you want to talk. I'll come by straight away, either of us,' Suzanne told him.

'Alright, but look, I'm no damn guinea pig yet. Just had a strange accident,' he told them.

'Yes, that's right. Rest up then, easy now. See you later, okay?' Steven said to him, and he and Suzanne left Gary alone in the room.

Walking between the zone area corridors, Jane saw some shadow of a person down the other end moving. She walked on, curious. The movement was irregular, unusual, like someone in pain or performing some strange physical act. As she walked on, the shape of the person was more defined, coming into focus sharper in the dark shadows. There was a disturbing silhouette before her, unlike any other she had seen while on the space station. She stopped walking then, stepped back a couple of paces, unsure. Was it someone she knew, hurt or dressed differently? An accident of some kind perhaps? she thought.

'Hello?' she finally said, approaching the dark figure in shadow ahead of her.

The jagged hunched outline of a person in shadow froze static, motionless suddenly. This almost disturbed her even further. It had seen her.

'Hello, who's that?' she called out.

Still the quiet continued, no audible response. Finally, the shadowed figure suddenly rushed away in a flash movement, and went back around the corridor.

The shocking complicated problems during the second minor journey to Mars had created growing, difficult arguments and tensions among the majority of people on the station. Now the control of Brian, Andrew and Suzanne was being questioned at first quietly with civil discussion but soon enough with overblown unrestrained statements and shouting. Individual separate groups from the zone areas wanted answers, wanted to have guidance, reassurance. Some then approached Steven, as he was the last scientist in the main leader group who had been quiet about his thoughts on the events.

'Tell us what you think. What do you think we should all do from now on?' one person from the endurance area asked on behalf of many there.

'You want to know my opinion?' he asked, seeming surprised but not in reality.

'You are one of the group specifically in control through talent and experience. Yes, tell us your view of our future now,' the man at the front said to him.

Steven looked around at them, pleased with the naive interest in his thoughts.

'I say... we take our time. Keep working as we have done. But Gary, on Mars... I think there's more to it. More to him, and to us. We need to look at ourselves. Maybe we're seeing things previously ignored...' he slyly suggested to the eager crowd.

'What do you mean?' another man up front enquired.

'Let's keep open minds, shall we? We could be easily frightened by unusual sights, happenings... but we're already in space, moving out in giant steps.'

'But the safety, the equipment on the station... Can we trust the rest of it now? Should we if we want to escape in any dangerous event?' the man asked.

'Can we trust ourselves? We need to be more honest – with ourselves, our tests, experiments – we need to open up and not fool our potential. It is definitely much greater than we at first believed, I think now,' he explained.

Steven was back to the bold, big sound bite statements, hyped polemics, and dramatic overstating he used to make back on Earth once more, which had been reliable personal strength. They saw this, some of them, but they also wanted to hear it right then. In the bleak loneliness of space, they wanted guidance, leadership.

'Maybe you should have more control, Steven,' the man said. Others then suddenly cheered aloud unexpectedly in unison.

Over the next few hours the population of the station cast votes. While Suzanne and Brian and others tried to warn of the rash defiance and danger of this reaction, the structure of control over the space station was realigned. Now the majority elected Steven beside Brian in all further decisions. He was quietly extremely very pleased with the decision of the space station population. Things would be so much easier. All kinds of things.

Steven returned to the hidden quarters in a greater mood and met Gordon in the dark light soon enough.

'Hey, things are getter much better. We've gone to Mars. One man breathed there, survived, we're studying him intensively. Progress like nothing else!' he announced.

Gordon stared back, half eclipsed in shadow, still ghoulish and decaying away.

'That... is... something. But what next.... then?' he uttered slowly.

'What? Give me a chance. Okay, I can set up more. I will, as far as it all can go, further,' Steven replied defiantly.

'You think... so?' Gordon said, taunting him.

'Look, how far did you ever go with it? Just how far?' Steven asked. 'Nowhere, no damn place at all, right? Until now, here with me.'

'Wrong... Nineteen... eighty... four,' Gordon said.

What did this mean? Steven thought. Another elaborate, provocative trick from his father?

'What happened then?' Steven asked, as if not too interested.

Gordon moved between darkness of shadow and moonlight, sniffing, yawning.

'I feel... pain now. Not... too long... now,' he told Steven.

'Come on, answer me old man. If you want me to know...' Steven said.

Gordon simply slunk away, hunched down, thin and crooked out of view once more. I will know, Steven thought. Truth or lies, I'll know what can be achieved by achieving it soon enough, he thought as the old obsolete man disappeared.

Chapter 26

In the quiet cool white medical rest rooms, Gary lay on the bed with his thoughts returning, logic and reason piecing back into his drugged mind. He thought about how he had almost died on Mars, a total alien planet, but lived. Completely unexplained, unexpected, a shocking bizarre event. He had survived, breathed... air? Or in some other unknown way managed to exist without his air mask helmet protecting him. Was it him then, his body, his organs different, special, and able to live on Mars like no other? Why and how? It was the only thought on his mind from then on.

He was different, he surmised. That was it. That was why he had come back alive after the shocking accident. A revelation was what it was. From that though, he of course, realised that this meant he was to be seen as very unique, a valuable specimen, a lab rat of human proportions. If he could breathe or exist freely on the surface of Mars, he then thought... what else could he do?

He needed tests, an extensive examination, he realised. Should he just let others poke him, sample him, as much as was necessary now, hand himself over for greater scientific knowledge now, he thought? How much choice did he honesty have?

As he lay pondering the right way asked for himself, Brian and Steven entered the room.

'Hello Gary. How are you now?' Brian asked sympathetically.

'Better, I think yes, a bit calmer now,' he told them.

'Well good, very good. Right, I'm sure you probably can guess what the leadership control team might be considering doing, following what you experienced. Do not be worried – we are all here to learn, but are all friends, peers and human beings with understanding, compassion and feelings. Yes, we discovered some interesting things on Mars, but we'll look into it as carefully and humanely as we can, okay?' Brian explained.

'Okay, thank you. I really appreciate that, I really do. So what are the next steps?' Gary asked with audible nervousness.

Steven moved in closer toward him then.

'Yeah, relax mate. We're going to look after you all the way. It's all going to be very easy-going stuff okay? You just watch some films, read a book or whatever in the meantime alright?' Steven suggested.

'Okay, thanks Steven. That's reassuring to hear. I'll trust you,' Gary replied.

That was just what Steven needed to hear and expected to hear, especially right in front of Brian then.

They left Gary alone and walked out together.

'Steven, I get the impression that a lot of people are almost ready to blame me or Andrew for the accident on Mars, but we were checking everything. Sometimes accidents happen,' Brian told Steven.

'I know, don't worry about it. He's back, living, breathing. No real problem, really,' Steven told him.

'You know, you can do many things now you're with us in a bigger way,' Brian said.

'I know, but wait – with you? They have elected me... right, okay?' Steven said. He saw that Brian was not letting go easily of the control across the station.

Being on Mars, if possible would mean starting again, from the beginning. New lives, new societies. A chance to begin and learn from humankind's sins, mistakes, and wrong steps. New resources and opportunity ahead of them. Could they, mankind hold back this time? Restrain themselves, respect their surrounding environment, each other, less overindulging in wasteful lifestyles, wasteful endless production of consumer items, damaging their own existence once again? Was it all to be possible? If so, were they prepared?

Or was it just too good to be true? To move from one planet to another when the first had been drained, used, abused beaten down beyond repair remorselessly?

What was the difference with Mars? Would it allow which had not been possible on Earth? Who would rule there? Who should? The ones who claim it, begin populating it and understand how to exist there?

Steven looked at him, then away, smiling to himself.

'Really? Well thanks Brian. That's much appreciated. Really is,' Steven said.

Things were working out well now, he thought. Very well enough for changes and surprises.

Eventually Steven made his way back along into the chambers of the hidden secret patients, who waited for him and positive news.

'Here he is, the wandering charmer schemer himself,' one of them said, seeing him walk back in through the entrance.

'Watch it, I'm not in the mood, okay?' Steven snapped at him.

'You're not in the mood? Shame, that is. Hey, trapped in dark claustrophobic squalor are you? Treated like some lower species specimen waiting for the inevitable torture and examination?' the man asked.

'Give it a rest. You have the same food, space and life as everyone on this bloody metal space village here, no different,' Steven told him and passed him by quickly.

He continued on down through toward the main study room and his desks with research and notes laid out still. In the room, a woman stood leaning by the wall and watched him walk in.

'Steven, how are things outside?' she asked, startling him suddenly.

'Oh, Gloria... you well? Yes, there are interesting things happening. You'll all be out very soon enough,' he replied, attempting to keep her pleased.

'You think so?' she asked. 'And we'll all be well, fit, as good as ever?' She moved out toward him around the desks, up close then, watching his eyes, his expression and response to her words. 'Steven, we are very grateful for what you have done with us so far,' she told him.

'I am glad that's what you feel, really I am,' he replied. 'All of you feel that?'

'Yes, but Steven, you do think of us, don't you, as people?' she asked.

'Right, yes, of course I do,' he said.

She leaned in, looked him in the eyes, then brushed his hair as she pouted seductively, her shirt open a couple of buttons down, he saw.

'Tell me what's happening? What's going to happen to all of us soon?' she asked.

'You know don't you? And it is happening. We're pushing the boundaries. We won't decay and get old early, and we'll stop many diseases that have crippled us and shortened our lives for too long now. It's all there, even on Mars – different chemicals, minerals, different possibilities of being. Real health, real existence, the lives we actually deserve. We, who've come this far now,' he explained to her.

'You're so thoughtful. Thank you then, Steven. You're sure of it all, then?' she said.

'We sent a couple to Mars three days ago. Then another two. They returned. Fantastic results back actually. They're being analysed now, so bear with me – just days and we'll all be moving along amazingly. That okay?' he said.

'Sounds promising. Are you promising?' she asked, moving even closer up to him, right next to his face, her chest on his. He felt her breathing, her heart beating close on him. Her breath in his ear, her closeness.

'I promise, I am promising, yes... I mean, certainly,' he responded.

He looked at her, into her sad hopeful eyes.

That night Steven experienced more uncomfortable, stressed sleep. A kind of nightmare or a surreal but topical dream haunted his unconscious mind until morning. He had returned to Mars again. Walking around freely, inspecting the terrain, the dark red rocks, crumbled open vistas all around. New hope, new potential. Unmarked land, untapped resources ahead of him there. No mistakes on this empty land, no bloodshed, genocide or wars yet. There were hills, mountains almost. He walked on, it seemed almost floating around, looking for something. Then he caught sight of a figure ahead, as impossible as it could be. This had happened before, he thought. Or it had been dreamt before.

The figure ran away, too fast behind mountains, rocks somewhere. Steven ran after needing to meet the person, to know who it was, how they were there too, and why. He ran, running hard and fast. He made it around the other side of wide hills, and came to find some kind of curious collection of things. He walked up, a little exhausted and knelt down to see properly. It was a small number of machines, metal boxes, which seemed man-made. They looked slightly old, vintage. Then a voice suddenly shouted out to him from behind. He spun around, shocked.

'Wake up Steven'

'What? Who?' he said, eyes opening slowly.

'Open... your... eyes... space god.'

It was Gordon, growling down at him.

'Jesus, father, I was asleep,' Steven answered.

'I know. So... what? No... time. Enough... relaxing,' Gordon told him.

'I am having some fucked up dreams, you know,' Steven told him sheepishly.

'Letting... it get... to you,' Gordon replied with a more tired voice.

Steven ignored the remark and got out of bed, then walked over to the desks. He looked over his files and notes, deciding what should be done next. He should stop at no sympathy for poor Gary, he thought. Was he finally becoming soft now that he himself was the one closely exacting the revolutionary acts? The times of simply watching Gordon doing such shocking, immoral acts in the name of science were truly behind him. There were many people on the space station, some he knew fairly well, and others he did respect academically, but now it just came down to the final acts of radical scientific experimentation to be done – it would be for their good, he told himself as he looked at his pale, weakened face in a mirror opposite the desk. What a truly exhausted face, an image of haunted confusion for a man to be a legend of future times, he thought.

'Use what you can... now,' Gordon told him in a faltering but stern voice.

'Yes, father, you're right,' Steven replied.

The whole area of the space station was by then feeling much more unsafe, each scientist unable to stop thinking in an irregularly illogical paranoid manner against their better judgement and great levels of education.

'We need to really think about who is leading us here,' one woman said as a large group of scientists congregated in the main recreation area four.

'We lead ourselves,' another replied.

'No, there's the four in charge, with Brian and Andrew, Suzanne messing it up, then Steven,' he told them.

'No, not totally just...'

'Yes, what about Suzanne and Steven? They could do more. They could lead. And Steven, he seems much more clever than at first, really.'

'Do you think?'

'No, she's right. He's said things that really sound right – about Mars, Gary, the mission, all of us here. He knows his stuff I think. Yes.'

They were all agreeing about the things that Steven was saying every few days – his suggested ideas, comments, and observations concerning events recently. He seemed a very likely leader, a clear minded, focused bold young man who knew what really could be achieved, unlike the others most were beginning to believe. They could all definitely trust him, it seemed. Perhaps they even had to. Andrew and Brian were soon enough confronted near the data collection buildings by a very large restless mob needing to make their case for change.

'Step down,' one shouted.

'We want change,' another said.

'We need different leaders now, or else,' another added.

'What? What's all this?' Brian asked, shocked and anxious seeing the approaching large crowd coming tight around them then.

'You both of you are not leading us from right now,' one woman at the front explained.

'Wait, everyone, just calm down. We all need to discuss this peacefully okay?' Andrew told them.

'Done that. This is the answer – you're both out. Sorry.'

'No, we know how to organise the station, the entire project as it is,' Brian argued.

'And as it is, we have had greatly dangerous results. Time for someone else to try,' the woman said.

'It has changed. We want someone else. You are just moving down in position in the team,' one stated.

'Steven will lead us. He knows what is needed more than anyone,' the woman explained confidently.

Andrew and Brian looked back with regret and turned away with no fight.

'Really? Leading the project?' Steven said, hearing the news from a scientist who had found him in the data selection rooms area.

'Yes, we have all decided this. With Suzanne beside you, and Brian and Andrew only now taking lower roles. Everyone believes this could be much more positive for the project.'

'And so how do you think we should continue forward now?' Steven asked, trying to sound open to any ideas.

'Don't you have a few ideas of how to take things forward now, after the first Mars journeys? From here, with the things we have collected,' the man said.

'You have the best ideas most of the time,' another man there added.

'Right. You believe so? Well okay, let's take it all forward. I do see potential we might have ignored so far. We know about Gary, we're investigating it now. As for how things were... Let me then organise a new approach forward with Suzanne,' he told them as she entered the rooms and saw them explaining things to him.

She seemed hesitant, possibly reluctant to visibly join in leadership with Steven. She already disliked him, his attitude and approach to working, his almost sexist character. But she did join him, because she could she how she herself could find new positive angles on this partnership ahead.

Jane watched this new leadership beginning – the mass majority agreement about Steven and Suzanne taking over control of the space station after the miscalculated mistakes caused by Brian and Andrew apparently. It all made her uneasy and she was shocked at everyone just so easily wanting Steven to lead them, knowing his reckless attention-seeking behaviour witnessed already. Not shocked, she then thought – saddened. Could not easily convince everyone just how unreliable he might be to them all in a very short time. She had seen how he acted around the projects back on Earth, and how Alan had been guiding them generally. Steven though, did seem to have some strange concepts in mind often, bizarre scientific theories that had disturbing and often possibly unethical leanings to them. It might have just been his sense of humour, being provocative as he often was, she considered. He saddened her now.

Jane did not believe that Steven would be able to keep all of the project going well, which frustrated her instantly. She was working so hard, her and many others. Besides this, herself and many others wanted to know more about how Gary was, and how he had survived on Mars. His return alive made her begin to question their health, and safety on the station much more closely from then on.

The change of control was decided, and so the next few days saw Suzanne organising different structure and communication across the station, with help at irregular intervals from Steven, and Brian and Andrew only just observing and offering basic opinions. It was all unexpected and difficult to work around, Jane thought to herself. She could handle trouble, things not being entirely as expected but this was a place hopefully without aggressive, uneducated working class bigots, itching for trouble. It was a different place. So distant, removed from familiar people, places, class tensions and regular problems, with any luck. If she was just simply homesick then fine, but she knew she was seeing some things that did not make sense. She was not pleased with Steven having a position of very great power on the station and she seemed the only one to think these thoughts at present.

Chapter 27

There were now at least a dozen or more on the space station who were experiencing some intense sickness, headaches, stomach pains, or slight fever. Nothing obvious to them, after a few basic initial tests carried out, but it was spreading fast though still individually each scientist was concerned and troubled between them they spoke little of it, each simply believing it to be short one-off symptoms. Besides the physical ailments, some could almost swear they had observed very strange unusual sightings around various parts of the station. Was it the confusion of being so far from home, so detached, removed from home, from Earth? They took breaks from their daily routines to recuperate and rest for short periods, and even then their own minds were such uncontrollable things it seemed. Some could not keep focus, some saw dots before their eyes on and off, blurred vision, shadows on the walls, even maybe strange whispers. One or two even mentioned possibly seeing specific figures – a hunched, tattered old man maybe, then also just maybe even the shape of a very young small girl running away up the corridors.

Shared mental confusion or paranoia? Were these psychosomatic subconscious images, signifiers of repressed thoughts, unified fears of poisoning from food or water or something else? Thoughts or their own family or friends or loved ones they simply missed too much or feared for so far away from them? These were some of the logical initial scientific answers they gave themselves to cope naturally, but they were still subtly disturbed. They saw a girl – too many of them saw her. It made no sense in any logical way whatsoever and it frightened each and every one who saw her. They saw her out of the windows soon, in deep black space. Then gone just as suddenly.

Some scientists walked through areas quickly, continually nervous and afraid. Their own personal logical perceptions of the station and space around them could not fully explain or help their tormented minds then.

'Paul, I just am not exactly sure what is happening here,' one man told another.

'Well, that goes for all of us, I'd say. It's a fucking mess. Just as bad as right back down on earth it seems. Bloody mess it is. We'll have to all get together in some safe area, but then how do we know if we'll have blocked out...' the other man was saying, when they both saw across the area the shocking sight of such confusion. Two tall red skinned people, naked, one almost female, the other possible male, were standing watching them.

'What the hell...? Jesus Christ in Heaven...' the first scientist said.

'Who... are they...?' the other began but lost his thought.

They watched the two alien figures as they too stood observing them for a long held moment. Then the taller red figure opened his mouth, black pupils of his eyes staring, and let out an unexpected loud shriek, some kind of scream.

'Move, let's run,' the first scientist suggested.

The other was in agreement and they fled right then, not looking back.

In the closed off room, with plenty of useful utensils, tools and devices to inspect with, Steven watched Gary lying quietly, occasionally moaning in his sleep. Gary woke then and was very surprised to see Steven looking down at him with a friendly face.

'Hello again. Feeling good?' Steven asked chirpily.

'Oh well, yes. Just about,' Gary said. 'How are things around the station?'

'It's going very well yes. A few changes actually, all for the best. But good progress on the horizon I believe,' Steven told him.

'That's great then. Steven, look, I've been thinking while I've been resting the last couple of days. This is going to sound probably very strange but... I think I want to go back... to Mars,' Gary explained.

'Okay. Well, look, you will when you're one hundred percent. That will be alright at some stage, I am sure. You will join the others, where you were before,' Steven told him.

'No, you don't get me – back to Mars. I think it is important for me, and us. Think about it. The way I am,' Gary suggested.

Steven certainly had been thinking about it privately in his chambers with the hidden patients. Should he send Gary back – use him, push him further on Mars, test just how different Gary was? But he was special and unique – or was he? How different was Gary from the others, waiting to be released right then? he thought. He knew that answer, or believed he did.

Steven was so very proud of what had happened to Gary, how he had developed so far. It was a very useful occurrence. Could he risk losing him now though, before the others were out? He had been studying all medical scans, samples and readings from Gary over the last forty-eight hours with close precision. He was seeing things which looked very hopeful – an almost kind of mutation of DNA within Gary, beyond present experimentation with the other patients, and change and progress of inner immune system, which could potentially suggest long term existence freely on Mars. He was seeing the difference between Gary and the patients hidden on the station as a significant sign of sorts. There were better signs in him – less mistakes, more improvements. His own work, more than Gordon had offered to him, he knew.

But could he seem to easily adapt the biological make-up of Gary now into these waiting, hidden away? They had invested much to him, paid him good sums of money, shares, trust personally in his offered promises he had sold them so convincingly.

He gravely doubted it. They were just perhaps redundant, finished with. It really could be a true possibility he knew, even thought it would mean a waste of his time, their travelling to the space station from Earth. Even their own individual health ahead of them was unsure, Steven thought, and he could not completely be able to save them. They might begin a slow, painful decline, falling away as simply beginning of a larger experiment, knowing they played a part in some way. Gary was the new key for Steven, following the theories of Gordon previously.

As around him all others were arguing and deciding how to remain safe, Steven walked back to the chambers discreetly, to ease his heavy weighing confused thoughts on his mind. He was beginning to almost think that he could be too weak in ways, that he really had fooled himself about how much he was capable of on the station. Along the dark narrow corridors he found the shadow of his father.

'Father, the patients are defying me now. Restless, annoying, miserable ones. But you know... I really could swear... Are you thinking of Lucy?' Steven said to his father.

'You have seen her?' Gordon asked.

'Well, I don't know. Could that actually really be?'

Gordon smiled back enigmatically.

'What do you think now? Do not worry my boy. They will stay in line for you,' he told him.

'I wish I believed it. I don't really think... It could be getting too much, I mean this is just me. My friend's on the university Master's project back home... I left them and I should have worked it out, I think. I really should have,' Steven said.

'It is fine. Forget that. Go rest for a few hours,' Gordon suggested with a knowledgeable smile.

'I'll go rest for a few hours,' Steven then slowly repeated word for word and then walked off alone.

He slept soundly, very easily for nearly six hours. He woke feeling better, and walked around his small chamber with returned optimism in some amount. The kettle was boiled for coffee, and he looked around for a snack to eat. He stood by the left wall and looked through the main door, down the narrow corridor and out beyond to the area zone outside. Into the corridor a small figure moved suddenly there. He moved closer to the door, looked more closely and watched with interest. The figure turned, stepping out gradually in half shadow. The frosted door glass hindered his view as he observed quietly. It turned, revealing a face – Lucy. Was it her? It really did look like his little sister Lucy out there in the corridor ahead. He opened his eyes wider, moved right up next to the glass door, shocked and looked away. He was ashamed at his stupidity, his foolish mind. Was his own sanity leaving him now? Could he no longer manage the pressure of the grand project he was involved in? Was this it? he thought. He had to know, to be certain of his state of mind, of what was fact and what was fiction before his eyes.

He opened the door carefully and quietly. Silently he moved up the corridor, so careful. She moved off immediately then, gone around the corner up ahead. He reached the end soon enough, turned the corner – no soul there in view ahead. Gone so fast. The girl, and maybe even his sanity.

The many talented scientists of various kinds continued the epic project, with Suzanne and Steven making the next decisions for them all. In time, they were all told that much incoming communication from Earth was receiving radio troubles, and possibly their own messages back were being distorted on sending them.

'That just can't happen,' one scientist said.

'We'll be fucked. Sorry, but we can't be left with no connection back to Earth,' another said.

'They know where we are, our coordinates, and they possibly see us still too. We'll be safe enough. We can communicate, only with some difficulty for now, but it will hopefully pass,' Suzanne told everyone at a meeting.

'Are we getting what we need yet?' Jane called out from among the crowd of scientists.

'Yes, we need to preserve it but we have certainly found much to interest us,' Steven told her then as he stood confidently beside Suzanne on the podium.

'Like what exactly? We all have a right to know,' Jane said.

'Okay, evidence of enhanced and boosted immune systems, biogenetic strengthening, breathing enhancement, among other findings. We should be proud, but keep working hard,' he explained.

'What about Gary?' another shouted.

It was a question Steven expected and wished to avoid, but knew it would come.

'He's doing well, alright, better now after a lot of rest,' Steven explained.

'Why is he alive at all?' another enquired.

Some looked at the person, as if a known taboo was uttered then, but all wanted the answer.

'He actually allowed us to... do tests within his chest, and with certain blood supplements. The result was... lifesaving,' Steven told them.

'You rigged his mask and space suit?' Jane said aloud and garnered shocked looks from all around her.

'Ha. Oh dear, no, not at all. But it happened like that, and it showed us hope,' he answered.

'Can he survive on Mars then? Live there?' another asked.

'We can't be sure of it. He'll stay here, safe with us. We'll simply keep doing what we're doing until the proposed time to return comes,' Suzanne told them.

Steven looked at her. She gave him a cold glance in return. He should be wary of her, he thought. She was definitely suspicious of him, and seemed to watch his behaviour far too closely. He had not minded so far, as he quite admittedly found her fascinatingly attractive intensely. He'll give her something to watch, he thought to himself. The attraction between them would be tested as far as it could go, he decided.

While Steven walked between area zones, checking the specific work happening he turned a corner and suddenly met Gary alone.

'Steven, I need to talk,' Gary told him.

'Hey why are you out of bed pal?' Steven asked. 'That's no good for you at the minute. You need rest, and we haven't finished our examination of you completely yet, you know that,' Steven told him.

'I know but I feel really good you see. Not very ill much at all. And Steven, I said last time, Mars – I do want to go back. Because I can – me, and only me for some reason. That's right isn't it? I am some special gift, maybe from... from God,' Gary said.

'Okay, right look, come with me. We'll talk back at the rest quarters,' Steven told him, taking him by the arm lightly.

Minutes later, they arrived back there and Steven locked the doors while Gary looked around and sat on the bed again.

'Okay now, Gary. We'll discuss how things can go, shall we?' Steven began.

Gary nodded looked at him, innocently waiting, and then Steven began. Steven walked around the bed, and as he did so, looked down at the tables and cupboards alongside, checking the instruments and utensils held there for operations and procedures.

'You have to really consider what has happened Gary, with perspective and objectivity from personal experience,' Steven explained.

'I have done, really. I understand your point, but I need to go back. This is probably my destiny, without wanting to sound corny. My body has been designed for this. I could be the bridge for us, to living there,' Gary suggested.

'Maybe... Yes, that could be right. I understand what you are saying, I do,' Steven began while walking around the room, behind Gary looking at the tables, workbenches, desks around them. 'I do see how eager you now are, that's very admirable indeed,' he continued, 'but right now unnecessary.'

Steven then produced a pair of extremely sharp knives, and thrust them urgently from opposite sides deep into Gary's throat, violently with rage. Blood poured out all over the floor as Steven stepped back, shocked at his own actions just then. He held the knives and ran out, quickly away down the corridors. Minutes later, he reached the hidden rooms and locked himself in securely, his bloodied hands turning the locks shut securely.

'Your blood?' a voice asked.

He turned and saw Gordon looking back, haggard and revolting in appearance, but still smiling at him.

'No, not.... Not... his... Not mine... his...' Steven stammered in a rush of hyperventilating tension. He looked around, fearful of others seeing him like that, in such a shocking and horrific state.

'We're alone. Just... us,' Gordon told him.

'Just us?' Steven asked, in some way not entirely pleased with the sound of the words.

'Where are the others?' he asked.

'Some here, some there, some hiding far from care,' Gordon said, a twisted macabre riddle of sorts.

'What's that mean, then?' Steven asked.

'Change. Change... We wanted,' Gordon told him.

'No, not yet. What have you... Not time yet, is it?' Steven said, panicked. He ran down the cleaning area. He scrubbed the blood from his shaking hands, over and over until it finally seemed gone, his skin sore and swollen.

'Out damn spot... Out' Gordon said, somewhere from behind him.

'Alright, hilarious. Damn hilarious,' Steven said. Finally satisfied his hands were decently enough clean, he then ran around through the corridor of rooms to find his waiting faithful patients.

Chapter 28

Steven slept another dramatic, tormented night of bizarre space voyages in his subconscious mind. He once more found himself walking the lands of Mars, freely if slowly. Looking at the astonishing views around, he walked past hills of red dust, canyons and crevices many miles wide. This time he reached the pile of mysterious metal small boxes again. He did not wake right then, but looked down further, closer. He could see the detail. There were markings on the sides, some vague cryptic symbols. Were they another language he thought, maybe Middle Eastern, or Russian? But that would make no sense, he thought. But then, just how much really was making sense? He stared hard, focused on each symbol... He was then almost sure that he might recognise the symbols from somewhere, some place before from in the real world, from real life sometime. He bent down closer, and touched the metal boxes.

He woke then, dim light of the table lamp vaguely illuminating the bed, table, his disturbed face showing in the tall mirror opposite. He looked haunted, like he had been given serious terrible news only a moment before.

'My dream, or nightmare I suppose, it is still of Mars. I walked Mars, like Gary has. But I saw someone there, then some strange things, boxes, with some codes or symbols...' Steven told Gordon. As he spoke he picked up a knife from down in a box near his small tables by the wall. Turned the blade on his palm, in his hands.

'I... could not see them clearly before they ran off. Then last night in the dream, I found some boxes just out in the vast sand landscape of Mars. Strange symbols, almost like some Earth language, but... not anything I recognised... But still familiar in some way,' Steven told him.

'A... mystery,' Gordon said.

'I'm so sorry,' Steven said looking away from him, with difficult pain in his face.

'I know. I... know,' Gordon said.

The wrinkles, the sagging skin on his old beaten face seemed to in some way decay much faster, crumbling, flaking in places, tearing at the sides as he painfully smiled at Steven.

'Sorry you... Sorry you died back there,' Steven said softly, so quiet as he held back tears and then struck out, punched at the mirror, cracking the glass into large fractured pieces in the frame, some falling to the floor near his feet.

'God have mercy,' Gordon said to him.

He disappeared finally then, a quick flash of decay and dust in the shadows of the quiet dark room. Steven stood alone finally.

'God save our wretched souls,' he said aloud to himself alone, then looking at his bloodied knuckles and the shattered glass.

He was one of the very few on his lead space station, who had planned his time and purpose there very far in advance of the journey there. He knew exactly what he was doing and what he was involved in, what would be happening and who was doing what. These stations were new original bold communities of highly focused professional scientifically trained people floating in the encompassing vastness of deep wide unknown majestic dark space. For some there, there was a level of uncontrollable excitement and unpredictable experience, for him thought it was all planned, expected coordinated precisely. This was the ultimate work venture for him, and it was just like the previous ones – he jumped onto another person's initial concept, talked it up, hyped it, met people, fooled others and here it was – life in space. He would be a legend next to Einstein, Galileo, Hawking, and all who had progressed humankind through existence.

There was truth in the work that the many hundreds of citizens on the space stations were involved in, but much of it was a distraction – something hidden, unknown to just about nearly all of them. Steven knew of an experiment behind the experiments known. They were very much important, though not perhaps how they themselves interpreted it. Steven knew it though, he watched it, and waited. He and a very small number of his co-owners of the successful European company – now galactic – timed their secret plans in synchronisation with leaving earth and what came next.

They kept in touch with another team of talented sociological observers and health analysts on Earth. Steven knew the direction that things were due to go on the station to the point of life possibly being highly predictable, boring if not for the endless fame and fortune. He was not just a celebrated now hugely respected and acclaimed scientist globally back on Earth, but he had wanted to know where he could take it next? How famous, how successful, how scientifically powerful could a man become?

There was, he would admit to himself and himself only, the feeling of slight possible guilt. Obviously – to him – he was not always entirely the scientist who found and made every one of the amazing breakthroughs that were associated with him alone by then, but he was always the one to join them all up, publicise and promote them with great success. His own PR man since the beginning, since it was simply just himself and Alan.

That was it. He had many things to consider on a daily basis, as part of the team which orchestrated the work there, but Alan came to his mind repeatedly, even while he wanted to forget him. Since their bitter, troubled and violent split and again, more recently, Steven's anger and resentment had been boiling away continually affecting his new careful plans out in space. As Steven had managed to take Jane away with her dreams of exploration and experience, Alan had followed, if only as a persistent thought and bitter memory.

And he wondered more and more since the very first horrible death. Steven was a showman, a celebrity scientist, a manipulator – he never really was any serious studious academic at heart. Having made the deals, talked so pleasingly, reassuringly to dozens and dozens of bankers, investors, millionaires, critics and real scientists who struggled desperately; he had escaped the nightmare scenario which could escalate to historic proportions very soon back on earth.

Back in the moment, Steven was a respected member of the exclusive united research scientists who steered and organised the entire existence and mission of the small number of initial space stations. They were extremely busy, as was he, and it felt so damn good, he thought.

'Give us your opinion Steven, do we go ahead?' one man by the name of McGuire asked.

'Hmm? Yes, continue on. We're all prepared here, all ready to try new paths aren't we? This is not our restrictive, limited Earth home. This is our man-made land of exploration and endeavour. Every challenge met head on,' Steven replied. He smiled with natural confidence.

'Very well Steven, we only thought perhaps things might take a more... a steady trajectory right now. Now that we're here,' McGuire said.

'We admire your work and decisions, but we are just concerned that you're pushing yourself just perhaps too hard. Maybe slow things down a little. We have achieved a great thing with these grand new space cities, soon maybe even space countries,' Valerie added.

'Look, I'll tell you when we slow down and it is definitely not just yet. This is going to advance man beyond any dream or vision ever, you all know this by now,' Steven declared loudly in a dramatic announcement and then abruptly stormed quickly out of the room.

They had made it. He had made it. His vision, his dream, made reality. He had worked the companies, talked people around, made the promises, made friends, used people, loaned huge improbable sums of money all for over five years. The result allowed them to be standing there in space right then. An independent British and European journey. He had people to impress, to make jealous, as always. That was what drove him on in many ways. He could not stop now though, but he kept that small niggling thought to the back of his mind, in the dark distant corner where any doubts might reside. If he actually wanted to, he really did not know if he could stop the secret meetings, promised tests, events and trials waiting on his next few actions and decisions over the following days.

They were waiting, these people like him. Not the many talented scientists on the stations, but the other presently well hidden ones. They had dreams of changing, evolution, advancing in life, past problems, beyond difficulties of the human body as it was, and Steven would help them because it was his greatest, most significant challenge, even if many would not understand.

He quickly ran along newly built quiet corridors, alone and deep in thought and pain. It was all part of the final experiment. No man could be so brave or defiant before God, he believed. He was the first advanced man. He was the best example of his own new work and still a careful secret. The wait was nearly over. All parts of the plan were almost in place. The pieces on Earth, the pieces in the space stations well prepared in advance. He had held out so far, controlled his body to the final degree. Every new limb, every nano-artificial compound timed, studied and monitored.

There were a collection of small private areas onboard the space station where he had housed some of his own secret research examples that he continued to study. They were restless, and confused though he kept them calm with a promise of magnificent new lives very soon. He wanted this, because he was one of them. No turning back.

He reached the hidden dorm, and stroked his right palm across the small detector light bar. A thin door opened up and he slipped through quickly, looking around behind him for any witnesses. A greatly distressed lady came to approach him immediately.

'Steven! Steven! I'm so glad you're here! Andy... he tortured Jenifer... again. And Paul... he is fighting...' she told him, all in gabbled panicked words.

'Can't you all wait? You're more than human, you should be more than civilised. Or be able to restrain yourselves at the very least for some short time. This is not devolution, okay? It is not,' He told her, shaking his head.

'Are you okay then? You?' she asked.

'Me? Who knows? I'm, oh I'm simply frustrated today like all of us here, hidden in wait. We will get what we deserve very soon, my darling,' he promised her.

'How soon? When? It's not happening and we're restless here, anxious, so... We want out. We're wasting away!' a shabby man called Rivers explained with an angered, wild stare.

'Trust me. I've got us all up here, haven't I? My word is good. I need it to happen, just like all of you. Trust me. Not long to wait. We are the privileged ones,' Steven replied.

He walked along the corridor with the young woman who studied his face as they went.

'How do you feel? We are worried that we won't last... We feel... strange, we're so anxious now... Too different...' she told him. 'The supplies aren't good are they? The medical provisions for the tests and more? It'll be good for our progression,' she asked.

'It's what I've planned for months, Alec. Don't worry. I'm in control. They all do as I say. I make the decisions, me and me alone. They may think differently, but that's not possible. I am the reason this all happened,' he stated. He closed his eyes tight as a pain numbed in his head then.

'You're very stressed, Steven,' Alec said quietly and patted him on the shoulder as they reached some small apartments.

'It's worth it, really. Who else can do all this in this way, for the same reasons? It's worth it. I'll be fine,' he said with sharp determination. They entered one of the quiet small apartments, well furnished, and clean.

Chapter 29

The clues were predictable yet important, an increasing sense of mounting unease as Jane worked away quietly alongside Douglas and Donald. They read the hand devices they worked with as they monitored soil, plants, air levels and each other. A young woman scientist came along briskly toward Jane and crouched down beside her as she worked.

'Have you heard?' she asked. She looked pale and frightened.

'What? What's wrong, Simone?' Jane asked.

Simone looked around, with pained anxiety and dread.

'Someone has died,' she told Jane.

'My God, when and who?' Jane asked in shock.

A group of monitor serving wardens came along from somewhere in that instant, interrupting their conversation.

'How is work going here?' one of the lead wardens asked Jane with a blank face.

'Well, quite good, I suppose. Has anything bad happened?' she asked him.

'We have meetings shortly. You must collate your statistics quickly, all of you, and then return to zone five,' the warden told them.

Jane and the others looked at each other, then back at the wardens. Jane, Donald and Douglas resumed their work then, completing tests, but each of them continued to contemplate the rumour of death and danger, even possibly murder on board the space station, which was intended to be of a new harmonious civilised level of society.

In less than half an hour Jane and the others concluded their specimen collecting and sampling work, and began to head down toward the instructed zone area for the meeting. Jane walked at the back of the group with Simone and as they walked, she spoke to her quietly.

'Simone, can you cover for me?' Jane asked. 'I'm not going to the meeting. I have to go sort something out,' she said.

'What? You have to be at the meeting Jane. It's important. We can't screw up in a big way. It'll look really bad. Everything is going so well so far,' Simone told her.

'Really? I though you said someone... I know. But I really have to go and talk to someone urgently. You know I wouldn't put you in a bad position but... please? You'll be okay. A white lie, that's all. A big favour?' Jane said.

'Okay, fine. You'll owe me? It does sound strange but I won't ask. I'm just nervous because of what I told you about...' Simone replied.

'Right, but don't worry. Call me if you need to, okay? See you later' Jane said, and seconds later she had discreetly split off down a small side lane street to another zone area.

So many of the scientists and engineers ran through the station then, desperate to find sanctuary. They moved between zones, scared and needing to protect themselves from the shocking horror that they were learning about from all directions. There was now most definitely something inside onboard the space station that was fatally threatening their lives and they had to know where it was and contain it. Then they appeared beyond, outside the station windows. One or two saw something, then a few more, all speechless and aghast, horrendous and illogical visions before their eyes.

There, outside of the windows, out in deep black space, there was a small girl. She appeared floating, so careless, and effortlessly. A beautiful sweet little girl, peering in at all of them, curiously.

'Oh my God...'

'Who...? How...?'

'I don't believe it... You see her?'

'Are we all going insane here?' another asked.

She smiled back, and watched them. Stopped, looked back at her momentarily caught in confusion. Then she screamed, she multiplied – she was dozens more in an instant. All of her, dozens of her screamed at them inside, she raged back at them. She caught the windows, scraped at them, and howled like a possessed creature. She scared the life from them.

'Come on, we should go.'

'But...'

'Don't look, stop looking at her...' another said, and they ran on, shaken and lost.

There was yelling, jeering and screaming all around Steven as he stood in the secret bunker quarters within the zone barrier walls. He felt embarrassed and nervous but knew better than to let it show to others around him. A large number of the enhanced people he had stowed on board were gone, escaped out around the space station in the last few hours he had learned. This could be it. His career, his reputation, hope and future lost to random uncontrollable mistakes. It was too early. Much too early, he thought. He had wanted this, the integration, but not so soon and not like this. It was so volatile, the whole personal project of his.

Behind the space travel, behind the healing the masses, the next level project had this instability from the beginning. He had almost thought that he would be able to keep it down, steer it along smoothly but... the experiment was progressing ahead of itself.

A lesser man might have simply confessed, admitted and handed himself over to authorities. For Steven, the occasion actually offered fresh surprising challenges and that was what he thrived upon. This fatal dangerous situation was just about perfect, he decided.

'We are going to use this right now. Our plans will simply move into action right now, ahead of time a few paces. No waiting, now is the time. We all move out as I order, and we take this space station as the experiment I envisioned,' he announced to the collection of diseased and mutated people around him in their crowded dozens.

'So who is out now?' he asked as he began to look over them carefully.

'We think that Decker, Crystal and Henry are missing. Others too, but obviously we're concerned about them being out there, with the scientists,' a tall thin man near the front of the crowds told Steven.

'Decker? Henry too? Oh God, that's no good. Damn it, the fools. Okay, right. I'm splitting us up. I want you, Nathan, with me along with...' He looked around, unsure, then continued. 'You, Mr Baxter, and Mr. Reynolds. Sterling, you take the first three dorms of people and... Moorcock the last three,' he announced. He had to quickly put together a plan of action which continued to make him seem all - knowing, ready and fearless.

He knew to be inventive, using what was around and right then that was all he could do. He left the secret rooms with Nathan, Baxter and Reynolds following. These three men were also experiments of his, willingly but also the most understanding and similar to him and his personal outlook and philosophy. While their bodies were undergoing changes, manipulations and tests following the enhancements from earth, these three were also scientists just like him. They understood the procedures but, like him, were ethically and morally lacking in many ways of thinking.

'I will control what happens from now. I will, and you will help me. We are better than all of them, you know that!' he told them with defiant vitriol. They nodded, agreed. Then Baxter spoke out.

'But Steven, the others... They are all at different stages of treatment and testing. How are they likely to act?' he asked.

'Don't think about back home now. I was not in control or responsible for many of the ill people, the strange sickness which broke out. Most were events, products of the other researcher's ignorant lazy testing routines,' Steven answered. 'Now let's take charge of this!' he commanded as they walked out together prepared to do anything to be in control and in the front of human evolution.

Two scientists stood around by a rest area with coffees in hand, talking casually, when across the way from them one saw two other strange men walking around.

'Hey look, who are they?' the first said.

'Who? I don't know. Haven't seen them around I don't think...' the other replied.

They both looked across curious of the two strange men nearly ten feet away across the corridor.

'They... They're not scientists, are they? Engineers though, perhaps?' one said.

'I suppose, could be. But look, what are they saying?' the other asked.

They stood and listened carefully to the words from the two men across from them.

'Russian, is it? Or Polish, maybe?' one said.

'No, it's not... Listen...' the other said.

'Space... Free... Change... Space... Down... Home... Space...' one was saying.

'Home... Down... Space... Father... Home...' the next one uttered.

'What does that mean?' one of the scientists asked.

'Bloody weird blokes,' the other said and began to step forward. 'Hey, you two, excuse me?'

They began to walk across but the two men when noticing them instantly turned wild and fierce. Their eyes bloodshot, green vile pupils, skin pale and flaking when they quickly moved toward them.

'Hey, wait – get back, okay?' one of the scientists said.

'Shit, Norman, we should go. Come on,' the other urged and they ran, they did not turn to look back.

They ran and the strange diseased men followed more slowly behind. The scientists almost fell over themselves, shocked and fearful. They reached the next area zone entrance gates, ran in and turned on the switches as fast as they could manage. Just before the two wild strangers came to reach the gate entrance, the door quickly moved out, meeting and locking them out.

'Right, let's radio this into Brian and Suzanne and the managers right now. This is fucking bizarre, it really is,' one said.

'It's just like those down on earth isn't it?' the other told him.

'Look... Don't say that, just don't.'

'But they are. Like them, aren't they?'

'I know. Yes,' the first replied as he turned to the communication panel.

Chapter 30

Across the vast station there would be no silence for a long time to come. Panic was spreading gradually along with gossip across the work zones and street lines. Not one person was working peacefully any longer, now distracted and fearful, just as when they had first seen the news of the sick attacks on the nation before leaving earth.

Hiding her face with her hand as she walked along the zones toward where her close friends Donald and Douglas worked, Jane could hear groups of people arguing nearby. Hours before, the station was a place of superior civilised living and peace, but now it felt like a claustrophobic ant farm. If anything truly unexpected and horrifying were to happen, she knew that they were all probably trapped, closed in on the space station. They weren't due to be taken back to Earth for months. They did apparently have some means of emergency escape evacuation vehicles but she could not really recall much about that. Could they easily leave the space station? It had rarely been discussed as they all became settled in the tranquil harmony of focused disciplined quiet work daily. There must be a way to get off the station, but then if they did, how many of them could?

She was moments away from the area where her friends should be at that time of day. She risked a quick look around and then noticed a kind of suspicious and strange new person across the block roadway from her. He stood with his back to her, doing something with his hands possibly, but she could not easily tell what. He did look different, in his movements, in the way he stood there, she thought. Then she realised that he also did not seem to be in the regular station uniform either. It made her uneasy and she silently backed away. Wisely, she continued on quickly as she passed the zone road, and the strange man turned and watched her as she went. He chewed feverishly down on his bloodied wrist, flesh mangling between his salivating lips.

Jane entered the working sample area three, and she saw before her people shouting, running, screaming in all directions. It had come to this area, the death and horror. She was late, or perhaps unfortunately right on time. She had to find Donald and Douglas somehow, but also keep safe at the same time. She saw some men she recognised and quickly approached them, dodging other hysterical women and men around her.

'Excuse me, what's happening?' she asked.

'Are you from another zone area?' the man nearest asked her, quickly, as he looked around, visibly anxious.

'Yes, but I want to find some friends – they work around here. Has anything serious happened?' she asked.

'Look, it might be too late for you to return to your area of the station right now. If you like, join us but stay close by. There was... There's been people... possibly dead. Possibly murdered... We don't... We're not sure exactly how. Just stay close with us as we go,' he told her.

Her heart nearly stopped. It was true, and it was not just one death. She had no idea that this kind of thing could possibly happen on this beautiful serene place away from earth. There was, it seemed, a murderer on the space station. Death was hunting down these skilled, decent scientists right then. No police, no detectives – only themselves to save themselves if they could.

'Do you know if Donald Davis or Douglas Brigson are around here now?' she asked the man at the head of the large group as they moved along through the quiet zone. He looked at her with exasperation.

'Who? God, I... Yes, I think so. Try over across by the tankard stalls across there,' he said and pointed in the direction. 'Go with Trevor here.'

She nodded and followed the shorter dark haired man pointed out to her. They walked off down the side of the stalls near the small buildings near their right where sleeping quarters where. The noise of the fearful people died down slightly which perversely increased their own nervousness.

'Where did the people die?' Jane asked as they walked. Without turning to look at her, Trevor answered.

'Over by the collection strips, then another by the shrubs and trees.' He sounded so unsettled, distracted.

'I'm right thinking that the killers have not been found, aren't I?' she asked.

'Stay by me. Nearly there. There are a group of people here. I think you're friends as well. Stay with them. We're communicating between the zone now, securing and defending weak areas and blind spots between zones,' he explained.

She looked around them nervously. The area was tense and foreboding. What would happen and what could happen could no longer be predicted anymore. Then Douglas came suddenly from around behind the stalls.

'Douglas! Hey!' Jane shouted. He looked over and went toward her and Trevor immediately.

'Let's go quickly,' he implored.

'What's happened?' Trevor asked suspicious.

'Another dead. It's all around. We need to close down the area, get weapons, defend ourselves. Someone's doing this for a reason and we have to stop them. As a group together we can do it, we have to,' Douglas told them.

'Back there?' Trevor asked, pointing behind Douglas.

'Yes, but let's get moving,' Douglas urged.

'But it happened back at the other zones too,' Jane told him.

'Really? Then we secure everyone. We find out what the hell is really happening. Catch the one, or ones doing it but protect ourselves first,' Douglas told them.

They made a pit stop around to the small apartment where Jane lived with Douglas and found Donald there with the same intentions.

'Who could have thought that this could or would actually happen?' Jane said, perhaps too naively.

'It can happen anywhere where people are. Maybe we'll just never change that much,' Donald said with grim pessimism.

'But everyone here is well educated, good natured, friendly and happy, or they seem that way,' Douglas said.

'Really? Maybe that's no excuse. Perhaps geniuses snap and go off it when things seem too right, too good to be true. All the thinking, the work, the intellectual pressure drives us to it,' Jane mused.

'Not us. Don't say that. So what's it like back over there?' Donald asked Douglas.

'Increasing hysteria, panic, shock, fear. Uncertainty. Just unexpected, you know?' he said thoughtfully.

They collected together an assortment of large, fairly lightweight things for protection-spades, mops, knives, and utensils from the kitchen and garden areas.

'What are we going to do?' Jane asked, feeling a little uncomfortable standing with a knife in one hand and a long metal pole in the other.

'Catch this murderer or just get off this death trap of a space station while we still can,' Donald told them.

A number of the more senior staff with many of the largest, most physically fit scientists, patrolled between the apartment zones of the station as Steven emerged toward a group of them.

'Hello. What is going on right now? All this noise and these confused statements I've heard?' he asked, acting ignorant of recent events.

'Steven there have been some deaths, I'm sorry to tell you. Haven't you heard? It's true, all of it,' the muscular man said.

'No, I haven't heard much. It's true? That's... unbelievable,' he answered with a sympathetic sadness on his face.

'So what's being done about it?' he asked.

'We're coordinating secure sections across the station area zones. Some of us are then heading across to look for whoever had done these things. People here are very skilled and we can probably very easily determine who did it and how to find them, we believe,' the man explained confidently.

'You could be right. But we still need to be careful, don't we?' Steven said.

'Of course. Who knows what could happen anytime?' the man agreed. 'Do you want to come with us now?'

'You know, I think I'd better check on some of the others. I'll be okay,' Steven told him.

'Sir, I know you are a very smart intelligent man but... Well, sometimes these people are unpredictable, you know?' he said.

'I'll call up some people close by. If they don't come, I'll come straight back. I'll call you in say, the next hour or less, okay?' Steven said.

'Well, alright then,' the large man replied. He then watched Steven walk off and then returned to keeping watch in all directions with his appointed colleagues a few feet away.

As dozens ran around in hysterics, losing their sanity and all fear that they had before leaving Earth came and returned to them, Brian and

Suzanne observed and tried to comprehend the situation is some sane manner.

'Where have they come from, these attackers?' Brian said.

'Have they been hidden here all this time?' Suzanne responded. 'Did you know, Brian?'

'No, not at all. I wish... If I had maybe... I don't know,' he sighed. 'What about you?'

'Me? God no. Who did? Some very bad shit has been set up here, or else it's just the worse fortune. Could it have been set up?' she said.

'You know... I wonder...' Brian replied.

They walked along together, with some intention to work together to solve the problem.

'One of them has been here. Perhaps more than that. We'll investigate now. I'll take control of the opportunity,' Steven told Baxter, Nathan and Reynolds as they all stood around behind the apartment side. They quietly moved along toward the central quarters zone. From there, Steven intended to manipulate the fear and paranoia of all the surrounding zones and scientists around while he found his estranged test people and made use of them all more effectively.

He had done reasonably enough tests to take a few chances finally. Besides, this was no longer Earth. Only highly educated, observant scientists of all varieties were around to take the fall. No media, no snooping reporters, paparazzi, or unpredictable curious citizens to interfere. This could be much more interesting and more free to creativity. He smiled to himself.

There was a sombre silence around as Jane, Donald and Douglas walked across the zones, with their make shift household utensils as weapons in their hands. They began to wish they were back on earth right then, where there were police, doors and locks and security to protect them much better than right then. Places to run to, to go to other than around in a circle.

'We'll be there soon,' Jane told the two men optimistically.

'I hope nothing more has happened yet,' Donald replied.

'I doubt it. We all know now, we're all intelligent people up here,' Douglas said.

'It was probably an intelligent person who did the killing,' Donald told them.

'Okay, right. Anyway, not far now. We'll be okay,' Jane reminded them.

They fell silent and concentrated on the areas around as they walked on. All kinds of fears and thoughts passed through their minds as they went. Jane wondered if it really could get much worse, if much more death would come to claim many others. She wondered if it was just the nature of having such a large number of people in space for the first time. They were free enough but really still inside the big metal dome that was the space station. A mix of cabin fever or space madness was obviously setting in, despite their mature awareness of these potential problems. Was this the inevitable result of so many people leaving earth? The curse of human nature that was simply inescapable?

'You know, I've seen something very strange here. I don't know if I can say,' Douglas began.

'Really? Like someone else?' Jane asked.

'Yes, that's it. How...?' he replied.

They looked at each other.

'A girl, maybe a very small young girl?' Jane asked.

'That's right but I mean... how? You've seen her too?' he asked.

'Not just me. Some others have started to mention weird things, spooky things and some said a girl, small. A few have seen this girl. And now you and me. I've no idea what it means,' Jane told him.

'Well, are we all ill? Could be some big social illness, our food supplies poisoned minds maybe, do you think?' Douglas suggested.

'Well, I suppose could be. It does worry me, I'll be honest about it,' she told him.

'What if she represents something, the girl? Like a sign. I mean, if she actually could be real or important to us?' he asked.

'Like what?' Jane said.

'A warning to us. Innocence. Safety onboard the space station or...' he trailed off then cautiously.

'Okay, right. But what if it's more like we've been drugged. Do you think? Someone here... Some sick game or, well, the work here is extremely valuable, don't forget,' Jane told him.

'I don't know. I don't want to see her again. I do know that. I'll... just ignore her. Yes,' Douglas decided aloud.

'Okay, but you know, she'll be there, kind of, anyway,' Jane said.

They looked at each other, neither happy with what they had told each other. Douglas was not impressed to hear that, and so walked away troubled.

'Wait, Douglas. Hey, don't get upset I just...' Jane called out after him, but she realised that she honestly really did not know how to calm him or herself. He was gone, decided on his way ahead.

Minutes later, they could see the next zone area clearly ahead of them beyond the testing grounds.

'Here we are then,' Jane said with apprehensive relief.

They all walked on and came to the large double door entrance. Pushing them open, they were confronted by two men with spades pointed at them.

'Hey! Wait! We're okay, really!' Jane told them, hands out to protect herself.

'We can't let anyone through right now. You'll just have to wait back at the other zone area. For safety reasons, while the perimeter is being checked,' the first large man explained.

'Hey, look we're not homeless junkies or criminals – we're all decent people right here,' Donald told them.

'It's not personal – you should understand that, I hope,' the large man replied blankly.

'Isn't there any way that we can come through?' Jane asked. She looked behind the guard, around at the nervous people shuffling around near apartments and the central offices and main laboratories. Among the crowd, one face stood out then, a familiar face that she had been waiting to look at.

'Steven!' Jane shouted across over other stressed crowded scientists moving along. He turned around fully facing her with a much vexed frown upon his face. He looked back at her for a brief moment and then slowly approached casually.

'It's okay, I know Steven well. He'll want to see me,' she informed the men before her. He came up behind them finally.

'Let her through, she's okay,' he told them. She turned to look at Donald and then back at Steven.

'Well okay, them as well,' he then said, acknowledging her friends.

The three of them then followed Steven into the central operations zone streets. He and Jane spoke with each other while Donald walked along behind cautiously.

'So, how are you dealing with all of these things that have happened?' Jane asked Steven straight away.

'Unexpected perhaps, but not unheard of. Part of mankind's dirty psyche sometimes shows these elements which tragically we still cannot escape out here in the deep darkness of space. Seems there are elements on this station we overlooked,' he told her.

He took long thoughtful glances at her, at her bright shining blue eyes, her long waved hair tangled down her shoulders.

'Is this the end of the whole project now? Do we call for help from Earth?' she asked.

'It need not be the end, I think. By no means at all. Life goes on. It always did back there, so it should here too. We'll overcome the problem and much more good will come. I'm very sure of that,' Steven told her.

'Really? That's unbelievably optimistic right now,' she replied. She found his constantly strange, unshakable hopeful outlook always in many ways suspicious. Although she loved Alan, she wished that he could be more like that sometimes, just a little more confident in his work, his plans, and with their relationship. This made her realise why he might really hate Steven in the way he did these days. It certainly did highlight the yin and yang to their partnership. Perhaps Steven's character was just too extreme and unpredictable for Alan to rely on. Perhaps Steven really could control this terrifying event, secure the safety of everyone on the space station, she thought. He did seem to get the results he wanted, every time, all of the time.

'Who's in charge right now then? Who's keeping us safe?' Jane asked him.

'I believe Benson and Kubrick have half the station then myself, and Hammett and Vonnegut are sharing the rest of the safety duties presently. Don't worry. I suggest you stay in one place and protect yourself,' Steven advised.

'Yes, we will. How long do you think it will take to get this sorted? To stop whoever it is?' she asked.

'I can't really say. But keep positive okay?' he told her and gripped her shoulder then, with unexpected affection which made her uneasy.

Donald coughed then noisily from behind them suddenly and looked embarrassed, and they all then walked on. They then reached a divide in the zone's wide stretch of road.

'I have to go and meet Benson and Vonnegut now. Look, let's meet again in short while. You three can make your way to your apartments easily from here, can't you?' Steven said to the others.

'Well, yes but...' Jane began, not expecting this.

'Good, good. So take care, and see you soon, alright?' Steven said, and he then quickly waved them goodbye and ran off away from them down the road and vanished behind some apartment buildings.

They felt deserted and cheated as the three of them stood alone.

'What now?' Douglas asked.

'We get to safety,' Jane told him with focused decision.

'But what if that's not good enough? I mean, we could get trapped. Could we really actually leave the station?' Donald asked them.

They silently looked at each other briefly, knowing that in reality, they just did not know the real truth to that question yet.

'There must be ways,' he said continuing.

'What, just us? What about the others?' Jane said.

'Look, really we can't all be on here without a real means of escape for us all. It must be built for us to leave if we really needed to, right?' he said.

'You really believe we will find a real escape route?' Douglas asked. Donald coughed again with irritation loudly.

'Can't we?' he asked. He looked exhausted and silky white then.

'Yes, we can. We will. Come on,' Jane said and walked out before them.

'You know where to look?' Douglas asked her.

'I think I do have a decent idea, yeah. Come on, follow me,' she told them. The two men shrugged and followed as she stepped out, bravely holding tight the spade in her gripped hands.

Chapter 31

Certain parts of the space station were gradually becoming empty, as many moved away from where they believed attackers to be heading from, as they messaged each other via cell devices. In these quiet empty rooms and corridors, there were still movements of life, footsteps and others wandering through. Some attackers did amble along curiously in these directions, with no strong sense of focus. They lumbered along, growling and wailing between each other's, these things previously conscious men and women. While they came through at the opposite side of the wide main area by the walls, others watched. Three red skinned figures observed, silent but learning. They wanted to know what the attackers were doing, where they were going. The three figures looked at each other quietly, thoughtfully and watched. There could possibly have been some version of a kind of sadness in their full black pupil eyes.

There were things that Steven wanted to say to Kubrick, Benson and Vonnegut as soon as he could. He wanted to organise the few steps with them very soon, lose no time and use them as best he could still. They must want to keep everyone safe and the future of the entire station in order, he thought and so they would do as he asked. He would work with them, secure a plan of action, a future that would hold much to be proud of – to him, at least, and any others who were as capable of understanding the risks and rewards before them then. They would thank him. He knew they would be too sceptical, especially as hugely gifted scientists – it was expected of them. His gift – they would be the most lucky, blessed people of our history so far.

As he ran along, he called up the other ones he could trust on his wrist phone strap.

'Hello? Nearly time. Give me an hour or less. We move in from all directions now. Begin the event. Glorious gift for all tonight. Trust me and thank me later. I'll find the ones who have... misbehaved. Just need to be, well disciplined,' he explained to someone on the other end of the line, and continued on toward the many dozens of fearful men and women of science.

After fifteen minutes, Jane and the two men reached the entrance to the next nearest zone apartment grouping area.

'Are we to continue?' Douglas asked.

'We should. If we still think and feel the same. Doesn't it feel like we're deserting the others now?' she asked them, unsure then.

'Human nature. Instinct. Self-preservation. We would if we could, and maybe we'll be able to if we get back safely. But right now... It's us or no one, I think. Like you said, there must be plenty of escape pods or whatever right? Somewhere?' he said.

Donald coughed and fell against the nearby wall in visibly uncomfortable pain of some kind then, and Jane and Douglas quickly rushed over to help him.

'What's up with him?' Douglas asked Jane as they caught him and looked at his twisted expression.

'I'm not sure,' Jane answered. 'Donald? Hey, Donald, take it easy,' she told him.

'He should get some rest. Maybe it's his heart. He needs to be looked at,' she said.

They knew this was an obvious problem for them leaving right then, but they needed to help him fast. She looked around about the quiet deserted front area of the next apartment zone.

'Keep going. Let's... continue,' Donald muttered with a great moan of exhaustion.

'Not you, honey,' Jane told him seriously.

'I shouldn't leave you two,' he replied.

'Wait in this area of apartments. We'll come back. Get back with a group and stay with them. We'll return when we know how to leave,' she told him. He nodded silently. He knew how bad he felt, and knew she was probably right. Jane and Douglas left him by the wall and signalled across a few scientists who walked past a few feet away.

'Help Donald here, can you please?' Jane urged them. 'Can you just keep him safe with you? He's in pain – sick in some way – maybe his heart. We have to go to check on something else just for a short while. We're returning very soon.'

'Alright, okay. But the... The station is not entirely safe right now. You both do know that, right?' the lead man asked them.

'Has it ever really been?' Jane said, and then she and Douglas quickly ran off in the other direction.

Fear stayed with Jane and Douglas as they continued toward the other side of the main communications and tests compound area. They both moved on thinking that they must find what they were looking for before they themselves were found by the killer.

'Is he going to be alright, do you think?' Douglas eventually asked Jane as they ran.

'I really don't know. Hope so. Let's not think about it too much. Let's just sort out our return flights for all three of us,' she told him. He looked at her while they ran.

'I do admire what you're doing now,' he said. 'I admire you.'

'Douglas... We're friends. Good friends. I need you as a good friend now. I'm not usually so brave or stupid as this... It's just me finally taking some chances,' she told him.

'Coming here was a bloody big chance to take, though,' he said.

'Maybe, or just another choice like any other,' she replied.

Douglas took her words easily, but still felt hurt slightly. At least he knew her. She might not be what he wanted her to be, but he appreciated simply knowing this courageous young woman in any way at all.

This awkward moment was broken thankfully, though unfortunately what came before their eyes would sadden them utterly.

'Jesus Christ, what the hell is this?' Douglas spat out as they both looked into another cul-de-sac in which they housed many of their fellow scientist peers. The majority of them sat in armchairs with wires hooked up into and over their eyes, ears, and mouths. They were playing the virtual games which were used in down time.

Jane ran in among all of them, and began to shake them in their chairs, the ones who had given up.

'This is not the time!' she shouted.

'They don't know how to handle it, and this is all they know how to do. This is their Heaven. They want to die and expect to die here, and so that's how they want it,' Douglas said quietly from behind her, watching her touch them and shake them individually.

'No, they don't. They've just lost all faith, hope and love,' Jane told him and continued to shake the scientists with tears forming in her eyes, while they just sat hooked up, connected digitally, passively blank. Not one stirred at her attempts to get their attention.

'Leave them, they've given up. That's their choice, that way. Respect that. We can still move now, us,' Douglas told her.

She looked at them all, quiet and sitting with vacant smiles over their faces.

'The killer or killers could be anywhere now... They don't care...' Jane said.

'They hope that they might be downloaded, and saved in the computer hard drives. Until... When it is all better for us,' he told her. 'Maybe we are trapped. Maybe they know it and so they've done what might be best. If they die, they might miss it, and die happy in a way,' Douglas said.

'That's just too selfish,' Jane told him. She moved away from them, thinking to herself.

'Where are you going?' Douglas asked.

'I'm not plugging in for death to creep up on me. I'm finding the way out of all of this alive, aware...' she told him. 'You with me?'

He looked back at the scientists – the VR chairs, sighed to himself and then walked up to Jane. They left the area together, and left them to exist in virtual peace, as long as it could stay that way.

Many scientists onboard were now extremely troubled, with terrible thoughts in their minds, and fear and panic not ending now. They kept close in large groups, trying to plan new safe means of surviving through it all. Two women stepped out around a narrow corridor to reach the female toilets together.

'I just can't believe all this, Ann, it's just so fucking scary,' one said.

'Well we're all staying close together. The others can hear us, we'll be okay, we will,' Ann replied.

They came out toward the wide-open section between station areas where it segmented, the toilets separating areas.

'I'll wait here, shall I?' Anne said.

'Well, okay then. Just right out here,' Susan replied, a little nervous. As she turned to walk into the cubicle they suddenly heard a strange sort of dampened moan then juddering scream out in the open area beyond.

'Oh shit, what's that?' Susan asked.

'I... Wait,' Ann told her.

She carefully stepped out, and moved to look around the near wall which separated the areas. With cautious inspection, she saw two people running – one fell suddenly, the other continuing along, but then turning to look back at the other. They seemed troubled, distressed in some way. Then the one standing sank down, right through the floor, or so it seemed, even while it defied logic. Through the floor, disappearing from plain sight. The other sat crying then stood and ran off again. Ann did not recognise either of the men she had been watching.

'Oh, my sweet Lord. Fucking shit,' Ann whispered quietly, her mouth open in shocked confusion.

'What's happened Ann? Tell me,' Susan asked from the cubicle.

'Wait...' Ann said. She watched as the other left the open area finally gone.

'Okay. Let's go when you're done. Very quick now, okay?' Ann said.

'What did you see?' Susan asked again.

'Hurry up. We need to get to safety,' Ann told her.

Panic and dread spread like an unknown rapid plague across the vast space station then, and Steven was taking it to his advantage as well he could. Now an undercover operation on the move, his secret private investors working with him to utilise the station as human experiment and playground beyond laws and ethics of Earth society. In the next few hours, he and his enhanced patients planned to take the station zone by zone, by manipulation, lies and of course unstoppable wild brute force as necessary.

In a narrow thin long corridor attackers ran along grunting repeatedly, searching for someone to hurt, abuse, or kill. That was their only desire, beyond more complicated moral thoughts of any kind. While they moved forward they looked up to see two tall red skinned people waiting ahead at the end of the corridor. They stood in silence, looking back. The attackers seemed to actually turn away a little, either confused or repelled. They looked back, possibly making some decision in their simple minds. They shuffled around, looking back at the red skins, then lurched away from where they came.

Having stopped at one zone storehouse, Steven supplied Baxter, Nathan and Reynolds with regular station uniforms to aid their plans quickly and efficiently. As they moved along, Steven ordered one to stay by a zone as the other moved to the next one along. Eventually Steven was left with only Baxter by his side. They came along the greater far eastern side of the station together as Steven checked progression by wrist phone with the others.

'...and so they are very confused, right?' he asked. 'Good... That's it... And no sign of the three who escaped us earlier yet?' He shook his head and cursed.

'How are things looking?' Baxter asked.

'We are in place around the majority of the station. They are genuinely afraid and malleable. Of course, partly because of the escapees, but it has only helped our plans. Maybe karma, even well... destiny! Ha. Or an all-knowing force guiding us along,' Steven mused in good humour then.

'Right. Can we take control of it all yet? Is that possible now?' Baxter asked.

'Not yet, but nearly. Be patient,' Steven told him.

'You know what you're doing then, do you? Everything?'

'Don't question me! Haven't I brought us all up here? Haven't I given you your legs back, improved your own health seven times over? My plans, my own skills. You're fitter, healthier, new again. Not just you, but so many of you,' Steven reminded him in a loud defiant voice.

'Yes, you did. I am thankful,' Baxter replied head down, eyes looking away.

The silence between Jane and Douglas had evolved from nervous embarrassment into a kind of objective determination as they journeyed on toward other parts of the station in the quiet semi dark half lit corridors around. They rested by a tall wall which was the side of some apartment bunks.

'We can think logically about our options, can't we? I mean, we might be running out of time. Just if say, Collins, Davies and the other major coordinators can't decide what to do or to defend us or to hunt the murderers... And your pal Steven – he's got a major role too, hasn't he?' Douglas asked. 'Do you think those guys have private emergency means of escape at all?'

'Oh that's... It wasn't meant to be hierarchal up here. Not like that, that was one of the things we were setting out to rise over. Okay then, let's consider that. Look, we will leave. We have to. I'm not dying up here. I need to go back. No matter how terrible life might be on Earth, in England, I still need to return, still want to. We keep going. Douglas if you want to forget this, go ahead and plug yourself in with the others back along there,' Jane told him.

'No, I don't mean that exactly,' he told her, but she was ignoring him then. Her eyes were taken toward movement across over his shoulder.

'What's that?' she whispered quietly to him.

'What? Who?' Douglas said then as he caught her eye line and followed her gaze, turned to look in the direction. Jane ran then, quickly across in the direction. There was a group of people, or some similar sized figures moving strangely. After a moment, Jane reached them, with Douglas somewhere behind her then.

'Don't ask. Go if you can. Find safety. We're moving to another zone. Steven is heading the safety monitoring but something's happened. He couldn't stop it... No one knows what's happening anymore,' he said, distraught.

'Well, can anyone leave? Go back to Earth somehow?' Jane asked.

He looked around, took in a breath then returned his gaze to her.

'There are ways. But to get to them might just be impossible now. It's happened. What was down there – the attacks, the violence – it's all here,' he said.

'Down where?' she asked.

'On Earth. The attacks, the ill people, the unknown disease or plague. They're here. They killed, not any of us. They're loose, and he can't stop them,' the man told her with a final kind of pessimism.

Jane could understand it. The entire space station did in some way now make a dangerous shocking new kind of sense to her. She knew how involved Steven had been, looking like the great entrepreneur, the genius saviour of modern man; the face of the whole mission, the one who everyone saw as doing his best to make things better in all ways. That was him, they had been led to believe – even Alan had told her that in the past. It was Steven's way. He was a scientist, sometimes a surprisingly decent and even hardworking one, but more often a shrewd opportunist, a charmer and showman. It now really seemed that he had very likely brought death and fear knowingly aboard the space station.

Had he really? It was possibly still only opinion and rumour. Was this a fatal kind of proof for them though only much too late?

Whatever was the cause of the deaths and panic onboard the station Jane still had to leave as soon as she could. She had reason, perhaps more than some others. She had a strong personal urge to go back to Alan, to know he was alright, to know they could be alright together. This new disturbing announcement only made her more focused than before.

'Can I reach Steven at a screen at your port document stall area?' Jane asked the distracted group of men who were then organising themselves and deciding upon their next actions.

'Sorry? Yes, possibly. Why, though? He's ruined the entire project! He's a crazed megalomaniac, he has no morals, no care for the rest of us at all!' the lead man told her.

'But I can reach him?' she asked again.

'If you want to do so... You want to talk sense into him? Beg him for mercy now that he has unleashed all hell upon us here?' he said, shaking his head in disbelief.

Jane looked across through the nearby corridors of the port stall entrance.

'In there?' Jane asked looking through the dim lit narrow passage.

'Go right ahead,' he told her.

'Well, okay. What are you all doing now, though?' she asked out of curiosity as she watched them.

'Plug in, zone, or... whatever feels right, or best or even easiest,' he told her with little shame.

'You don't know the escape routes then?' she asked.

'Never mentioned, was it? Strange that isn't it? But we never gave a damn, it seeming so perfect before...' he said. 'Alvin Seeder.' He and his team knew about it all, or so I have been informed. Find him, and just maybe you'll know then.'

'So where is he, do you think?' Jane asked.

'I've no idea right now. Quadrant zone... I just don't know... Between two and four? Good luck, we're moving on now,' he told her and they walked away, their large pack of troubled and nervous men and women together as they moved equipment.

Jane walked on through the narrow corridor alone in her hope and quest. She looked back and saw Douglas stood still.

'Are you coming?' she shouted back. She suddenly coughed with a painful jerk of her head, covering her mouth. She and Douglas looked at each other as he came along toward her then.

'That's... Nothing, not what you're thinking okay? So you're coming now?' she said, trying to sound positive.

'We could see what the others are doing. Make calls out around the station, keep connected,' he offered.

'They're not doing a damn thing that will save us. They're... just surrendering,' she told him then turned and continued toward the small desk area of the communications area monitors and call switch boards screens terminals ahead. The whole area was quiet, deserted and left screens bleeping, processing figures as normal.

Jane sat down at the desks and began to look at all of the buttons, level controls, processing controls before her and the numerous keyboards. She eventually logged in on three separate computer screens, and clicked up a number of windows, and quickly read over information about the current state of zone security, health and access right then. The monitors let her reach all others quadrant zones of the entire space station, though there were not currently any other scientists online then. Even so, she decided to leave messages for a number of them in the half dozen most significant zone areas, and then continued to surf and access the other station zone files and information. After opening up various contact lists, document files, she almost miraculously found the contacts for the main Earth base communication bases and immediately sent down help messages to them. She turned and Douglas was standing behind her, observing her actions.

'You need rest. We can just hide in a safe zone for a short time while we wait for responses. An hour or two at least. Get back to Donald even. So what have you managed to find?' he asked.

'I'm not resting now. Don't deserve it. None of us do,' she replied. 'I've mailed out to all station zones. No one's online or in an office right now – no doubt too busy trying to keep safe, defend themselves or jacked into digital nirvanas until death takes them. What I have done that's more impressive is I've reached the Earth bases, I think. Again, no live connection yet or response, but we can only hope,' she explained.

'So we can rest then. We're only waiting, right?' he suggested.

Jane nodded, surprisingly in agreement finally.

'We can wait here for a short while,' Jane said grudgingly. 'But any shit comes along nearby and we run like hell out of here, okay?'

'Fine with me. Any meds in here, then?' Douglas asked and began to look around them at the cupboards and shelves. She shrugged as he looked around. She amused herself by scanning across many collated files concerning the recent studies on the conditions affected inside the space stations.

There were many photos of specimen deposits and the scientists themselves working peacefully and with dedication. The side monitor buzzed and shocked her into looking across instantly. Douglas looked over while he rummaged in boxes in a corner of the room.

'We've got some responses,' Jane told him and began to open the main screen's mailboxes.

First was a reply from zone five 'Things are finished, plug yourself in, wait for Earth to send help.'

Then zone two: 'Collect supplies, find safe area, lock yourself in, hide. Contact Earth.'

Then zone six: 'Steven was leading us. He organised defence and planned escape routes. He knew about the attackers, how to defend ourselves. He is gone. Believe him dead. Plug yourselves in. Wait for Earth.'

Jane was shocked and dismayed. Could Steven really be dead? This was the genius, evil bastard who seemed to have organised the whole horrific sadistic event up there, she thought. If he could not control them at all, if they killed him, could anyone then defeat them or restrain them now? she wondered. Was that it, then?

She did not like Steven now, she was definitely sure of that, but she had never wished anyone dead in life. And if he was the one who could stop these people or well, things that they now were, they all might just have to suffer the consequences and die along with him.

'My God, that's no good,' Douglas said. He was reading the onscreen mail over her shoulder. 'Could he be dead so easily?'

'Who really knows? Anything could happen now. Yes, maybe. But I am not so easily convinced. I don't know. I would prefer to find him alive so that I can kick the living shit out of him personally for all of this,' she answered.

'Look at the other mails,' Douglas told her dramatically with enthusiasm as he pointed at the screen. 'They say Steven was organising escape routes. Sounds like there really are some somewhere then. Ask them if they know more about them,' he urged.

Jane then scanned down through quickly.

'Okay right, yes. That one group. They repeat that they knew of instructions and briefings concerning escape possibilities. That's zone six,' she told him.

'Well, do you want to go there now, or rest up some more? Or is that a stupid question?' he said.

Jane coughed, then held her hand against her head for a brief moment.

'Jane? Are you okay?' he asked as he stepped closer to her.

'Tired, I think. Just tiring, this. What the hell, can't... Can't stop now, can we?' she replied.

'How about Earth?' he asked.

'It seems... Seems to be taking a while to make a mark... or... I don't know,' she said, reading and checking the email in boxes. 'Can't wait around right now, and we have to check out what we have learned. We should just... move.'

She watched the computer screens and loading monitors. Colours merged while codes throbbed loaded, moved up the screen, changed and were replaced, and repeated over.

'Who's that?' Douglas asked, pointing one out.

Jane flicked on the speaker receivers and played out the audio message.

'... Station one, this is station three. All kinds of unpredictable shit happening. Some attackers are on our station. Inhuman or post-human. So strong, unstoppable. They've killed a few of our crew, blood all over. We just can't stop them. Tell Earth, watch that your station is safe from any of this. Tell Earth! Get help please...'

Jane and Douglas looked at each other in silence briefly. She then typed out an email and sent it back to them.

'We move now,' she told Douglas and they stood and walked out of the area.

Chapter 32

While Jane and Douglas moved back out across the station again, in other further zones many of the scientists were battling the unpredictable and deadly killers and attackers in any way that they could. The attackers at first seemed to be moving around in a stealthy preconceived manner, almost like some wild jungle predators, all-powerful and conquering. After a few hours, it did change.

They were less concerned about being caught but simply attacked in the most savage, careless and nihilistic way, having scientists and themselves in the clashes together. In the time since Jane and Douglas had gone on ahead, Donald had joined with the closest zone group in defending themselves against the wild attackers.

'They keep coming. I don't want to kill anyone really,' a physicist, Ben Foster, said openly.

'So you want to be killed instead, do you?' Donald asked in response.

'Of course not, but...'

'Then keep working,' Donald said as he and the other half dozen scientists pushed large shelves over the entrance doors to the zone lounge room area.

'Do you have the sanitation utensils here?' Donald asked them.

'We have some, not all kinds. This area is not the key mineral research area field zone so not everything is at hand here,' one man told him.

'Get what we have got then, and be prepared,' Donald replied with serious certainty.

'You seem very knowledgeable about all of this,' one of the female scientists commented.

'I trained in the Territorial Army for a year or more in my early twenties. Learnt a hell of a lot more than most of the narrow-minded cretins there. Now I can use it finally. Let's see what else we can do,' he said with determined authority. He coughed again and grimaced visibly then.

'You seem just a bit sick there, Don,' the red haired woman observed.

'You… You're not wrong. Not much I can do about that right now. I'll help the rest of you while I can, though,' he told them.

'No, look go and rest, Don,' she said.

'What? Plug up in virtual like the others, leave my body to be beaten and torn to pieces anyway? Don't think so,' he said.

'No, just rest up, is all. We'll move the rest, us,' she offered. She and the others admired him, but saw his fatigue so obvious then. He watched her and the rest look at him, with admiration but sympathy, and he agreed.

It had been a long while since romance with a fine woman for Donald, the last relationship having ended badly nearly three years back bitterly for him. He did not expect much, but he did notice how she smiled at him so warmly then with a unique affection in her eyes. It was good, making him feel human and manly once more.

The woman – called Jessica – and the couple of dozen other scientists of that zone barricaded the quarters and office block around them in under an hour. As the group took a break and then talked about options, Jessica came to see Donald privately. In a small sparse room, Donald sat slouching down on a couch tearing pages from a magazine in quiet anger when she stood in the doorway and observed him.

'Can I come in?' she asked.

'Please, yes. Sit down,' he said, shocked and remembering to be gentlemanly. She joined him and sat opposite in a chair by the desk and smiled at him.

'Feel better?' she asked him.

'Not greatly. Funny, don't know where I picked up this unexpected cold sniff, or whatever it is,' he replied.

'Yeah, weird, I suppose. Do you think we can survive this? I mean, we won't…' She could barely utter how she really felt, so scared and terrified of the mysterious deaths.

'Hard to say. Of course I hope we can, look there are more of us than this loose cannon, whoever it is. Probably got cabin fever. I think it must be all overblown, exaggerated really. I have two friends who are making their way across the station, trying to find the escape route among other things,' he told her in trust.

'Really? I thought we were just going to be collected in a couple of months, right? Wasn't that mentioned?' she said. 'That's pretty dangerous then, right now. You think they will?'

'Well, my friend is very brave, or just stubborn but she's certainly determined. She wants to be back on Earth. She seems to know a lot or knows someone who might help,' he said.

'That's good, I suppose. You think she will leave now?' she asked.

'Possibly. How about you – do you regret leaving Earth at all?' he asked.

'Well, now with all this danger, maybe. I came as a scientist who wanted to help, to do good, to make progress, beyond our problems with fuel, population growth, disease; all of that,' she said and sighed to herself.

'I think that I came to escape. I am a scientist of course, and I enjoy the pioneering experiments here, the research, pushing boundaries, but I see I was running...' He coughed, then continued. '... from some mistakes and fears in my life.'

'You want to go back now?' she asked quietly.

'Now's a very good time,' he replied with a weak smile. 'If this had not happened... Now that I've seen my misperception of my problems... What kind of life do we have here? Don't we ourselves need some different kind of life?'

'Almost like some monastery or religious servitude in a way, ironically. I wonder how everyone is down there. We just don't really know, do we?' she said.

'I miss real social life, I think. The problems of the day. The simple nuances of daily life, however crap and irritating. Simple things, personal things – shopping, walking past different strangers, paying for things, seeing the clouds above, the rain and night sky...' he told her thoughtfully.

'If we go back, we could go to a restaurant, as friends if you want to?' she offered.

'If we go back... Yes, I would like that. Very much I would like that,' he answered her and they smiled at each other as he touched her hands.

Chapter 33

Between the station zones there was a desperate quiet, a cold echo of fear through the long stretching corridors. It was the sound after death and before other shocking sounds to continue on. Any voices heard were quiet, nervous, hesitant and whispering. The many scientists on the large cavernous space station locked themselves away by now in the building quarters at each zone, either leaving themselves for death while in virtual bliss, or hopefully planning at coordinating defence against the unknown amount of ones who were somewhere waiting or approaching to kill or inflict many kinds of pain and suffering, wherever they were.

One of them suddenly appeared, running out into the open quickly, along haphazardly through the empty zone streets and lanes to the next place it wanted to hunt and savagely attack anyone before it. It was or had recently been a man, and he had a purpose, though he only marginally recalled some of it. As it came closer to the front of some short bunker rooms, someone jumped out and pulled him inside instantly.

On the inside stood other sedate enhanced people, and between them all was Steven.

'What do they all think? How are they acting now?' he asked, as another held the returning attacker still and yet another stuck a needle of some calming fluid sharply down into the arm of the savage man.

'They... are scared... They... talk... talk...' he said as he struggled and then gradually calmed slightly.

'Think now. Did you tell them, what you were meant to?' Steven asked. 'What do they think of me? Now?'

The attacker looked back at him blankly, then closed his eye lids slightly as he seemed to be thinking with concentration.

'You... are... dead. You're... dead,' he told Steven.

'Excellent, good. Thank you. Job done,' Steven said, nodding then.

'Does it change things yet?' Baxter asked him with interest.

'Yes, you know it does. Now we can get on with other things freely. I don't have to worry so much now. Now comes real revolutionary science,' he explained with a look of profound austerity.

'We're like scientists now too, right?' Baxter asked with enthusiasm.

'Yes, we're helping you with this pioneering special work at last now,' Nathan said, rested from his run back to join them again.

'You are important. Of course, you were investors initially, men and women with very good business sense, that's obvious. I am grateful that you're here now to help me. It's going to be very special alright, no doubt about it,' Steven told them.

He teased them once again, charming them, offering compliments though they barely registered it, having been diluted with a good mix of various pre-selected powerful potent chemicals in the last few days to keep them the now obedient, faithful dogs by his side which they were until their end might come.

His ill-timed mistake with the enhanced attackers breaking out earlier than planned was now his carefully utilised opportunity to begin his grand plans before any of the many scientists onboard the space station might uncover the truth and actually see how to stop it all. As his death was now believed as spread around the station to all, Steven lost the fear and guilt that could possibly stop him and could then begin with no more setbacks. He believed now that almost all of the scientists on the station must have given up any and all hope of escape or return to Earth, and even survival.

Steven walked along the cramped room past the watching attackers, and opened up the shutters and locks to a hidden wall of monitors and secret equipment – various bottles, vials, jars and measuring containers filled with numerous mysterious substances and fluids.

'From now on, I am in here. Baxter, you and Nathan and Reynolds now do what I talked about. Keep in touch, okay? It is simple for you all individually really, but I want it synchronised together, for it to happen all at once. I have more to organise from here. Now go. Make me proud!' he told them.

They looked at him for a brief moment, then at each other, and then all three ran over the entrance and out, to do the work requested of them. Steven really hoped that they could do what he had asked for like he had explained. They could definitely be unpredictable at times, which he realised was part of their beauty, but they also were his teammates now, his new colleagues until the end of it all.

As the flock of obedient attackers milled around behind Steven, simply waiting, roaming, and some fighting, Steven began operating the computer desks and small apparatus on the tables before him. He entered the communication board's access programme of the space station, and used the passwords he had been keeping until this moment arrived. The screen changed and a list of other contacts came down the screen, with the same space station experiment programme name. These other significant names – referring to Greek mythical literature, old politicians and biological discoveries – were not groups he could reach back on Earth. These were groups unknown to practically everyone back there. These names, which he looked at on the screen before him, were other space stations out there in the deep darkness of space around them.

The station was open to the attackers, they finally were free to roam and explore, fight and torment, and demand what they desired while their savage nature eventually would kill so many soon enough. Steven was gone somewhere soon enough. Had he deserted them? Was he afraid or ashamed of his mistakes he knew he had made all by himself? Two attackers – Gloria and Richard – stopped and looked down the corridor before them.

'We are free now, finally. Out and we can rule here, no judgement, no prison. Take control here,' Gloria said joyfully.

'It won't last. We can't do that,' Richard said. 'Not the way we are. We will only kill or... No, we won't be any good now,' he said.

'But it feels right here to me,' she told him.

'No, just another step in the experiment.'

'We can survive, can't we?' she said.

'Let's take our freedom while we can,' he told her.

They ran along, to gain what they could, while they could until it was over for them.

All the while Steven had been a quiet, dedicated member of the large flagship space station which all of Earth had known about, and thought so unique and special, there had been two other smaller stations not too far away from them in space right then, as Steven was very aware. All three had been financed and built out there for a decade or more in secret negotiations between Britain, American and other European connections, though the reasons for them and reasons of their present use had changed several times up until then. Gordon had told him, or had tried to explain a while earlier. When Steven came to get involved, he was immediately welcomed by just about all of the very well hidden money men and women involved in the operation and use of the four stations. He was the international rising star of the science world, a prodigy and genius of a new generation, and they instantly wanted to invite him in, welcome his skill, and could hardly refuse any of his wishes at all.

Steven clicked up windows on the monitor screens and then flicked on the speakers to quiet level.

'Hello station two. It's me, Steven. Has it started yet?' he asked to a man on the screen looking back at him. The man twitched slightly, yawned and grunted before replying.

'Hello Steven, yes right now, it is happening all around right now,' he told Steven.

'You are following the instructions I sent to you via email, aren't you? No mistakes? No confusion at all?' Steven asked anxiously but calm.

'No problems yet. Yes, as you instructed us. It is really very interesting, fascinating work now. What will happen next?' the man asked.

'There are a few possible outcomes I predict but only one or two which we are aiming for specifically. Do not go off the plan or away from instructions. It is in all of our interests to see this through right to the end, no matter how... challenging it may seem, okay?' Steven warned.

'Okay then. We're working at it. Count on us like you wanted,' the man answered.

Steven nodded to himself, thinking about what was happening then, across all three of the space stations. It was the real science, the experiment he had been waiting to begin since going up weeks earlier. It was a phenomenal endeavour, with himself at the reigns, in control of it all up there. He did have the help of several of the enhanced attacker people on his station and on the other two smaller stations. A number of them had been well-educated, trained and experienced scientists themselves and had volunteered to be used by him and now he was using them, and pleased at their individual progress.

Clicking up more windows on screen, he then set up audio channels for the third station.

'Hello, station three? Steven here. How are things progressing now?' he asked.

A long silent moment passed by while he waited patiently. Loud rumblings came from outside of the room then. It shook him, distracting him from what he was focused on briefly. He considered checking outside but then decided to try again.

'Hello, station three? Steven again here. Come in,' he said. Static crackled back through to him pessimistically, but then finally someone replied.

'Steven, is that you?' a voice rasped anxiously all of a sudden. Steven sat up right alert then.

'It is, it's me. Who is that?'

'It's Jackson, Sir. Things are a bit lively here right now. Done what we were told but it's gone crazy. This how it should be, Sir?' the man asked.

'Why? What's happened?' Steven asked.

'Well, most of what you wanted – just it's unbelievable to see it really happening right before us,' Jackson told him, clearly amazed and even scared possibly.

'Keep me updated here okay? It's all go now. The instructions are there. For the greater good remember. For us, all of us in the end. Call back very soon,' Steven ordered calmly still.

Two space stations of varying size and potential – all changing, all potent with new advances and fresh dangers. Anything could happen, Steven saw that. All three stations were together part of one larger plan, an unknown experiment of mankind – for mankind – but unknown to almost all people of Earth even then. This would be his legend, his peak of creation, Steven wished. No god had done this much to save mankind in centuries, if ever at all, he thought. He too coughed alone, a sudden abrupt pain in his throat twice and took a deep breath ignoring it. He was exhausted, he realised. Getting to this point had been a long, hard trip, weeks of dedication mostly in private. He fumbled inside his jacket pocket and found some pills to swallow.

He then stood and walked over to the other set of monitors and computer desks which flashed and blipped in harmony. He clicked open a monitor board and accessed the channels to communicate again.

'Hello Baxter? Reynolds? How are things now? Come in,' he said. He looked at the screen charts of mineral and numerological tests from around the station as he waited for the response.

In the last hour, Baxter, Reynolds, and Nathan had spread out over the main space station to control the scientists on board and test their levels of defence, immunity and mortality as they chased them and attacked in any way they deemed fit.

The scenes became almost simple primitive animalistic attack, mirroring lesser mammals and ignoring centuries of civilised growth and endeavour. With Baxter, Nathan, and Reynolds being enhanced men or 'attackers' they were having a ball just going wild scaring and chasing the scientists, with some tragic fatalities as were to be expected. They performed the most reckless stunts around zone pathways, off room walls, against themselves and the scientists too slow to hide from them or too foolish enough to approach them.

The attackers revelled in the bloody heightened strength, immunity, and senses now being finally allowed to express their joy, rage and gratitude in such disturbing ways. All of the enhanced attackers on the stations had welcomed the experimental treatment months previously, most facing potentially fatal illnesses or extreme advanced ageing, Steven had found.

Steven himself was proud of the bold new work with these patients, even with the known negative media backlash and accusations which had begun to escalate. Though while they did exhibit signs of positive progressive physical improvements on disease and individual ailments their long-term psychological outlook had not been monitored or even anticipated at all. Or if it had, Steven could not let any bad signs stop the ultimate results that he though must be possible soon enough.

In a quite dark, shady area of research preparation rooms, a handful of attackers walked in, each moving apart and sniffing around at tables, devices left out when scientists left quickly earlier. They looked, possibly remembering the meaning and the names of some things from deep inside the darker clouded areas of their minds. Perhaps not even that – they were possibly just roaming like simple savage animals. In the room at the opposite end stood two of the tall red skinned people. They stepped right up among the attackers, who immediately wailed and muttered. The first red man clutched hold of one by the neck, looked very closely at it, into its eyes. The other red figure, looking more female, then grabbed the attacker closest to her. She too inspected it, silent and focused. They seemed to want to find something. They needed some response or defence from the attackers. The attackers all around simply remained very quiet, like humbled dogs, their masters watching over them. The red man and woman made some personal complex vocal sounds between themselves, communicating opinions. They put the attackers down, stood and looked then at all of them. The attackers looked back, and there was just possible some telepathic communication, some understanding. The two red skinned ones slowly turned and walked out of the rooms, with the attackers silently watching them leave.

Douglas watched Jane with tired admiration. They had been walking for nearly two hours toward a corner of the station which might possibly hold a kind of salvation or just simply point to their unavoidable deaths. The chance of escape just possibly outweighed death, at least to Jane. Douglas was not any kind of spiritual man – not too many of the scientists aboard were, although some did see scientific exploration as looking for the clues of God's handiwork, and His blueprints. The ones who did express their quirky kind of 'New Age' difficult yet dedicated faith in God were few, and he guessed even fewer right then. Jane had been one of them, he remembered. At least he thought she did hint at a belief at some point. He almost laughed, as he thought to himself that if her faith got them off the station he would definitely not mock her for it. Finally they sat in the darkened safe room, with computer screens and radio panels around, small lights bleeping and flashing in regular sequential patterns.

'Well, we're here for a while. Jane, what about all the rest around the station now?' Douglas said.

'I know, I've been thinking about that. I don't know how well Brian and Suzanne and the rest will listen to me, but I am going to communicate messages through the station to their management mail code addresses. There should be a chance they can all collect together in one side of the station, lock down certain areas and survive. They can close off and lock out the attackers, then decide how to deal with them, or just wait until they can escape. More pods need to come or be found, or another shuttle to pick them up. That should work though, I'd say. It will have to,' she told him.

'Not far off now, I think,' she said, turning to face him.

'Good, it's about time,' he replied.

She wheezed and coughed once again, lurching down in obvious pain beside a looming wall at her side.

'Slow down. Nearly there. Let me go on ahead,' he offered.

'If I didn't have you...' she said and smiled up at him.

'You do, and more, I think,' he told her.

'Sorry?' Jane said, missing his point.

They could see the next few blocks of sleeping terraces and offices only perhaps a dozen yards ahead. It was dark and shadows engulfed the buildings, cloaking the streets around. Anything could be waiting deep within the quiet darkness for them, Douglas thought as he look ahead.

Then a movement. A person, Jane thought she saw.

'See that?' she said to Douglas, still coughing.

'Where...? What exactly?' he asked.

'Right... there. Where we're heading. Look,' she told him, pointing.

He looked, but could not see much of anything in the darkness of the zone ahead.

'No, nothing. Do you... want to go now, continue?'

He thought her sickness seemed to be conquering her, attacking her senses.

'We go on, Douglas,' she told him as she stood up again beside him. But again, she glimpsed something, or someone dashed along ahead of them further into the dark streets.

'I... I saw something. Wait, just... I'm not sure of this,' Douglas said.

'We have to. We can defend ourselves, can't we?' she said.

He did not reply but continued walking forward slowly. As a handful of minutes passed they eventually came along to the end of the station's loading and boarding hatch entrance bay area. It must have some way of leaving, Douglas thought, looking at it as he approached with Jane.

'We start looking now, quickly,' she explained to Douglas as she stood beside him.

They heard something behind them not too far away. Douglas turned around and stared into the shadows. He looked back to Jane.

'I don't know. Might be nothing,' she told him hopefully. They both looked back again, unconvinced by themselves.

'You start looking here. I'm just going out there a bit. Not too far. Just to see,' he told her. He saw the uncomfortable anxiety over her face, but knew he had to go.

'No, Douglas, you... Don't,' she said, sounding scared at last.

'Find what we've come for,' he told her, then began to walk back out.

Jane sighed, and then turned to inspect the wide front area of the loading bay entrance. Douglas walked out, cautiously holding onto his spade and looking in all directions around as he walked. All around seemed deadly quiet, a brooding dangerous quiet to fear.

Did they just imagine the worst? Were both of them simply too paranoid and fearful to focus and think logically then he wondered?

It had been an extremely long day, the longest, and they were so tired to their bones. He stared into the long zone pathway ahead. Nobody, no one. He simply laughed then.

And then Steven.

'Hey! Hey, you there!' Douglas called out, seeing the silhouette of him.

There was Steven. He stood alive and smiling his usual though now more disturbingly polite smile. Damn creepy bastard, Douglas thought. They made eye contact in that very brief moment and then Steven ran off somewhere, vanishing among the shadows once again as suddenly as he had appeared.

'God damn you, you...' Douglas began saying aloud and almost threw the spade in the direction of where Steven had been. He waited a moment, then decided it best to just go back to Jane and leave if they could. Steven was alive but he could deal with the horrific mess that he had created, Douglas thought, as he ran back down the path to the bay area.

There were numerous instructions, dials, monitors, level meters along the sides of the bay doors Jane observed as she waited alone. She felt like she was blindly guessing at what should be there. Nothing stood out to her, nothing grabbed her attention immediately. It had to be there, in some way. The other group had known of it, she thought. They did not seem unsure, but could they just have been wrong, misled or confused? Perhaps it was opened at another zone control point? she wondered. That would not be right thought, would it? she thought, trying to find logical reason to the planning of the space station and their being there. She continued to gaze at the bay doors, vast and tall. Behind them was the deep freedom of space. Beyond that, Earth itself.

A loud growl, a scream, and Jane turned and held up her spade, gripping it tightly in defence. The sounds came from somewhere ahead of her, most likely she believed, but was not absolutely certain. She held up the spade...

... It jumped out and launched hard onto her, growling still. She pushed against it with her ailing strength, startled and unsure. She coughed and could feel the strain to keep it back. She had little energy in her to fight this deformed, rabid person. She could possibly lose strength and then...

... No, she strained and then managed to push the attacker to one side. She kept the spade before her then as the man laughed and growled again bizarrely. Jane moved and he followed, snatching at her, grabbing randomly in her direction. He jumped at her again. She fell down then but struck out at him with the spade quickly. He toppled, and tripped on her legs and so came down onto the hard blade of the spade. His head was sliced instantly down, deep with blood seeping onto the ground. The blood began to pour out over Jane beside him. She almost threw up, but held back and pulled herself up. She pushed him off her, onto the ground and, looking up, noticed a light flashing on the panels by the loading bay doors behind her. Somehow the attacker or the spade had knocked the buttons, and something was different. She looked at the small flashing light on the bay side panel curiously.

'Jesus, what's happened here?' Douglas asked in total shock as he arrived behind her looking at the dead bloody attacker on the ground with the spade protruding straight up from its head.

'Look,' Jane said, turning toward the doors then. She flicked on a small switch and then they both watched in stunned awe. Slowly the huge, heavy bay doors began to move apart. As they watched, behind the doors was revealed the vehicle that they had prayed for. A reasonably small shuttle, maybe eight or twenty foot long and around twelve wide, was docked to one side of the doors. It almost made them slightly nervous looking at it, but they knew that it was created with the purpose of taking people back to Earth. It must therefore have all of what it needed to do so, Jane thought. The area was used before the station was fully operational and finished in design. Having not been used so far in the months since they all arrived, there was growing level of grey dust over the desks and panels around. Jane walked in quickly, not wanting to waste any time.

'Hey, careful now,' Douglas said behind her.

'Of what? This is it, Doug. We're away,' she replied to him, and smiled. It was the first time he had ever really seen her smile properly while up there.

He wanted to tell her about Steven. No, he did not want to tell her, but wondered if he really should then. They could be gone in minutes perhaps, no more trouble. Wasn't that the point? he thought to himself while watching Jane look at the controls and buttons over the desks.

Jane was instantly occupied looking around the shuttle. Immediately it seemed to be surprising to her how simple the controls of the shuttle seemed to be. She seemed to understand the symbols and marked instructions as far as she could see, and this then gave her even more hope. She opened the shuttle doors in a few seconds using a section of the controls, sudden grinding and aching sounds as it happened. Then she stepped inside the shuttle. Douglas apprehensively then followed her in, watching her moving around confidently.

'Right, this is it now. You're coming, aren't you?' Jane asked him.

'Yes, I am. Of course I am,' Douglas told her, and came inside the shuttle, sitting down by her in the area at the front, most likely the cockpit.

'You drive don't you?' she asked him.

'Yes, I've a Capri classic back home. Does this thing look difficult to handle?' he asked, pointing at the controls before them.

'Well, actually no. Not too much difference to a car or big van I think. A few other things like altitude, pressure and that, but pretty average I think,' she replied.

'Still, would you mind if you actually do the driving? I'll help if I can, of course,' she told him.

'Well, okay. That's fine I suppose. You need to rest anyway. So... now?'

'Now,' she replied nodding back. She looked over all the dials, monitors, levers, and switches. After quiet consideration she began to tell him what to press, button by button. They disagreed a couple of times, but then chose the right selection.

The bay doors began to close outside the shuttle pod behind them. Before them then, another grand tall pair of doors, unnoticed until then, slowly began to open once the inner bay doors were shut. Loud noises thundered out around them, moving the shuttle around on some lower platform to face the second doors.

'You ready for this?' Jane asked Douglas.

'That doesn't matter. We're going anyway, somehow, in some way,' he told her.

'Amen to that,' she replied and winked at him. She pushed some buttons before her and on the small monitors, maps and coordinates came up gradually for her to programme and click on. Back bay doors locked, front opened fully – they launched open suddenly. They rocketed out, a hugely powerful blast of energy propelling them far out, with sudden startling speed to the darkness of deep space.

Chapter 34

The main space station was behind them. They were out, away and finally free from the death which chased them. Out into space, but their problems not ended.

'Will they survive back there?' Douglas said to Jane after a while of concentrating on the controls and flight pattern ahead of them.

'We... can only hope and pray. We were all pretty resourceful people. I've no idea how long it could now take us to return to earth yet. We will return, but we have to really understand the controls of the shuttle,' she told him. He looked around the quite small closed space of the shuttle control cabin then replied.

'Took about a week last time, didn't it? Or less. But this little thing we're in... Who knows, it could be longer. I'm guessing we've food and other essentials back there,' he said, not entirely certain.

'Oh yes, I think so, that's what I remember about these. We should have a few weeks of food and toiletries. Exactly, I think we can set up the coordinates and sit back soon enough,' she told him.

'You really think so?'

'Well, yes. I think we can't go too wrong, by the looks of it. The hard part is over now,' she answered.

'Good. Then I think I'll go look for any kind of medicine for you. You can now rest properly like you need to,' he told her considerately.

'Yeah, if...you insist,' she said with forced sarcasm, against the nagging pain she experienced still as she smiled back. They made a good enough team, she thought as she put in orders to the main direction control, selecting navigation paths for their journey home.

In the next few hours Douglas found some creams and treatments to calm Jane's coughing and lower her temperature considerably, and then he opened up a number of small tins of meat and fruit for them to eat as they relaxed in the shuttle.

'Can we contact earth from in here right now, do you think?' Douglas asked Jane after a while of just sitting joking about.

'We should try really, shouldn't we?' Jane replied in agreement with him.

'Then the station too?' he said.

She looked back at him, and they were silent for a moment.

'Yes, you're right,' Jane said as she ate the fruit then thoughtfully.

She paced the back area of the shuttle deck as she wondered about the future for them. But not just them, people back down on earth right then too. What had been happening down there? she thought. Just how had things continued while they were away? They had reports, but none of it really fully informed them. It was a small space inside the shuttle, and could have been claustrophobic if it was not for the number of strong but clear windows revealing the depth of space around them. The stars and distant planets passing some way from them but out there just like them, floating, moving but still. Jane looked out thinking to herself. There was darkness, nothing around them, only unexplained mysterious galaxies light years away.

Then an object came past a window, startling her. It shocked Jane and she stumbled back, stammering aloud, putting her hand to her open mouth. Regaining balance, she stepped back to the window once more. Something was there, some other thing close to them somehow in space. She instantly ran down the corridor to Douglas.

'Hey, come look now, quickly!' she told him, grabbing his shoulder. He was worried and curious immediately. He followed her back along to the small windows. They both looked out together.

'What did you see?' he asked. There was nothing to be seen out there then.

'There... Wait... Over there!' she said, excited and pointing right over in the corner of the window. He bent his head at an angle. He saw it then. He saw the other shuttle out there.

'Who is it?' Jane said aloud with dramatic shock. Douglas looked at her then away, down the cockpit area of the shuttle. 'Who?' she asked again.

She followed Douglas and stared him in the face with frustration. She saw him holding something back. She could see that he knew something and did not wish to speak. There was a secret deep in his eyes then, she saw. She realised then that he knew something significant.

'There's a chance... Did you check the signals of the station and earth signal frequencies?' he asked, suddenly turning around.

'Yes, and nothing coming yet...' Jane answered, waiting for more, with suspicion and unease toward him.

'Flick them on again, just in case,' he suggested.

She gave him a look then stepped to the control message board area. After a minute or so of dialling through to the correct lines, something buzzed in. A voice spoke through crackling static from somewhere.

'... Keep it going... Can... trust... soon... for you...' they heard, snatched cut up pieces of distorted dialogue, part of a conversation.

'Is that... it's Steven?' Jane said almost in horrified disbelief as she looked at Douglas.

'He's out here too,' Douglas replied in a quiet, almost guilty tone.

'What's he doing? How insane is he? So he's escaped too. Leaving all of them. It's his fucking mess!' Jane said loudly with bitter anger.

'If he gets to earth, he'll just lie to everyone, deny every damn thing,' Jane said.

'Well, we'll get the truth out. We need to keep trying to contact earth base of communications as soon as we can,' Douglas told her, trying to be positive.

'It's all we can do, isn't it?' Jane said, then coughed again suddenly. She rubbed her forehead with irritation. The dizzying pain would not go easily from her head. She could only wonder where the illness had come from so suddenly on the station when everyone had been tested for being almost completely well and in good health before being allowed up there. In a way, she really did not want to know why she was ill then.

In the other small quiet space shuttle not far from them in the depths of space, Steven tried to calm down and relax for the journey back down to earth. He looked forward to receiving the expected warm welcome back, the continued adulation and respect from the many media people, scientists, politicians he would meet again. Would they offer him even more money, deals, help and freedom in his work and life on returning? he wondered.

He had left the main station which contained possibly one of mankind's greatest and most unnatural follies on board. The guilt and confusion that he felt was immense and unrelenting. But he was certain he could lay the blame elsewhere – that was his great skill and he needed it more than ever now. Should he have left the enhanced people there to kill and torment the scientists? he thought to himself. He was one of them, a good, respected scientist. A good passionate scientist should come up against difficult results, problematic findings in their work. This was no different, he thought. It was going to be a magnificent experiment, advancing all of mankind. As with many historical changes to society and culture, the majority often were oblivious or simply did not care while those taking the trouble to move things on saw the tremendous effort taken and appreciated it always. They were just too... uncontrollable.

Something inside the enhanced patients would not sit well with the prepared gene mapping, and DNA shifting processes. Even since leaving earth, no final successful change had been found to please him. Gordon had lied, it had seemed. He had not known the total full answer, and only wanted to get Steven up there. Interesting, fascinating changes, but too early hoped for results... Still so far from him or anyone it seemed. The journey back to Earth was to be longer than he would like to know, he realised.

PART 3

Chapter 35

The attacks across all England by the many hundreds of diseased attackers had continued long after the scientists had travelled up to the space stations many months before. Police all up and down the country and special defence combat groups from the military and other elite lesser known units had increased their strength and efforts in stopping them and ending the attacks, trying to capture some in good enough condition to provide for doctors and scientists to continue studying. Somehow the attackers just seemed to continue to increase, even though it was never thought to be a contagious or infectious disease initially.

The symptoms of the attackers had in effect become a new man-made epidemic, unstoppable in growth, and the attackers continued to slaughter all in their paths and often each other in random but brutal ways, often though that barely decreased their increasing horrific numbers on the streets, towns and cities of the country. England was in a cataclysmic state, mass hysteria, fear, despair and suicide. The life known from the twenty first century so far was now gone, all modern living eroded, stolen, ruined. No daily routines of nine to five work, shopping malls, restaurants, quiet walks in the parks. Few people did anything like what resembled work as was known before. Work now was a jumbled mix of hiding, stealing, hunting, surviving in among dirty, smelling, neglected buildings. The majority of people stayed indoors continually, keeping away from the danger of the attackers, not knowing where the next would appear to try to kill.

Some lost relatives to them, while others became attackers themselves mysteriously and were quickly then forced out, or painfully killed if their loved ones could find the courage to do so in time. The news media had fallen apart, reduced to irregular and largely uncontrolled nationally spread phone messages from the news channels. Almost all institutions such as hospitals, supermarkets and pubs were torn open and robbed. Regular papers, television and Internet news only now functioned as normal, very rarely and accessible to any who found solar power or similar energy supplies. In just over half a year, the nation of Britain had changed to become almost like some Eastern Bloc or even Third World country of desperate simplicity and basic existence, danger and death stalking the streets every day and haunting the minds of everyone as the cause was still unclear to them.

A number of people tried to set up hunts for the attackers, and to organise groups to catch and kill them, alongside the official teams. The public were scared and fiercely angry, and had seen that ultimately the nation's police forces had not been able to predict or control and suppress the attackers to any successful degree at all. Communities tried to remain together, strong and resistant to the killings, but some inevitably became attackers while fighting the original ones. People took to wearing protective scarves, masks and goggles over eyes as the cause and spread was still unclear to them. Members of the police, Army and Navy, along with politicians, tried to keep alive a sense of civilised brave living, decency, to focus people on what they knew and had to fight for as humanity, but the fight was unrelenting and brutal.

When people were not scavenging for food and drink outside, people actually often began to go to churches, temples and other places of worship, hoping for God to hear their pleas for mercy and forgiveness. They were looking for God again, for salvation and answers to the horrors around them. Any place of worship seemed to console the confused and terrified souls around. They prayed for help though some even cursed God and saints for abandoning them, it seemed. The surviving elders, priests, and vicars told them many helpful other things, words of hope and grace, patience, and love, but most people could not understand or were simply still angry and eager to try to fight the increasing numbers of attackers daily.

After being so afraid and angry of the attackers, the media still surviving had managed to continue to direct the masses hatred and anger toward any scientists, specifically any left on earth connected to the work that Steven, Alan and their group had been accused of doing before they went out to the space station. These science researchers, professors, assistants, analysts and technicians among others kept very low profiles often going outside in disguise, or after dark tentatively. These scientists themselves were frustrated and angry – at Steven, who had left them to take the blame and accusations for his unsuccessful experiments which now ravaged and ruined the country without solution. They had, of course, all begun to wonder how the spread of the attackers could be stopped with scientific means. Some had met secretly, or at least communicated a number of times over the following months. They studied patterns, movements of the attackers, their human biology, and body language when they watched them from safe points. Some caught samples from dead attackers and tried as best they could to analyse the tissue and genetic makeup, studying the blood and cells for differences or clues. They discussed and debated the problem, whether it could be like many had initially thought a virus, disease or spreading germ, almost plague-like, and then they looked at other theories between them. There must surely be some people somewhere who could solve the problem, treat the attackers or put an end to them somehow, and that was the hope of many all over the land.

Without access to regular electricity and water, their limited testing barely scratched the surface of what created and continued to produce the attackers. While these defeated and tired jaded scientists struggled and some simply even gave up hope, there was one more who had not begun to personally really consider the solutions just yet. Many people had met this man, as he had made his way around the country alone, travelling for months. After many months with no end to the attacks everywhere, and no stop to them, this man became a whispered hero. He was known to have saved many from the attackers, but mostly found the ill and helped them, aided them with medicines, cures he had found or created. Many believed he was a very clever man, skilled and a mystery. He knew the symptoms of the attackers prior to their full change, seemed to know more than most men, and could sometimes treat people, save them from changing – or so some said.

So many across the country had heard of this mysterious man, but no one was sure if he used to be a doctor, scientist or from some other trade, but they all prayed that he might visit them when trouble seemed too close, when attackers were coming. The rumours and talk of him were still so vague, unsure but hopeful that it seemed to sound like he was almost some kind of mystical shaman or healer who could actually genuinely help them. He was the new mythical hope of everyone eventually. Some were unsure, thinking that he was simply a story created to give people hope, a new kind of modern folklore, some positive hero figure to keep everyone hopeful. This made Alan extremely tired.

He was so tired now. He was tired but free, travelling around and not himself. He should not feel tired he thought, as he was, he had heard a kind of myth, urban legend of sorts to all he met and helped. He went at his own new pace, travelling around, finding, meeting and helping those he could in some way.

His life had finished, he had decided not long after the last space shuttle journey. That shuttle taking the talented, useful scientists of Britain and Jane away from him, and from everyone. Constantly feeling he had been in the shadow of Steven's spectacular work and persona almost drove Alan to severe deep depression. At the end, it had been just so suddenly confusing and demanding. Steven had pushed him just too far, and Jane had acted so confusingly. Then finally when she left, for whatever real reason – he just was not sure completely – he gave up his work in his research projects altogether. As the country fell victim of the hundreds of wild savage attackers, most regular accepted work ended anyway, people having to simply defend themselves and families and friends before any other capitalist ventures could be entertained.

At first Alan was simply just one of the many who protected his family and friends from danger in any way he could, bravely and without a second thought. After witnessing the killings and torment, then the changing of someone from man to attacker in such violent and shocking ways, he set out to do what he could. Using his own specific skills, knowledge and information from his research work and scientific past and developed theories involving partially natural remedies and biologically developed serums and compounds, which he soon created to the best level he could, he healed others like no other around could. He helped those close to him, then left for his own safety when many began to hunt, torment and victimise any scientists they could find to blame and hate.

It had been weeks of healing people like only he could, and it drained Alan. He did not stop or stay in one town or city really long enough to think or question his path deeply – he simply did what felt right as a capable human, ethically and with selfless virtue, while the country turned to tragic ruin. He was alone, with short supply of his crudely mixed and brewed antidotes in a number of small vials as he went. He would rest and wait. Now, like many more people around who hid or waited for change, he also waited in some way for God to speak to him – if that could, or would, be likely – for guidance, for someone to take the burden from him. He was eventually beginning to feel he had done his part. He was, after all, only one poor man – a man of science but also of flesh and bone, mortal and emotionally beaten and lost.

As Alan moved out by himself, shedding his academic nature, his scientific habit and rigid outlook and living like some mysterious nomad, he did take with him some notebooks and files. They held information, notes collected which he had written concerning his own studies of the growing food and plants back home, and the changes and tests he had begun and developed over three years gradually.

There were no secure or easy ways for him to continue his investigations right then, but in his mind he did continually consider the ways his findings could go forward, possibly connecting with the work of the group project before the nationwide chaos of the attackers. He even knew of what now seemed very likely terrible connections of Steven's father Gordon, and his company's work to the attackers were a mystery previously. Were they man-made in origin? Results of very recent, very local work gone wrong? he wondered. There had been trouble between Steven and Gordon, he knew. But he also believed that Steven was a very interesting young scientist in Gordon's eyes, in a professional way. No matter how Gordon had seemed to ignore him or the work their university group had been doing, it had been more important that they never knew at the time, Alan thought.

Chapter 36

Somehow, in some way, Steven came to reach Earth before Jane and Douglas. His shuttle came down in the sea near South Wales and Cornwall. Getting out, he swam the small distance over to the shore. If anyone did notice his descent back down, no one came out to greet him and welcome him back as he walked into the nearest small town carrying a compact tightly strapped shoulder bag with him.

He was back. He had tried to navigate and plot the shuttle close to the original launch base, but it proved too difficult. No communication to or from the shuttle base had been possible, he had found and so he had to simply guide his own return. He seemed to be near the top of Wales, not too far from the northwest coast – close enough he thought. Once he met up with the shuttle and space project base staff, he could explain the dire events which had so unexpectedly unfolded up at the space station. Whether he confessed to being the cause of it all, he had not decided for certain. Perhaps he could actually find an angle on it whereupon he could set himself out as knowing how to end it all, and it would continue his grand celebrated work and success as before. He had though endured such quiet, lonely time travelling back to Earth in the shuttle by himself. He had been with his thoughts, his deep, twisted, guilt fuelled thoughts of regret, sorrow, fear, and hatred, and could simply not avoid thinking things over, questioning his actions, his immoral acts. He had seen his faults, his sins and what should never have happened, but he was so afraid of the reaction and punishment he expected. Such a phenomenal coward and fake, he thought of himself as he walked quietly over broken roads and cobbled streets into the small town. If anyone could reverse the whole situation, surely he could. He had been capable of such marvellous, unbelievable things, he knew he could surely do the same but with actual good intentions – couldn't he? With some help, of course...

As he walked along the quiet streets, crows flying low overhead below the heavy dark dismal long clouds, he noticed the lifelessness all around. Where was everyone? he thought, looking then in all directions around him suddenly. It was beginning to disturb and trouble him. Where was his welcome, his applause, the rows and rows of adulated many fans, spectators, reporters even? Where was the England he knew? The voyeuristic, curious, obsessive society needing information, news, scandal constantly like a drug?

He had been gone months – long months admittedly but not more than a year. Thinking back, he knew there had been troubles, he could not in any way forget that the initial patients and participants in his secret experiments had escaped and done such shocking unpredictable – mostly – things. That could not account for this total lack of life out here could it? he wondered. Just what had happened in the months since he had been away in space?

The last few voice-cast messages to the main space station had, he now vaguely remembered, mentioned something remote about the problems the British police were experiencing with catching all of the attackers, and that it was on the potential verge of epidemic proportions if they were not quickly caught and examined. Could it really have grown so big, so dangerous or out of control in a few months? he wondered. To actually ruin and silence a whole entire country, a land of sophisticated advanced civilisation? Those kind of events were just medieval or biblical horrors, and they just did not happen these days, especially not in the West of the world. Plagues, mass horrors, nationwide spreading diseases... But then he remembered the bird flu, swine flu, the anthrax scare, and biological warfare fears. Many bad things were very possible, he knew. And while some of those were elaborated and distorted in real truth by the news media, they often did happen in some slight way, killing some at least.

Before him then, he noticed a thin man abruptly creeping closely in the shadows of some buildings up ahead of him. The man appeared silent, but visibly bothered, agitated in some way, scratching at himself, yawning as him came up the path. Even so, the man was quiet, so Steven decided to very carefully meet the man, and approached him then.

'Hello there. Excuse me, are you well?' he asked. The man gasped suddenly, then began to turn away for some reason, with a strange look of haunted shock or fear over his face.

'No, wait. Talk to me sir! What has happened? Where is everyone? Tell me!' Steven demanded, walking after the man. He grabbed the man by the wrist, frustrated.

'Let me go. We... shouldn't be out long, out on the streets. Are you mad?' the man said, whispering back, eyes darting around paranoid and fearful.

'Then let us talk somewhere else,' Steven suggested, trying to observe what the man was afraid of out around them then.

The man, short and apprehensive, sighed to himself but then nodded.

'Follow me then' he said. They quickly walked away under the cover of many tall densely spreading trees to a place of safety.

The two of them moved quickly along dark alleyways, winding narrow streets avoiding the main town streets carefully. After a few minutes, the short thin man led Steven to a neglected but sturdy looking building, and stood by the doorway.

'In here,' he told him.

Steven walked in after the door was opened for him, the man leading ahead.

'What's going on here?' Steven asked bemused as he followed the man.

'Want a coffee or even a beer?' the man asked more cheerily then, and turned to quickly offer a surprising smile.

'Well, yes a beer would go down really good right now, thanks. Look what's down here? Do you live in here?' he asked.

They came to the end of the long twisting corridor, opening two heavy doors, the man revealed to Steven where they were finally. Looking around, Steven saw the local town shopping mall ground floor filled with many groups of people with looks of focused but extremely undernourished fatigued faces, vacant stares of despair and mourning, moving around. They seemed to be collecting things, moving items, here and there, some arguing quietly. Were they all criminals looting the mall? he wondered. Where were the police of this town right then?

'What's going on here?' he asked.

'We're coping how we can. There are some things in here we can still, not too much but, it is still a useful place in ways. I'm sure you've seen this elsewhere, right?' the man asked.

'Oh yes, right,' Steven said, lying to him.

'We're got some tinned food in here, equipment, but some have managed to successfully catch live animals – foxes, sheep, rats, perhaps dogs, cats... I just can't. But how much longer can we be like this? America is still meant to help some time, in some way... Yeah, right. Or even Europe if they care. None of them care. Where are you from then?' he asked.

Steven looked back and was almost annoyed, offended that the man did not instantly recognise his face.

'Me? Well, I'm from... from near Suffolk but... I've been away for a while. It... really is bad now...' he replied. He thought about what the man had told him, and he was just so simply but overwhelmingly shocked and saddened.

'Those goddamn street devils. We'll all be like them soon enough. Fucking scientists ruined everything we ever had. Had to keep testing, knowing, finding, looking for... fuck knows. Now all this,' the man told him 'Everyone was all excited about the damn space travelling, so proud, so bloody proud of them... If only... and we were all left here. It all went to hell.' There was visible anger but also almost tears in his eyes as he spoke.

'We have to survive, though,' Steven said as he observed the many people pottering around within the quiet mall area.

'Survival, yes that's our thing. No one can stop them though. The country is a dead country, total mess now. A leper to all other countries of the world, a place to be wary of, to ignore and steer well clear from. We'll be left and only we'll see how we end,' the man said with terminal pessimism.

He then passed Steven a beer from a nearby display freezer running on solar electricity from the roof.

'So are you people doing much? I mean organising anything, testing things, opportunities?' Steven asked between drinking.

'What can we organise? We are the ordinary men and women on the street. Many of the police officers and army folk are dead now or have moved out further. They may return but... politicians and anyone else, safe from the shit happening down here and don't care,' he replied.

'Maybe they know but well... They might be stuck like everyone now, right?' Steven asked.

'Hmm. Maybe so. I think Americans or someone like Germany might save us. Us... Little chance of help really,' the man, named Christopher said and slurped hard on his out of date beer.

'He might come soon, really,' a woman said, suddenly coming near them. She smiled kindly at Steven.

'Forget about him, Cheryl. Please, it's just a tale,' Christopher advised.

'Who is it that she means?' Steven asked, curious.

'The man known as Saint Alan. Here, everywhere and nowhere. Could come at any time to help us, it's what he does' she told him, with that warming smile.

'Who... Sorry, Saint... Alan?' Steven said, looking at them with stunned, simple confusion.

'Yes, well that's what some call him. Others have called him the helper, the Samaritan, or simply the Saint,' she explained further.

'No one is really sure if this person is a real guy. If he actually really exists at all. He is talk from hopeful people, a myth to get them through, a thing to cling to in all of this, these desperate shitty days,' Christopher added with doubt and cynicism.

'He's out there, Christopher. You know it. I'm sorry you lost your brother to them, but he could still be our real hope. Keep praying,' she told him strongly.

'I don't pray for him... Never did before, haven't started now. It isn't even 'written' is it? Saint Alan? Bullshit, Cheryl. We have to be the heroes or nothing else,' Christopher replied and walked away from both of them. He turned back to face Steven.

'Welcome to our charming lovely town. My name is Carl,' Steven told them, deciding to withhold his real name from them. 'Enjoy your time here, however long it may be. You can stay but you'll be expected to help with the rest of us okay?' he then continued on his way between the small crowds across the open mall shop floor area.

Steven looked at Cheryl then awkwardly.

'How are you finding it now?' he asked her. She was a pretty young lady, possibly in her early thirties he decided. She wore lipstick, some make up but seemed unkempt as the rest must be also he thought.

'It is a sad time. Judgement is on us maybe. Some think so. My family are weak and hungry. Where are you from? You look very smart, clever,' she told him.

'I came from... down south. I... yes, I used to be an academic, teaching sort of,' he told her, quickly thinking of some alternative life history.

'Well it's very nice to have a new face here. Good to know you. Everyone is confused about what is going to happen, why this happened to us all. What do you think?' she asked.

'I suppose I know as much as anyone, really. Could be a number of things. We have to try to look at things in different ways now, don't we?' he told her.

'Yes. Some think it is meant for this country. Like it was part of our times, natural. Others still blame the scientists, some others. I don't know. So you came in from the sea?'

'Yes, my boat. Travelling. I don't know how many survived. I will have to get home soon, to Durham in the north if I can,' he told her.

'Hard to believe,' she said.

'I'm sorry?'

'Because of the attackers. Same all over. So unexpected. It was just news at first wasn't it? Then more and more... then... now. Everything gone, lost. All of my old life, and yours too, right?' she said, almost shedding a tear then.

'Here, sit down. Take it easy. We're alive. Free in a way. Life is still... Hey look.' He sat here down on a chair by a doorway and reached over to a nearby clothes rack. He put on a dusty, but warm jacket.

'How do I look? Bit George Clooney? Or Ricky Gervais?' he asked her and struck a pose. Cheryl stopped sobbing then and began to gradually smile again.

'That's it. Better. Want to show me around then?' he said. She nodded, sniffed then stood by him. She took his hand and led him on through the crowds around the shopping mall.

Chapter 37

Over the next few hours, Steven spoke to many of the scared poor souls who moved around inside the shopping mall. Some left, others came in quietly and carefully, bringing food and other items and clothes. They were stealing, he thought, but then realised that really they were simply surviving. Something had happened all around to bring down civilised life – everyday things, ways of living, work, relaxation, everything you would expect from day to day – cars driving by, people talking, laughing in the streets, people at work. This was how things were now, somehow. His fans, his respect, adulation and greatness could actually be gone now, he thought with sudden panic. All lost, his carefully built reputation and persona in the media, his identity, or at least the false, exaggerated one. The laws that the country used to stand by barely existed now. Social, ethical and national laws gone, eroded away, mostly forgotten. Now only primitive desperate basic laws existed, like from many centuries before. It was a more simple and desperate land now, unpredictable and totally changed.

Was it actually his fault? Were these people really hiding from the few sick attackers that had been chasing and terrifying people those many months before? he wondered. He desperately tried not to think about it, but his mind returned to it again and again. He tried to just relax and rest a little, adjust to how things were now, what it meant for him, and how to then get along.

'What did you do in Durham, Carl?' one of the many men around asked him later as they played chess.

'I taught at a school for a while. Then not too much. Then all this. You?' Steven said.

'I was a campaigner for charities and a PR person. I really liked working with the charities, children and families needing help with problems, addictions, money issues. Now... we all need help. Good work. Gone,' the man explained.

'Sounds very worthwhile. Interesting,' Steven said, genuinely fascinated. What had he done to this country, with his thoughtless out of control schemes, he thought.

'Kind of a relief now though, isn't it?' Cheryl said lightly.

'A relief? How come?' the man wanted to know.

'Right, now there's no nine to five, no bills, no jobs really like before, no rich or poor like before. The usual repetitions from before gone. Things are kind of even in a way,' she offered.

'See, what sets us apart from being basic primitive animals? We're hunting and hiding right now. We've devolved backwards. Is that a relief?' he asked, infuriated at her whimsical light remarks.

'So we don't have our cable television with hundreds too many channels, we don't have our plasma screens, our nightclubs, state of the art electrical goods, work deadlines? We are still decent people if we want to be. Still able to be thoughtful, conscious, rational, reflective, intelligent, caring, creative, deep. I'm a good person, not one of them, on the streets,' Cheryl said defending her opinion and beliefs.

'There's all kinds of potential in everyone. We've got language, art, philosophy. Look at the work of Da Vinci, Hawkings, Gandhi, Plato, Martin Luther King Jr., Jesus... People can do all kinds of things,' Steven added.

'True, but what the hell can any of us do right now?' another man asked.

'Hey, we can do a hell of a lot, man! Pick yourself up! There's nothing to lose right now. All to gain,' Steven told him loudly then. He stood, and looked around.

'Where are you from?' asked the older man, staring with scepticism.

'Somewhere I should be right now,' Steven said then walked away from them all.

He felt he had to be away from there – he was wasting time, he had seen that much. He needed to know how his mother and family were then, if they were safe. He tried to look at things practically then. He needed a car he realised as he walked back outside alone. He stood in the back entrance of the alley and looked up and down the street. He really did not want to actually steal a car, but it might be the only option. Hell most people probably already have by now, he thought. He cursed himself and began to walk away up the alley to the main streets.

'Carl, hey!' a voice shouted from behind. He looked back to see Cheryl standing by the entrance doors, and so walked back to meet her.

'You really going to try to go back to Durham now?' she asked him.

'Somehow, yes. I have to get there. It's very important, family issues and that kind of thing, you know,' he told her.

'You're taking a car then?' she asked.

'Probably, yes – I suppose so.'

Cheryl reached into her shoulder bag and eventually took out a set of keys.

'You can have my car if you like,' she offered, waving the keys.

'Oh, no Cheryl. Really, I...' he began to refuse but he could see that she did seem to really like him, and he himself had warmed to her honest caring personality quickly. He felt embarrassed and guilty of his uncomfortable lies.

'Please, it's important for you, I won't need it really soon I don't think,' she added.

'Cheryl... Carl is not my name,' he told her.

'I know. I could tell. I don't mind. I know that it is important though, whatever it is you need to do. Take my car,' she told him.

He looked at her, seeing that she was much brighter and sharper than he had initially taken her for.

'Okay then. Thank you very much. I'm... Steven,' he told her with slight hesitation.

'It's just up around the top of the street there – a Toyota, silver. Toy cow in the window. Good luck,' she said.

'Thanks Cheryl. I'll bring it back some time, I will. Take care,' he said and kissed her on the cheek before walking away up the alley again.

The roads were unbelievably deserted as Steven drove along the M6 steadily, the mid-afternoon sun setting on the horizon alongside him. The only other time he had seen it like this could be New Year's Day or Christmas Day, and even then it was not as barren as this. The lack of life, of movement of any kind heightened the guilt on him once more. It almost already suggested the end of mankind from this small island which had seen all kinds of history, from brutal battles to unifying times of peace and balance.

It had to be a priority before other plans, he might have had, Steven thought to himself while he drove along quietly later. He was back, there very visibly terrible things happening everywhere around. He was keen to get involved, do what he could with what he now knew since the space station.

Before that though, he had to visit his family. It was what remained of it – Gordon gone, and Lucy... where she was, in her way. He managed to travel along to the town in a couple of hours, while occasionally hearing the sounds of attackers off the roadside, fighting, harming others somewhere close enough to fear it.

The house looked as it always had done, but the garden was overgrown, neglected and forgotten. There were broken bricks strewn around, rubbish and vandalism. He could not be so sure what he was going to find, but stepped up, took out his keys. He entered with quiet caution, moving slowly into the dark shadows of the house.

'Hello, mother? Nathan?' he called in a soft tone.

He looked around, saw an umbrella by the hall, and armed himself. He walked down by the kitchen doorway, and peered in slowly. There was Nathan. He was putting together a sandwich and other bits quietly.

'Hello Nath,' Steven said.

Nathan, in a split second grabbed his knife and turned and stared right at his older brother.

'Steven?' he said, amazed and shocked.

'Yes, it's me. I'm alright. How are you?' Steven said.

'Holy shit man. Yes, bloody hell. Good, I'm good. You're fine?' Nathan said.

They hugged then, a long emotional moment for them.

'Where's mum?' Steven said.

'Right, she's down in the basement. We stay there most of the time now. Where have you been?' Nathan asked.

'Me? The space station' he replied.

'I knew it. I said that, I did. Just knew it. Do you know anything about our father, Steven?' he asked his voice quieting.

'He... He was there too. He passed away. But died happy I think,' Steven told him.

'Oh God. Steven, and... Lucy?' Nathan said.

'Yes, she went there. He took her there.'

'He did? Well, it was right, wasn't it?' Nathan asked.

'It would seem so, yes,' Steven answered.

Nathan then took him down in a while, through the back hall passage to meet their mother. There was no guessing how she would be down there, having lost her precious little girl months before. He had to confront her, he knew. The long wide room was dimly lit with many small candles, only a small window to the top left giving some vague light behind thick dirt. To the far corner she sat, she seemed to be occupied with books, many open books, spread out across a large table.

'Mother I've brought food down. There is someone here to see us too now,' Nathan told her calmly as they walked in.

Beatrice gradually turned around, and revealed a dried worn old face, drained of life and hope.

'My Steven. My bloody bastard,' she whispered out.

'Hey, hang on mother. Don't be like that,' Steven said.

She turned and stood as Steven came closer to her at the table where she stood.

'What's all this here? Books, all these books...' he said but realised as he looked much closer at them. They were books about space, planets, and the galaxies around earth.

'Tell me why? Why help him like that, Steven? Why?' She screamed out and sighed, as she hit at him repeatedly, again and again. Nathan stopped her and pulled her back.

'Mother, please calm down. He tried his best. Only tried to understand it all, but Dad, he did it. He is gone now anyway,' he told her.

'Hiding now, scared, guilty like he should be,' she said.

'He died, Mother. Up there,' Steven said.

'Where is my Lucy, Steven? Where?' she asked.

He leaned in, pointed down to the biggest open book, down at the planet Mars.

'There,' he told her.

Beatrice was silent and sat back down again, looking at the books. She looked at Steven, then over at Nathan and finally at her meal on the table.

'She'll cope. Let's go back upstairs,' Nathan said to Steven.

The two brothers talked about what had been happening around the country, space, the space station. After some food and coffee Steven explained his plans ahead.

'I'm very glad you're here with Mum. Glad you're both well, but I do have to go elsewhere now, and meet others. I have to do some things that could change all of this now,' he told Nathan.

'I know, I thought you would. Do what you have to then. You'll be back, will you?' he asked.

'We'll see. Goodbye then, brother,' Steven told him and took his things up again and in minutes he was back on the motorway driving away again.

Chapter 38

He decided to keep in mind the interesting rumours of 'Saint Alan' the redeemer, however bizarre. It made him almost laugh out loud as he drove thinking of it. His old friend Alan, quiet super-intelligent Alan, now moving around healing the sick, helping others across the country after the failed science projects, and academic work for years which he had put himself into. How possible could it be, to really be him? But then it did almost make a kind of cruel sense, or justice – karma, even – Steven thought. He felt deeply ashamed, as the sun dropped below the horizon of the land.

On the road ahead came a man running at his car suddenly. Where the hell had this crazed loon come from? Steven wondered. He swore and quickly swerved the car to the other side and around the man, dangerously careening over to the other lane of the motorway and back. One of them, he thought. As he continued to drive away, the wild man still came running steadily behind the car, like some rabid dog on the loose. Steven changed gear, moved up in speed and noticed signs up on the road ahead. The man will get tired and fall away, he thought. The next signs on the road came up – North East, Newcastle, Gateshead, Durham, Sunderland. He breathed a long sigh of relief.

As Steven looked ahead, beyond the signs, around the next corner, as he got closer, he saw a group of people running along the road. They came down toward his car as he drove up. Mad people with a death wish. His people. Jesus Christ, what is wrong with them, won't they stop? he thought. He slowed down the car a gear, easing the car over to the left but they seemed to see this and followed him in that direction. He just could not be sure of how conscious they actually were, or how much they had devolved. He stopped the car finally and watched them run toward him. They came closer, did not stop. Would they want to talk to him, or just simply attack him, kill him if they could? Hard to really know, but not really worth the wait was it? he thought. Were they just like the ones he had left up in space, he wondered, or different? Did they know that it was he who had ruined everything, had made them like that now, could they know that? No, no way, not at all he thought. They then came within a few short feet of the car, and he finally put his foot down and the car sped away instantly. As he did, he could see one of them, then knocked it, and smashed it into the road with blood splattering instantly all across the motorway. He gasped as he saw it in his mirror. Oh God, he thought, oh hell. These were his people, his experiment. He realised that this was in no way the first one he had killed. They had all been slowly murdered or tortured by his megalomaniacal plans for months.

Everything had obviously become much more volatile, dangerous and unpredictable than before they had left, Steven realised. He had returned a different kind of man, so far pushed beyond his earlier careless self only months before.

This new chaotic, ruined Britain must hold with the beaten cities, the secrets of what Gordon had been attempting to create and arranging while Steven had been a teenager, and then finishing his university education. The family business would be his now, but what did that really mean now, among all the abandoned twenty first century western capitalism, business, life and known society neglected.

He remembered the basic connections that Gordon used to hold through his many frequent business partners and projects over the years – there were at least four very close companies Steven could remember. He knew them to be closely connected and involved with the space station shuttle launch when he himself personally took a major role in the final arrangements. There was one close to Leeds, one down near Bristol, another close to London and then the last possibly beside Bristol as well. He would then, he decided, travel out to each of them if he needed to do so, if it was really possible. It would just have to be. He needed answers. Gordon, the bastard, had taken it away with him, a frustratingly mysterious final family secret kept away too long.

Steven saw that not too many expected rules of civilised living still stood proud – the population everywhere stole cars, electrical goods, clothes and certainly food when and where they could. It all apparently was much easier. Less social moral guilt and personal conflict over wrongs and rights over basic survival and need blurred with selfish desire. Steven had noticed how some police officers were still admirably trying to control society and protect it, but ultimately the masses had seen how little control they had now. Safety was not guaranteed anywhere – not from police, the Army, or any further institutions of the land once relied upon for such dour times.

So with a new kind of positive freeing joy, Steven broke into and stole a respectable modern car and began his journey. He had been driving nearly two hours along the quiet motorway south when unusual sounds came in toward him from around. Canons, erupting. He continued driving but the surprisingly loud explosions continued, random and intimidating.

He took a turn, on a junction down, then saw ahead the source of the noises. He could not believe it – here were some of the still active police force of the land, but they careened wildly along in a large wagon. They hung out of the wagon windows and from the roof and two or three visibly fired out rockets or fireworks as they drove the wagon speeding along. Could they really be actual police? he thought. These crazy wild hooligans were the ones maintaining law and order in some bizarre way here?

They saw him easily enough and their car turned in his direction then.

'Oh, holy shit,' he said aloud.

He quickly spun his steering wheel, changed gear. He could not waste time with a bunch of testosterone rabid wild 'postmen' living out their crazed macho sadistic fantasies. They tailed his car, both driving along empty off roads, beside the motorway. The sky was clouding over, nightfall engulfing them. These crazed punk police had no problem speeding right hard up by his car, crashing hard, metal on metal. Sparks burst out, wheels grinding across the roads.

'Hey stranger! Pull over! Stranger! Stop your car!' one from the police wagon shouted to him.

Steven struggled, swerving to move away and keep distant, but something in his thoughts wanted him to get closer. He did slow the car, moving down the hard shoulder and the punk police wagon slowed clumsily down alongside him. He saw that the journey across this ruined new Britain might need the help of others. Who could he call on though? There were certainly a very impressive list of science industry associates he had collected while acquiring funding and promoting the university post-degree project. He could try to contact some of them, but it did seem that means of communications were much less accessible. It could be just too difficult to make deals or arrangements now with how things were, he thought to himself. His closest friends had probably been his scientific project group after university, but where were they, and what would they think of him now? There was Jane, who he had last seen somewhere up in the space station. He did feel regret at what had happened, but she had made her own choices too, he knew. And then there was Alan. Left behind with his fears and doubts and overseeing their initial science project before the space journey. His old close friend, who could still be there, but in what condition? Steven wondered. No, they did not agree with him, had not been interested and even voiced concern at his truly challenging and fascinating ideas. Other help would be out there, people to use and make deals with, he decided. He would find them and impress them, because that was in his nature.

He was alone now, where he had been followed and listened to and supported by dozens until going out to space. Now the time ahead to him could hold many unknown dangers and hazards to confront. A few aggressive and powerful men and women of law could take the blows and danger before it reached him, he thought. They would deal with the crowds, the public, and he would deal with them.

'Hello guys. Good to see you all,' he announced in a relaxed manner.

'Who the fuck is this? You diseased? Know who you are?' one asked him from the police wagon.

'Yes, I'm Carl Stockham. I'm heading up for a while, to find friends and family,' he explained, watching their faces. They looked eager for some brutal action, the anxious hate in their expressions apparent.

'Oh really? Okay then, Carl. Steal the car, did you?' the lead police punk asked him.

'It belongs to a friend. That's okay though, right? I'm taking it to him you see,' he replied.

'Yes... For now. Down south then?' police punk asked. 'What was your job, Carl?'

'Journalist mostly, writer for magazines and papers,' Steven told them, making the answer up on the spot. 'You guys are the real police around here? Protecting us all, right?'

'Hell yes, that's right. Putting all the scum in their place. Better than the government ever could. We will, until things get back to normal.'

'Okay, that's very admirable, really good to hear. But I see not much really bad things here. I mean, it is yes, but around the country

I hear the trouble is lower down. Help is needed urgently there. They just so desperately need people like yourselves there,' he told them with serious conviction.

'Is that true?' one of the officers asked, listening with interest.

'It really is, from the messages I've been receiving. Really deserving well-trained professional police help like all of you lot,' he added, with a look which urged compassion.

They looked among each other in thoughtful silence, nodding, agreeing together. Would he have to prompt them further, really make the situation seem so perfect for them, and offer many more flattering platitudes on them to rub their egos? They did seem slow to react, he observed.

'Well, we're going around this town. Protecting the town we live in, our people. Where we used to all work, before...' the second officer began to explain, but then lost his thoughts.

'Yes... and we are, but... Damn freaks around, God damn scientists and government messing...' the first began, struggling with his opinion.

'You did work for this town, but now everything is different. The country is different, rules to living, and surviving different. People everywhere, the country all over needs protecting now, unlike before, doesn't it?' Steven suggested reasonably.

'What do you think?' the second officer asked the others behind him who listened in the wagon. They looked at him, at Steven with uncomfortable confused but thoughtful glances.

'He had a fair point of view,' one said.

'Yeah, that's true, really,' another said.

'But this town, us…?' the first countered.

'Well look I do have to continue along on my way so the rest of you do your own thing...' Steven said casually, and looked up the road ahead through his windscreen through the dark clouds

With that statement, he had done it. Two of them joined him, the others turned back to the town. He now had brute force, some well-trained and disciplined muscle to protect him on his passage down to get to the places where he would find the remaining information from the ones who had worked alongside his father.

Chapter 39

Hours passed as Steven travelled in the car with the two police officers, passing quiet streets, town centres smashed up, robbed and ruined shockingly. They spoke to each other, and they told him more about how the increasing violent devastation had pulled down the veil of civilised modern living from all around them.

'So you haven't seen much of this, have you?' one officer, Malcolm asked.

'Well, not really, no. Where I live it was very closed off, tucked away. It's... shocking, just horrific but there has to be... hope,' Steven said.

'Who fucking knows? But we'll go down fighting these bloody freaking monsters. We're not letting them bring down this great land,' one man, Alec, added defiantly.

'When things get better – they will – if they find the nutcase scientists who did this, who caused the illness, the mutation of these people... They say it was man-made, scientists tinkering like they do and what do you know, here we are. You won't be seeing many scientists out and around,' Malcolm explained.

'Is that so? Very probable, I suppose. We'll have to wait and see. We'll get there, we'll get through it together,' Steven said.

'Some aren't sure of that. Could be just natural, some disease just bound to happen, a cause of nature taking its course. But we can still try to stop it, fight it into submission. That's our job here,' Alec told him and punched the inside door of the car. He certainly had some restless angry men on his journey for company, he thought.

The journey began, driving down as bitter rain lashed over their car windscreen. Steven gave directions, feeding them a tale of admirable honour and family ties to keep. The two officers themselves had lost a couple of close family members each – wives, parents, even a baby boy – to the relentless rabid attackers back home. Besides possibly saving many more towns or cities together, they also simply wanted to fight. They had desperate urges, probably too long repressed primitive, carnal desires, to release so much unending anger and rage onto as many of the unpredictable abominations as they could for the loss of the lives they knew before.

They would enjoy it and feel a possible amount of vengeance they could acquire from the often immoral retribution labelled law or justice now.

'You seem to know so much more that most people around. How is that exactly?' Alec asked finally.

'Well you see, I travelled up and down when it was all just beginning, far from home. Seeing family and part of my job really. So I heard things from people around the country. I began to get a bigger picture of the whole thing,' Steven told them, putting a few vague truths in.

'So we're first going to Birmingham – why?' Alec wanted to know. He was far too curious for a stupid, dumb macho alpha male police guy, Steven thought. He could not simply guess these blokes so easily – they might not be the stereotypes they usually were.

'Some family, friends to save. Heard some people there were coming together and trying some interesting things. Maybe more recent news about the disease progression of the attackers, its weaknesses,' he told them.

'Disease? Or plague do you think? We could all deserve this, like a rapture. Some of us are believers, with a kind of faith. A kind of fear of the wrath of God. This might be due to us, and we have to endure it, show that we are better, and that we can just survive it. So how do we stop a plague? Do we just burn them finally?' Malcolm said.

'Depends, I suppose. Might be a few things possibly. Might be hope of change. So yes, also Birmingham had some strange thing happening I heard, they were defending themselves in a different way. Could be well worth seeing,' Steven told them.

'Alright, man with the lowdown,' Alec said, smiling firmly at him as they drove along together.

He could use these two trained, skilled strong men, if only to get so far. They would help if he could get just enough of what he needed, what his father had hidden from him, the frustrating game demanding respect of scientific achievement never fully completed before death. They came then past signs on the motorway, diverting off at a junction down into Birmingham. At first, it seemed just as quiet and ruined as further up north, not a great deal of difference to look at. Desolate shops, broken buildings, a few dead bodies festering by the roadsides as they moved along in the car.

'Okay, so where to now we're here?' Malcolm asked, driving slower.

Steven leaned in, staring hard through the window at the streets outside. He had been to Birmingham, and he had seen the city before a couple of times. Gordon had told him of the company his own had been working with a year or two previously to the ruin. He had begun to really think hard about it... street names, names of possible companies it could be...

It was all just too nondescript, too similar, especially in the increasing dark of night.

'Let's just drive through, toward the centre, see what comes up,' he suggested.

'Hey, we don't just have loads of petrol anymore, you know,' Malcolm told him.

'We can get it from other cars, petrol pumps even. Improvise right?' Steven replied.

Then the screams came. Piercing wails, groans and then screeching and scratching on the outside of their car windows.

'Holy shit, what the hell?' Malcolm said.

'Them, they're outside, here on us already,' Alec told him.

'Okay then drive, just... Go! Now' Steven shouted.

Malcolm seemed to wait, not immediately increasing the speed and moving.

'What's up? Let's move,' Steven told him.

He saw Alec and Malcolm glace at each other then, a silent message, some shared thought occupying their minds.

'No, look we should go on, no time. Not the time, not now, not yet,' he told them.

The wagon shook then with sudden powerful force, swaying before Malcolm then put his foot down and they finally drove away, speeding on through toward the town centre.

'Too close,' Steven said.

'You think? Or not close enough. Like you say, time will come,' Alec replied.

Moments later, the town centre came to view, a tall regal town hall, community centre, then to the far left what seemed like some music area, maybe the famous arena.

'We'll kill some though, we will, new ones down here. Kill them all the way down,' Malcolm told him as they went.

'Shit, yes we will, damn right,' Alec agreed.

'Alright, okay but... Look here,' Steven said then, seeing some interesting split in the road ahead. 'Try going right, the right again,' Steven said.

Malcolm did as he was told, and they did eventually come out at an open wide car park with some long building at the far end.

'This looks familiar to me, it does,' Steven told them, with optimistic thoughtfulness.

'Great, I'll park closer up. We'll go with you, take the weapons, stay close,' Malcolm said.

'If you really have to,' Steven said quietly.

'Hey – we don't really have to protect your clever intellectual arse, you get me?' Alec told him.

'Yes, fine. You just got me wrong. Come on,' Steven said.

The three of them parked and walked along close to the grand building. It was difficult to be sure at first what the building had been used for exactly. Getting much closer however, Steven soon recognised the large company logo adorning the entrance wall.

'So – what's here then?' Alec enquired.

'A place where a friend worked. Could be some useful things here. He said he'd leave some information, diary or press cuttings. That kind of thing,' Steven explained.

'Right. You want in then?'

Steven nodded as they looked around. There were windows higher off the ground to their right, some smashed.

'Well there's up there, but could cut ourselves to ribbons,' Malcolm observed.

'No, maybe no need,' Steven said.

He walked around the front, with a golf club in hand for defence. Reaching some side entrance, he delved into his coat pocket, and retrieved a strange set of key fobs and locks. He held them up, shining light on them with his small pocket torch. Looking at the door locks, he matched up a key. The doors then opened with ease.

'In we go,' he said looking back at the two stunned police officers.

'How'd you manage that?' Alec asked.

'Seems it was left open,' Steven said.

'Bad sign but hey.'

'Maybe not entirely,' Steven told them and quickly entered the building.

Using his pocket torch, Steven walked and illuminated the walls around, going further in. It was certainly a vast impressive business building of sorts. Obviously it had been built with a huge investment of money and wealth behind it. He knew there was some kind of actual testing labs though, Gordon had spoken of them, he was sure. He walked on further, Alec and Malcolm behind him a few feet commenting on what they were seeing inside.

'Very impressive place. What kind of company was this, do you think?' Alec asked.

'Some kind of huge multinational. Whatever. Big business of some sort definitely,' Malcolm said.

They wandered on, following Steven, darted in and out of a number of rooms, looking down corridors.

'You sure there's anything useful here?' Alec wanted to know.

'Yes, had to be. Definitely,' Steven replied, though he was not convinced by his own words.

Maybe there just was no obvious useful research information there to be found, he began to consider eventually. It could have been taken or destroyed, or both he began to think. He heard some small sound, somewhere then. He turned, shining the small torch up a corridor then walked on quickly not finding the source.

'Hey, wait will you?' Alec warned.

Steven ignored his advice and ran on, determined to know what the sound was, and where. It seemed to come from a room up ahead, toward his left a few feet away. Some paper rustling, a voice muttering, mumbling possibly. Steven waited then stepped into the room.

He saw a strange image before him – a man hunched over a desk, knotted, ropey hair, dirty, glasses on but broken, and he was looking over many papers, charts spread out before him, some with bloody prints smeared over them. The man continued to mutter to himself, until Steven stepped in right up closer to him.

'Hello there, friend,' Steven said.

The man quickly looked up wildly then.

'Get out. Leave. I'm... I'm busy here,' the man told them seriously.

'You... worked here. In what way exactly?' Steven asked quietly.

The man laughed then, looking up at him.

'I'm... I did many things,' he replied cryptically, still looking over the many papers, documents and notes frantically.

'Did you know Gordon Lowell?' Steven asked him.

The man turned to slowly give him a strange look then. He stared hard then at Steven with suspicion and distrust.

'Who are you?' he asked.

'I'm his son. I've been travelling. I'm interested,' Steven told him.

'Really? Feel guilty?' the man asked.

'Sorry? Why?'

'Why not? We all should now. Good for the soul,' the man answered and laughed suddenly and loud. 'I'm Ernie Stoker. Tell me something Gordon's son would know'

'Okay... I know what you're looking for, or what I can guess. It involved very secret work of my father, right?' Steven said.

'... That's right. Well, good to meet you then, Steven,' he replied, a little calmer.

Steven leant in then whispering 'I'm with two police officers. They don't know who I really am. I see how dangerous that could be. You being here... Do you have anything that my father kept very secret or know of plans he had?' Steven asked.

The man – Ernie – stood and walked slowly over to some filing cabinets, opening them up.

'He had many plans, your father. Many which just remained simple ideas, dreams or questions,' Ernie told him.

'Yes but... With your company here? Any help he had or things he might have been testing early on?' Steven urged.

Ernie then brought out a file, with tight double bindings on the front.

'Here, take this. Your answers should be inside I believe. Where is Gordon, is he alright?' Ernie asked.

'No, no he passed away I'm afraid to say. Very recently,' Steven told him.

'Oh, not... Them, was it them?' Ernie asked with difficulty.

'Not exactly. But it was... expected. More illness, really. This should be very helpful. Thank you Ernie, very much.'

'You are doing something? Now?' Ernie asked him.

Steven looked at him, saw that this man, while obviously shaken, traumatised, still was a wise observant old fellow.

'I might be, if I can. I think I really can and should – don't you?' Steven told him.

'Look, it's just... Science is dangerous. In a way outlawed since... The fall, fall of the country,' Ernie said.

'Yes, I heard something like that. Sometimes you have to just do things where danger lies – usually the hardest but most important things,' Steven told him. 'You staying here?'

'I did think I might have to,' Ernie replied.

'Maybe not. Go home, get some rest. Check on family, friends. I'll get your details,' Steven said.

They joined the two police officers and as a group left the large forgotten business building together.

'This guy's a friend, is he?' Alec asked Steven.

'A good, honest man. Needs to go home now,' Steven told them.

'So what went on in there?' Malcolm asked.

'Food research, right? Testing cereal or something. All that kind of boring stuff – minerals, vitamins. Big business, that kind of thing. We should look for some food ourselves now though right?' Steven said to them, hoping that would tell them what they wanted to know.

'Yeah, great idea that. I'm so hungry,' Alec replied as he watched Ernie with curious suspicious eyes.

Chapter 40

They drove around town, took some supplies from a supermarket, then stopped down by a pub somewhere. They ate a selection of tinned meat, tinned vegetables and chocolate washed down with some warm beer. Steven moved away alone, and took time to look through the secured files from Ernie earlier. Such secrets could be revealed, a new path to lead him safely now. There was so much, dating back years he saw. All various project concepts, messages back and forth between Gordon's company and the other. Some interesting ideas, fragments admittedly, but so much seemed sadly irrelevant or useless and unfathomable to him. It might have been that he had been getting his hopes up much too early, he decided. It could really take longer than he wanted to admit to himself, as the country decayed and fell to pieces, all civil modern ways further from memory every day that would pass.

Alec came down beside him suddenly, a can of flat lager in hand.

'What you reading there?' he asked sounding slightly drunk.

'What? Nothing really. No, just some stuff from that... the business building. And other things I've found. Just keeping my mind active, I suppose. Passes the time in a way,' Steven told him.

'Oh, okay. Have another beer if you want. We got a few left. I'll leave you to it then,' Alec replied, slightly perplexed.

They decided to camp down in the back of the pub they had found. Alec and Malcolm blocked up the doors, and secured the windows tightly. They were travelling together, but suspicions were inescapably there between them, their minds tired but restless.

The following day was brighter, a strong blazing sun shining high over the desolate streets. Malcolm drove the wagon, Alec and Steven in the back seats. They headed down the motorway, toward London then further west Steven believed, giving directions every couple miles. Around London should be the bases of a couple more companies Gordon had dealt with and in them, more information, or plans or something more to help him. As they drove along, Steven took out the documents again, looking for more obvious meaning, rereading parts, reconsidering text in other ways, statistics, numbers, theories suggested or any great significant clues to come out at him.

He remembered how Gordon had used to like to boast. He had been a distant man mostly, but there would always be sporadic unexpected grand boasts of new theories and projects he had in mind, which he would suggest to Steven, in small parts, as if only to tease and test him occasionally. He saw his own grand boastful behaviour right there in those memories.

There could be something, he thought. There were pages of recorded results of special experiments from a few years back, tests involving diseases, immune system, and cell structures. It was certainly very close to what he needed. So close, he thought. Almost close enough.

The car slowed then, and Alec and Steven leaned to see why Malcolm had done so.

'What's up now?' Alec asked.

They saw out ahead of them on the open road a large group of people standing simply arguing with each other loudly, fists shaking, some pointing, shouting. They eventually looked up to see them in the car.

'Who the hell are they?' Steven said.

It could be unwanted trouble, unavoidable crowds blocking their road ahead, an angry mob, fighting with no direction or focus. Were these people mentally ill? Steven thought. Don't they move when a large vehicle speeds up toward them? he wondered. He then opened the side door, and stepped down and out to meet them.

'Hey, excuse me here, could you please step aside for us please do you think?' he said loudly, getting their attention. 'We need to drive past,' he told them.

One man at the front looked surprised and possibly insulted even.

'There are greater things around us now,' he said cryptically in reply to Steven.

'Sorry, what are you talking about exactly?' Steven asked.

'The Saint man has been seen, close enough to here. We could be saved soon enough. We can all praise God of future times, and grace of hope after our self-harming ruin and fall,' the man said, sounding like some overexcited televangelist preacher.

'Saint man? Oh...' Steven said. 'Look, I need to get past. I hope you are all safe and well, and that sounds very... nice. We will not interfere but can we simply pass and we'll leave you, okay?'

The large group shook their heads with sadness, but generally seemed to hold joyful expressions over their faces. What was all this new religious crap? Steven wondered. But then he thought logically it must just be expected. It was simple anthropology, the ways of human life – forget God or faith, but after tragedy, return to pray for help to unknown higher forces. He could always envy religious people – it seemed so easy, he thought. Not that he pitied or despised them, or looked down on people of faith, but he personally looked to science, tests and logic before even considering an all knowing force somewhere, somehow.

'The Saint man heals, stops the attackers. No one else can, not police, not government. Only the Saint man and his angels. He is close, we have heard good word of it. Be thankful,' another one of the crowd explained to him.

'Right. Someone did mention him... but... Okay. That's very good. I'm very pleased for you all. I am. But really, I need to pass. Please?' he told them.

Would they get angry? Was he blocking the path of their saviour, even?

They looked at him, seeing how he really did not seem to be so impressed or amazed at the good news they had for him. They did move though, away to one side as a group. They watched him get back inside the car with Alec and Malcolm, and quietly Steven waved goodbye as they drove on past them.

'So what were they saying? Why were they standing there like that?' Malcolm asked Steven as they drove on.

'Oh, they think this mysterious Saint bloke is near, coming soon and going to save them. Like the old myths and religious faith, a distant hero will end the suffering – gives all hope to continue. To be expected, country fallen into shit, people get spiritual, desperate. I suppose prayer costs nothing, while it wastes time,' he said.

'Watch your words. I myself believe there is a God over us, in some way, maybe even Jesus Christ himself. Got me through some hard shit actually, so just watch your opinion,' Alec told him.

'You believe in this Saint guy though too?' Steven asked with more empathetic caution.

'I might actually. Maybe, where's the harm? Look at the crap we're in. I think things were always much simpler than we liked to believe, than we tried to make them.'

'But really, some mythical man who can actually heal people... who no one actually seems to have witnessed first-hand... It's just... Fine, you have your belief, I'll have mine,' Steven told him.

'Better to believe than follow science like those bastards who ruin the country. Too busy then?' Alec said.

'Never mind. Just... you think you'll go back up north later then?' Steven asked.

'Wait and see what's down here first, then yeah I suppose. See how bad things are though. Right now, maybe as a police officer, I should be like a saint too, and just save souls I can. Simple as that,' Alec told him.

'Right, fair enough. Good intentions,' Steven replied.

Steven could not help but be amused and perplexed at what Alec had told him, but he knew it took all sorts. He knew even there were many scientists with strong faith, which seemed a contradiction to him. It took all sorts, he thought.

Closing in after a couple of hours, they came down into the outside of greater London, but the roads then suddenly seemed to become much busier.

'What's all this? These cars... Hey they're police cars, look,' Malcolm enthused.

Alec and Steven leaned in seeing the increasing line of roaming cars, some with lights flashing, even a siren then.

'What are they doing?' Alec said as they watched.

Steven was not pleased by it. It seemed to be another obstacle in their path, he just did not need another then.

'Try to keep driving forward,' he told Alec.

'No, hey they're just police. I think we'll stop, meet them. See what it's all about,' Alec explained, nodding to Malcolm.

'No, wait come on,' Steven protested. It did not help, and they slowed down by a roadside.

As half a dozen or more police cars drove in a large circle, one came down by them and pulled up. The two men inside came out to come along by the wagon and met Alec and Malcolm, Steven sheepishly standing in the doorway to the wagon.

'Hey, what are all of you doing?' Alec shouted over the noise of the cars driving around them.

'We're patrolling this area now. We're the police, the authority keeping the laws strong now. And you?' the lead officer said.

'We're police from up north, near Newcastle,' Alec told him showing his police badges.

'What you doing here then?' the Officer asked. 'Far to come with the state of things how they are.'

'We've been told some really big trouble happening south, and we might be of use apparently,' Malcolm explained.

'Well, shit yes definitely. There are some strange damn things going on. We got all the fucking attackers out still, but also some have reported a number of people stirring shit up, making trouble, messing things up even more. Anarchists, vigilantes and stubborn locals but just causing big problems,' the Officer told them.

'Right, we can help with that,' Alec told him positively, and he then turned to look at Steven.

'This what you were talking about? Crazed vigilantes, idiots stirring trouble up around here?' he asked.

'Who's he?' the first Officer wanted to know.

'He's not police, just this guy. He heard, told us about things. He's a traveller,' Alec explained.

Steven stepped down, cautiously joining them all then.

'Hello. I'm Carl. This looks interesting but I have to move on,' he said.

'Look, you said there was some bigger shit happening down here – this seems to be it,' Alec said.

'No, it's not. I mean, it is, but that's not it. There's more, something else to see further...' Steven said, almost running out of lies to feed them.

'How do you know so much in the first place anyway?' one of the police officers asked suddenly.

'Me? Like they said, I'm just a traveller, that's all. Picked up information. I'm going to find family and friends,' Steven said in defence quickly.

'Bad time to travel now. So?' the new police Officer said, waiting for an answer.

That moment, a number of people suddenly ran out of the side streets, screaming, yelling many panicked wild things. The officers and Alec, Malcolm and Steven all looked across at them.

'It's happening. We've on the right track. Get them!' the Officer ordered.

'What? What's he doing?' Steven asked. He just could not predict the ways of any police now things had changed so much.

They watched the four other police cars circle in closely, screeching as they quickly parked up, the officers getting out and chasing the hysterical people running wild near them through the open street crossing way ahead. They pulled the people down, cuffed them, pushed them back toward the cars quickly with little effort. Steven was shocked, but not entirely surprised really, he thought.

'Does this happen a lot?' Steven asked.

'He asks too many questions,' one of the new police Officers replied, hearing him.

'Look, traveller – just be quiet or do some travelling,' one told him.

'I intend to' Steven said and moved toward Alec.

'Hey can we get going now?' he asked.

'You know, we think we'll help out here right now. For a while,' Alec told him.

'No way, damn it. You can't do that here, now,' Steven argued.

Then they heard the noise growing louder. Attackers were approaching, they knew instantly. The police rounded up the people they had caught, some running off successfully. They packed them into the cars, then began to drive away all at once together. Malcolm looked back toward Steven.

'Hey Carl, you coming with us?' he asked.

'I... Wait,' Steven said. He stood and listened – the sound of these attackers was different; some unusual tones to the screaming, different moans as they came into the main roads.

As he stood, he picked up an abandoned metal pipe from the ground while two attackers ran out, straight toward him. He readied himself, waited, and they split off, running past him on either side. They continued on, disappearing up further streets. It was not right – they did seem just like other attackers, but they seemed distracted. They were annoyed, it seemed, somehow.

He walked forward, listening carefully. He could hear more distant sounds, then they gradually built up, becoming more audible. Again, suddenly two more attackers ran out, screaming but passing him by, running on beyond him as if he just was not even there. Steven took a chance then, and walked on quickly through the street where they had all come from, looking around for answers. A lone man appeared, looking slightly pleased and amused. They made eye contact then, each seeing the other with hesitation.

'What did you do?' Steven called out. The man casually walked up to meet him.

'What do you mean? They just didn't see me,' the man said.

'That's a lie. Tell me your trick,' Steven said.

'Okay, I just tried something. Just an idea I had with the attackers, not much,' the man told him.

'No, you are a skilled person. Tell me, what was your past?' Steven asked.

'No past of interest, mostly paying the bills,' the man said.

'Don't bull me. What? What did you do? Here's some truth, worth something these days – I was in scientific research. Now you,' he told the man as a careful offer.

'You know what people think of those who worked in science, right?' Deacon said.

'I have heard some things,' Steven said.

'I am Deacon. And you?' he said.

'My name... My name is Steven,' Steven said, deciding to be honest.

'So then, don't even begin to bullshit around. If you are saying that you are like that or had any connection to that kind of work then you really need to know what to expect, and be really fucking careful,' Deacon warned him.

'Should I really?'

'Damn right. Any kind of unwanted kinds of really terrible danger could come to you if you're talking like that in these times. Got a death wish?' Deacon said.

'You know, I am beyond that. I have a wish of another kind. And you, perhaps I might not even believe what you tell me of yourself,' Steven responded.

'We are both obviously either very brave or very foolish enough to align ourselves with what people believe of modern science. So we want to both be in the same line of danger it seems at least,' Deacon judged thoughtfully.

'That does seem to be true,' Steven said.

'So then, show me what you know. Let's play our game,' Deacon told him.

'Alright. Follow me quickly,' he said.

Chapter 41

The slim, paranoid blond man lead Steven away, back through streets, quickly running between buildings, to finally stop at the back doors of some faceless building among many others in a long row.

"You might have heard of my father. Gordon Lowell?" he said.

'I am Deacon Blakelock, psychological neurologic research. Yes, yes I certainly did know of him. Your father did come and meet with the heads of my projects group a few times I recall. And you – you were on television, I think. Come inside, Steven,' the man said as he opened up the entrance carefully.

They walked in, and inside were dark passages, illuminated by spaced apart small lamps, flickering fragile light around them.

'Like most places, this building is a mess now but I use it and the equipment as much as I can. I come and go very carefully,' the man explained.

'So what had you done to the attackers running by me back there?' Steven asked again.

'I was testing out some theories, psychological, biological... Sounds, symbols around them... It made a difference, defected them, usurped them. I'm pleased,' Deacon told him.

'These theories – they came from you originally?' Steven asked.

'Good question. So where did you come from? What are you doing around here if you too came from the most dangerous of backgrounds, science?' Deacon asked.

'Travelling, like I said. But you know Gordon, my father. This your place of work – before?' he asked.

'Yes. Good times until the attackers ran loose. Cherished, good memories,' Deacon said.

'There can still be many more to come,' Steven said.

'In all this? It's just about survival now. However long that can last,' Deacon replied.

'Honestly? You've found something right? Have you been in touch with others, people from here or others with similar work, theories and knowledge?' Steven asked.

'Only just. It's so dangerous to try or even take the chance. But yes, just,' Deacon told him. 'Want some chocolate? Some beer?' he asked.

'Yeah okay, thanks. Sounds good. But tell me about my father's work,' Steven said.

'You think it's very important still? Maybe. I knew him to be connected to projects linked to the eventual space shuttle mission and bioengineering, right?'

'That's right. What else?' Steven asked.

'A mysterious man, powerful, very respected but often disliked if I am honest. Some did not wish to approve his ideas. I heard that a number of times. You did not know him very closely?' Deacon asked.

'No, I did – probably too well eventually. But like a son knows any father really. The business side just as vague as anyone else seems to know. So can you show me anything?' Steven said.

'Should I? Aren't you travelling on soon?' Deacon replied.

'I might be, or then again... Actually, I am looking for things my father did, or did not do. Things which could be relevant to right now,' Steven said.

'You...where did you go? You were on the news, on the industry websites I remember now. What happened since? Just travelling, then the attacks?' Deacon asked him.

'Travelling, that's right. But work, away. Problems in work. Now all this. So...' Steven said.

They moved on through the building, upstairs Deacon leading them into other rooms, even computers buzzing showing information, data, programs running.

'I'm impressed at this,' Steven said honestly.

'Thanks, it takes a lot of effort with the god damn police swarming around. Got to keep your eyes and ears peeled constantly,' Deacon told him. 'Okay, look at this.'

He directed Steven's attention to some pages of information on a computer screen before them.

'I've seen that project mentioned before. My father was involved,' Steven said, moving closer to inspect it better.

'Right. And what a strange project it was indeed. This is really pretty vague, but it does at least suggest what could have been researched, looked into. These theories – very radical things, deconstructing DNA, splicing genome structures, mixing, adapting, immune levels and more...' he said with serious grim tones.

'It's true he did seem to have plenty of bold ideas ready to go, but he managed his international pharmaceutical projects firstly,' Steven told him.

'Yes, well you have to pay the bills before winning the Nobel prize, right? We both see very intriguing possibilities in your father's ideas don't we?' Deacon said.

'It seems we do. But this is only one part of a bigger puzzle involving him,' Steven said, trying to dampen his interest.

'So can you tell me more?' Deacon asked.

'I only know so much right now. That's why I'm travelling.'

'You see something hopeful in the things your father was trying to do, don't you?' Deacon said.

'I see something unfinished, and I am his son, I trained in the same line of work. Who have you been in touch with?' Steven asked.

Deacon looked back and was coming to feel a suspicion of Steven. He was thinking that something was not too good about the questions Steven was asking. Steven watched him and waited for the reply.

Police sirens wailed from outside the building walls then. Crazed screams followed behind.

'We'll have to move again soon. How did you get here?' Deacon said.

'Me? Honestly? Got a lift off two police officers,' Steven told him.

Deacon stepped back then, worried.

'Relax, I told them about things happening here. It was a safe easy ride for me. Just used my head, and them. Now I'm here,' Steven said.

'Right, well come on then, with me,' Deacon told him.

They packed up laptops and left the building, moving out quietly and quickly through dark back alleys toward another place.

'Okay this – this is where I am staying at the minute. I like it, and it's safe so far,' Deacon told Steven.

He unlocked the door, and they entered. Inside was like some retro bohemian commune, a messed up hostel with techno geeks around, more computer hardware, books, and some scientific apparatus spread out between them and over table tops.

'These are some of my fellow co-workers. Neil, Sandra, Liam, Emily,' Deacon explained pointing them out. 'This is Steven, everyone. A new friend of ours.'

They casually said hello and each looked at Steven apprehensively then.

'Deacon? Where is this bloke from?' one said.

'Yes, really Deacon, you can't just...' another began.

'Hey, listen – he is okay. My decision. Alright?' he said to them.

They looked at him for a brief moment, and then continued their individual activities, focused on studying various clocks and monitoring levels and readings. Deacon took Steven through to a separate room where more laptops were set up waiting to be used, various programs running.

'Look, I'll show you what I was testing out with the attackers,' Deacon said, moving in toward the computers, starting up a program and opening files quickly.

'So what is it? You trying to just peacefully move them along?' Steven asked.

'Well, no, maybe more than that – I don't know, look at this,' Deacon said and he pointed to the computer screen.

'Some reacted to this – it's scents of different kinds – it calms them. Then others reacted to this – these sound waves from a reformatted handheld radio. It deterred them, like you just witnessed. Not for too long but long enough to get past them,' he explained, visibly pleased with his findings.

'That is actually very interesting. But that's it?' Steven said.

'Well, look, I don't exactly have the same levels of research and experiment equipment apparatus as I used to,' Deacon told him.

'Right, right. So you have plans with these techniques?' Steven asked.

'Well we – mostly I – have been trying things, like you saw. It really could help us to survive. To cope, reach supplies, and maybe help them,' Deacon told him.

'Really? What state are they in now? I know that's a very difficult ethical issue, but shit, the attackers are so... distant, so vacant. If people are in there, deep down inside still, it would take so much extreme testing, neurological research, probing – those times are pretty much gone for a long time I'd say,' Steven told him.

'So you think what? We just stamp them out? Survival of the wickedest?' Deacon replied.

'No, no but there must be other things possible. In fact, I know there are,' Steven told him.

'Okay that's fine – you have your opinion, I'll have mine. I was actually preparing another test for later. You can watch if you stick around long enough,' Deacon offered.

'Alright yes, I'll help out if you want,' Steven said.

They decided on an agreeable kind of way to move forward together. In the town, Deacon and his friends knew of some unfound food and electronics hidden beyond the industrial estate, near the town cinema hall. They had monitored the police groups and groups of attackers for nearly a week continuously in preparation to this occasion. The police could mostly be timed predicted when they would patrol near the estate, the attackers were of course less predictable but that was where Deacon and friends would implement the discovered techniques.

When early evening arrived, the sky darkening about, they all moved out together careful and silently. They took with them knives, rope, torches, and cricket bats to defend themselves if they needed to against any oncomers. Steven looked around the base before leaving, making a mental note to himself of where things were kept and how to reach them.

After around twenty minutes of walking carefully under shadows of tall trees and high city walls together they reached the place. The city cinema hall was coming into view.

'We've communicated with people outside of the United Kingdom, you know, over the Internet, webcams, just a few times as mostly the connections are just terrible but still there to varying degrees – it all still works fairly well, depending on battery and solar power sources. Signals have to be hooked up, but yes, we have still reached outside,' Deacon revealed to him.

'And what? What's the news? The response to our nation's problems?' Steven asked genuinely interested.

'Well, America and Europe intend to help at some time, but when that might be... It is taking them so damn long. So long. Apparently they might send troops first, medics, maybe but we wait. Breath held still,' Deacon explained, showing low expectations. 'Okay, see the police cars – wait,' Deacon told them quietly.

'Yes, they're driving away now. So now you move in?' Steven asked.

Deacon waited, watched the sight of the cars going back away from the place gradually then... gone.

'Right. Wait. Everyone got their equipment?' Deacon asked.

The others nodded in agreement and so they continued on. It was most probably only a few minutes across the lengthy car park of the deserted estate area, but time seemed to draw on with intense paranoid fear escalating on them. They moved on and seemed good, and then the noises came.

Wails and demented groans carried through the night air toward them. The attackers were arriving, as expected at some point. The group split apart a few feet, two of them spreading the drops of specially designed scent over walls and ground further away in opposite directions, then Deacon himself using the radio advanced handheld device in preparation.

'You know what you're all doing then?' Steven asked him as they did each acted out their parts of the experiment.

'Hopefully, yes. Just keep close to me, okay?' Deacon told him seriously.

'Yes, right,' Steven replied.

The first couple of rabid attackers stormed forward from an alley to one side quickly then. They ran hard, any trace of previous human soul lost deep in their eyes, or hidden behind disease and mystery. The group had come back together, the trap set and could now simply just hope they could make it.

'It's going to work right? Deacon?' Emily said with obvious nervousness.

'Wait. Just wait,' he told her.

'But they're coming, not separating or spreading yet Deacon,' Neil said.

'Let's go on. Fuck it, right?' Sandra said.

They stood tight together, attackers almost at them. The scents were discovered, attackers coming to reach them. The attackers turned slowly, stopping like confused dogs, agitated but obedient.

'It's working now,' Emily said, surprised.

'Right, that's really amazing...' Steven added, watching, honestly in awe of the work of Deacon and these others.

'Knew it. Now let's get what we need,' Deacon told them with satisfaction.

They ran on forward, attackers way behind them, far too distracted by the trap and the industrial estate remained deadly silent.

They passed the side doors. Deacon opened up the locks with a crowbar with unexpected aggression, the security alarm long since redundant.

'Made it. Very good,' Steven said.

'We still have to make it back later,' Emily reminded them.

'We should be okay, I think. Follow me,' Deacon told them.

He walked on, through quiet corridors and opened up a door, to reveal a large room which contained a surprising large quantity of long life food, computers, hardware, and more useful equipment.

'Oh my God, this is better than you described. It's unbelievable,' Emily said.

'Yes, there is a lot here. I prepared it myself at the beginning with a friend. He's gone now sadly,' Deacon told them. 'So let's fill up our bags. Choose wisely, we can return though soon enough I think,' he said.

Steven was definitely impressed – the way they got past the attackers, and now found all of these sought after extremely useful goods carefully hidden away. Deacon was certainly a very clever guy, Steven thought to himself sadly.

Chapter 42

Almost fifteen minutes passed, and then they appeared at the back exit again. They once more prepared themselves, then set out to move with their cargo bagged up. Deacon led them away, looking cautiously ahead. They did expect to encounter the attackers, they knew them to move around near that time and it seemed the prepared new techniques would help them again. They just had to time their defence and everything would be fine.

'I'm certainly impressed with how it has worked,' Steven told Deacon in a whispered tone as they moved out together.

'Thanks, but we're not back safe yet,' Deacon told him.

They entered the route they had come by, and in a couple of minutes heard the sound of attackers close enough.

'Watch all sides carefully. Have weapons ready but trail the scent away, and I'll prep the noises again,' Deacon told them.

They continued – three attackers burst forth, arms flying around, screaming in tongues as they rushed toward them manically. The scent did confuse them in seconds, but one ran on still, closing in near them. Deacon flipped on the noise box, frequencies skipping, to find something offensive to the attackers. It was jamming unexpectedly to his annoyance, he found. A problem was occurring, and the attacker stepped right up toward Deacon easily. Emily came back, and began hitting it with her baseball bat violently, blood spurting wildly.

As they tried to cope with the trouble, Steven quietly made off alone. He went unnoticed right then, during the difficult fight against the stray attackers, until the noise box was restarted, tuned and powered again. In that time Steven made his way back, quickly and alone to the base. Entering with a key he had stolen from Deacon, he found the laptops and equipment and bagged up what he wanted to keep and take with him. He rushed out, careful of any witnesses around, and headed for one of the cars they had ready to use.

He had learned enough of what Deacon had been up to there. It was certainly very useful, interesting to him with great potential at least to help him on his journey, he thought as he drove back out onto the motorway again.

Outside the dirty windows, Jane only saw guilt and regret reflecting back at her. She saw her fault, her mistakes out there, waiting to inflict pain upon her if she would let it. She knew Steven and Gordon had been involved in extremely dangerous things, Alan had warned her, the email message and even before that she knew he had tried to suggest something. She had used him to begin with, for the job, the experience, but then she did find that she loved him, without seeing his genuine honest love from the start. He had been such a passionate, honest young man, so special. She had been thinking of her own career far too much. She had been brought up that way, but that was no excuse. She did it, she had acted like that and lost him. He was gone now, somewhere out there hopefully, out among all the broken streets, ruined society around her.

Her own town was as quiet, dead and broken as most others she had witnessed. Such a sad state of things. She found her parents and sister still living in their home, but they had boarded up windows, put up wire and only went out with neighbours or in large groups to find food. She rested over night with them, found her bearings and decided on her way ahead. She would find Alan. He deserved it, if she did not deserve him even.

In the morning, under dark clouded sky Jane walked out with a bag on her shoulder holding food, drink, and a baseball bat in her hands. She walked out of town, met a few people, then a couple of friends from her streets, but many had disappeared or just possibly been murdered, died or become attackers, she realised. It was difficult news to hear as she continued on. She had asked about Alan – some were not sure who he was, and others knew but were not optimistic. She was feeling increasingly bitter and angry with herself while she passed the ruined town streets, a way of life lost and becoming memory totally.

Perhaps she had to return, defend her family and home with her sister and neighbours? she wondered. That could be the way. The sky was darkening around her, taking away the light and view ahead. She knew it would be the wrong thing to be out there still soon.

'It is Jane, right?' a voice said.

She turned and saw a lady she knew from her life in some way.

'Yes, I'm Jane. You...?' she said.

'Jenny Bealson. Technician at the university you came to, remember? Where have you been?' Jenny asked.

'Me? I've been away. Just returned. Jenny, can I ask? – have you seen my... Alan, Alan Blake. We worked together before all of this happened,' she said.

'Alan? That Alan? No, haven't seen him myself in months. But hey, I've heard a lot about him, haven't you?' she said.

'Really? Like what?' Jane asked.

'He's out across the country. He's the one they all talk about now. It's unbelievable really.'

'They talk about him? Why? I don't get you,' Jane said.

'He's out helping people they say. Like some doctor but more like a healer, sort of. You know, being trained how you all were,' Jenny said, lowering her voice.

'What do you mean?' Jane asked.

'They call him Saint Alan, or the Saint man,' Jenny told her.

'You're joking, right?'

'No, not at all. Some really hope he is. So are you staying around here somewhere?' Jenny said.

'I was but... Where did you hear of him last, what direction?' Jane asked her.

'Over toward Birmingham, that way down, they say.'

'Right, okay. Well, I might see you around hopefully, Jenny. Goodbye,' she said.

'Yes, okay then,' Jenny replied, watching her walk away.

So there were plenty of brave scientists spread out over the country, in hiding for their lives, stigmatised, unfair propaganda spread about them, fear and hatred aimed at them if ever they appeared on the streets, but they were some of them doing special things, trying to change how the country had become in a number of ways. That could be a threat to Steven, but he seemed to be successfully gaining what could be of use each time he was finding another person or company related to his father's work and theories.

He drove along, his own obsessive thoughts and tragic memories alone for company. He was admittedly feeling lonely, and wondered what might have happened to some of the business friends he had come to meet over the last couple of years. Were they alright, were they alive? he wondered. Thinking like that was getting him down too much, so he eventually drove along by a large abused supermarket. He parked up and walked up close. There were police officers guarding the doors bizarrely.

'Hello, can I get some food possibly, please?' he asked the first one he met.

'Yes, but rationed. Only two bags. Essentials. We'll check them when you come back out,' one officer told him.

'Okay, fine. Fancy a chocolate muffin or tin of spam you know?' Steven said, but got no laugh from it.

He went in, spent around ten minutes gathering some tinned food, biscuits and chocolate bars. He even poured some beer into juice cartons and closed the lids carefully. They did check his 'purchases' when he left the building.

'Take care pal, and be very careful,' the officer told him in a friendly but suspicious and stern manner.

'Thanks guys. Good to know men like you are here, doing this for all of us. See you around then,' Steven replied as he walked back to the car.

In an evening after travelling, Steven stopped near an industrial estate and took out his palm computer. With saved power, he turned it on, and began writing emails, in the hope that they would be found. He spent over an hour writing and sending half a dozen to begin with, using a handful of significant international web addresses of people and companies he used to know, some his father was very close with. He was spreading the news to parts of America, specific institutions; that things were very much under control and getting gradually much better now. That the real state of the country had been very much exaggerated weeks ago. They did not need to come straight away, the emergency had ceased now. He created several new names and user identities, assuming a number of locations within the United Kingdom. He explained away problems with news media, coverage and contact with masterly contrived lies, but they would very likely convince and satisfy the present foreign concern.

He took his food and drink into the car, along to an open park area up the motorway next to a picturesque lakeside area. There, he got out some of the files and a laptop with some beer and a chocolate bar to the side of the lake embankment to do more investigating. It took hard focus and study, noting various names, concepts, giving them serious thought. The company names, projects, theories written about, some eventually reoccurred, ideas which signified a few important things to him. The old crazy scientist and Deacon were finding useful results, but were still far from bigger more revelatory ideas. They did not think like Gordon used to, only seeing smaller broken down parts of his more whole bold radical puzzle. Piece by piece, it was revealing itself to Steven, it was becoming clear slowly but it was, he knew it. And with it came more truth of the life of Gordon years before.

Going by the notes he was keeping, there were two more places he had to visit as soon as possible. He was alone now, no police escorts, no other scientists to manipulate as he travelled. He had only himself to figure it all out, he could not give up. Judging by what he had seen, other scientists around the country, while hunted, hated and in hiding, were still likely to be testing the attackers just as Deacon had been. That was what Steven hoped at least, as it could make things easier if they already had tried to fathom the theories of Gordon when he would reach them. Gordon had been viewed as too radical, too extreme, eventually too much of a risk taker, possibly unethical but they individually had parts of the theories which Gordon had tried to get funding for years earlier. Now it was important, much too late it was just what the country needed Steven thought.

While resting parked at a motorway service area, he turned on his laptop, and using a couple of aerial modem connectors, tried to attempt reaching the Internet and outside of the United Kingdom. A very long silent moment passed, loading signs onscreen teasing him, barely changing as he watched. Others had apparently managed to reach America, Europe, and further, surely he could do it as well, he thought. There were possibly some others he could contact, ask questions. Just how much could other countries actually intervene right then? he wondered. What was the real chance that they were going to come over any time soon he thought. Slim chance, he believed. What he wanted to know was more about how the country was operating – police, government, especially scientists out there.

It was beginning to seem like a waste of time, and then all of a sudden the page on his laptop screen loaded up – 'connection made'. Thank God indeed, he thought with relief. In the next few minutes he logged into various science research social sites and message networks. There it was – there had been contact. He was a topic of discussion in sites. He laughed aloud then, impressed and satisfied with his reputation. A number of respected and influential scientists were wondering where he had gone, if he was alive, but most interestingly just what he had actually been involved in personally before the attackers broke loose on the streets.

Some had made guesses, speculating, cynically, some discussed his father and his influence on the science world and on Steven. They were very close to actually finding some of the reality of things he saw, reading posts and blog messages. Then over some national news sites, they warned him to be careful if he was out there, along with the many other scientists of the country taking blame for the way things were.

Noises came, growling, feet running manically. Steven switched off the laptop, packed up and prepared himself. He had learned a good few new tricks since space. They came from behind, from the far left around the service area shops and cafe, screaming and falling like a stampede as they tried to reach him, clawing toward him relentlessly. He ran back, held up a cricket bat, smacked one of them, then another. He ran back further, then grabbed hold of some useful devices. He flung out two vials of mixed scent samples, strong and potent. It worked, it seemed, thankfully, attackers turning from him, curious and distracted easily. Another was left raging up toward him still. It looked him in the eyes, as if about to accuse him of its state of existence, but then grabbed his left arm tightly and pulled.

It tugged at him, Steven punching then, blood on his knuckles instantly. He fell, and moved over, finding the noise box he had stolen. Flicking the switch, it worked fast and effectively. The attackers screamed and moaned, moving back turning from him. Yes, he was obviously well equipped he observed. He rushed over to the car with laptop and equipment in his arms. Seconds on, the car was back on the motorway, Steven confident and optimistic for the place he was to reach soon.

Chapter 43

As days had passed, Alan had met many people as he walked through towns, between cities while he moved on. Some nights he was offered a bed, some nights a floor in some disused building, other nights he slept in an abandoned car somewhere. On this bright morning it was a ruined, beaten house where Alan sat with a kindly woman and her young daughter. He drank the tea she had brewed as she watched him.

'You have been travelling around, haven't you?' she asked him in a curious and friendly manner.

'I have, yes. Since things fell down, I have found that I have been able to... help others out and around. I've met some who do it very well – paramedics, doctors, Army people, Red Cross, nurses... They trained in the areas necessary unlike I. I do know some things. I know remedies, medicines, compounds, solutions, sort of potions, techniques of healing. Though the doctors and nurses know much, a lot of their resources and equipment is gone, missing or not available to them. My techniques seem just as helpful now – maybe much better it seems,' he told her in a quite humble way.

'Thank you again for helping me and Katy. She is very grateful to you, you must know that. You came at just the right time,' the lady told him. 'More tea? We have some good cake, even vegetable stew.'

'Well, if you are cooking some it would be very welcome,' he replied.

'Oh yes, I will bring you some, definitely,' she said.

She looked at her daughter then, in a proud way.

'Stay and talk to him,' she suggested.

'Yes, alright. I'm Alan,' he told her.

'We know,' she said.

'Right, yes. That makes sense. Strange, but I understand,' he replied.

They both looked at each other. The lady then walked away into her kitchen.

'You are a very brave man,' the girl told him suddenly then.

'Me? I am just helping others, I think it's what has to be done. What we should all do, especially now. You would help someone else if they needed it, wouldn't you?' he asked.

'Yes, I think so. I would try my best. Like you,' she told him.

'That's good. Listen, don't be too scared now. I know there are things around to be afraid of, unknown things, evil in a way, but there are good people too like me who want to help us. Help you and your mum, okay? We'll be okay,' he told her.

'My mum already heard of you – you're the Saint. Saint Alan,' she said with an innocent wide smile up at him.

'Really? Maybe. You never know. Maybe he'll turn up. Things are alright now though, for now,' he replied.

'Mum's going to call people now. People want to know where you are,' she told him.

He stood then, alarmed by her words. Her smile was charming and lovely, but she did not know what she had told him. It brought him dangerous news.

'Thank you Katy, thank your mother for me, for the tea. Say your prayers sweetie, and I might see you in future again. Take care,' he told her and then quietly and carefully bolted to the front door.

It was simply yet another place which too soon became dangerous to linger around. Either attackers surfaced to chase him unexpectedly or there were people who blamed others like him, and wished to strike, and take out their pain and suffering on him when the chance arose. He was a scientist, or used to be. Now, he was not exactly sure what he should call himself. He did what he could with things he knew, which after a couple of weeks in this ravaged country seemed actually really unique and special.

Back on the open streets now. Careful vigilance on the turns ahead, around the slightest sounds to suggest danger, coming attack or trouble. It was comforting to stop every couple of days with new people, discuss how things were, offer advice or hope even in his small personal way. He had to move, the mother must have made a message to local police or other angry mobs, who waited for a chance to meet this mythical helpful mystery man. He stayed in the deep shadows around as he moved along, near close to bushes, under trees. He heard groans then, somewhere close, then footsteps in odd movement it seemed – attackers, he thought.

He stepped quickly up toward the side front of a closed up café and shop at the small village centre. He saw two lurch out, rambling out and moaning in their painful movement. Alan thought quickly and took out a small glass vial from his inner jacket pocket. He waited until one more attacker had stepped out, increasing the group, the three then moving with more united focus in his direction. Alan then threw the small vial with steady powerful anger and careful aim, and it flew far ahead, crashing to pieces on a wall right by the attackers.

The three figures turned, moving apart slightly in angered confusion, but distracted to look around, confused. They sniffed around, then took to biting at each other and clawing at the wall beside them. Without wasting any time, Alan then ran out fast past them and across through the open road on the other side of the village centre. It was a successful personal trick, science as makeshift defence and it was seeing him very safe in his travels.

He was not sure why he had become this new modern myth, a folktale in desperate tragic times, suitable but unexpected urban legend. It had begun accidentally, with him covering up his well-learned academic scientific knowledge with the first he had helped those months back. He had joked then quickly when he realised, saying religious healing. But in such dramatic times, people took it to be the truth, reality, probably because it sounded so helpful, good and comforting. He had told a few how to do some basic things with plants, herbs, chemicals around the house, or found naturally to aid healing and so his myth continued on while he moved down the north, then steadily south of England.

There were rumours significantly building up in the last few days over which Alan had heard while he moved along alone. Some people, seeing their known attackers running around as had become expected at some point every day, had witnessed very unusual sights, apparently. What he had heard from a few hysterical strangers was hard to fully understand, and believe, but given how things had become, he was open to more similar doom laden news. If he was now being described as a mysterious, mystical prophetic saint healer, the news that some attackers were changing physically, and seemed to have gained a number of strange unsettling new powers was obviously containing a form of truth woven somewhere inside.

No actual scientists had managed to successfully find the real cause of the attackers before the country had fallen but a few did come very close, Alan remembered while he himself kept notes, thoughts jotted down, scribbled in a useful old pocket notepad. They were close to finding the truth of it all, the cause and reason, or it had begun to seem that way, but then things continued. People died, lost equipment, were taken away by the police groups. They had not fully begun to really investigate the cure or solutions in the way which Alan would personally look. He was finding very interesting personal success there, even without weeks of official research and academic testing beforehand. He had done his experiments privately, it seemed he had found much of great use. With Steven away from him, up there, now Alan was much more confident with his secret discoveries. What used to waste time, and seem immature to others, was possibly to be highly valuable soon enough, he found. He finally had admitted their worth to himself.

Chapter 44

Weeks spent roaming the north of England alone between helping people here and there, Alan was viewing life in a number of different ways now than before. Civilised living was gone, twenty first century Western jobs and careers, lifestyles gone – for now at least. No academic scientific research for him, no nine to five for others, or minimum wage exploitation, even. He could be another person, not the Alan who would be working as usual. It was a relief in some ways, he thought repeatedly, though almost with guilt. So he did think of himself as 'Saint Alan', the moving myth between the dangers of tragic Britain. More incidents were confronted, attackers avoided, fought but also viewed and in a sense studied over time. He could not help but do so. They were fascinating, in the same way that a deadly exotic spider or scorpion would be. They were mysterious too, like him now. Not in the same way at all, but their creation and symptoms still curious after months. Eventually he did witness unexplainable things involving them-laws of known physics seemed to be over turned, ignored at times, distorted in slight but shocking ways. Was his mind weak, too tired beyond logic finally? he began to wonder.

Even previously known famous viruses and diseases from the past of mankind history, none were so elusive, exotic, unexplainable or indefinable as this. There had been sickness, dementia, rabid violence, cannibalism, painfully slow deaths but nothing like what was seen right now. This was a new species potentially, a tribe of monsters previously as human as the next man or woman, now... Something deadly but fascinating to all. Their strange continued mystery quickly prompted him to increase his own level of mystery, his vague known existence to others more unsure, indefinable but hopeful still.

The more mysterious the attackers remained, the more mysterious he himself would be, creating hope, having no known flaws, weaknesses or mortality while only for the more part existing in only spoken words and minds. While he privately began trying to find scientific details and information, he would be mysterious hope to the fearful people who hid and waited in the towns and cities around the country. He was hope, more so then, than any idea of an injection or hospital cure like before. A community was afraid but desperate to find some help, while police and corrupt local politicians were taking control without justice or equal peace or notion of any form of democracy now. Around behind some houses, near a dark back alley street, a group of almost brave enough local people met up together in quiet shadows.

'Listen Joe, cheer up. We got some great wine this afternoon. And here's more to cheer you – the Saint has been seen today,' one man said in a low voice.

'What? No fucking way. The real one?' the other man, Terry asked.

'That is what we've heard. He came along by Middlesbrough today. Coming close by now,' the first, Andy, replied.

'Well then, praise our moody, forgetful God. It's finally our time,' the woman added.

'Don't go praising the newly reinstated bloke in the clouds yet, but we could think of meeting him, contacting him first, before others, and before he leaves,' Andy said.

'We could make it out there if we have to.'

'No, he's probably moving on – we won't catch him.'

'Don't be so damn negative now. We have to try, shit. What else have we to depend upon? What other hope is there around here now? There's only him now. Only the Saint to save us from these times,' she said.

'Right, okay, but there's the damn police blocking our main roads before we can cross over in the direction where people have said he was heading toward today. My own family and others do need his help, and I know his importance. You know I do. Can we hold back the police then?'

'It could be done. It is worth trying right? It is, it's just that... We might have a difficult time of it.'

'But then there are the attackers as well. They've already fucking done us in in a right bloody serious way, you know that. If they come out at the wrong time, we'll again be totally fucked over. No damn prayers will help out there.'

'We should try, you know we should.'

'You really think so?'

'Andy, we really have to now. He is justice, he can help now finally'

Under two hours later, they had organised their group. There were at least twenty minutes of walking to go to be close to where saint Alan had been observer that afternoon. Cold winds blew over them defiantly against their wills. They began their walk. In the same quiet, broken grey town there were egomaniacal sadistic out of control police groups roaming, taking out their overtly hyper masculine anxieties, and insecure frustrations and confusion with extreme violent effort on any who questioned them with the simplest of looks or remarks.

'So this bloke can really heal? Not like some kind of freaky TV preacher from America but like proper biblical crazy shit?' Andy asked with his known cynicism.

'That's what some have said they've seen him do in front of them, before their jaded eyes,' she told him.

'Even now? Without any big religious television company around with dogma and lies? What is he, a cult leader?' the other asked. 'Because I'm not joining any mind-warping nutty group for simple gullible or suicidal dopes. I've got a brain thanks, no matter how bad things get.'

'Yes, I agree, me too. I'm no bloody idiot either. Weak people want someone to lead them, guide their directionless lives,' Andy agreed.

'He's not really a leader at all. He's a gifted man, just a... He knows God. Just helps people, that's all. Some people are simply just gifted, that's it. We need that now,' she explained.

'He knows God, does he? Can he ask why the fuck all of this crazy evil bad shit has happened to us then? Get the answer for us will you? I'd love to know,' Andy said.

'Look, let's be honest – we as people have not all been living or working in a wholly decent, morally right manner for a long time now have we? All kinds of mistakes, all kinds of sins. It could be karma, grace, or righteous punishment from the Lord, or chaos of the universe, but we still aren't at all innocent in our actions, and that really could have some part in things I think, but that's just me,' she added.

'Okay fine, that's... No, you are right in a way. You are right there. Okay,' Andy said, nodding thoughtfully finally.

Sounds were building then, they heard commotion some place close to them.

'That could be attackers now.'

'Great, I want to bust some heads in about now,' he said.

'Stop talking like that please, I told you I don't like it,' she told him.

'They are in our way. They're not us any more now. They're either going to get us, kill us, tear us, beat us, or just get right in our damn way,' he told her.

'They still live. They feel, in some way. You don't agree, but respect my view. They feel,' she said imploring with humanity.

'A scorpion feels, a wild jungle tiger, or lion, even deadly snakes feel but...' he began.

'Yes, and you just stay clear of them, respect them and their ways,' she said.

'No, this is different. They are a problem to us,' he replied.

'Look, we'll see what is up there, and deal with it,' the other replied.

Turning the final corner at the top of the long stretch in toward the open area of the town, they saw the sad sight of police officers beating and harming people caught out in the wrong place at the wrong time for them unexpectedly.

'Shit. We'll have to wait.'

'No, fuck it. I want to go with the damn police. They need putting right,' one said.

'What? No, not now anyway.'

'Yes, we can get them down. There's what... five or thereabouts? Just go in hard, fast, knock the hell out of them with focus.'

'We'll wait until they go. Just hold on,' Andy said.

'We can't wait though,' she urged.

'We have to now.'

'See? That's two against one. We go fight like troopers,' another said.

'No, just... I don't know,' she replied.

But then he ran out before them, right out quickly into view of the punishing police group out on the streets. One of them turned to see him in seconds.

'What's this? More losers wanting a knock about, eh?' he said while kicking down another hard to the ground with satisfied relish and cruelty. The police colleagues around continued hitting out, beating civilians to pieces, blood spraying over abandoned cars and pavements. Andy and her watched speechless and shocked, not sure if they still could move in with any sure hope then.

'We can go now,' he told her.

'What... What do you mean?' she asked.

'He has helped us out, see?' Andy said and slowly stepped out forward.

'Look,' he said and they watched the scene longer.

The other police officer eventually stopped and finished with their initial victims, to view this new cocky, mouthy bloke defying them and their actions. He was brave or simply suicidal.

'He'll get beaten to his death,' she said, saddened.

'No, we'll step in. If we're careful, just follow me, okay?' Andy said to her.

He took her hand and ran around a number of neglected, burnt out cars, and kept to deep shadows while the other provoked and challenged the police officers.

'What's happening in this town?' he asked loudly. 'Are we all going under with no dignity like animals now? I mean, who is leading us out of all of this? This was a proud country, bold and civilised, modern and hopeful not too long ago you know?' he told them.

'Hey, you can just go back to your hole or take some medicine just like this lot, okay?' one lead officer threatened then.

'Can I have questions answered at least? Will we have work again? Freedom, safety, opportunities? Prospects or even peace?' he asked.

'You ask too much all at once. We are looking out for everyone. Be thankful for it. Things have changed for now. Deal with it,' the officer warned him. They all moved in close for him as he walked around steadily aware of them.

'Are you guys all safe? From the diseased sick attackers? Where are they? Do we know? Can we just hunt them, kill them?' he asked.

'Forget it, close your mouth, guy. Your family must be waiting for you now. Or do you need real instructions now? A clearer way to understand how we rule?' the Officer said.

They moved in closer to him, watching his movements. He casually looked around him, and saw the shadows of Andy and her moving away higher up the open area.

'You know... Not right now, fuck it. You're all too god damn dumb to explain anything to at all it seems to me, poor lower mammals,' he said quickly.

In a quick flash moment they jumped forward at him, as he also instantly leapt away, with an extremely well timed quick desperate movement from them. Without stopping, he ran on, up ahead, through shadows and alleys away and to a safer path.

'Andy? Hey, hello?' he shouted with caution as he ran on.

Had he missed them? Did they just decide to continue on not risk waiting for him? Shit, he thought. He needed to go now, whatever they had decided he had to find his own route to safety. Brutal police waited at his back, eager to deal out pain in bludgeoning painful amounts. He looked around him, pissed off greatly. He should just maybe turn back, it seemed. He slowly turned around, as he considered his narrow options. There were the police officers coming up closer, only a few feet away.

Andy and the woman, Lindsay, walked on quickly, knowing they just had to continue for the sake of their families and people who cared.

'He will be alright, or at least... he helped us in a good brave way,' he told her.

She remained quiet as they went on together.

'So, do we have the right directions? I mean, he could be anywhere really, couldn't he?' he stated.

'No, he'll be where he needs to be,' she told him with quiet sudden confidence.

'And so, where will that be?' he asked her.

She looked up, where long open grey roads and tall grey buildings stood. A dreary dark cloudy sky hung over their thoughts, pressing down as ever though heavier then.

'Let's go over to the left, near the long open roads,' she suggested.

'You sure? We'll be open targets then. Not entirely safe, I say,' he cautioned.

She gave him a look suggesting a need for sincere trust then.

'Alright then. You win,' he replied.

There were no cars really, maybe only one or two out along the horizon on the further wider motorway, more bold people taking risks to protect loved ones, or look for better conditions wherever they could be.

'You used to work in a florist, right?' he asked her as they walked.

'Yes, but not all the time. I was studying again, a degree in social studies,' she replied.

'Oh, that's... a good thing. I miss being at work like back then, on the buses,' he told her honestly, looking so sad.

'Even all the flowers I see now seem to have lost some amount of colour, never as bright as they were before,' she remarked.

'It'll get better. Bad times don't last forever. They can be the most painful times, but they end, sometime' he told her, with some kind of hope.

'But sometimes it takes generations. We didn't know such bad times, until now. Other countries had all this, all the time, every day – the Middle East, Africa, war-torn, brutal, corrupt, tragic places, not nearly as much life or freedom as us but now... All they ever know in their lives. We had dour digital possessions, styles, fashions... If only we never knew it all, all of that,' she said with a sad tone.

'Right, I see what you're getting at. Wait, look; over there – what's that?' he suddenly asked, pointing out to the horizon.

'Some people, groups moving along. Who do you think?' she said.

'No idea. You think we should go nearer them?' he asked, looking out at them.

'That's near the direction we should be going in,' she told him.

'You're right, I know,' he replied.

He looked at her and decided they both seemed to think that was their path to follow. They moved on ahead, nervous yet determined. After another fifteen minutes they came close enough to see the groups clearer.

'Hello? Are you alright?' Andy called over with caution.

They continued and then met them a moment later.

'Hello. Yes, we are okay. We have been walking all day. We heard... The Saint, he was coming, supposed to be near here... You know of the Saint man?' the lead man asked them.

'Yes, we came out here to find him too. He... he's not around here yet? Where have you been?' she asked worried.

'We walked through past Middlesbrough, got a lift so far after that. Go back out now. If he did come this way, he is definitely gone now. You should probably get someplace safe too now, quickly,' he told them.

She turned, and looked so sad finally, and Andy patted her hard on her shoulder to comfort her.

'That's it then,' he said quietly.

She looked around, still unsure, still wanting proof, reassurance from somewhere or someone.

'Yes I suppose that's...it...' she slowly agreed.

The other two small groups walked on past them looking tired and regretful. Andy and Lindsay stood on the open roads looking at each other, then back in the direction they had come from.

'Lindsay...' he began.

'No please, don't say anything now,' she replied.

They began the walk back home together, disillusioned and feeling foolish. Nightfall was darkening deeper over them, taking any remaining clouds away into the blackness of night. Nearly another twenty minutes down the road, a loud dramatic series of screams and wails broke out from the direction to their far left.

'Jesus, what's that?' Andy said.

'Oh God, let's walk faster,' Lindsay responded fearfully.

They picked up their pace, the path they walked darkening, disappearing ahead in shadow. The pained moans and wailing continued on for minutes still, and so they eventually ran hard and fast to reach home. It was quiet around soon enough, but dark, deep blackness engulfed them, keeping familiarity of any kind away.

'Are we close to home yet?' Lindsay asked Andy.

'I think we're getting there, just a while longer,' he said.

'I heard someone,' Lindsay replied. 'Footsteps near us, somewhere close.'

'Okay, we'll hit them hard. We have our weapons, we'll be alright. Get ready,' he told her.

They stopped, and equipped themselves – golf clubs, knives, baseball bats out, held tight, ready.

'Okay then. Anyone there? We're ready for you. We want no fight, but we'll defend ourselves with the hardest bloody hitting attack,' Andy declared aloud then.

Someone did move closer to them from within the darkness and shadows of the tall trees around them. Footsteps came closer, they could hear them.

'Hey, watch it,' Andy said.

'You are definitely strong, brave people,' the voice told them.

Lindsay took her flashlight and moved it up slowly. It revealed a smiling man before her, in loose jacket, dirty worn jeans, a bag over each shoulder.

'What are you doing out here?' he asked.

'Us? We're heading home mate. Do you know of the Saint man?' Andy said.

'I do. That is a name I have picked up,' the man told them.

'Alan?' Lindsay said.

'That's right. Saint if you want, it seems familiar these days. My new name. How are you?' he asked her.

'What? It's you? Him?' Andy said looking at Lindsay for a response.

'I can't really promise visions, raising the dead or bringing down angels to help, but I just do what I can. Bit of this, bit of that,' Alan told them modestly.

'We have come to find you. Like everyone seems to want to now. Others we met half an hour ago said they did not see you,' Lindsay said.

'Oh well I'm very sorry. I'm sure they'll get through. Like I say, I'm not sure certain salvation, for the troubles, no hero or miracle man. Not how people are telling it anyway. But that's what happens right? People just exaggerate,' he said.

'It seems so, yes,' Lindsay agreed.

'Are you busy? I mean we hoped you might come to help our families in some kind of way,' Andy said. 'Well, we hoped the Saint would help...'

'I'm pretty tired, actually. I've just found a guy over here who needed some help, took some effort, serious attention,' he told them.

From within the shadows to the side of him, another man came forward then.

'Hey, you lucky ones. Here he is then right? You were so right, Lindsay,' he said to them, smiling.

'Oh my God. You, you're okay,' Andy said.

'Well now, yes. Just missed a full on gang beating from those maniacs back down there. Then this guy came in, threw in a few strange impressive tricks of his own, saved my arse in seconds. A true Samaritan alright. He's a clever one for sure I'll say,' he told them.

Together they all then walked back down to town, but through different paths, Alan near the front ready to help defend them. Reaching their own enclosed neighbourhood, they took him in, inviting him to rest and eat if he wished.

'Thank you for this hospitality. It is actually good to meet so many genuinely pleasant, reliable good-natured people. I will do what I can, I simply want to say that you can't expect me to cure people for sure, okay? I cannot guarantee it, alright?' he told them.

'Yes, we do understand. But you are what people talk of now, you are hope and faith and love. Something, someone to look to through this darkness,' one told him.

He knew that, no matter how uncomfortable it seemed to him. He understood what he was to many now.

Chapter 45

In the morning, Alan was taken to meet some of their family members and friends nearby, ones feeling sick, people with injuries and sores. He was no real doctor or medical professional, and he only had some basic knowledge in first aid, but had picked up advice from those who did know more. This he combined with his own extremely unique personal chemical formulas and that was what counted. What was really significant he knew, was the potions he had made up and which he brought with him. He took time to make a quantity of the medicine he had come to define in the last few months, but which originated from the allotments earlier. He offered it around, gave small quantities to those in severe pain and suffering. He had seen the impressive results ever since his findings at the allotments and the following tests in private.

'I hope you see good results from what I have given them. I have seen it do good a number of times – not every time, but most. Now, I must go on. I am travelling to meet people elsewhere. Thanks again and well, pray for much better times ahead. Goodbye,' he told them.

'I have seen some disturbing things among the groups of attackers. Though I have found some solutions to keeping the disease at bay, they themselves seem to be gaining unexplainable strange abilities now. Quite honestly, just shockingly strange things I have seen. Do not be too alarmed, it seems more to be about how they act together than their aggression or acts toward us,' Alan explained to them with serious urgency.

It was mostly a long arduous journey that Alan undertook through the country, down the Midlands to the south eventually, but he did meet similar men and women that he knew. With a couple of weeks of careful emailing and internet communications, he did send messages to some fellow scientists and postgraduate friends who understood the work and theories of which he described to them. They all knew to be so very alert and weary of letting others know their profession and their whereabouts if they already knew. They, like him, knew many people would so eagerly wish to harm them repeatedly and with great pleasure given the opportunity, but with careful, coordinated planning they could still work through continued tests, and help each other.

They did not follow Alan, these few chosen scientist friends from his and other universities and science companies. There were five of them – two women, three men and all were between twenty one and twenty five years of age. Some were back in their home town still, and three – two girls and one guy – were spread between Coventry, London, Portsmouth and the south of Britain. As Alan moved down the country, hitchhiking and occasionally driving some of the way, they all separately heard the growing myth; the modern folk legend of him as 'Saint Alan'. With his blessing, they individually and collectively continued to elaborate and embellish it, add to it and strengthen it as whispered rumour and spoken sightings.

Three weeks in, Alan came to meet with Jessica – a graduate Biology Master's degree student in Coventry. She helped her disabled father and cancer stricken mother, but found time to offer help to Alan also when he appeared eventually. He thanked her as she let him stay in a spare room for a few nights. They spent time exchanging theories and scientific concepts concerning the attackers and the fallen country together. She asked and was honestly very curious about how he had so easily and quickly become this elusive, inspirational figure, giving hope to so many around the country while attackers roamed and police beat others.

He explained that while he did know much expected academic scientific information and theory, he also had come to discover some very helpful but strange personal findings.

'I just cannot explain it all fully yet in pure scientific terms, not while I cannot do the expected level of industry testing and monitoring, but I have helped a good few with some chemical and biological techniques I have found,' he told her.

What he tried to tell her next she found difficult to believe immediately, and with total seriousness though she did want to.

'I know how crazy it sounds. You must think that I've simply lost the plot, right? I do not want to boast at all. You know, as much as I love science, many decades, even centuries ago; before we have obtained the most basic scientific knowledge, testing devices created, and procedures we saw things around us in much more... suspicious, superstitious ways. And that, really might not have been a completely bad thing. Not knowing laws of physics, biology, chemistry, the universe around us; many believed more easily in ghosts, witches, demons, spirits, ghouls – all that stuff. The unexplainable was all around, respected, everyday back then. I think so much still is, and now we can be in honest helpless awe and respect once again,' he said.

'But we are scientists, we work to understand things around us, existence, solve problems of life around us,' she told him.

'Yes, but we should also see there will always be things to stir us, amazing, unexplainable things in our lives. Whether the work of God, random chaos, quantum mechanics black loopholes, we will never know everything. Right now I don't know the why or how of this, neither do the public, maybe that's good.'

'Really?'

'I tell you this – times are frightening now but people have belief, they have sorts of faith, in someone or something. That can get people through, despite the illogical foundations of it,' he said.

'I have faith in science,' she said very quietly.

'Do you, do you still?' he asked.

She seemed quietly unsure but so was he, he knew. But some faith in some unexplained mysterious positive force seemed good to him. Beyond his analytical, calculating scientific rational and logical mind, a notion of a force perhaps like God seemed to him increasingly possible and uncomfortably but inevitably present against his better judgement. But that might be his new outlook, he came to finally admit to himself. He would not ignore it any longer, and no longer deny how things seemed.

'I can take you to someone needing help, from the attackers. Your talk about unusual help could be much desired, from the rumours,' she suggested.

'Alright, before I leave tomorrow,' he agreed.

In a short enough time, he was led out to a house a few streets near. Inside a family was quietly occupying themselves, playing cards, reading books, some even praying silently in one corner. She led him through.

'Good evening. This is a friend, and he might be able to help Daniel. We'll just see him – is that okay?' she said to one of the people by a table.

'As long as he is not asleep, yes,' the man told her.

They then ventured on upstairs, stopping at the second door on the right. She knocked, then entered inside.

'Hello, Daniel? You awake in here?' she asked quietly.

A young man, possibly in his early twenties looked up from his bed. He seemed feverish, pale and sweating yet thin, drawn in the face.

'This is a friend of mine – he has some unique knowledge of medicine, treating sicknesses,' she told Daniel.

'Hello there, Dan. Have you been feeling bad for a long while?' Alan asked.

'Around three weeks. I'm... I'm worried about things,' he admitted.

'Cough up any blood at all? Or just feeling sick, like a fever? Throwing up, dizzy or confused?' Alan enquired further.

'Yes, some of that. I did cough blood first time, two days ago. I don't have much hope, I mean I try, I want to see my friends and get out again but... it could be wrong,' Daniel said.

'Okay. Daniel, I'm going to give you a drink which I'll make up now, and also some special mixed compound too. Rub that on your sore muscles, your face and neck every four or five hours. Have the drink again tomorrow, around the same time, okay?' Alan instructed.

'Will it... Can this cure me?' Daniel asked.

'It might. I will not say it definitely will, but it might. It has worked before on others. It is hope, not a definite cure. It's just strong hope, okay?' Alan told him 'Nice to meet you. You have good friends and family, that's a blessed thing'

He then gave him the drink and applied the mixed compound in a small container, leaving them at the bedside table. Alan and Lindsay then left him, smiling and waving goodbye hopefully.

She took Alan out and they returned back through the streets to her own home again. He slept in relative comfort for a change, then woke with warm, powerful sunlight over his eyelids in the morning.

'I will pack up, wash and be going again very soon. Thank you for your kindness here,' Alan told her, finding her in the kitchen downstairs making coffee.

Less than fifteen minutes later she led him out, back toward the main roads near the outskirts of the town.

'Do you want to see how Daniel is now, before you go?' she asked him as they stood looking out at the open roads ahead. Alan looked up with a simple smile.

'No, I hope he is good, that is enough. He has hope in him and more to go now. Take good care of him and yourself now. Goodbye,' he said and then began his journey alone once again. She watched this lonely, mysterious saintly man go from her, but he had left a mark, she knew as she smiled.

He walked out alone across the streets again, but felt a sadness. Alongside the grey burnt out shops and vandalised windows he cursed as he moved on.

'Goddamn pressure... Too much to know, and too much to consider...' he said to himself.

Chapter 46

Some hours passed by, Alan walking on between shadows of abandoned tall proud buildings through small villages and towns, past great tall trees, parks, forests, some that had burnt down tragically. He came close toward an area where he knew some acquaintances should be, he hoped. He had contacted them days before, they had discussed the state of things, and the journey he was taking. He followed roads on, then found street names which he needed to see, they led him close in near the heart of Coventry. Before he could begin to search, he was confronted by two men suddenly.

'There you are. Are you well?' one asked him, walking up quickly.

Did he know these men at all? Yes, or the one speaking to him at least, he thought.

'Good day to you. I am well enough, thank you,' he replied.

'We've been waiting. Expecting you. We need you. We have tried things, like things you suggested. Do we need longer? Can you look at our work please?' they asked.

'Yes, alright then. I will come with you,' he replied.

They took Alan carefully away through a maze of back alleyways, behind doors, into a well-barricaded and fortified building behind well overgrown bushes and trees. Inside, they checked the locks and bolts were again secure, and then continued deeper in, on toward a room where a series of tables waited, all with scientific equipment sat out, prepared and functioning.

'We haven't been caught and it is very tough getting the supplies for the tests here,' one told him.

'I am very much impressed, but this is not my own goal,' he told them with respect.

'But you have to help us out, you know so much more. They all are thinking all kinds of things about you, you know that?' one said.

'I know, I've heard much of it. It is no bad thing right now. You can't deny that, can you?' Alan said.

'No, true. You will help us though?' the man asked, still hopeful.

Alan stepped around the long tables, and he looked at the experiments set out before him there.

'We have done as you said, and we listened to your words carefully but...' the other began saying then.

'Did you?' Alan asked 'Did you listen to my words or yourself? Listen to something else now – the answers aren't in me, or you completely.'

He walked up, observing one of the test situations laid out over a table, the tubes, flasks, then wires and conductors.

'Show me now, what has been happening here – the test itself, the problems you've encountered then' he said to them.

They guided him through, then began the test he had suggested they begin when he had emailed them previously.

'Brian – fuse, pour... Mark...' one said.

'Yes, yes... Pouring...'

'Good, but... Then move...' Alan replied watching the liquids running through tubes, mixing as the chemicals heated up.

But he pulled away, something right as the other lit a fuse and moved in too close, much too fast.

'Shit, no!' he shouted loudly, reacting.

'God above, holy...' Alan said, obvious pain in his words. He quickly pulled away his hands, some blood splashing the table surface then. His palms were burned badly, the smell of freshly burnt flesh in the air.

'I'm so sorry, I really am, oh God,' the scientist told him, looking so distraught.

'It's... okay. Not your fault really,' Alan told him. 'Any bandages?'

They did quickly cover up and dress his bleeding scarred hands, but first all three observed the deep shocking marks in both of his bleeding palms. The electricity from the test had been a short but extremely powerfully hard burst of electricity. So powerful, it seemed the flesh on the backs of his hands had been damaged with such an intense shock all the way through to the other side of the hands. With bandages wrapped tightly and wounds seen to, Alan laughed loudly to himself, rocking in the chair as he sat near to them. They could not believe his reaction then.

'You alright?' one asked.

'Finding my humility, I think. Never better, I'd say,' Alan told them, with a wise smile.

'Is that it then?' one asked.

'We can try again if you like?' he said.

'Are you really sure about that?' another asked, as they all quietly sat and stared at his injured hands.

'Oh yeah, but I'll just watch this time,' he replied.

In the morning, they did begin their tests anew again, with calmer steady focus. Alan only observed from a desk at the side of them, with occasional advice as it began.

'Can you see what's not working? You must see it, right?' one said

'It's your concept, it's working out there, isn't it?' the other said.

'Yes, it has been... I don't see it, though. It just works in its way. There's something else but it's still not totally clear to me,' Alan told them.

They took careful measured steps, and went through it all again with close precision. He told then what he knew, calmly with care.

'That's it then, I suppose. No fucking use here then, is it? Forget it all then,' one said dejectedly after a while at work.

'No, you both know it. You know what I told you, that's enough,' he said.

It confused them, but they thought about it with consideration. After that he then left them, and while the time may not have been successful in producing large quantities of his potential cure medicine, they did know enough to continue on without him in confidence.

The journey back down to Earth for Jane and Douglas had been a challenging ominous ride. They had only been able to do their best at guessing how to set the coordinates and create a path for getting back. They prayed and hoped and simply let the hours and days go by them. It had been all they could do. Finally, they came down, a massive impact right into the sea along the coastline. Both after some difficulty managed to escape the pod, and swim out across to the shore. They walked into land together, exhausted but relieved to be back. It did not last.

Things were unbearable, cold air around, dark bitter clouds over her still. Jane saw them coming out, arriving and moving in their recognisable manner. Attackers approached the street ahead, as she stood hidden and observing from behind the shop waste bins of the alleyway. They stumbled out, like feral dogs, savage and stupid but dangerous creatures. This time though, Jane was shocked suddenly. Between the group of speechless attackers, she saw something come up from the ground, it seemed. What was it? What dark effigy was rising in such a startling and disturbing manner? she asked herself.

They parted there, the attackers, and between she saw two more simply rise up out of the ground below between the others. They all then joined together once more as a group, and continued to amble off ahead. Jane waited, just thoroughly shocked in disbelief of what she had witnessed right before her, and once they had gone she stepped out forward to where they had been. She investigated the area where they had been moving, right where to two new ones had seemed to come up out from nowhere, easily emerging from below. There was no sewer or manhole opening as she had initially thought, no apparent opening or ditch there even, no visible apparent possible reason or explanation for what she had seen moments earlier. Things could not be more truly confusing and disturbing now, could they? she thought to herself as she looked around her for answers.

Chapter 47

The long dark months had been lonely and fearful, with a bitter discomfort between the family for Steven's mother, his brother and younger sister. They stayed at the mother's house still, through the ruin, but it had been ahead of time prepared in surprisingly good form by Gordon, with eventual thankful paranoid caution. He had pondered some of the potential and now resultant tragic chaos which would happen. They were thankfully secure for a good selection of all kinds of food and drink which had been stored in their lower basement wide larder rooms, and the house itself very meticulously secured and ready before the many groups of attackers began roaming after both Gordon and Steven had left them, travelling up into space away from them and earth.

It had hurt the brother and sister deeply and emotionally painfully, giving them so many unanswered questions about why both their father and older brother Steven had to leave them so suddenly. Not only that, but why both had gone out to space together as far as they knew? It did probably make sense in some way, they understood, knowing that both Steven and Gordon were incredibly successful in science work and research, but it was such a hard thing for them to accept as they were left with their mother, and around them the country was faced with a daily increasing danger and uncertainty. They spoke little of their haunting and troubling thoughts, which all three experienced continually – the most disturbing being the question of whether Steven would return to them at some point.

It had been planned of course – they knew that really. It had been well announced, and all of the public nationwide expected the many scientists to be returning after at least five or less months, it had been said. That had passed now, but since that time so much more had taken the immediate attention of everyone nationally, every day for all of them. The panic, hysteria, accusations and fear escalating to an unending level. Beatrice had not been personally too emotionally concerned about Gordon returning to them – there had been years of distance and bad feeling which had kept them apart, and they were only on civilised terms for the children. She did though, of course, wish her son Steven to come back to her, even if she had warned him about his wild, often careless risk-taking habits. She had in some way expected him to fall into some similar problematic situation, but this was about as big as it could have been. She wanted him back safely, and then she would keep him from Gordon for good. She cursed Gordon for it all right from the very beginning, but then also blamed herself – she knew she had to in some way – for a good deal of the troubles to her family, and even the chaos around them all out on the streets, all across the country. She knew she could have spoken out, could have told someone like she had often considered to herself.

Only a thought, that was all it had been. Too much guilt, and shame for marrying such a surprisingly immoral, thoughtless work-obsessed fool, she thought. While she had long ago divorced from Gordon, she did know him probably better than any other person around him, than anyone who worked with him. She had admired his skill back in the day years ago, and had been taken in with his charming bold creativity, his strong admirable pursuit of practical solutions in medicine and scientific research. The mistakes came after a while, the excuses then, and all apologetic lies which built and surrounded him, separating them day by day. She knew and expected it, and let him continue for a time.

America called Gordon over then, all those years back, then they abruptly returned, secretive job changes and quiet rumours then fights, threats and the final pregnancy. After the girl, Lucy, had been born, Beatrice left Gordon but knew his secrets still, like no one else ever would. Their children needed safety and calm, so she tried to keep them away from their erratic obsessive scientist father while they grew up together. College had been difficult, but building up a strong persona, he eventually headed for university, and then did spent more time with Gordon, two men now with similar career opinions, though he soon began to regret it quickly enough.

The two other children – Nathan and Lucy – lived with Beatrice always, knew her well, and preferred her mostly to their estranged father and his suspicious behaviour, who had been shown a troublesome side. Now only Nathan remained with his mother, and he watched her sanity crumble and decay like he knew it always would do.

With another scientist who met with Alan along his secret journey, questions came fast enough as expected. It had been some useful luck, Alan had thought. Finally some conversation that he could really get into, academic debate and scientific discussion to ease his mind after so long.

'The attackers – I have my own theoretical scientific thoughts about them,' he told Alan.

'Oh really? Please share them with me if you care to,' Alan said.

'Haven't you been thinking outside of the box about it all after so long? Or outside of known earthly diseases and viruses? There is something much more obscure, hidden with them. A few doctors and scientists over the country have done at least some basic early tests, as much as can be done until the way things are now. There are some things we need to consider in much more open ways, from new perspectives,' he explained.

'Go on, do you think so?' Alan said, with a kind of bored, distant scepticism.

'Yes, or we'll not end it all or even use it in any way we can while we have the best opportunity,' the man told him.

'Use it? Their sickness? I am not sure you and I are thinking the same way right now. Do you trust my experiences?' Alan asked.

'I, well... Yes, despite the strangeness of it all,' the man said.

'Then trust my words. I don't claim to know the absolute reasons, but I see how my own actions are relevant somehow. So certainly relevant, which I say without intended egotism but honest truth. I will continue my travels, play my part, see what happens and accept it. I do want us to live like we all did only months ago, but I do believe only this will help us at this present time,' Alan said with absolute belief. 'Agree or not, but I will continue on.'

'What happened to your hands, can I ask?' the man said.

'No answer there either. We see what we see, but how we interpret it, that counts so much more right now,' Alan told him.

They regrettably parted earlier than planned, Alan sad that this obviously very talented fellow young scientist now denied any personal belief or agreement since their first communication – for no real clear reason, it seemed. It in no way stopped Alan, a man known as a saint, with selfless acts to perform somewhere, taking his own opinions and views along with him.

On a briskly cold and bitter morning, Beatrice walked out alone from the house, leaving Nathan inside, asleep still. She needed this quiet time alone, a long walk to think to herself, contemplate deep problems and dark issues in a mind still so troubling to her. Many thoughts had been weighing down so badly on her mind, so much guilt and anxiety mounted up, hurting so much more since her husband and Steven had fled, exhausting her, wearing her down so mentally to almost breaking point, it seemed. She could not tell how much longer she could bear the anger, rage and huge sadness alone. She believed that she saw a different view of the terrible violence over the now uncivilised streets and towns and cities of the country. She had been the wife to a man so closely involved in what might just possibly have so greatly began the entire catastrophic events.

If her thoughts were true, her beliefs correct then she was certain that she should definitely take some of the blame for it herself. She had not taken the chance when it had been there to step in, to intervene before Gordon had left earth. She knew his long brewing dreams, his unending, rarely disclosed personal ambitions and real prized personal scientific theories which meant so much to him, but ones he had barely spoken of over the last fifteen years or more. Such radical, lunatic, arguably immoral theories which had many years ago only received ridicule and confused, hesitant responses before others made clear their advice to forget the suggested theories immediately. It had taken such effort then to save his reputation, rebuild his company and career in a different direction, and move over to England with the family. She knew the mistakes he had made, cover ups, and the denials of some highly significant governmental international circumstances. Much had been left unresolved when they had moved as a young family, the boys very young then.

So much weighed down on her alone, painful visions and dreams unrelenting to her. No punishment though, no trial, questioning, verdict upon her personally yet. So she walked out. She knew by then the areas around them to fear, the directions where the attackers usually appeared from, the alleys to be weary of so far. So that was exactly the direction in which she decided to walk in, alone.

Minutes passed, tears coming down her cheeks gradually as she approached the dangers waiting. She stopped, stood by a wall and whistled, clear and loud. A tune, possibly of Celtic folk origin, some hymn or regional old tune of thanks and mercy from many, many years before. They came so quickly and suddenly she was torn, beaten, knocked down to the ground soon enough. The blood spilled, her groans and screams falling around, her life eventually brutally taken away.

Steven spent the next couple of hours driving, observing how bad the country appeared now. Ruined town centres, smashed in office fronts, shops boarded up, overgrown parks, and gardens nearby. If things were to get back on track in any way, how would people live again? he wondered. Things had been so good, and so much was so obviously taken for granted before. Lives and ways of living easily established, jobs, careers, popular culture built up and depended upon. Could he still be the kind of person he had been before? The answer was something he barely wanted to consider then, and he could only focus on his actions ahead necessary in the present. He was simply on a different journey now. Possibly one of redemption, or one of sacrifice, and while it happened he could only battle his own difficult turmoil inside.

It was the outer main area of London he needed to reach first, to find the centre of the Otomo-Vision company. He could remember a vague direction to go down. He drove on, but then found main roads ahead blocked up by an incredibly long car pileup. Discarded burnt out cars and trucks left, some overturned blocking the entire stretch for a long way forward.

'Oh shit. No way,' he said aloud to himself.

He had not been looking forward to this time, but knew it was to happen. He stopped the car, and packed up his most essential things into a large rucksack and another bag strapped over his shoulder. From there, he had to simply walk, at least until the end of the motorway stretch ahead. There was a very sickening unusual smell rising out from the long stretch of parked, abandoned vehicles he passed. A pungent mix of death, gasoline, burnt meat and clothes, he expected. Nauseating, but he held back the strong urge to be sick as he continued. There were sounds in the distance from around – very likely attackers and police punks fighting them. They could all just do each other in, he thought. Save him the trouble. No, that was no way out, he knew.

It was a long stretch to walk, and with his laptop and folders and devices carried with him more arduous a task still. Out of breath and tired he thankfully could see what used to be the beginning of civilised London town in clear view before him.

As he approached the opening wide town streets, leading into what had arguably been the most multicultural city in the world, the sounds increased, still coming at random intervals, shocking and bizarre, wild and violent sounds. He knew something was happening there. Things were waiting too, there for him to find. He had to move forward, ignore the sounds, go on still. Should he wait? Could he? He remained, waiting in deep shadows before the streets connected with the first part of the town area ahead. There were voices, only a few, talking, discussing some problem it seemed. He waited, listened, hearing their conversation.

Two men, maybe a woman also, he thought.

'... They're coming, looking for them, they'll find them, then we're all screwed.'

'No, we don't need them. We don't. They're not even scientists, they changed. They're different.'

'That's why we need them. We have to find them now.'

'Look what happened to the other ones – no scientists have survived. We're just fucked. Bloody police fascists controlling us for food and anything worse.'

'Look, we'll find them, help them,' the female voice said.

The voices stopped, moved away, growing quieter. Steven stepped out then into the open town area before him. Things actually were moving along while he had been gone. He should have guessed really he thought. He should not have been so egotistical and naive about it. But it was a challenge, and he liked that, knew he needed it to keep him moving forward. Things were getting too easy, he told himself. It was a good thing that he had grown a decent beard and worn a woollen hat recently, as everyone had seen his old image in the news months earlier, his face known as a specific prominent new young scientist making waves in the news.

He ran out, with an idea to find the people he had heard talking moments before. Anyone and anything could be out there he thought as he ran out clearly under moonlight and morning dawn rising. Who to reach first? he wondered. Were the police punks down here as reasonable and clueless as those before? He probably could not just chance that. They did all seem extremely totalitarian and power crazed, enjoying the lack of law courts to defend civil liberties or human rights. He saw then a small group up ahead of him.

'Hey! Hey there, hello!' he called out with dramatic but still low level of voice.

One of them turned to see him, and watched him come up to meet them.

'What's up mate?' the man asked, eyeing him with suspicion.

'Are the police gone? Just trying to get food and blankets. I don't want their trouble again,' Steven said to them.

'No, they've moved on. But attackers could be anywhere close still. Watch yourself. Where you from?' the man asked.

'Came from Bristol, up north before that. Car broke down, trying to meet friends, find them. Do you people know about some powerful scientists down here?' he asked.

'Hey, any around are either hiding, afraid to show themselves, or dead at the hands of police and ones who do not forgive them for the state of things. Yes, there are two, though – they've survived unlike most others. More like vigilantes doing really strange things. They have some crazy weapons apparently. Really clever bastards, it seems like. Been around, tricking police groups, sabotaging defence areas. Bit like hero figures kind of, they have done things to redeem themselves almost. Almost like Robin Hoods, leaving supplies and food in safe parts, helping us but sometimes just dangerous, wanting us away,' the guy explained. 'I'm Lewis.'

'Hello Lewis. I'm Carl,' Steven told him.

'Why do you want to know about scientists?' Lewis asked.

'Doesn't everyone want to know? I'd heard something about these ones a few hours ago from some people on the road. Well, I'm just curious to know what's happened to them around the country, how things are. With no real news any more – no papers, television or Internet updates, news just stopped really, didn't it?' Steven said.

'They're unpredictable, and they've got some bigger plan going on, the two of them. They seem very organised, focused with some unknown agenda. They're not just messing around, pissing off the police for the hell of it. They know what they're doing we believe. They are extremely organised – weapons, tricks, almost like a kind of new magic. Clever guys but yes, they've killed a few themselves for some reason,' another man added seriously.

'Unbelievable. I thought the police and attackers were all we had to worry about,' Steven said jokingly.

'Oh no, things are much more interesting around these parts, mate. Hey come with us, we'll get some things for you. Just a few okay?' Lewis offered.

'Well, thanks very much pal. Thanks a lot, Lewis,' Steven replied, smiling his old devious smile.

Chapter 48

Around the whole of London now, two men were infamously known for their unexpected defiant wild acts against the police and gangs of attackers for the last few months. Some supported them, some hunted them if they could, failing to locate them endlessly. These two scientists had become something else since the change to the country. As with all scientists nationally, they were blamed and hated, but all the others had taken their previous professional skills and knowledge and used it in many highly creative, powerful ways.

Peter Sheldon and Victor Harris joined together early on already, and that friendship saved them from the emerging questions and anger facing them soon enough from public and police groups. In only a few weeks, the attackers had finally shockingly grown in total number, they spread somehow across the country, and no one could stop them. Many were hired to try, with so much pressure and scrutiny from the news media daily. No one could turn things around in a short time. So soon after the whole population had been completely positive and optimistic from the sudden unexpected space shuttle mission launch from the south of the country, things became so horribly bleak.

The two scientists came together, and while their fellow workers were eventually threatened, abused, chased and jailed they, like only a very small minority, escaped into safe hiding. Like many great scientists in the past, they still looked at wider future implications for everyone, at the way the diseased attackers lived and existed nationally, and how the whole country had reacted against them. Peter and Victor planned their own defences, as they did not want to be taken down when they knew they could together do necessary vital work to stop the spread of the attackers and help everyone if they could find some kind of cure. Privately and in secret, they were being incredibly resourceful, applying techniques of biological and chemical research and experimentation to their survival from police, accusers and the attackers around them on the streets frequently.

There could be a variety of possible futures – both Peter and Victor saw what could be done, and what might happen if they simply gave up. They saw the government lose much of its known power in a matter of less than two months, politicians chased, killed even. Police though, were lifted up nationally, some strange respect to begin, then weeks later, only weapons and training allowed them to rule in effect, deciding who was to be punished, jailed, caught or freed. That was not any real justice or democracy, not as they had known it to be. And so they became new kind of defenders – mysterious, radical men, using reason, intelligence with chemical tricks and ingenious weapons, stopping the police and attackers where they could.

They managed to communicate to other scientists and then outside the United Kingdom – the Internet offered hope and guidance to an extent. America said they would help them shortly, as did France, other parts of Europe but time continued to pass quietly along with only themselves to depend upon.

Peter had been a future professor in biochemistry, and good friends with Victor who specialised in scientific theory principals for the later stages of many major national projects regularly. Working well, no one could begin to guess who they were, what they were doing or how they were doing it. Their plans remained secret to only the two of them, such carefully prepared plans.

On the hour Steven reached greater London, they were deciding on how best to use the attackers to their advantage when ready. Peter had been studying them in the close areas, knowing them well. It was a very sad thing that these strong, determined monsters were only months before conscious, emotional, individual, caring and real human beings, just like both of them. They hoped to end the whole dark time in a few months, or even sooner if they could be so lucky. They could not know when exactly, but they did not wish to harm them, as difficult as that was, knowing some of the attackers had very likely killed family or friends of theirs. Laws had changed, as the times had, and many rules could be broken without consequence.

It was a tall regular building of offices barricaded up where Peter and Victor spent most of their time together. They had managed to so far continually confuse the police gangs with decoy clues to their whereabouts, leaving them safe to carry out their private experiments.

'Victor, are you sure this is the right way to do this?' Peter asked, crossing the main second floor room.

Victor then took a careful considered view over their pile of many drafted notes and documents on his laptop.

'We've planned this with close consideration, it's the next step right? The attackers are obviously reacting well,' Victor told Peter.

'True, very true. Almost seems to be going too well,' Peter said.

'No, come on. We had a hell of a time holding off the police. We nearly bought it too,' Victor reminded him. 'They don't know how we do these things, we're well secure. They didn't study much hard academic science like us. Now, the way you want the attackers to be is in three large groups, splitting the way of police. My own weapons can hold them in place from that point. There is nothing else to stop us. Everyone needs this. No other countries obviously give a single damn in any serious way. You know that, right?'

'Yes, we agree there, we do,' Peter replied.

'And this is us, us being the important, significant scientists we intended to be back then right now. Right?' Victor asked.

'Right. I agree. That's us, no one else. Science as revolution in post-apocalyptic nightmare,' Peter agreed, smiling.

There were some quiet, recurring thoughts troubling Peter still while they planned their mission. Victor had his own unending confidence, boastful, egotistical plans growing more every day, along with their array of ingenious modern magician tricks of chemical compounds crafted into handheld capsules and bombs. But Peter... he was the one of doubts inside. While they became talked of as wild, rogue neo-magicians of technological sorts, they had heard some talk of a mysterious man, somewhere around the country, acting in similar ways to them but offering safe hope, healing and guidance in the dark days of present. Not everyone believed the talk, and Peter was not exactly sure of what was true from it. Hearing of this compassionate mystery man hero only made their own selfish flaws stand out even more to him, and made him feel ashamed.

'Victor, we know people... I see them, don't you? People from our old lives. They are out in those streets,' Peter said with difficult pain.

'I know that, Peter. We've seen them, yes. It is difficult for both of us. Think big, that's how we'll rise over this. Science created the situation, our science will get us out of it. The police don't understand any of it, can't be trusted, or depended on. Everyone knows that. Government politicians are hiding or dead, right?' Victor told him.

'You do convince me yet again. Nothing better to do is there?' Peter agreed.

'So the plans continue, right?' Victor asked him.

'Tomorrow night. Like prepared. We are the unknown element,' Victor told him with a confident smile and a pat on the back firmly.

It had taken them nearly a month of very focused study and planning around the city by day and night, between stopping fights and violence between public, police and attackers when they felt they had to do so. They did not hang around to gain respect and glory, but hid after learning what they needed quickly and fast. Unfortunately, things were just not simply black and white and could not be, however much it could make surviving easier for them. Like wars and genocide overseas in Africa or the Middle East, this was truly a dangerous and extreme time, severe situations with a lack of time to stop and reflect or debate the moral rights and wrongs of actions, but merely acting to live.

In among the constantly brutal police groups patrolling London and the entire country were individual officers, themselves afraid for their friends and family, who survived still somehow. Not all of them had wanted this new way of control and forced oppression over the public but societal rules had eroded too much, too soon. Many regretted inflicting horrendous power and violence on public and attackers, wishing they had retained what they told themselves was a kind of justice or normality to their acts like before.

Chapter 49

Douglas returned to his town, a broken house but he met his family at the town hall. Still he thought of the return to Earth with Jane, concerned to her. It really did not take very long for Jane and Douglas to learn of how far into chaos the country had fallen as they walked along into a city centre. They saw shocking damage, ruin and mostly empty streets, bare of any people as they usually would be. It just left them speechless. It made Jane so sad ultimately. They took it in, absorbed the horror, but continued because they knew they should. They had to get home, check their families and just perhaps see how they could offer their talents toward finding a solution.

'It's them, isn't it?' Jane said as they looked around.

'Yes, I'd say so. Looks like we left before it become some kind of horrible mess. Can it be like this all over? Everywhere?' Douglas asked.

'It is. I know it,' Jane told him, with a sad but focused look over her face.

They walked on together.

The two of them explored what seemed to be the lower part of Wales for a while. They did soon enough spot some people, but they only just briefly ran out across the streets and avoided their efforts to communicate with them.

'We can't just walk around like this. Look, I'm going to take a car,' Douglas told her eventually.

'What? Take one? Like steal?' she asked.

'Jane, things have really changed now. We need to get safe, and know our families and friends are safe also. Are you joining me?' he said.

She looked around at the abandoned streets and vandalised shops and buildings around.

'Count me in, Doug. Let's go home,' she replied.

Around London there were at least five large mass police punk groups, maintaining defence and a high level of control against attackers and any foolish rebellious ones who challenged them. The groups each acted quite spontaneously most of the time, just simply beating innocents and showing their intimidating brute physical narcissistic power. It was all about control, dominance, fear and indulgent violent acts without apology to higher authority finally. They were only police – only ever serving to protect the public before, never thinking or questioning society or themselves, never theorising in a deeper manner. Not to say some police could not be thoughtful and humble, but the majority at this time of nationwide horror were taking out their frustrated, impotent and helpless anger at not ultimately being able to change anything for the better in reality, but only simply increase the sadness, fear and despair all around.

They could not think like scientists, really theorise about the cause or solutions to the attackers, but they were thinking of only darker, sadistic vengeful things. They thought very seriously, especially in London, of much bigger, definite means of halting the attackers surrounding them daily, always returning.

Half a dozen of the police viewed as leaders were the heads of deciding how best to coordinate their coming brutal showdown which had finally begun to be planned after months of simple killing, torture and fighting back. There were known streets and roads which they had chosen to close off, once luring the majority of attackers inside, though this could take a number of times to fully defeat them more or less, with many fatalities on the way. They all were focused on the idea of this glorious epic battle, a mass slaughter in defending England, and eventually then ruling undoubtedly – no more ignorant, distant government using them like before, they decided.

One or two did, however, spend time trying to hunt down remaining scientists, and now these two notorious troubling men, who somehow performed strange, arcane, dark magic tricks to fight them, elude them and ruin their efforts just kept returning at the worst of times. Too often, many of the police fell deep into losing any moral virtue and committed acts too bloody, indulgent and remorseless in public view to keep and lost respect and now they saw that more and more people around seemed to be supporting these irritant modern rebel magicians.

People on the streets talked about all of these dangers they feared while trying to just survive. On the further greater London streets, a small group of eight people ran along, searching for food and even things to entertain them from the past.

'We should not come out this far any more. I can't see the point,' one young woman stated as they looked around with caution through piles of broken machines and furniture.

'We find good things all the time,' a thin man with unkempt hair and beard replied with annoyance.

'Yeah, not helped by the fucking police groups. They'll get us all killed eventually. God damn macho killers,' another said.

'But they just want order, rules. Justice, we need some form of it. We need some kind of what we used to be – civilised life,' the woman said.

'Not like that, their hypocritical insane useless violence,' the thin man responded, scratching himself.

'The tech two will help. They know what they do,' a shorter man added behind them.

'Don't even begin. The tech two can't be relied on – and they are wanted like any scientists are. They're dangerous just as much,' the thin man said.

'Says you,' the shorter man replied.

'Say plenty of us. We just have to be aware, be careful. We can survive until America help us, or France,' thin man told him.

'That's just as dangerous – waiting around doing nothing, waiting for their help if it ever emerges at all. That's suicide in a different way,' the short man responded.

The short man slowed, meeting a woman at the back of the group.

'Hey, you met them didn't you – the mystery men, the tech two?' he said.

She nodded without saying anything.

'We have to talk,' he told her quietly.

In the quiet narrow paths, near abandoned coffee shops and pubs, Peter stood in shadows and was eventually met by a woman who knew him only very briefly.

'Thank you for coming here. I do understand your risk in coming, and it is worthwhile. So, can I ask? – have you done the things I asked?' he said.

'Yes, I have – it was tricky but I did do them eventually. It will definitely help the two of you to change things for us all now, I hope?' she said with fragile hope in her eyes.

'I cannot truly promise anything, but I very much think so. You see how we have acted so far, please trust in us,' he told her.

'I do. I think you are so very brave, real heroes, the kind we need now more than ever,' she replied.

'Thank you. Keep safe, please. I care so much about this town, and the country I live in. We see a way out of the dangers around us. There were mistakes, man-made as usual, but we can also find solutions. We are not simply animals, even if we once came from them,' he told her. 'See you soon, maybe.'

He ran off alone, knowing that parts of their plan were secure and waiting for them to proceed now. Meanwhile, near the base of their research, Victor was working on traps and distractions, chemical weapons and more. He could always hear noises, so paranoid and tired as he worked, barely ever stopping for long. But he was a new legend, a living myth, elusive, still pushing science in practical terms, an illusion and a lie to all.

Were attackers near him then? Was it police punk gangs ready to detain and torture him and Peter? It could even be furious angry people of the streets, desperate to punish him for endangering them just too often with his homemade weapons and rebellion. The noises stopped.

So he continued to tinker, prepare weapons, getting ready. He knew everything out there that might threaten him, or he thought so at least.

The night came and allowed the London police gangs to enjoy another night of debauched sadistic ultra-violence and fighting against the attackers. Coming to open paths, they waited and a few attackers ran through, screams and wild limbs thrown around in the night. Then gone.

The police group watched, waited speechless.

'This is different now,' one police Officer said.

'Just wait, watch it,' another replied.

Then a sudden burst of screams from the left, attackers separating, moving then but actually in a more calmer manner for some unknown reason.

'What's this?' a police Officer said. 'They're different now – why?'

'I've no idea. Move, keep watching. Wait or just hit out but together, tight still,' the lead Officer commanded.

They were all nervous, unsure now, seeing this uneasy change before them, challenging them suddenly.

'Wait, watch,' he said.

Eventually, two attackers walked or they were just about sure they were attackers they were seeing then. They had slowed, calmed, seemed just almost normal.

'What are they doing?' an Officer asked, confused

'Let's take them in. They're unusual ones,' another suggested. He then moved in, ahead of the other officers around him.

'Wait! Connor, you stupid shit!' another whispered out to him.

They had to go after him. They followed, and all three reached the quiet, calm attackers who stood thoughtfully by the back doors of a closed up restaurant then. The attackers were so quiet, disturbingly calm before them. The next ones were so wild as ever. Six more rushed out across behind them then, crossing the roads madly, over past the police group entirely as if the police were invisible. Confusion and fear suddenly held the police, as they were standing finally overcome.

The attackers – thoughtless, post-human beings no good for much at all anymore – had tricked them, whether by accident or some more unsettling occurrence somehow.

From a window high above out of view, in a chosen building, Victor had seen the event and was definitely very pleased. This gave him valuable hope in his coming actions. Beyond the interesting smaller gadgets and chemical weapons he and Peter were perfecting, this was a much more potentially significant discovery for him. It was not his or Peter's own truthfully, so they could not hold complete credit for this result. The initial basic scientific theory of this test upon the attackers below was the idea from Gordon from more than two years previously. Thank you Gordon, you truly weird mad bastard, Victor thought to himself as he watched the panicked police group below.

The attackers could be utilised and used in a number of ways, Victor had found. By using various compounds, chemicals and sounds, they would react almost on cue. With just enough time, he and Peter would have the many groups of attackers to use in bringing down the police authority and control. It did in some way feel to be not entirely right – they had been people, the attackers, with jobs, characters, lives, families, ambitions, hopes, fears, personalities – but it was just so obviously worth doing, he believed. Peter might not think so, but it was too late for his opinion.

'So these two blokes, the tech magicians, where do they usually turn up then?' Steven asked the two men he sat with as they ate some fried meat with tinned onions.

'Well, they are very clever, they move around. They don't want to be caught by police, so they are extremely careful. They were down by Morgan Street one time I know. Then a week or more later they saved some folk near Barkley crossing. But it would be anyone's guess where or when they show next. They have their own agenda, do their own thing,' they said.

'Sounds like it,' Steven said.

As hours passed, Steven took the time to do some research. He had not studied like this since working with Alan and the others. He thought back then, remembered the times together, the way they worked, how he engaged with them and Alan. He took out maps and books, studied roads, buildings, streets and directions. These two men were of great interest, and he knew they were very definitely important. If not specifically connected to the things he wanted to find, they could offer valuable use in making his way safely through London and help him gain access he needed. He felt almost overshadowed, neglected or forgotten. These mystery men were now entertaining the masses, pushing boundaries, testing theories of grand significance and gaining respect and awe once he had in endless supply. He should find them and tell them they were in his place, in the wrong path. They would step aside, he thought. They had to for some price or some offer, he decided.

As he looked over maps of London, he thought of what little he knew, but it did come down to some valuable level of information. He could practically guess almost certainly where the two scientists – they definitely were – had come from, and where they had worked. They then returned to the places of work, possibly returning still now frequently. The police might know that much, but perhaps not much more; or not as much as he knew then. That was the difference, he thought.

Chapter 50

Having re-secured the entrance to their present sanctuary, Victor walked in, thoughtful and contemplating his marvellous scientific magical tricks. He wondered just how much longer he and Peter could act like that, their weapon devices, chemical tricks and distractions relying on a depleting source of chemicals, and other elements. What would they be then? he wondered to himself. Simply intelligent, hopeful men, who knew of things no longer useful to the future of people in the country. He found Peter in the upper second room, reading.

'I'm back,' he announced.

'Good, I'm glad. Just browsing a couple of books here,' Peter said.

'Are you confident about our plans right now?' Victor asked.

'I see possibilities' Peter replied.

'Peter, this next few steps, looking for more equipment, and others... What if we don't get much further?' Victor asked tentatively.

'Don't go there. We can, we have to. Stop fucking being defeatist. You're so negative right now,' Peter said.

'Hey, it's been great, amazing good times, but it's not going to last,' Victor offered.

'Listen to me – what we have. What we've found between us. The space shuttle journey. It means something, you agreed,' Peter said.

'I did, I know... But we might just not get any further information. Maybe we need to think differently soon,' Victor said.

Peter stood then, displeased with what Victor was saying.

'But we'll do the next things we've planned, right? For me at least, then just fuck off if you need to. You do that,' Peter said, with jaded drama in his voice.

'Shit Peter... We'll do it, go as far...' Victor said. He turned, sighed, then quickly walked out.

He left the building. He walked out on the dark street alone, angry and frustrated. He was some special scientist hero bloke in some way, but did he have to be or even try? he thought. Could he just be like anyone else out there? Forget big grand scientific theories – just hide, attack, scavenge and survive like the others. Easy, simple, he thought. It was just a matter of time. That was the future, he thought. These strange broken beginning theories they had found at their company buildings could stop, incomplete.

He had been giving some personal thought to the attackers, and how they were. They were human physically, with all known senses like any man or woman. Deep inside a brain operated in some distorted way, but surely it still contained the same make up of memory processors, connections, signal routes inside still capable of acting like they once did. Just fighting them like the punk police groups he had seen differences, and he knew different ways. With these thoughts in mind, he walked on.

In another place, but only less than half an hour away in London, Steven looked around him. He came to see buildings and places others had mentioned before. He kept a note of them in his head, observing street names and directions. He was going to try something, take some chances now. It was time. The sounds of police cars came out of the air, rising clear and wailing. They were around, close enough, he thought. But closer still, the sound of attackers, but in a pained, unusual manner. What was up with them now? he wondered. He was close to something useful, he thought. He walked out carefully, holding a steel pole tight in his hands, ready for violence, ready for confrontation.

Crouching low at the side of some rubbish bins overflowing, he saw then a tall man performing some bizarre, unlikely act. Peter stood between two small groups of attackers, calm and focused, he seemed to possibly be communicating to them. He moved his hands like some macabre conductor of the diseased masses. The two beaten, feral groups followed his actions, it seemed. Steven watched as Peter then walked out, away from the groups, ran ahead, the attackers only following casually but loyally. What was happening here? Steven wondered. This man he watched was like him, he was doing things that he had been doing up in space, it seemed. He had found one, he thought.

As the two small groups of attackers separated, one keeping behind Peter, the other disappearing off down an alleyway, Steven walked around behind, amazed. Then it was time to join in and be sociable, Steven thought. Only right to do so.

'What's happening here?' Steven asked, loud and clear but in a friendly manner.

Peter spun around surprised at being caught then.

'Very impressed, most certainly,' Steven added.

'Keep back. I must go, they're likely to turn. Just go,' Peter warned, but Steven remained, watching with relaxed interest.

'No, I don't think so. Don't stop on my account, really,' Steven told him.

Peter was distracted from leading the attackers then. He looked at Steven, with caution.

'It's a technique I know. They can be used, calmed for a short while,' he explained.

'Yes, I've noticed. It might lead to more though, right?' Steven suggested encouragingly.

'It could, maybe. I suppose,' Peter admitted.

This man did not seem like a police officer, but still he should be careful.

'So they can be used, manipulated... Maybe they could be turned on the police,' Steven told him.

'Who are you?' Peter finally asked

'Me? Carl Dryer. Traveller, observer. Friend I believe. You – a scientist, I am right?' Steven said.

'Carl, I appreciate your thoughts but I am moving on now. I suggest you do too,' Peter told him.

'You're trying to do something, some unfinished thing, aren't you?' Steven called out to him as he began to leave. Peter stopped in his tracks, a few paces from him, then turned back to face him. Someone seemed to want to listen to him finally, someone who understood how things should be, Peter thought as he walked up to Steven.

The books let Victor escape the surrounding bleakness, if only temporarily, delving deep into theories and complex biological and scientific dilemmas. He then drifted, wondering about how he could have been a successful bold research scientist, winning prizes, gaining respect, and pushing boundaries. But gunshots, cries and loud shouts broke the waking dreams suddenly for him. Some new wild drama outside was taking place. He stepped over by the window slowly, and peered through the blinds.

There were half a dozen police officers below, near the reinforced entrance, beating at it, smashing away with raging aggression repeatedly. This was much too soon, he thought. Not expected just then, not yet. Where had Peter gone he wondered looking around,. He swore to himself, then collected up the weapons, strapped on his shoulder bags, and walked out to the inner staircase, ready.

It had been Peter and him up until then, the magic mystery men. What now that he was alone? he thought. Well, it would allow him to do things his own way finally. A challenge was always good for creativity he thought. He ran out through the building, deciding his direction. With the police below, sounding like them actually getting through into the building then, he knew he should go elsewhere – he had to.

He continued up along the outside of the building, carefully climbing down and around to the other side, and jumping down into a main street, hitting the bins. He steadied himself, climbing out. Took a breath, then took from his shoulder bag on the left some smaller wrapped pack. Opening it up, he found a syringe, which he held out before his eyes momentarily. Quickly he plunged it, deeply but carefully into his left lower arm. He grimaced, flinching then shook his head. Looking around he then ran off, away between a street up ahead into deep dark shadows.

With groups of powerful attackers roaming free in many parts around London then, and police punk groups oppressing the masses, somewhere between Steven and Peter moved along together, with much to discuss.

'It's good that you understand my ideas, somehow can grasp the possible plans I can see here. You surprise me, but that is alright, I suppose,' Peter said as they walked on.

'Well I had read some things, and I spoke to many kinds of people. I have an open mind, that helps.'

'Very true, I agree,' Peter replied.

'You are with people, friends?' he asked.

'Not exactly. I have time to spare if you need any sort of help at all,' Steven said in a deceptively kind way.

'Yes, if you want to. You could actually really help right now I believe,' Peter said, pleased with this unexpected meeting.

They moved on, coming toward a wide-open split road area, with large crossing between before a cinema and nightclub buildings.

'Wait, I hear them,' Peter said, holding his pocket chemical bombs.

Voices, familiar, stern. It was police coming toward them then it seemed.

'We're going up then left? Let me handle this,' Steven offered. 'You go on, I'll meet you shortly,' he told Peter.

In only seconds, two cars drove along and stopped by Steven, who acted like he had been running fast from some near danger approaching then.

'Hey you, stop there. Wait,' an Officer called to him.

Steven turned, looking relieved to see them.

'That guy, one of the weird tech wizards – he was here. Bloody flames and strange shit coming off of him. He went down there, ran off,' Steven told them urgently, seeming shocked and angry.

'Did he attack you?' one Officer asked him.

'Well, no, just fucked off down there just now. Go, stop him. He'll be gone soon,' he warned them.

The police stopped, turned the car then moved down the street to the right ahead.

Steven laughed to himself. Gormless brutes, he thought. He turned away, but a noise came at him. Screeching, an attacker ran out, reaching for him suddenly with wild force. Steven caught it by the shoulders, held it away from him. The face contorted, screamed at him, as if possessed. It was a hell of a strong man, muscular, athletic even with its arms grabbing out at him. He could barely keep a tight grip as it tried to get free.

Then from behind an explosion, blue smoke, then another, orange tinged smoke billowing up around the attacker. It was distracted, confused then somehow it calmed and stepped away from Steven. It moved away, sniffing around, turning off toward another street. From behind it stood Peter.

'Are you just hanging around with these guys?' he asked. 'Come on now, follow me.'

Everything was timed and ready to go with the plans of Peter and Victor. Or it had been until they had now separated, their differences taking them in opposite paths of interest. As Peter took Steven around London, Victor remembered the streets and alleys around which had been marked, just waiting. Groups of brooding attackers milled in those forgotten areas. They lived almost, finding food and if not – which was often – finding and eating people. Warm, bloody flesh was a reasonable substitution for them.

It was all simply instinct, thought it did sustain them, while corpses then lay randomly rotting after their feeding events. Other foreign countries, less financially and economically sustained were like this – wild untamed animals free to pick off innocent passers-by – but here it was not dogs or savage other mammals on all fours. Now this was England. Where poor countries had simple shepherds to watch the flocks and livestock, this land had only a few former scientists caught struggling with their morals, and a mysterious rumoured Saint man somewhere providing some means of hope.

With the whole of London set out ready, Victor moved out with plenty of opportunities ahead of him. He and Peter had been the mysterious heroic vigilante duo for months, but several times recently each of them felt the other would not listen, could no longer agree with plans ahead. The attackers were an opportunity, and Victor could do the tests he wanted, he really could. If the police groups were to show – fuck it, he could surely find ways to hold them back. He would do it now. The people would be his people. He could be in charge, a king, a president, leader now the government was in pieces. Now it came right back down to real power, power of the mind – intelligence and technological solutions which he knew. If he could control everything, then he should, he thought. Wasn't that obvious?

He ran along down through the streets for a couple of minutes, checking a map he had. At one corner he stopped and looked around. He knew the place, and knew what to do – he took hold of his shoulder bag, and found a small device. He walked toward a doorway up ahead and sprayed something. He then repeated this, again and again as he ran up and along a couple more streets. He waited – then heard the noise.

So he then ran on, ran further, checking the map. Another street to find, he thought. Once there, he withdrew a different labelled device, sprayed some other gas around the building before him then again ran along leaving a trail of the sprayed gas scent upon a number of areas. Once more, he stood quiet, and waited, and then heard the groans, and footsteps increasing, running. He ran on in a different direction. He could do this, it seemed. Alone he could carry out the devised plan, and much more.

Chapter 51

The winding, twisting streets held restless groups of attackers, where they regularly rested or ate in their disgusting manner. They were beginning to move, curious of the changing scents which now lured them forth, their simple animal behaviour betraying them. It was a tragedy to see these bungling groups, containing all kinds of people who could have been from many kinds of walks of life earlier – lawyers, salesmen, artists, teachers, chefs – anyone and everyone. Would it be possibly for anyone to save them and return them to what they had been in their lives, their individual selves and human personalities?

Over the next two hours, Victor moved out, around the town, following his maps, and setting up the synchronised routes for the attackers of action. That was one side of the plan. It had to essentially coincide successfully along with the police gangs being led out, and carefully executed collision would occur. Some attackers were for distraction, others to be very special test efforts.

That was what Peter had been working on, and Victor had been expecting him to take care of that. With Peter gone, somewhere unknown, this too would have to be done by Victor if he really wanted to pull off the whole grand scheme himself. After just a brief time, he was spotted, seen by police punks as expected. He could hide then, he knew, he could just quickly stop the work, flee and save his skinny arse from a violent beating alone, or worse some medieval grisly end. The chase then began.

No more casual observing his choices and possibilities. He had his bag of chemical tricks, some knives and a baseball bat for defence.

'They know not what they do,' he said and ran off, not looking back.

'There. The tricky tech shit! After him now!' a police Constable shouted loudly from a car window.

The small row of cars moved down the road, increasing speed, on him fast and gaining. He ran past bins, bodies, turned over burnt out cars. They were on him, in cars close behind but he knew his location and could lead them where he wanted. There were tricks waiting for them, he was sure of that. As he ran the rising sound of pained moans and distorted voices of attackers came up through the streets around. They were moving, he thought. It was his doing and hopefully it would help just in time, he hoped.

Though the attackers were audibly coming out and responding, so too were the many police punk groups around him across London. He was getting very tired, the plan was exhausting him so much finally. His legs ached so badly he felt. He was probably verging on malnutrition and mental depression severely which added to the overall pressure. The cars were coming, closing in, only a couple of streets from him he heard. His weak legs stumbled on, his thoughts drifting haphazardly and uncontrollably.

What was important, he thought – safety? The plan? Freedom, or was it food, the attackers or... Peter? Was Peter close somewhere? Was safety somewhere he could reach for a short time? Safety used to be police, judges, the law, community, home, family... Police... Were police safe? Police...

The sound of cars driving fast and close had stopped he then realised. Footsteps running were then heard somewhere, moving in, coming to get him... To get him... find him...

He was losing grip of where he had come to, what street he was on, what he was to do next.

They came – half a dozen police officers walked into the street then, seeing him in his weakened, pale state, vulnerable and unsure.

'Finally we've got one of the bastards,' the Officer announced. The officers stepped in, moving apart and observing him.

Victor saw them coming in around him, his steps much slower then. Time to pull out a bunch of final showstopper tricks, he thought. From within a pouch, he drew out a small capsule, flipping it across the air, toward the police there. It sparked quickly, gas spilling out. They moved away in shock, knocking each other.

'Watch out! His fucking tricks again!' one shouted.

'Just get him, he's alone!'

Some of them coughed, stumbled, dizzy. More of them moved in, following him as he walked off quickly behind the smoke and sparks hiding him. They kept following and he pulled out another pellet. This one hit a police officer, different smells coming from it, affecting them, creating a sickening atmosphere. Then, in seconds began to feel painfully sick, twisting violent pains in their stomachs creasing them, stopping them as Victor looked back. He was having some luck, but he knew that he didn't have much else. Feeling inside his pouch bag, there was nothing else left to try. All his tricks were used up and his supplies gone, and now he had to think of something else to survive the night.

He thought of the streets. Where was he right then? These streets were possibly familiar – he had been close to this place not so long ago, he thought. He looked up as two policemen came right up on him, almost grabbing at him. With a strained push of energy, he ran up onto his left further. He looked around, down the next long alleyway.

'One of them, is easier than two. One down, here he goes,' a police Officer stated as they walked up, satisfied. Only a few feet from Victor they were stopped, shocked and turning back immediately, as an unexpected pack of attackers came suddenly storming along from the alley beside them.

'A fucking trap! Get out, get back everyone!' the Officer shouted, moving away.

Victor himself stood nervously while the attackers came in around him, stumbling, raging in a slightly different way to usual. As he stood just too tired to run, he saw that they just did not come near him. They were more concerned with other things, something else around the area. He knew what, and he was extremely pleased. He looked back at the police, who moved back defending themselves and he simply walked away casually off down the dark alley. His new tricks were working it seemed, very well and right on time. He had to see what more was happening and he could – very easily it seemed now.

As time passed, Steven got to know a great deal more of interest and use from Peter. As he gave him plenty of compliments, Peter told him enough gradually. Steven got to know a good deal of what Peter and Victor had been preparing, where they were safe, where the police groups patrolled regularly, where the London attacker packs roamed.

'I am going to go see some people I know. Look, the longer you hang around with me, the more chance you have of getting into some serious trouble with the police punk groups as well. They see us together, then you're hunted and wanted along with me and Victor,' Peter explained as a serious warning.

'They'll hurt and hunt anyone who disagrees with them eventually. They're not the democratic decent law system we tried to uphold before. Now it comes to individual ethics, needs, and our own views of right and wrong. Our views are right, not wrong – right?' Steven said.

'Yes, we are,' Peter agreed, pleased.

In a very short time the pair moved along London, between roads, streets to a place between places of safe refuge mostly. Peter led them down between walls, through narrow gates, into a hidden entrance. He knocked in a cryptic manner. A voice spoke from behind the doors.

'Who is there?' it asked.

'One with virtues,' Peter said.

The door opened to them then. A tired seeming man greeted them, with a once beautiful lady beside him.

'Hello Peter. You are well?'

'Good enough for now. This is a helpful friend with me. So how are you all now?' Peter asked.

'Come in please, we'll talk,' the man offered.

Peter seemed slightly reluctant, but followed, Steven joining him. They entered a quiet but visibly cared for place. A few other people busied around the place. There was a quiet calm and unbelievably even a couple praying in a far corner.

'You know, we wait for you still,' the man said to Peter as the group walked through the building.

'I made no strong promises, you know that. I simply told you of some ideas we had,' Peter said.

'How much longer? We are dying here. No more cures, no more drugs, medicines. No democracy, freedom, only hope and not all have that,' the man told him with honest regret.

'Well, look, I am at least pleased that things are still... Well,' Peter said, pausing then continuing. 'Tell me, any news about what I was asking about the last time?' he said.

The man leaned toward him closer.

'We think things, see things...'

'Things like I asked? Things found?' Peter asked further.

'Things seen not with eyes earthly. Honest things seen,' the man said. 'Beer?'

'Yes, of course. Thanks,' Peter agreed. 'Anything stronger?'

The man then reached back further, they shared from a fine expensive old whiskey stored away safely. Peter turned to Steven, then the man and woman.

'Thank you for this.'

As they began to leave a while later, they were met by a hysterical younger man, eyes frantic, wild.

'Barry, the attackers are fucking different tonight. Moving different. It's wrong. We can't go around tonight. Not now. This is difficult,' the younger man told them.

'Honest things seen,' the older man replied gravely.

Peter watched and listened with cynicism.

'The routes are still as usual though, right? We're going still. See you again,' Peter told them, patting the old man on the back and gesturing to Steven. They moved out once again.

He and Steven walked out together, thinking about what the younger man had been suggesting.

'He was some crazy stressed little guy, right?' Steven said.

'They talk about all kinds of things around outside. Not like I've helped. Fuelling their imagination, but it's hope I think,' Peter told him.

'Yes but he was saying...' Steven began but was then drowned out by some unknown loud chaos. There was something, many things moving, noisily close to them.

'Attackers coming,' Peter said.

They took no chance, and instantly moved up by some higher placed stairway to their right. Climbing up higher, they knelt silently and watched. In seconds a large lively group ambled in through the street, attackers with their usual fever, rabid and chaotic but focused unlike in previous times before.

'What is up with them?' Peter whispered.

'Sorry?' Steven said but almost wondering the same thought. He knew their routines just as well from miles up in the space station. He had studied and observed them personally – he had to.

'They move... differently. Look, what is this they're doing. The way they move now. Very interesting...' Peter said.

They observed the attackers who moved along, seemingly with some new collective mission, and just possibly some significant level of conscious communication between them.

'They've been prompted, moved to change, to go after something. It's not their action or desire. Something had done this to them, motivated them like this,' Peter said.

'I agree, yes,' Steven added.

They moved on then, both looking for something new now, attackers with some different capabilities. It interested both, both men seeing the possibilities, the potential.

'You know those ones?' Steven asked.

'Yes, I... I recognise them. I actually do,' Peter replied.

'You know where we are too?' Steven asked.

'Yes, okay then. Follow me. There just could be more close by us here,' Peter suggested.

As they walked on, Peter spoke of his thoughts then.

'This does seem to suggest a few changes, some change very similar to...' he cut off.

'Just where is your partner, Peter?' Steven asked.

'My... He is... Well he's... preparing things, or he was. Back at the base,' Peter told him.

'Really? That's a pity then. So can I help now?' Steven asked.

'Yes, yes you can. Absolutely,' Peter replied in agreement.

Chapter 52

After only minutes passing, they crossed a few more desolate streets. Between dark alleys walked out a line of quiet but focused attackers. All torn clothes, scabs, and dirty, greasy tangled hair, they ambled along with some urge taking them forward.

'Here we are. Like the others, just as strange' Steven said as they carefully watched, from a doorway alcove.

'So what's happened to them?' he asked.

Peter waited and watched. He saw eventually some characteristic of the results he and Victor were theorising together. He then decided to approach them as they moved along the street. The attackers simply quietly walked along, moving toward some destination unknown.

'They don't act like this normally, do they?' Steven asked, following close behind Peter.

'No, never have. This is… It's been caused by something,' Peter said.

'Right. Could be something due,' Steven agreed.

They followed the line of attackers from a few feet behind. Suddenly the sounds of many cars were heard arriving streets away, and then wild shouts and screams in the night.

'The trouble is coming, just on time,' Steven said.

'We'll watch them though,' Peter told him.

There was no way they could not. They stopped once again, standing behind large creeping trees in shadow as the line of somnambulist attackers moved along. They then suddenly came to a stop at the end of the next street, crowding around and then groaning together and scraping at the walls and ground. Outside them, before the street, the police cars drove up stopping. Some officers came out fast and they approached the attackers.

'Why are they here?' one officer asked and they tried to push them, move them then. The attackers resisted, waking slightly enough to unite and increase their aggression.

'They take the beating, that's a lot of hits there,' Steven said.

'Yes, and why? Why not just move?' Peter said, thinking about it carefully as he watched. 'Let's move on now.'

'Really? Don't you want to see what happens?' Steven asked.

'I want to see what happens elsewhere now,' Peter told him.

They quickly ran on, away through other back streets past closed pubs, takeaways and offices. Peter watched the street signs they passed, stopped and led Steven in other directions remembering where he wanted to go more clearly. They were seen then as they moved, by a handful of people also moving along.

'One of the tech blokes,' a man said, pointing at Peter. Peter looked then, startled and unprepared.

'Come on, keep going,' Peter said quietly.

'But they like you, right? They support you?' Steven said.

'Not necessarily, not all of them,' Peter said. 'Look... could you...'

'Be the other? Yes, but give me some clues, right?' Steven said.

Peter then subtly handed him a couple of small capsules and vials as they looked at the people.

'We are very busy. We hope you are strong, fight the brave fight. We'll know tomorrow,' Peter announced boldly.

This prompted a large cheer from the people who stared back possibly waiting for some impressive sight, or a miracle of sorts.

'There will be change, soon enough. Patience will reward us, science will save us. No mistakes like before. Clear thinking and change,' Steven added, then threw down a capsule. It exploded some wild colourful gases between them and the group.

'Let's move,' Peter urged.

Running on again, Peter eventually turned to give Steven a hard accusatory stare.

'Why did you say that back there?' he asked.

'It seemed like what should be said. No more bullshit. No embarrassment of what we can do and how we will save the country now,' Steven told him.

Peter looked around feeling speechless, confused and then in some way very disturbed. He did certainly appreciate this man he had met, especially at this time when he had walked out with his angry lonely thoughts, away from Victor and their disagreements. But this man was, he came to realise, most definitely much more than he first seemed to be. It could be luck or it could be extreme danger, he considered to himself.

'You want to keep going anywhere else now?' Steven asked him.

Peter looked at him, made his decision.

'Alright. Let's go on. I know what's next,' Peter told him.

Police drove around in their stolen cars painted with police colours, sirens wailing; they beat random people on the streets around, chased some along scaring them, threatening them. Many honestly did prefer their more simple straightforward violence from the attackers when it came, than the calculated sick darn out sadomasochistic pain from the power-mad officers around them, who hurt and beat them to control what little was left of civilised known culture.

Between the regular bouts of crime fighting, distorted warped visions of law and justice and order now, the police punk officer gangs around did begin to communicate the strange problems arising with the attackers around the city. They beat and hurt them, but the attackers were obstructing them from crossing many areas of London and causing many unexpected problems which quickly became very difficult to deal with.

'John has given word of more like this; it's all across the city now too. It's some kind of big freaky fuck occurrence here. The damn attackers are organising themselves, thinking or just getting one over on us in some damn way,' one Officer yelled.

'Just fucking beat the bastards. They can't stop us, not these half dead inhuman things.'

Again the police were having more of the first real surprising problems they had encountered in a long time on the streets. Their feeling of supreme control and dominance was faltering, and they were feeling now lost and anxious. The order and control was slipping, the masses were rising they saw.

'I'm seeing things with the attackers – the differences,' Peter told Steven when they crossed the streets together, both just waiting for truth and the next steps together that would reveal how things were to be.

'Right, interesting, yes. I see it too,' Steven said.

'Tell me... anything, anything you know,' Peter said.

'What's this? If I told you everything or anything more it would blow your mind my friend. But you know, we can definitely help each other, you know it and I know it,' Steven told him. 'This whole thing... How does it end? How far does it go? You tell me that.'

The answer was held away when a gang of men came around toward them suddenly.

'Good evening, you creepy shits. Law and order has arrived,' one man yelled out menacingly. The police were there to put things right, if they could.

Peter and Steven quickly looked at each other, the decision made. Peter led the defence. Unexpected, the police moved in wild and aggressive. Smoke capsules exploded, they moved through. The police lurched in, smoke clouding around them, choking them, confusing them. Supplies running low, both Peter and Steven simply threw out the last chemical bombs to confuse the police while they could. One grabbed out near Steven, another almost reached at Peter but missed, they struggled, punches thrown but missing. Steven got a hard crack to the jaw, then ribs, and Peter was kicked down but managed to stand again and run away. Leaving the police officers with the smoke gradually dying down, they both escaped to search for more strange phenomenon.

All police groups then witnessed a hugely distressing sight with many of the attackers they found in different parts around London. Paths and streets were blocked, attackers crowding over openings, simply building up with no clear reason but to highly irritate the police. When police fought against them, the fight was though tougher than it ever had been before – attackers seeming stronger, more in some way intelligent or at least aware of things possibly as they avoided harm, moving away from punches, strikes, and even bullets. After only a couple of hours, the unexpected new movements of the attackers was taking a toll on all police easily.

'We can't handle this, we just can't not now anyway. They're getting better, learning,' one Officer shouted to the others.

'Are they returning, I mean... to what they all were before?' another asked.

'What? No, no way at all,' one said.

'No, they could be, I mean... Really, look,' another suggested.

'No, fucking way. They are scum. Monsters, our scum to put in line. The scum of the streets that we control,' another said with loud anger.

'We'll sort them like before. It's just tonight. A small problem. We will handle this. We will stop this,' the lead officer told them all with determined focus.

Each of the individual small groups of attackers had been led out in a specific direction to play their own part in the earlier arranged and well organised synchronised experiment which now finally was executed. Originally, it would have been the work of both Peter and Victor, based on the basic theory notes they had found at their separate company research buildings months before. This present occurrence was now solely the work of Victor, the anger and frustrated isolation having just built up to too much to handle. His insecure wild paranoid mind simple took the reins and let go, the plan happening as Peter had rebuked him once too often. Victor could not wait any longer for Peter who had too many unsure questions and personal ethics, concerns for the small elements of society and more. With him gone for some reason, Victor had also just taken too many chances. And one seriously fatal chance too many.

The police could be heard shouting in confusion, their cars backing up, stuck in roads unable to move through. Every part of the plan was working so far, it seemed, not that Victor had necessarily been closely keeping exact track of events after the beginning. He was simply moving along, setting up each step a part at a time, then moving on, not looking back. There was a constant continuing distraction in him, some undiagnosed and unrecognised symptoms tormenting inside his body, taunting his mind, his logical focus on things. He was ill in some way, various kinds of unpleasant sensations buzzing, throbbing within him. His blood was cold, hot, his arms and legs shaking as he walked on, eye sight blurring slightly on and off. His idea had been a bad one, an instant regret with no reachable obvious solution as he stumbled through the London streets alone, the mad events he had set off exploding in all directions around him.

Through the night, Jane walked in toward the city centre. She really had to be coming closer to where Alan could be, or else she was lost completely. She could hear people around close then, and she knew the dangers that it could be. She heard groups of people, shouting, talking loudly somewhere very near. She walked on, moved along around another street, out down toward a main open court area – what she saw then shocked her unexpectedly. She had found him. There was Alan, but he was not helping others, and they were definitely not helping him either.

The gang around Alan were tying him down, kicking him violently over and over with visible pleasure. She ran in, unable to hold herself back.

'Let's give this scientist saviour what he deserves, shall we?' one shouted and peered down at Alan.

'He thinks he's a martyr anyway, he should act like one. That's how real Saints are,' another yelled, mocking him as they took turns tormenting him.

'Get away from him, you fucking bastards! Step away from him right now,' Jane shouted as she came up to the scene.

She ran in with her baseball bat gripped tightly. The first got it hard in the face – broken nose, smashed jaw. She turned, punched the next man, kicked him down. Moving to one side quickly she hit the next two fast, kicked one in the stomach, turned and hit one again, knocking him down over his friend. She reached Alan who slumped down on a large makeshift crucifix, which lay against a wall behind him in the alley.

'It's me, Jane, Alan. Oh God, I'm so glad I've found you. I'll get you out,' she told him.

'Hello. Don't... bother...' he uttered slowly.

'What? No, you're coming now,' she told him.

She quickly looked around, at his bound hands and ankles. A couple of the men began to lurch back and returned toward them then.

'Who are you, bitch?' one asked.

'We'll take you down with him, you cow,' another said.

'You're wrong, you idiots. This isn't him. Wrong guy here,' she told them as she finished untying the rope holding Alan down and picked up her bat again.

''Says you? How'd you know?' one asked.

'It's him okay? He's one of them, and he's the Saint,' another told her.

Jane stood and wielded her bat toward them.

'Okay, I've kicked all your arses. I'll kick them again, worse so fucking stand back' She announced and gripped the bat. She was pissed but she was uncertain that she could actually hold them back for much longer.

'My... left pocket,' Alan whispered behind her.

'What?' she asked. She took a brief glance, understood, and quickly delved in. She grabbed two small glass tubes.

'Throw... down,' he told her.

They smashed down at the feet of the gang of men, steaming gasses unfurling, and blinding them instantly.

'Let's go,' Alan said.

Jane helped him up to his feet, and they walked off as quickly as they could, hidden by the smoke and gas around them. They found their way out and into another alley, then up another and away to a different part of the city centre.

So many gangs were coming out into the city centre gradually, and police groups drove out around them, but all were being manipulated and tricked into position by the work of Peter and Victor. It was almost the perfect time for them, but both had separated from each other. The opportunity could be lost to them, but more was there to challenge them they had not predicted. The entire city was working for Steven – it had been a challenge but one he had enjoyed and had to confront finally. He could see where the pieces were heading, and he made his way for the set up.

The many gangs crowded around the open street city area were moving in, looking for opportunity and revenge.

'Everyone, people out on the street, listen – the tech two are here, down this way. Everyone is after them,' Steven shouted down from up on top of the entrance to the mall building. He then ran off, while checking they had heard him and began to follow in the direction he suggested. He led them on, where he knew both Peter and Victor were due to arrive soon enough. He moved on then, to where he would find the attackers, as long as he called them in with the techniques he had learned of on his journey down there from the others.

Under an arched doorway, in the night shadows Jane held Alan, while he took a short rest, his pains and bruises aching him.

'I am so sorry I left you. I let you go. Forgive me?' she asked, tears streaming down her face.

'I forgive... you. I forgive,' he murmured in uncomfortable pain.

'Look, we can head back when you feel up to it. Take a car from around here or go back to the one I brought,' she suggested.

'Steven... is here. For them, his plan,' he said.

'But... can you manage it?' she asked.

'We... have to,' he told her as he gradually stood once again.

When Peter walked down carefully, unsure of what he would find, he seemed to be early. No attackers were out in place where they should be, he thought.

'Good evening, my confused friend,' Victor said, stepping out from the other side of shadowed buildings.

'Finally, what's been going on?' Peter asked.

'You tell me, or would that be a real waste now?' Victor shot back.

'There's no time now. Look, there's another guy. He can help us out, he understands so much really,' Peter tried to explain.

Victor grabbed him by the shirt collars.

'No damn it, no way. What have you been doing all this time? Telling strangers all of our plans? Is that it? He's probably the god damn police Peter, you absolute fool,' Victor shouted hysterically.

As they stood arguing then, gangs and crowds began to enter into the area from around, police groups as well, charging right in toward them.

'Fuck it, they're coming now?' Victor said looking around them.

'No, it's everyone else,' Peter said, noticing.

They all moved in as Peter managed to slip out, Victor losing hold on him. It was difficult, a painful struggle, but Peter knew a route out.

'They're in here,' one man shouted at all of the crowds around.

'Stop them, get them now,' another yelled.

Victor was left alone, grabbed and pulled under, punched, kicked and mauled while the police gang tried to make their way to collect him. They would be lucky if he was in one piece when they finally found him.

While the many gangs moved along in the direction Steven had led them down, the streets cleared behind, in the other direction, right on time as the many separate groups of attackers emerged, finally directed by the signs and scents Victor had prepared, but which Steven ultimately made use of for his own plan. He stood over the entrance of the city hall, and waited, watched while gradually he saw them all come in a few dozen at a time, until eventually there must have been a few hundred at a good guess, he thought. It seemed to work. Now was time for the completion of the plan. This was it, the end to all of what Gordon had wanted. The end of it all, he thought.

From one side opening of the city centre area, Alan and Jane watched the shocking mass of diseased attackers all collected together.

'So tragic to see,' Jane said.

'Our tragedy in time,' Alan told her.

'It can be stopped, you think?' she asked.

'Steven is here?' he said.

'There, up at the hall. The other end. He's watching them,' she told him.

Alan then began to step out, heading down toward the mass of increasing attackers, all scratching, moaning around down there.

'Wait, what are you doing?' Jane said quickly, afraid.

'Steven... He's... down there... Need to meet him,' he told her as he walked in.

Alan looked up and could see his old friend standing on the hall steps across the way.

'I'm here now. We made it here,' Alan shouted across.

It shook Steven when he located the speaker and found Alan down in the city centre about to walk right in among the attackers. He heard the words.

'Get away from here now, Alan. Leave please,' Steven shouted down to him.

'We're not finished. The project's not done,' Alan said, continuing.

Steven was ignored as Alan stepped right in, between the savage wild diseased crowds. Steven had the same idea, but he had planned to use them, his own blood and flesh, to finish their evolution. It was him that Gordon had needed for this final act at the end.

He jumped down, right in with the attackers, and with his prepared syringe. He had prepared himself, his blood and the intermediate stimulant to connect their cell makeup into one. They worked in, grabbed at him, scratched and pulled, while he stepped through with difficult force. He knew Alan was in among them all then, and would prefer him to get out, but if that could not happen then that was the way it would be.

It was difficult to see, only arms, shoulders and rabid green eyes flashing past among the shadows around in the dark of night and the crowded mass. Moaning, screaming attackers pushing in, around, fighting for him, for each other, for flesh and blood to spill. But they were confused and distracted, unlike every other night they came out.

'Alan, leave... here,' Steven shouted as he made his way in deep enough for his work. It was difficult to move, but eventually they did seem to ease slightly, enough for Steven to step through easier somehow. He took out his syringe, pulled up his sleeve on his left arm, and looked around at all of the vile, diseased tragic beings all around him. It was a terrible horror to behold, he thought. How did it all happen? Had it been destined? It had been his father, and then it was now him. Evil men, doing evil things he thought. He held up the syringe, and the attackers moved in watched in some way.

A hand grabbed onto him tightly from somewhere. Something stabbed into him, pierced his arm. Not his doing, he knew. Between the crowd of attackers around, he saw human eyes. He saw Alan looking through at him. Then gone, back into the dark mass, away. Between the many attackers Steven struggled, he fell around, pain in his eyes and his limbs suddenly. They reacted, attackers pulling at him. They bit and scratched at him, some tore and scraped him, over and over.

Down at the opening to the alley, Jane watched and waited for Alan to return. She was unable to see him beyond the lurching mass, and was extremely concerned. Alan appeared suddenly to her.

'My God, Alan,' she yelled and ran over in his direction. She took hold of him, pulled him away to safety near the alley opening.

'What happened in there?' she asked.

'I... found him,' he replied.

They turned, watched the many dozens and hundreds of attackers still crawling, struggling and scratching around at each other. Movement began to slow after a long moment. They could see them now biting each other and scratching at each other.

'Is that it now?' Jane asked.

'Watch,' Alan said.

The attackers did seem to slow and cease their movement, some of them even falling down, weakening in places. They seemed to be sick and weak, all of them, but their complexion altering visibly. They all were dropping down, losing their aggression in some way. From within, over the limp, piled up bodies, another climbed up and out.

'There he is,' Alan announced.

He and Jane watched Steven make his way over in their direction. Looking sick and different, a quiet Steven found them down by the alley opening. Steven felt something gone from within him, like he had been cured. Lucy had left him. Her thoughts could not be heard within his mind. Just his own.

'Come with us. That's enough now,' Alan told him.

They moved along a few streets, found the car Jane had driven and drove away from there. Over the next few hours they travelled back home. Between them, they repeated the process on the many more cursed ones waiting for them. A process had begun, a reversal in one sense, or progression in another.